KNOW THY ENEMY

Nermesa charged the murdering brigand. But as he neared, a huge figure outlined by the flames dropped down from the trees between the noble and his adversary, a figure so massive that he easily stopped the knight's horse in its tracks.

Nermesa's mount cried out as gigantic hands crushed its throat. The knight was tossed aside, landing hard. He looked up to see the giant approaching him. There was something not quite right about the way this monstrous brigand moved, but Nermesa could not worry about that. He desperately searched the ground for his sword, but could not find it.

A harsh, barking laugh made him look to his left, where the bearded, wild-haired brigand watched in amusement. Nermesa stared at the face and the Pictish tattoos, recalled bits of accounts he had heard . . . and knew then that it was Khatak the Butcher who so reveled in his imminent demise . . .

Millions of readers have enjoyed Robert E. Howard's stories about Conan. Twelve thousand years ago, after the sinking of Atlantis, there was an age undreamed of when shining kingdoms lay spread across the world. This was an age of magic, wars and adventure, but above all this was an age of heroes! The Age of Conan series features the tales of other legendary heroes in Hyboria.

*Don't miss these thrilling adventures
set in the world of Conan!*

AGE OF CONAN™
HYBORIAN ADVENTURES

A SOLDIER'S QUEST
Volume 1

THE GOD IN THE MOON

Richard Knaak

ACE BOOKS, NEW YORK

THE BERKLEY PUBLISHING GROUP
Published by the Penguin Group
Penguin Group (USA) Inc.
375 Hudson Street, New York, New York 10014, USA
Penguin Group (Canada), 90 Eglinton Avenue East, Suite 700, Toronto, Ontario M4P 2Y3, Canada
(a division of Pearson Penguin Canada Inc.)
Penguin Books Ltd., 80 Strand, London WC2R 0RL, England
Penguin Group Ireland, 25 St. Stephen's Green, Dublin 2, Ireland
(a division of Penguin Books Ltd.)
Penguin Group (Australia), 250 Camberwell Road, Camberwell, Victoria 3124, Australia
(a division of Pearson Australia Group Pty. Ltd.)
Penguin Books India Pvt. Ltd., 11 Community Centre, Panchsheel Park, New Delhi—110 017, India
Penguin Group (NZ), Cnr. Airborne and Rosedale Roads, Albany, Auckland 1310, New Zealand
(a division of Pearson New Zealand Ltd.)
Penguin Books (South Africa) (Pty.) Ltd., 24 Sturdee Avenue, Rosebank, Johannesburg 2196, South
Africa

Penguin Books Ltd., Registered Offices: 80 Strand, London WC2R 0RL, England

This is a work of fiction. Names, characters, places, and incidents either are the product of the author's imagination or are used fictitiously, and any resemblance to actual persons, living or dead, business establishments, events, or locales is entirely coincidental. The publisher does not have any control over and does not assume any responsibility for author or third-party websites or their content.

THE GOD IN THE MOON

An Ace Book / published by arrangement with Conan Properties International, LLC.

PRINTING HISTORY
Ace mass-market edition / August 2006

ISBN: 0-441-01422-4

ACE
Ace Books are published by The Berkley Publishing Group,
a division of Penguin Group (USA) Inc.,
375 Hudson Street, New York, New York 10014.
ACE and the "A" design are trademarks belonging to Penguin Group (USA) Inc.

PRINTED IN THE UNITED STATES OF AMERICA

10   9   8   7   6   5   4   3   2   1

1

"—AND LO, THE foul sorcerer, Xaltotun, who would have raised the ancient and monstrous land of Acheron up from the dead, was smote by magic more powerful than his! Shriveled, he became, once more, the mummified corpse raised by Aquilonia's enemies! Smote by magic secured by the king, who had already escaped black Khitan assassins and Nemedian treachery!"

The tall, balding orator in flowing white robes gazed imperiously at the crowd in the open amphitheater. Torches lined the upper walls of the round stadium, which seated some two thousand. The orator's lidded gaze and proud standing added emphasis to his remarkable baritone voice, perfect for effect for this particular tale . . . or so Nermesa, son of Bolontes, scion of House Klandes, thought as he listened, almost mesmerized.

One hand on the upper fold of his robe, the player continued, "And with Xaltotun no more, the betrayers quickly fell to the king and his men! Valerius, blood of the foul tyrant Namedides and usurper of the throne, slain with his followers by the sacrifice of those brave citizens who most had suffered torture during his short but terrible reign as king of our realm! For Valerius, a score of arrows to pierce his black heart and a sword to sever his head! Then fell Amalric, Baron of Tor, who found doom impaled in the heart on the lance of Pallantides, commander of Aquilonia's host! Lastly, Tarascus, who rumor has it only gained Nemedia's throne through the sorcerer's dark arts! Brought to his knees by none other than the king himself and spared life only in exchange for restitution to the peoples of Aquilonia and the release of she who now sits beside great Conan on the throne, our beloved queen, fair Zenobia!"

From the stone benches upon which they sat, the audience abruptly arose with several shouts of, "Hail, Conan, King of Aquilonia! Hail, Zenobia, Queen of Aquilonia!"

When the crowd had quieted again, the speaker concluded, "And so peace was brought to the realm! Aquilonia grew strong again, and our tale, for now . . . is ended . . ."

The listeners clapped. The robed figure bowed, then strode from the stage as if Conan himself. Musicians began a piece designed to prepare the audience for the next entertainment, a play concerning two young lovers from vying Houses.

But while most of the audience looked forward to the next piece, the young, brown-haired aristocrat seemed almost oblivious.

"Amazing . . ." muttered Nermesa, blue eyes round despite his having heard the story a dozen times before. He never ceased to enjoy hearing of the astounding events, even if they were only a little over four years old. At the time of their happening, he had been a youth still caught up in his learning, and so everything that had happened had taken on a larger-than-life meaning for him. Yet, now, even though he had just become an officer in Aquilonia's military, those events still guided his dreams and his very existence.

"Poor Valerius," mocked the grating voice of his companion, a dark-haired, bearded man with a squat, crooked nose that compared even more unfavorably against Nermesa's well-angled one. "After all these times here listening to him ending up full of bolts I can't see him other than a red pin-cushion!"

Nermesa chuckled slightly at his servant's jest. Quentus might have been in the employ of House Klandes, but, having been assigned since a boy himself to the House's heir, was more of a friend despite their differences in status. Of course, Quentus never completely forgot his place and always urged Nermesa to do the same, for the latter's father considered rank and blood of the utmost importance in life. The son of Bolontes, however, generally ignored the servant's advice when it came to that subject.

"Are we staying for the play, this time, Master Nermesa?" But even as the ursine servant asked, the robed aristocrat stood. Quentus shook his head. "Of course not. Such a foolish question."

"I've got to prepare, Quentus. I received my orders."

"Eh?" Black eyes narrowed. "How's it I've heard nothing?"

Nermesa smiled again. "You'd have had to have been standing near the doors all day as I did. When the messenger came, I stopped him before he knocked and took them from him directly!"

"Are you saying that this here's something even your parents don't know yet?"

Now it was the noble's eyes that narrowed. "No, and that was the way I intended it. I wanted to wait until the last minute . . . when they couldn't put up a fuss."

Quentus grunted, his life as a servant having given him a much more basic perspective. "Oh, you think they'll not?"

His master grimaced, well aware that Quentus was likely correct but refusing to admit it entirely. "We'll see . . . we'll see."

HOUSE KLANDES RAN with order. Bolontes, his stern, patrician features clearly marking him as Nermesa's father, insisted it be so. As head, he oversaw all of Klandes' affairs, including their vineyards, granaries, and smithies. Klandes had agreements with every facet of Aquilonia's government even though Bolontes himself kept some distance from King Conan.

Klandes was one of the oldest, most stable Houses in all the realm, and its bloodline had flowed through more than a few kings. Thus it was that, even though he outwardly wore a respectful face in the presence of his monarch, Bolontes did not entirely accept the outlander—a Cimmerian, no less—as such.

And to find out that his only son now intended to serve Conan and serve him willingly was nearly enough to tear asunder the mask the patriarch ever wore.

"How . . . could . . . this happen?" he demanded of Nermesa. "How could you do this?"

"I spoke with some friends close to General Pallantides, Father," Nermesa quickly answered. "You shouldn't be too surprised! I've been taking training for so long—"

"As any son of House Klandes should! As any future master should! Not as the lackey of a barbarian conqueror!"

"I will be an officer in the Aquilonian military, Father! A proud tradition that our family has included for most of its existence!"

The gray-haired Bolontes sniffed, his expression turning imperious. At six-foot-three, Nermesa was taller than average, but his father was two inches taller, enabling the elder Klandes to gaze down at the son as if the latter were still a pimpled child barely out of his first decade.

"A proud tradition, when the military served Aquilonian kings."

Nermesa would not let his father intimidate him. They stood in the great room of the Klandes residence, where each wall gave tribute to past lords of the family. Busts of ancestors from centuries past lined much of the chamber, and each seemed to join Bolontes in eyeing his son in disappointment. The painted marble heads looked so very lifelike that Nermesa did his best to focus only on his father, the true impediment. He did not need to feel as if generations of Klandes condemned him. It was enough that the immediately preceding one did.

"I suppose that you would have preferred Valerius to continue to reign, or even Namedides."

"They were Aquilonian, at least . . ." But here, at last, Bolontes faltered. Even he had been no friend of either. Pursing his lips, Nermesa's father turned and walked behind the large oak table he used to conduct most of his business. Scrolls covered the six-foot-wide table. Several quills and a flask of ink sat on the far left corner, Bolontes favoring that hand.

Nermesa, too, was left-handed, and he knew that it was likely the fact that he and his father were so similar in many ways that had them butting heads like two rams so often. Yet, when it came to what was best for their homeland, the two seemed quite far apart.

The banner of the House hung high behind Bolontes. A red lion in a golden field, with twin swords—also red—crossing over the rearing beast. That Klandes and the Cimmerian-born king both had the animal as their symbol—Conan's a golden lion on a black field—made no impression on Bolontes. After all, the banner of Klandes went back centuries, whereas the current monarch's went back only a few years.

"Understand me, my son. Aquilonia and our House are intertwined as no other clan is. A thriving realm means a thriving Klandes. That you'd wish to protect Aquilonia fills me with pride, but I have difficulty in seeing our home survive under this Conan. How many times has insurrection and war come to us since he took power? He draws danger to him! Is that the sort of ruler we need?"

"I will be leaving immediately, Father. I'd like to leave with your blessing."

Bolontes adjusted the neck of his tunic, a sign that only Nermesa could have recognized as a hint of anxiety. He smoothed his cloak, red with a gold lining, before responding. "Immediately? A quick farewell to your mother and myself and off you go? That's to be it?"

"I thought it best," the younger Klandes insisted. "The better not to draw *this* out."

"Ever thinking of your parents. And what, may I ask, do you plan to do about Orena?"

Mention of the name caused Nermesa to grit his teeth. "I've written a letter that should reach her just about now. I'd hoped you could speak with her, too . . . especially since it was you and her father who arranged our betrothal when she was born."

"Lenaro is a House with a breeding almost as pure as our own! I chose the best marriage I could for my only child! Is that what this is? Are you running away from all your responsibilities? Klandes will end up in the hands of one of your cousins if something happens to you, you know. It would be better if at least you had already produced an heir . . ."

"My marriage to Orena will still take place. I told her so in the letter, Father. It'll just be a little later."

Bolontes planted both fists on the table, ignoring the parchments he crushed in the process. "You will be the end of me, my son."

Nermesa began to turn. "Do I have your blessing?"

"Come back alive and in one piece."

It was less than Nermesa had hoped for but more than he had expected. His father remained behind the desk, eyes unblinking. Nermesa nodded, then left the chamber.

Household guards came to attention, their red-and-gold tunics marking them as property of Klandes. Nermesa barely noticed them. His sandals clattered loudly on the shining marble floor that covered the entire ground level. The symbols of his House had been etched at great price in every tile.

From behind a fluted pillar burst his mother, Callista. Almost as tall as her son, she was a slim, handsome woman with just a touch of gray in her brown, upswept hair. Her alabaster gown, bound at the waist, trailed behind her. She had softer, rounder features than her husband, with full lips and a petite nose. If there was any similarity in looks with Nermesa, it was in the shape and hue of her blue eyes, which matched even more closely those of the younger Klandes than the father's.

Those eyes were now red with tears. "Oh, Nermesa! Please don't be angry with him! He's being harsh with you in part because of me! He knows what it will mean to me for you to go! Please, don't leave in such a mood!"

Nermesa softened. "I'm not angry with Father or you, Mother. Just a little disappointed in him. I'm doing what I believe right, and I'm not leaving Klandes forever! *He* served for four years, remember?"

"Bolontes was a second son, Nermesa. If not for the death of his eldest brother, he would have stayed in the military . . . but when that happened, he chose the House over all else."

"I'll be all right, I promise." He kissed her on the cheek. "You needn't worry about me."

Callista returned the kiss on his forehead, as she had done since he was a child. "I will worry nonetheless. That is what a loving mother does." Her expression softened. "And when the time comes, I will speak with Orena."

It was an unexpected gift. "Thank you. I promise, I'll still live up to the betrothal . . . since I have to."

"She is quite a beautiful woman, Nermesa. Would it be that terrible? I know she can be a bit . . . autocratic . . . but, without sons, as eldest child, Orena *has* had to take on the reins of their House. She'll be giving up much when you two marry. Lenaro will be absorbed into Klandes, its name lost to history. Imagine if the reverse would take place. How would you react?"

"I understand what you're saying, Mother. As I told you, I'll be going through with the betrothal. Give me time to make my mark. I'll come back with more glory for House Klandes. That can only increase our prestige, aid our holdings, and even perhaps make me a bit more impressive in Orena's eyes."

"As if you weren't so already." Wiping away a tear, Callista added, "At least, whenever you come back to Tarantia, you can visit us."

"Naturally!"

He gave her a hug and another kiss on the cheek, then departed his home. Outside, Quentus was finishing packing Nermesa's horse, a chestnut stallion . . . and *another* beside it.

Quentus's own.

"What's the meaning of this?" the noble demanded.

"I'll be coming with you, good master. Think I'd be leaving you to the mercy of the military?"

"My father would never—"

"Your father arranged it all. Three days ago." The bearded servant grinned. "Looks like he's as good at keeping a secret as you are! He may not want you riding off, but if he couldn't be stopping you, then he wanted someone to keep watch! Who better than me to do that, eh?"

Shaken, Nermesa gripped the other man by the shoulders. "Quentus, I'll go speak with him! I never would've risked you so! I know you don't have a choice, but to be forced into the military without—"

"Master Nermesa! I proposed that I be the one before he even had the chance to ask! You think I'll be letting you go into battle without me around to save your hide?" He slapped the blade sheathed at his side.

In truth, Quentus handled a sword at least as well as the noble. Small wonder, since, as was common among the aristocracy, a trusted servant like him trained with their master. Nermesa had needed someone with whom to spar, and Quentus had proven perfect.

"But . . ." The protest died on his lips. He had thought himself so clever, yet both his father and servant had outwitted him.

Quentus held Nermesa's horse while his master mounted. The servant then mounted his own beast, an older, brown stallion that the noble realized was not the horse that he had at first thought it was. "Is that one of my father's steeds?"

"Yes, but a lesser one. Wouldn't do for a humble servant to have a better animal than his master."

"But why?"

"My lord Bolontes felt I might not keep pace with you in times of trouble if I rode my own mare." In truth, Quentus's own horse was more useful for carrying loads around in town. Stockier, she was not built for speed as a horse in war necessarily was.

Nermesa did not have to ask, but he knew that his father had used this horse to pay Quentus, the better to guarantee that the servant would indeed watch over the heir to Klandes. With each passing moment, Nermesa was feeling less and less clever.

He hoped that General Pallantides and the king would not find him so.

Although they had an estate outside of the city—as did most of the affluent Houses—Bolontes preferred to make his home more often in the clan's original home in Tarantia itself. This allowed him to be more in touch with those elements upon whose business Klandes depended. Thus it was that only minutes after departing the gates, Nermesa and Quentus rode through the throng-filled streets of Aquilonia's fabled capital.

Tarantia was the nexus of western civilization, a place where all came to learn, to marvel, to envy. A great, stone wall with battlements surrounded it, and four gateways— set at the compass points—allowed entrance from the surrounding plains. Tall marble structures dominated the interior, many of them the traditional blue and gold towers first built by the city's founders. Tarantia was actually a more recent name, and some elders still called it *Tamar*, a name whose meaning Nermesa had never discovered. Most of the major buildings had a series of fluted columns marking their exteriors and stone roofs sharply slanted, with masterful carvings over the columned entrances.

Statues decorated buildings of particular purpose and also marked intersections named for famous personages of the past. As with the busts in Nermesa's home, these were brilliantly painted. Life-size warriors and statesmen in colored garments watched over visitors and inhabitants alike in so real a manner that every now and then someone could be caught stealing a glance at a statue as if feeling the marble eyes upon him.

The pair passed one of the massive, arched city gates just as a troop of breastplated Gundermen with long pikes resting on their shoulders marched out of the capital. Nermesa watched the unit with pride despite its consisting of the gray-eyed, tawny-haired fighters from the northern edge of the empire. Gundermen were not Aquilonians in the traditional sense; their home, Gunderland, had been seized early on in the realm's formation. The people of that land were of an independent nature, but were among the most trusted soldiers in all the military. There had never been anything resembling an insurrection in Gunderland. Men such as these had battled beside King Conan when he had saved Aquilonia from the sorcerer and traitors and held a place of honor with the Cimmerian-born leader.

Despite Aquilonia's presently being at peace, wary guards watched from a walkway near the top of the city wall, which extended all the way around the capital. The king did not take his victory four years prior as a sign to relax; no, Conan had a healthy distrust of his neighbors . . . and even some of his own people. It was something that any good monarch soon learned . . . if he lived long enough.

An Aquilonian knight rode past them. The nose guard on his helm, shaped like that of a dragon's muzzle, gave the mustached fighter a fearsome look. He wore chain under his breastplate and at his side hung a huge, scabbarded sword that Nermesa doubted he himself could have easily hefted. Yet, if all went as planned, Bolontes' son would soon be a member of this fabled order of defenders.

High buildings with iron-railed balconies overlooked the market through which Nermesa now passed. With the day well under way, people of all castes flocked the public area, making travel slow. In addition to many whose blood could be traced back to the same stock as Nermesa, there were more Gundermen—mostly acting as hired guards— and darker Poitainians, with whom Quentus shared some blood. There were brown-eyed Bossonians, often with bows over their shoulders, and a wary-eyed figure in a cloak who might have been a Stygian. A group of short, stocky Argosseans had set up a tent of their own and now dickered with customers over pearls and golden goblets, perhaps brought from beyond the southern land of Zingara. Nermesa even saw a pair of yellow-skinned travelers in long gowns, who he had to assume came from Khitai. If so, they surely had committed some terrible offense in their homeland and been cast out by order of their god-emperor. Although their kind could be found in goodly numbers in such places as Stygia, few of the almost-mythic race came to far-off Aquilonia unless forced to by circumstance.

The market abounded with fresh produce, fish, meats, and products from within Aquilonia and beyond, even silks from the Khitans' homeland and beyond. Lush animal skins from Kush and copper trinkets from the Pictish lands were among some of the other unusual items to be found in the capital's market.

Nobles followed by slaves and servants wandered around, buying whatever struck their fancy. More serious figures in the garb of House officials picked and chose among the various wares, especially the foodstuffs, seeking what would please their lords. Freeborn citizens argued with sellers for every coin they could keep, their savings kept in tiny leather pouches clutched in one hand.

Several women of varying social status looked up with interest at Nermesa as he rode past, eventually causing his cheeks to burn. Having been betrothed for nearly all of his life, he had not had much interaction with women other than his mother and Orena.

Quentus chuckled. "Would that I had your face instead of this crag of mine . . ."

"You've had your share, so I've noticed."

"No complaints, but I'd be always willing to take what you've not had."

Nermesa returned his chuckle . . . then suddenly had to rein his horse to a halt as a group of riders bullied their way directly toward where the pair were located.

"Aside, you!" snarled a muscular guard in blue-and-black garb. A Gunderman by birth, he treated Nermesa as if the young noble were the outsider, even kicking at the latter's horse to shove both out of the way.

Quentus, one hand slipping to his broadsword, immediately pulled in front of his master. Despite the Gunderman's obvious skill and armored torso, the servant looked more than willing to take him on. "Treat my lord Nermesa so again, and I'll be cutting that tongue of yours and feeding it to some Kushite as a delicacy!"

The guard snarled and reached for his own weapon, his four comrades following suit.

"There will be no need for violence," clipped a cloaked figure whom the fighters obviously protected. "Be not so eager, Betavio, that you ignore the mark of a House so respected as that of Klandes embossed on the saddles of both men."

Betavio bit back some retort, then bowed his head at his own master. "Forgive me, Baron Sibelio! You ordered haste, and I thought—"

"Wrongly." The other noble rode up next to the Gunderman. "Now, apologize not to me, but rather to one I believe Nermesa Klandes himself."

As the guard bowed his head to Nermesa, Bolontes' son eyed the other aristocrat. He knew of House Sibelio, a far more recent but quickly ascending name among the nobility. Known in previous generations mostly as a rustic House in the agricultural lands north of Tarantia, it had, in this last generation, transformed itself into a capable competitor of Klandes . . . and mostly because of the man before Nermesa.

Baron Antonus Sibelio was perhaps a dozen years younger than Bolontes but looked closer in age to Nermesa. Sibelio was an athletic man with lupine features and black eyes that seemed to burn through the younger Klandes. Clean-shaven, with pale, brown hair, he resembled some of the emperors of old.

His garments marked his success in trading, the robes

made of rich, colored silk. His voluminous cloak was clasped around his neck by a gold disk bearing the House crest, a heron with one leg raised. In the bird's talons was held a ready sword.

Pulling himself from the baron's powerful gaze, Nermesa bowed his head. "I am honored to be known by the illustrious Baron Antonus Sibelio. Your reputation precedes you."

Sibelio smiled, resembling more the wolf than ever. "But it is the House of Klandes that is most illustrious of all and, to encounter its heir is *my* honor, to be sure." He snapped his fingers. "Betavio! Let us stand aside for Klandes, first among Houses . . ."

The guards began to make room for Nermesa, but the young noble's eyes were not on them. Instead, he noticed the glittering emerald on a ring worn by the baron. It captured Nermesa's attention the way it might have a magpie's. Bolontes' son felt drawn to it—

"I said the way is clear for us now, Master Nermesa . . ."

"Hmm?" He had not even noticed that Quentus had been talking to him. Belatedly nodding to the baron, Nermesa added, "Thank you for your kindness. May we meet again soon."

Baron Sibelio smiled graciously, revealing many teeth. "I am certain we shall . . ."

He led his guards away. Nermesa and Quentus rode on and only after a few minutes did Nermesa realize that he had been all but holding his breath.

"There's one to watch, my lord!" commented Quentus with a growl. "Ambitious to the core . . ."

"He's made much of his House. I won't fault him for that—" A building rose in the distance, and all thought of competing nobles vanished from Nermesa's mind. "There it is!"

His dark-haired companion grunted. "Aye. The palace. We see it all the time. You've got a good view from your balcony, remember?"

But to the Klandes heir it was much more than just a
towering structure with high walls and the banner of the
lion flying above. It was a place of power, the place from
which he whom some called the lion watched over all
Aquilonia.

"The palace . . ." he breathed. "King *Conan*."

2

FOG WAS NEVER a good thing in the Westermarck, of that Captain Trajan had long grown certain. Picts and devils— and sometimes both—used the fog for foul deeds. Many a time a courier or even a small patrol had been waylaid by disaster, each head often left on the end of a spear or . . . more unsettling, not found at all.

And then there was the brigand chieftain, Khatak.

The constant struggle to secure the border meant an incessant need for supplies for the various forts. General Boronius, commander of all territorial forces, believed that the fate of the entire expansion westward depended upon allowing no single location to fall into disorder because of insufficient materials. Therefore, despite fog, it had fallen to Trajan's men to guide the wagons to one of the central forts of Oriskonie, the northernmost of the four provinces of the Westermarck. Thinly settled, Oriskonie often proved the most tempting target for the Picts, and now Khatak, who was half-Pict himself. Through the frontier province, the brigand leader struck at the richer land of Conawaga to the south, sometimes even daring to rob caravans near Scanaga. Scanaga, the largest town and the seat of the territorial judge, was also where General Boronius kept his base of operations.

The fifty soldiers and six wagons had been on the journey for four days without incident. Trajan knew that the fort could only be a short distance ahead, but, until he saw it, he would not relax. True, he believed his force more than capable of keeping Khatak at bay, but one never asked for trouble. That was something ten years in the Westermarck had taught him well.

It was with relief that he spotted the first hints of the fort. All concern of bandits and savages vanished from Trajan's thoughts. Even Khatak was not foolish enough to take on the combined might of the garrison and his fighters. Trajan's force would stay the night, then return to Scanaga in the morning, none the worse for wear.

A few torches dimly marked the top of the large wooden structure. Trajan grumbled under his breath at the miserly attitude of the fort's commander. They would have seen the fort at least a mile earlier if the proper lighting had been put in place. It was not as if this region lacked for wood. They were surrounded by virgin oaks, pines, and more. Fuel for a fire was never a problem out here.

"Prepare to give the signal," he commanded the company trumpeter. "On my word."

The soldier brought the horn to his lips and waited. Trajan let the small column get almost within hailing distance before nodding.

The horn blared, echoing long in the otherwise silent land. The captain leaned back and waited expectantly.

But no reply came.

Frowning, Trajan muttered, "Try one more time."

But the results of a second blast brought only more silence . . . and increased wariness on the part of the column.

"Dralos! I want you and five men to go scout that place, but be on your guard! No heroics!"

The officer in question saluted, then called out the names

of five others. With two torches to march their way, the group cautiously rode off toward the fort.

About midway, they came to a halt, then quietly led their mounts to their destination. Trajan watched with rising impatience as the twin torches vanished moments later. That they did so made him assume that Dralos and the others had found a way inside. That bothered Trajan. Had the gates been left open?

Minutes slipped by . . . then suddenly the thunder of hurried hoofbeats made the captain stiffen. Dralos and his men came riding back as if their mounts were on fire. Watching them approach, Trajan snarled, "All weapons at the ready! Be prepared for anything!"

Dralos reined his mount to a halt. A huge man with a face like a hungry cat, he had, to Trajan's memory, fought bloodthirsty Picts with all the emotion of a bored shepherd. The captain had watched Dralos run through adversaries with utter detachment, then move on to the next. Now, though, the soldier stared wide-eyed at Trajan, his face pale.

"They're all dead, Captain! Every last one of 'em! The gates were wide-open, and, when we went in, they were everywhere! Slaughtered!"

The heads of those who had ridden with Dralos bobbed up and down in stunned agreement. Trajan sensed restlessness from those behind him and realized that he had to seize control of the situation.

"Remember yourself, Dralos!" the captain snapped. As the soldier instinctively straightened, Trajan glared past him at the darkened structure. "I will see this for myself! We ride for the fort!"

"But, Captain—"

With a sharp cut of his hand, Trajan ended the protest. "Would you rather we camp out here? Move!"

His appearance of defiance somewhat comforted the men. Captain Trajan hid his own uncertainties well. Still, as he had indicated, what choice did they have but to enter the fort? The woods could not be trusted at night.

Yet, when they reached the gates, he almost regretted

his decision. One body lay sprawled just at the entrance, the arms outstretched as if imploring the newcomers to flee for their lives. Trajan had a torch brought up.

"Mitra . . ." he whispered. The dead soldier's expression was one of outright fear. Worse, whatever had slain him had done so in a manner not at all like what Trajan had expected. To his trained gaze, it looked as if something had shattered the Aquilonian's bones—even battering the breastplate to ruin—and only then had *ripped* out his throat. The mouth still lay open in midscream.

"Stand ready . . ." Trajan commanded unnecessarily as he led the column inside.

The scene that slowly unveiled itself in the light of their torches resembled something out of nightmare. The corpses of the garrison's complement lay strewn throughout the area. The dead hung from the walls, sprawled on the ground, and, in one particularly macabre case, stood pinned against the door of the barracks.

Despite the grisly scene, however, some of Trajan's horror changed to fury. There were men who appeared to have been torn apart like the sentry at the gates, but many others, including the one by the barracks, had died in a more familiar fashion. The bolts sticking out of the throats and chests of several were proof enough.

"Picts!" he spat. "Picts or brigands, it matters not which! This is their work!" He looked around, and the absence of what he searched for further verified to the captain the source of the villainy. "Not a sign of any of the friendlies," Trajan added, referring to those natives who lived in the fort . . . especially the officers' kept women. "One or more of them clearly opened the way, likely after slitting the throat of the guard."

"But the way the body was mangled—" began Dralos.

"Picts're *beasts*, as I've always said! Done by them to shake our nerves!" He grunted, more at ease despite the butchery. "They brought this on themselves, keeping those females here! The rules warn against such fraternization! Aye, that's how it came about, mark me!"

His words did not entirely ease the thoughts of his men but did put the massacre more into a perspective that they could understand. It would not have been the first time that so-called friendlies had proven to be spies.

"Gather the bodies. We've no time for burials. Get a pyre started just outside the walls and make certain it's well tended. And get that body off the barracks door!"

As the men moved to obey, Trajan located the officers' quarters. With Dralos behind him, he shoved open the door and stepped inside. Two more bodies lay immediately within, one of them the fort commander. Unshirted, he had easily fallen victim to a stab in the back.

Dralos, his composure much returned, knelt by the corpse. "This is no Pict weapon, Captain. Looks like good steel did this!"

"Brigands, then. Likely Khatak's bunch. He's got his Pict ties . . ." Trajan moved on to the next room . . . and suddenly stopped still at the doorway.

Dralos rose. "Captain, what—"

"Shut the front door, Dralos . . ." his commander snapped in a low tone. "Now."

After the soldier had obeyed, he joined Trajan. Dralos peered past him and swore.

Two other officers lay dead, obviously stabbed. Near them, however, also lay the bodies of four young Pictish females.

Trajan looked over the latter. They had been as brutally treated as the Aquilonians. "Dralos. I want two men who can be trusted to keep their mouths shut. I want those bodies wrapped up so that they can't be identified, then tossed on the pyre when it's burning strong."

"Maybe . . . maybe there was another wench who did like you said or some other Pict who worked at the fort—"

"That's likely true, but if the others see these bodies, it'll get them all worked up. They'll start wondering about that body at the gates or the others like it. Truth be told, Dralos, nothing human did that, not even something so base as a Pict."

"But you said—"

The captain gave him a harsh look. "I *know* what I said. Find the men and deal with these bodies. We stay the night, then tomorrow leave half our troops here with supplies and ride back in haste to tell General Boronius everything."

Dralos looked more uneasy again. "Leave half *here*?"

"They're soldiers of Aquilonia. Besides, it won't be maybe a little more than a week before they get some reinforcements."

"More like a month . . ." the other soldier muttered. Nevertheless, he saluted and went off to find the men whom Trajan had requested.

The veteran officer eyed the bloody display. One night. It would be more than enough for Trajan's taste. The sooner he got back to Scanaga, the sooner General Boronius could properly take care of the matter. It would be out of Trajan's hands.

"Damned wilderness," he growled as he made his way to the beds. Thankfully, at least they were bereft of blood. He could sleep here tonight . . . once the bodies were gone.

He lit an oil lamp that had somehow survived the chaos, then tore a large blanket from one of the beds and began the task of wrapping up the first of the Pict bodies. Dralos returned a few moments later with the two men in question, both of whom Trajan knew to be trustworthy. The small party quickly finished their morbid work, and the two began lugging the first of the women out.

"Treat her like she's heavier," their commanding officer reminded them. "The others must think them the bodies of our own."

When the last of the corpses had been removed and Dralos reported that the fire had consumed them, Trajan finally relaxed. He had men guarding every wall and the pyre under strict control. Dralos and two other seasoned fighters had command of the troops for the night. There was no hint of trouble outside. The fort was well secure.

"Report to me when you come off duty," he ordered Dralos before dismissing him. Because of the native girls' bodies, the beds were bereft of blankets, but Trajan had slept out in the open enough in his life that the loss mattered not a whit. Not even bothering to remove his breastplate, the captain fell back and shut his eyes.

A sound on the roof made him open them wide again.

The oil lamp still flickered with life, creating shadows on the walls. Trajan blinked, his inner clock—trained through years of service to Aquilonia—immediately informing him that he had probably slept some two hours.

The captain waited, but the sound did not repeat itself. He finally started to relax again—and then shouts and screams shook him to the core.

"No . . ."

Trajan leapt to his feet, his sword already half-drawn. He ran to the door, wondering why his guards had not alerted him.

A bright light leaked through the cracks. Trajan smelled smoke. He tore open the door.

Swarthy figures wielding axes and swords filled the fort.

And the gate was open again.

As for his two sentries, both lay dead, one with his neck broken and the other with a gaping hole in his throat that brought back visions of the body found at the gates.

A wild cry was all the warning Trajan had before the brigand nearly severed his neck. The captain leapt back, recovered, and pressed his would-be killer. The bearded and unkempt thief was no match for his expertise. Trajan's blade artfully cut open his chest.

As his foe collapsed, Trajan grabbed hold of a soldier running past him. "You! How did this happen?"

"Someone opened the gates!" the other answered uselessly.

"Ridiculous! No one in this troop would do so, and the walls are too steep for any man to climb without gear!"

Yet, the gates *were* open . . . but how?

He had no more chance to discover the truth, for suddenly an arrow caught the soldier in the back of the head. With a gasp, the man slumped against Trajan. The captain unceremoniously tossed the twitching corpse aside, then ducked a second shot. Swearing, Trajan slipped behind one of the supply wagons and attempted to collect his thoughts.

Everywhere the clang of metal resounded. A voice shouting commands stirred the officer. Dralos.

"Re-form ranks!" his second called. "Watch the horses!"

Trajan followed Dralos's voice, spotting the other Aquilonian outlined in the flames of a burning wagon. A small band of soldiers stood with him.

He started for the band, certain that with this as the nucleus, they could rebuild and counterattack. There were not so many brigands that a squad of well-trained soldiers could not run them off. Surprise had been the only reason for the disaster—

Then, to his astonishment, a single, huge figure leapt from one of the walls. The drop should have slain the reckless attacker, but, somehow, he landed unharmed . . . and in the midst of Dralos's fighters.

They should have cut him to ribbons, but, instead, the giant brigand raised one Aquilonian high and threw him into several of the others. Another who sought to attack the newcomer was seized by the arm . . . an arm that, a breath later, cracked audibly. The shadowy brigand then crushed in his victim's skull with a huge fist.

What sort of man is he? Trajan wondered. *Could that be Khatak?*

As he started forward again, a sharp pain caught him in the thigh. The end of a shaft thrust out from his leg. Trajan stumbled down on one knee.

He looked up in time to see Dralos lunge at the berserker. Dralos was almost as large as his foe and with his skill with a sword should have easily cut down the brigand, but the latter moved with inhuman swiftness, leaping atop Trajan's man and—

The captain nearly lost his last meal. The fearsome figure had thrust his head forward and *bit* Dralos through the throat.

"Mitra!" Ignoring his own pain, Trajan pushed himself

forward in the hopes of coming to the rescue. However, a bearded figure with wild black hair and a crooked grin suddenly blocked his way. The robber had no shirt, only a jerkin, and on his chest were tattoos of Pictish design.

"You would be their commanding officer, yes?"

"Away, you filth!" Trajan slashed, but the easy kill he expected never materialized, for the brigand parried his sword with ease, then forced the wounded captain back. Trajan quickly realized that he faced a master swordsman.

The captain was pushed farther back. Trajan gritted his teeth as desperation filled him. All around, his men were being slaughtered, and he could do nothing.

In his foe's steely eyes Trajan saw that this was just what the brigand intended. Without a capable commander, the soldiers would be easier to slay.

"Ungh!" A red cut now graced the Aquilonian's right cheek. He knew then that he was outclassed. This half-breed fought with skills far beyond most of Trajan's fellow officers.

At that point, he realized who it was he faced. "You! You're Khatak!"

The crooked grin grew pleased. "Ha! Yes, I am Khatak! Khatak the Sly! Khatak the Black Fox!"

Trajan had little doubt that he would die, but, if he could take the master brigand, then his own death would have some worth. Summoning up his remaining strength, the captain pushed his skills to the limit. He succeeded in halting Khatak's advance, then forced the ebony-maned bandit to retreat.

Yet, Khatak seemed, if anything, entertained by his situation. He laughed. "Good! Very good!"

Growling, Captain Trajan sought for the throat. The point of his sword slipped past Khatak's guard—

And an impossibly strong hand grabbed the Aquilonian by the nape of the neck. Trajan dangled in the air, then was turned to face the one who held him like a child. The putrid stench of a carnivore filled his nostrils.

The face . . . the face was a nightmare.

"Mitra protect me! What is it?"

He heard Khatak chuckle. "My own personal god."

Yellow fangs four inches long buried themselves in Trajan's throat as the Aquilonian screamed.

THE CLASH OF blades echoed through Nermesa's ears.

"Again!" thundered the officer in charge, a thick-necked veteran with several scars and a patch covering one eye. He strode among the combatants, studying the various duels.

The torchlit chamber held three dozen men, most of them aristocrats hoping to prove their worth as knights of the realm. In the old days, all a noble had to do was pay enough gold, and he could gain the rank he desired. That had changed with the coming of Conan. Now the value of a man was in his wit and his sword arm, not his birth. That rankled many old families, but the results could not be denied. The Aquilonian military was at its best level in decades.

Even Nermesa had secretly hoped that, as a noble of Tarantia, he might be able to gain the posting of his desire, chiefly the Black Dragons. The king's personal bodyguard was known for its strength and allegiance, and to become one was a mark of achievement few ever attained. Only about five hundred men at any one time wore the crested breastplates with the stylized beast emblazoned on the front, five hundred out of the fifty-five thousand and more that made up the Aquilonian military.

But even though Nermesa considered his skills up to the standards of the august company, it had become clear to him in just a few days that such a dream was not yet to be his. Exactly where he would end up was, to his knowledge, derived from some arcane and perhaps even random formula. All the young noble understood was that in another two days, he would be sent *somewhere*.

"Watch that sloppy bladework!" the senior officer, Garaldo, snapped. He was, in fact, a knight of Poitain who had once served directly under Prospero, not only commander of the forces of Count Trocero of Poitain, but also one of the king's most trusted advisors. But minutes after first introducing himself, Garaldo had picked out several of the most prominent of the new recruits and beaten each of them handily in combat.

"Just so each of you know from here on why you young blue bloods won't be given instant command of some part of his majesty's army," he had said afterward.

The lesson had taken with Nermesa. Now he wanted only not to embarrass himself before the highly skilled Garaldo. If he succeeded in that, then perhaps there might be hope that his posting would not be in some backwater area where the greatest danger was the risk of dying from boredom.

Garaldo stalked past him, watching each move carefully. Sometimes, Nermesa wondered whether the eye with the patch was actually useless; the Poitainian seemed to see things even to the side of it.

The fighters wore padded vests and helmets over pants and shirt. Today they wielded swords, but, in the past few days, they had trained with a variety of weapons, both on foot and on horseback. Veterans like Garaldo continuously monitored every action, however minute.

Nermesa's current opponent tried a foolhardy lunge, no doubt in an attempt to impress Garaldo. Bolontes' son easily dodged it, then brought his own blade over the other's guard. The blunted tip jabbed the other noble right above the heart.

Garaldo stepped between them.

"You're looking like a true leader," commented the veteran knight . . . to Nermesa's adversary. As Nermesa stared incredulously, and the other fighter started to grin, Garaldo wryly added, "Yes, you'll lead your men straight into the afterlife with foolhardy stunts like that!" Turning to Nermesa, he added, "A good, strong return, but you want the blade *here*." Garaldo guided the tip to where the center of the heart was located. "He might've lived long enough to gut you in turn. Always aim for the vital areas."

"Yes, Sir Garaldo."

Only then did Nermesa notice in the background a figure who seemed to be studying the group in earnest. A rich, purple cloak with silver threading draped over the watcher from his shoulders almost to the floor. Narrow brown eyes that missed nothing swept over Nermesa with obvious interest.

The heir to Klandes held back a frown. The dark complexion, vulpine features, and thick, long black hair reminded him of the people of Ophir, whose lands lay beyond the southern mountains of Aquilonia, yet there was something familiar about the man, obviously a noble and a knight.

Only when the figure turned and strode away—slightly limping—did Nermesa realize who he was . . . and how much of a fool Bolontes' son must have looked, staring back so.

The cloak had shifted away just enough to reveal laced, silver armor . . . and a breastplate upon which a hissing wyrm of ebony stood. It was an emblem worn by only one man in all the kingdom . . . Pallantides, commander of the Black Dragons themselves.

Garaldo did not hear his groan, the senior knight having moved on to the next pair, but another did.

"There something the matter, Master Nermesa? You suddenly look ill."

"Nothing's wrong except that I keep doing things to make my dreams stay dreams and never reality, that's all. Do you know who that was?"

Quentus frowned. Like his lord, he was covered in sweat. He trained with the young nobles, although how Nermesa's father had arranged that the son did could not fathom. It showed the great influence of Klandes in the royal court despite any misgivings Bolontes might have concerning Conan. "Somebody important," the bearded man muttered. "All that silver armor and all."

"General Pallantides," Nermesa revealed. "Of the Black Dragons."

"Aaah. Maybe he saw your fine swordplay, Master Nermesa."

"More likely he saw me gaping at him like a fool. Not the sort of demeanor one would look for in a future Black Dragon . . ."

"All right!" snapped Garaldo to the group. "That's enough for now! Your time's your own for the rest of the day, but we'll all start new before first light, so you'd be wise to see yourselves to your beds soon!"

Nermesa exhaled in relief. Quentus passed him a water sack, from which the noble greedily drank. "I never thought it would be this difficult . . ."

"You've done yourself proud, Master Nermesa."

"We'll see."

As they left the gray-walled practice room, they heard sounds coming from other chambers. During the reign of King Namedides, this far-off section on the right half of the vast palace had been reserved for torture. At any one time, dozens who had run afoul of the tyrant's lusts had been condemned to it. Iron maidens, racks, and cat-o'-nine-tails had been only a few of the monstrous tools in use then.

King Conan had disposed of all of those and remade the chambers into training areas, yet there were those who swore that the ghosts of Namedides' victims still wailed from the corridors.

However, it was no phantom's wail that startled Nermesa, but rather a loud, enthusiastic roar from the room to his right. He and Quentus paused in the doorway in time to see two giants grappling with one another. The one facing them was a tawny-haired Gunderman with beady eyes, a broad jaw, and an even broader grin. He stood a good hand taller than his opponent, who was also some outlander, although of what people, Nermesa could not say. The square-cut black mane and sun-browned skin clearly marked him as from far away. Even though the Gunderman outweighed him, there was something about the latter's catlike movements and muscled body that made Nermesa choose him as the better of the two.

Sure enough, a moment later, his choice proved one of wisdom. The black-haired wrestler twisted, pulling his opponent over his wide shoulder. The Gunderman sought to counter, but leverage was with his foe. The huge fighter went flying over, landing with a thud on the cloth mat covering the floor.

Not taking any chances, the other outlander shifted position, forcing the Gunderman onto his stomach and bending one arm tight behind the back. He then planted one powerful knee on his adversary to complete his victory.

The pinned wrestler let out a groan, then rumbled, "I yield, your majesty!"

"Your—" Nermesa blurted before catching himself.

Smoldering blue eyes glanced toward the doorway, then, apparently sizing up the young noble as of no concern, quickly returned to the match. The victor released the Gunderman, who rolled over and accepted his monarch's assistance up.

"Well fought, Varom!" roared King Conan, patting the man on the shoulder. "Well fought, indeed, by Crom!"

"But with the same results as ever . . ." returned the loser, rubbing his arm. "None's the man who can beat you, your majesty!"

The blue eyes grew steely. "But I'll trust they try their best! I want no mock victory simply because I sit on the throne!"

"I think we all understand that, my liege," said another. General Pallantides materialized from the right. "Now, if you are through for the day, I've matters that must be presented to you."

"Crom! Don't you always?"

The appearance of the general urged Nermesa to a hasty departure. He had already been caught once looking like a gawking child. It would not do for Pallantides to see him so again.

"Truly the king is unique among mortals!" blurted Quentus as they hurried through the corridors. "Such raw power! Like a wild but graceful animal!"

"He is *Conan*," the noble managed to answer. Had his face registered with the king? He hoped not. Bad enough if General Pallantides thought him a buffoon, but if the lord of Aquilonia also did, Nermesa's hoped-for military career was already at an ignominious end.

As he came in sight of his assigned quarters, he noticed

a figure who seemed to be waiting for him, by his black tunic with the gold lion emblazoned on it, a messenger of the palace. Fearful that he had already somehow slighted King Conan, Nermesa met the man.

"You are Nermesa, son of Bolontes and heir to House Klandes?" the functionary crisply asked.

"I am."

"It was requested that this be handed to you personally," the other informed him, holding forth a parchment.

"What is it?" Nermesa asked, taking the item. However, the messenger had already turned to leave and seemed disinclined to look back and answer. He marched away, quickly vanishing down another corridor.

"From your father?" suggested Quentus.

Turning the small, flat parchment over, the noble saw a seal that was not of his House . . . yet, was almost as familiar to him as that of Klandes.

"No . . . it's Lenaro's seal."

The sudden intake of breath from Quentus matched Nermesa's own quickening pulse. The young Klandes quickly broke the seal and read the contents.

"Lady Orena wishes to see me."

Quentus tugged on his beard. "We could still pretend that the missive didn't reach you or that you're so busy here that you don't have time to ride to her home—"

"She's already thought of that," Nermesa returned, crumpling the parchment. "Orena wants to see me *immediately*." He handed Quentus the note to dispose of and girded himself for what was to come. "She's here at the palace, waiting . . ."

3

THE GREAT HALL was some fifty feet high and required some time to cross even at a good pace. Every few yards, wide, fluted columns of marble stood sentry duty and, between them, the heads of kings past stared out from friezes painted most lifelike. Conan had been wise enough to understand that, when he had conquered the realm, it would not do to wipe away the Aquilonian people's entire history. One could find nothing of Namedides in the palace, but rulers long dead—and, therefore, no political threat—were allowed to retain their places in the annals of the kingdom's prestigious past.

There were living sentries in the hall, too—a half dozen crack members of the Black Dragons. Clad in armor, their stern gazes fixed straight ahead, they made for an imposing sight. Unfortunately, they also remained some distance from the torchlit entranceway where Nermesa's visitor awaited. Knowing just who he would be facing, the would-be knight wished that their strength would accompany him and Quentus.

As Nermesa neared the iron doors, Orena Lenaro rose from the plush bench set aside for those awaiting entrance.

She was the vision of classic Aquilonian beauty—thick blond hair bound tight behind her head, a slim yet patrician nose, sculpted cheekbones artfully touched with a hint of red powder, full, crimson lips, and eyes as green as emeralds. Lady Orena Lenaro was a statuesque woman who stood not much shorter than Nermesa.

Her white-and-silver gown, bound at the waist to best accentuate her alluring figure, came within an inch of the floor. Nermesa's betrothed looked like nothing less than a goddess . . . a cold, imperious goddess, in his eyes.

Behind her stood two other figures. One was a broad-shouldered, ponytailed Gunderman with a square jaw and very patient look. Although Orena's servant for the past three years, Morannus, had, at times, become something of a friend to Nermesa. The noble often wondered how the earthy guard could tolerate his mistress's imperious personality.

The second figure, barely seen behind Orena, was a shorter, almost boyish female who bore some resemblance to Nermesa's betrothed, but in a rough way. Her auburn hair hung straight and unadorned, and the brown gown in which she was clad did likewise. Most appealing about her was her eyes, which were green like his betrothed's, but softer. Those eyes stared wide at Nermesa, and a hint of red suddenly graced the pale cheeks.

"Orena," Nermesa murmured, taking her proffered hand and kissing the back of it. He looked briefly at Orena's younger companion. "Telaria, you've grown. Someday very soon, men will batter at the doors of Lenaro for your favor."

The blush grew deeper. Orena glanced dismissively at Telaria. "My sister is fortunate that I am seeing to her future. I will find her a respectable match, one that will benefit House Lenaro."

Nermesa did not bother to remind her that House Lenaro would be absorbed into Klandes upon their marriage. It was a sore point with Orena, even though Klandes offered new life to her dying line.

"One hopes it will be a pleasing match," Nermesa agreed, with silent sympathy for Telaria. The sisters' mother had died after delivering Telaria, and their father had passed only a few years later. He had been in negotiations for his youngest child's betrothal to a very prominent family, but, upon his death, Orena had put an end to that. Since then, she seemed to be waiting for the most advantageous arrangement.

"So long as it is of value to both Houses, it will be." Her lidded gaze fixed on Nermesa. There were many among his friends who envied his position, for Orena was among the most desired women in Tarantia, but Nermesa, who knew her better than anyone save perhaps the pair with her, would have preferred to trade betrothals with just about any of his comrades.

"Thank you for your wishes, Lord Nermesa . . ." Telaria belatedly piped up. She immediately shied back when Orena looked over her shoulder, and in the torchlight, Nermesa thought he saw a mark on the side of the young girl's forehead. Dark thoughts filled his mind, but he knew that he could do nothing. As mistress of Lenaro, Orena had utter domain over her sister's life, including punishment.

Again dismissing the presence of her sibling, Orena said, "Your letter caused me much distress, my love. To hear of your imminent entry into the service of the king—a proud and worthy service, of course—and to hear of it in so distant a manner as a message carried by a servant, shook me to the core! Our marriage date was to be set within the next year, but your impetuous desire, no doubt to prove yourself worthy of our match, places that date in jeopardy . . ."

Nermesa steeled himself. "As I stated in it, I ask forgiveness for my actions, Orena, but it was something I felt I must do. My soul demands it. Besides, it can only bring more prestige and advantage to our Houses . . ."

A subtle change in her manner indicated to Nermesa that his last words had struck Orena well. Prestige and advantage meant more to her than even to his father.

But still she would not let him slip free of the noose. "There is certainly truth to what you say, my love, and I applaud what can only build an even more prosperous future for us, but with our Houses yet unbound, I fear what might happen to both of them without a formal declaration of our unity."

Nermesa fought back his anger. To hear her speak of it, their betrothal sounded more like a peace treaty between two warring kingdoms . . . which might not have been so far from the truth. Worse, she clearly indicated with such words that she wanted some legal right to his estate should he fall victim to battle or accident while serving the king. Understandable in some ways, but the tone in which she suggested it made it sound more like a simple business consideration than concern for what might actually happen to him.

"Should *tragedy* befall me," he responded, emphasizing the word since Orena had not even used it, "my father will do whatever must be done. You have my assurance on that."

She started to say more, but Morannus suddenly interjected, "Noble lady, the hour draws late, and you have guests coming still."

The blond woman nodded slightly. "Thank you for reminding me. It would be remiss of me to make them wait." To Nermesa, Orena added, "Very well, if that is how it must be. Be careful, my love. Come back to me so that we may be wed as soon as possible."

She leaned forward and kissed him. What should have been a caring, wondrous moment had, to Nermesa, all the emotion of ice. Orena's lips pressed against his, but that was all.

The Gunderman opened the way for his mistress and her sister, but, as he did, he leaned back a bit and, with a brief nod, muttered, "Fare you well, Lord Nermesa."

"You're a patient soul," the noble returned, also speaking low.

Morannus glanced at Lady Orena's back, then again at Nermesa. With a momentary grin, he answered, "Very patient, yes."

Only when the door had closed did Bolantes' son relax. Beside him, Quentus shook his head.

"Glad as a lowly servant my choice of brides is mine, not that of some patriarch."

"So why haven't *you* married, then?"

The bearded man grinned. "Because it's also the *bride's* choice, and, so far, whoever she is, she's decided to keep herself from my sight."

Nermesa started to chuckle, but, at that moment, one of the other young hopefuls came barreling down the hall. He spied the pair and, with clear annoyance, growled, "Here you are! Garaldo sent me to look for you! You're wanted in the main practice chamber!"

"For what?"

"How would I know?" sneered the other. "If you're in trouble with him, I want no part of it! I've given the message, now it's up to you to face him!"

Nermesa and Quentus glanced at one another, then rushed to where Sir Garaldo awaited them. As he ran, Nermesa went over everything that he could think of that might have caused the veteran fighter to find fault with him. Unfortunately, in his mind the list stretched far too long.

To his surprise, Garaldo was not alone in the chamber. There were four others from Nermesa's group, all looking as concerned for themselves as Bolontes' son did.

"Good. You're here, too," Garaldo commented in Quentus's direction.

The servant grimaced. "What did I do?"

"Hush," his master quickly ordered.

"Nermesa of Klandes," continued the senior knight, ignoring Quentus's outburst. The eye with the patch seemed to fix on Bolontes' son. "I've had some trouble tracking you down."

"Forgive me . . . I had a . . . an unexpected visitor."

"A lady, no doubt. Hope you saw a lot of her, Nermesa of Klandes, for you'll not have another chance for some time to come."

"I don't—"

But Garaldo cut him off. Instead, he surveyed the entire party. "You've all acted quite eager to join the finest military in all the known world. You all say you desire to serve the king, may he reign supreme for many years." Again, the eye patch appeared to be facing Nermesa. "Well, lads, now you'll be able to prove yourselves."

He said no more, for then a cloaked figure entered who caused everyone to stand at attention. Garaldo slapped a fist against his chest in salute.

General Pallantides nodded to the assembled group. "These are the ones, Garaldo?"

"My opinion, General."

"And one I greatly trust." Pallantides looked over each one. He towered over them despite Nermesa and the rest being themselves well over average.

Nermesa expected an escort of Black Dragons to follow the general into the chamber, but it quickly became obvious that Pallantides was alone. True, here in the palace he was likely very safe—and could readily defend himself against most threats, anyway—but Nermesa was used to government officials and stout nobles who paraded through Tarantia's streets with so many guards that one had to wonder if they assumed themselves more important to the realm than even the king.

The general abruptly paused before him, squinting. Up close, an anxious Nermesa noticed the small scars decorating much of Pallantides' face. He also read in those eyes a man entirely devoted to his liege and his position. Pallantides would have cast himself over a cliff and let his bones dash on the ground below if it meant saving King Conan.

"You've a skilled arm, Nermesa of House Klandes. Is his wit quick enough to keep pace with it, Garaldo?"

As Nermesa fought to keep from quivering, the one-eyed knight chuckled. "I thought so, but he may be a bit distracted by the ladies . . ."

"Aren't we all. What say you, Garaldo?"

"Aye, he could survive it . . . and help others to do so, I think."

The heir to Klandes wanted to ask just what they were talking about but was certain that, if he did, he would be lowering himself in the eyes of both men. What did they have planned that they had to ask about not only his ability to survive, but how well he could keep others alive, too?

"What about this one?" The commander of the Black Dragons indicated Quentus, who stood as frozen as Nermesa.

"A finely matched set for a master and servant. You'll get good value."

General Pallantides nodded at what Nermesa thought a very enigmatic statement, then addressed the group. "Sir Garaldo tells me that, of your band, you lot are the most capable fighters." There was some swelling of chests until he added, "But capable fighters are easier to find than honest politicians. What Aquilonia needs and what I, as the king's general and commander of his loyal Black Dragons require, though, are those who can fight and think at the same time. Those who can command others and keep them, as much as possible, from losing their heads to an ax or having a canyon slit through their chests by a sword."

Although he tried to hide his growing excitement, Nermesa felt his mouth twitch upward in the beginnings of a smile. He and the others were meant for something important to the realm!

"The Black Dragons are the elite guard of the king, and I'm proud to be at their head, but my duties extend to all Aquilonia. That includes the Westermarck . . . which is where you lot come in."

The Westermarck. To Nermesa, the vast wilderness area was a place of legend, where brave soldiers and intrepid colonists sought to tame the lands of the bestial Picts. Many were the astounding tales a young Nermesa had listened to with round eyes from servants who had, in their earlier days, fought as men-at-arms. He had often imagined himself battling tattooed, loincloth-clad warriors who wielded axes and shouted war cries in their unintelligible tongue.

Now that boyhood dream was about to become a reality.

"Garaldo will give you each your orders. You will be the

equivalent of captains to start and will respond by that title. Bear in mind, the Westermarck is no place for games, so if any of you think yourselves not up to the task, you likely aren't. You can tell Garaldo yourself and save us all a lot of trouble and a lot of lives. That is all I have to say."

Garaldo stepped forward to say something, but what it was, Nermesa would never know, for, as Pallantides turned to leave, he nodded to Bolontes' son, then patted him on the shoulder. Nermesa stood silent as the general departed, entirely undone by the personal gesture.

"The Westermarck . . ." Quentus finally mouthed, stirring his master. "Had an uncle who fought there . . . and never came back."

The comment finally drove home exactly what they might face. Nermesa looked at Quentus. "You're not required to do this. I'll send you back to the house with a message for Father stating that I refused your company—"

"Do you take me for a coward?" Quentus snapped, ignoring their different statuses. "Master Nermesa, I'm as willing to serve Aquilonia as you!"

"Good to hear that!" Garaldo joined them. "I don't like looking the fool! I told the general that you two were worthy of what he wanted, and if you'd backed down, it'd have been my hide . . ." The elder knight leaned close to Nermesa. "And then it'd be your hide, young *master*."

"I've no intention of backing down, Sir Garaldo . . ."

"Then we're settled, aren't we?" He handed Nermesa a small, folded parchment. "The orders. Written in Pallantides' good hand with the king's signature to mark them! Come the ceremony, you'll be a true knight of Aquilonia, lad! Then all you've got to do is prove it . . ."

Nermesa gaped at the parchment and the power held within. He had thought his life transformed just by his decision to join, but truly the most dramatic change had come now.

The Westermarck . . .

• • •

THE DRUMS BEAT faster and faster, stirring the warriors' blood as they danced around the great fire. In the wild, flickering flames, the tattoos covering their bodies seemed to writhe of their own will. Short but broad-shouldered, the warriors moved smoothly and swiftly like the animals of the thick forest around them. They wore little save loin-cloths or deerskin breeches, and their thick black manes were bound tight by copper bands. The flames reflected in their narrow black eyes, and the patterns painted on their faces only added to their demonic appearance.

Now and then, one would howl, often revealing teeth sharpened to points. Sharp teeth also hung around their necks, those of the fox, from which this particular tribe took its name. Each Pictish tribe chose an animal or bird spirit as its totem. The Fox Tribe was not among the largest, but they were known for their slyness and ferocity.

The five drummers continued to beat madly. The taut skins on their drums came not from some beast, but rather slaughtered enemies. The Fox people believed that this bound the souls of their adversaries to them, making the tribe stronger.

And around the area of the ceremony, atop poles towering over the Picts, the skulls of other enemies stared down sightlessly. Some had the squat shape of Picts, for feuds between the tribes were common, but several had the longer look of the invaders, the Aquilonians. A few of the latter were especially fresh.

Huts encircled the opening, and from one rounded wooden structure emerged a bent, skeletal figure who wore upon his balding head a complete fox skin that draped down in the back and ended with the skull of the animal atop. Despite his tremendous age, the eyes were so piercing that any upon whom he looked cringed.

A sleek, well-curved young female, wearing little more than the warriors, walked behind him. She carried two bowls, one with a dark liquid, the other a white powder. The shaman crossed the dancers without any hesitation, for it was they who made certain not to interfere with his path for fear of their souls. The female followed quickly behind, cautious not to spill a single drop or crumb from either bowl.

The shaman stopped before the flames, then reached to the side with his hand. The girl, her face fearful, brought the bowls under his fingers. From the powder, the elder took a pinch. He threw the powder into the fire, and the flames briefly exploded skyward.

"Jhebbal Sag!" the shaman called in the Picts' guttural tongue.

Around him, the dancers paused and all shouted the name again. "Jhebbal Sag!"

He took another pinch, tossed it in, and as the fire shot up, called out a different yet equally fearsome name. The other Picts repeated it, their eyes wide and devoted.

At last, the skeletal elder took the bowl with the liquid from the girl. So close to the flames, the crimson color of the contents could readily be seen. The shaman uttered several words, then, raising the bowl over his head, roared, "Yana Gullah!"

"Gullah!" came the cry from the rest.

He threw the liquid into the fire.

A tremendous hiss rose and, instead of even dousing the flames slightly, the liquid fueled them in such a manner that the girl and several warriors nearby stepped back. Only the shaman remained close, laughing at the results.

Then he whipped his head to the right and growled to two warriors near another hut. The stone-faced figures ducked inside and, a moment later, removed from it a desperately struggling Aquilonian.

"No! Please! No!" he cried. What was left of his soiled garments marked him not as a soldier but a merchant. Formerly fine, silken robes now ended in grimy tatters. The once properly plump physique beneath had shriveled to nearly the boniness of the shaman. The merchant's head had been shaven with no regard as to cutting the flesh in the process. His face was freshly painted, a skull symbol embracing his features.

His hands and legs bound, the Aquilonian was dragged to

a spot just before the flames. He ceased pleading, but continued to look around in panic, seeking that which was to be his death.

At a silent signal from the shaman, the warriors forced the victim into a kneeling position, then tied his arms to his legs. They staked both to the ground so that he could not even roll away.

The drums beat. The shaman danced around the Aquilonian. He threw a bit of the white powder at the merchant, calling again the name *Gullah*.

Suddenly, the drumming came to a halt. The shaman waved a hand to the people and, as one, the Picts rose and began to walk off. There was that in their steps that showed a barely held eagerness to be away. The merchant anxiously watched them, aware that he was being left alone for a reason.

Only the tribal elder remained. Grinning darkly, he put both hands by his mouth, and shouted, "Yana Gullah! Yana Gullah zin!"

And with that, he, too, vanished from the area.

Shaking, the Aquilonian peered around, but, after several seconds, nothing happened. The lack of action did nothing to assuage him and, in fact, heightened his fear. He struggled, attempting both to free himself from the stake and tear apart his bonds. His contortions caused his shadow, created by the lusty fire, to dance even more madly.

He gasped with revived hope as he felt the stake loosen. It had a sharp point to it, which the merchant could possibly use to sever his other bonds. His tugging grew more determined . . .

In the midst of his struggles, he happened to look up and see that the shadow had grown to gargantuan proportions. The merchant started to look away again . . . then noticed the giant shadow move to the side, revealing the smaller one that truly belonged to him.

With growing horror, he forced his gaze to that direction in order to see what could be so huge yet had moved as silently as the shadow it cast.

"Mitra!" the merchant gasped. "No!"

Huge hands seized him . . .

THE INHUMAN HOWL that followed made the Fox people kneel and chant. One word . . . or name . . . they repeated over and over.

Gullah . . . Gullah . . .

But one there was who did not chant, instead watching wryly as the Picts abased themselves. Khatak the brigand, arms folded, smiled as the tribe concluded its bloody ritual. Tomorrow, a new head would decorate the poles . . .

He let the chanting go on for a minute more, then located the chief. The wiry, deep-chested warrior rose quickly when he saw Khatak coming toward him. He treated the brigand with as much regard as he would have the shaman, possibly even more.

"The people of the fox are pleased with this blessing, great one," the tribal leader quickly said in Pictish.

"Then there should be no trouble doing as I asked," returned Khatak in the same tongue. "The power of the Fox Tribe is strong now, especially with The Hairy One Who Lives in the Moon having shown his favor, yes?"

The chieftain grunted proudly. "Spirit of Gullah fills us all! We will crush the Wolf, the Raven, the shelled ones . . . any foe that is asked of us by you!"

"You know what is wished by Gullah through me, who speaks his words on the mortal plane. Do as is desired, and greater yet will be the Fox Tribe, for it'll be a part of something so powerful that the shelled ones will be driven from the Land screaming!"

That uttered, the bandit leader turned from the chief without any farewell. He strode through the camp, finally leaving it entirely. A short distance through the moonlit forest, he came upon three riders, his companions on this trip. Two were fellow brigands sworn to his service. The other was a form so completely cloaked, one could not have sworn whether it was man, woman, or even human.

"It's done," the half-breed declared to the others. "The Fox Tribe will fall into place with the others."

The robbers grinned. The hood of the unseen figure dipped once.

A slight shuffling of the foliage above made Khatak glance up. He smiled in the direction of the sound. "Done already? Well, then, we can leave."

The brigand leader mounted, then led the others off. In their wake, the only sound of the fifth member of their group was the occasional rustle of leaves in the treetops behind them.

4

KING CONAN WAS not one for the long, pompous ceremonies that from time immemorial had so marked Aquilonia's aristocracy. Thus it was that on the evening after he
was informed of his posting to the Westermarck, Nermesa
and the others selected—all clad in the colors of their re-
spective Houses—stood before the former barbarian and
his magnificent queen, Zenobia.

Nermesa was very taken by the queen. In much the way
that Conan's exotic look and manner made him so distinctive
as ruler, so, too, did Zenobia mark a change in what Nermesa's people expected of a royal consort.

The queen was said to be of Nemedian heritage, but she
had burned all ties with that kingdom when she had risked
herself to save Conan after he had been stolen away to Nemedia by black sorcery. Some said that she had originally
been a harem girl who had been in love with the king since
gazing upon him from afar years before. Whether or not the
truth, these days no one doubted her deep love and devotion

not only to her husband, but also the people over whom she now ruled.

A dark-haired beauty, Zenobia was not merely a showpiece for the king. She had a quick wit about her, spoke her mind whenever she felt, and was clearly well respected for it by the former barbarian. Clad in a silken gown that draped to the floor, Zenobia sat at a height equal to her husband. No one who stood before them could not think them as other than a perfect match.

The throne room was large and elaborate, capable of holding almost a thousand people standing. High tapestries, with the golden lion prominently displayed, lined the stone walls. The marble floor was draped by a wide, intricately woven rug with gold lacing brought all the way from Khitai. Elaborate carvings covered the walls between the tapestries, carvings of the heroics of the man on the throne. The last had been done on the express order of the queen, for King Conan was not one to advertise his prowess so. Zenobia, however, wanted everyone to remember of what her husband was capable.

The thrones were strong oak with gold trim throughout and ivory seats of the plushest down. Despite that, the king looked decidedly uncomfortable sitting on his even though he had already ruled for several years. It was said that the only place where King Conan could sit relaxed was in the saddle during a heated battle. The luxuries of civilization were things to which he could never completely become accustomed.

Whatever their qualms, Nermesa's parents, of course, attended his knighting, as did the families of those of the others. Orena—her sister and Morannus behind her—stood just to the side of Bolontes. Nermesa knew no one else there save for Quentus, who had been made a man-at-arms earlier, and, to his surprise, Baron Antonus Sibelio. The baron was evidently the cousin of one of the young Klandes' comrades, but Nermesa still found it a bit curious that he would be there.

True to his nature, the monarch of Aquilonia made the

ceremony short and perfunctory. After heralds blew welcoming notes on long, brass horns, Nermesa's band stepped up to the dais upon which the thrones sat. Rising from his, the king eyed each man in turn. The young nobles immediately went down on one knee, bowing their heads in the process. Coming up to them, Conan drew his sword, a long, menacing blade with a jeweled hilt.

Once more, the horns blew. One after another, Conan—dressed in simple if richly woven garments and wearing not a crown but a plain golden band around his head—took his blade and tapped each of the kneeling figures twice on the shoulder. Nermesa shivered with excitement when his turn came.

When he had finished, the king sheathed his sword, took up a goblet of wine with his bride, and, with the other guests, drank a toast to the new knights.

"May your arm be swift and strong and your blade sharp," the muscular figure intoned. Then, with a brief, sly smile, he added, "And may your enemies lie piled at your feet, their women wailing their loss the song in your ears."

Several of the nobles looked askance at this last, but Nermesa, after a momentary shock, realized that King Conan had, in addition to an Aquilonian blessing, given them a Cimmerian one as well.

The heralds signaled the end of the ceremony with a long, martial blast that echoed long after they finished. As Nermesa rose, he momentarily caught General Pallantides standing with his father. The encounter appeared a fleeting one, but there was a familiarity between the two men that surprised the knight. Did the elder Klandes know the commander of the Black Dragons?

General Pallantides joined the king and queen, who, with very little fanfare, departed the proceedings. Nermesa went to his parents, who hugged him.

"An . . . interesting ceremony," Bolontes remarked.

His mother did not hold back. "I was so very proud of the way you looked!"

"Thank you. Thank you both."

"A pity you've no chance to return to the house at least for this evening," Nermesa's father added. "Since we will not be seeing you for some time to come."

"I'm sorry, Father. We ride at first light for the Westermarck."

"The Westermarck!" gasped Callista, her pride giving way to fear again at this reminder. "Oh, Nermesa, please watch out for those horrid Picts! And where will you sleep? Bugs and serpents crawling all over the ground—"

Bolontes took hold of her shoulder. "Easy there . . ."

Nermesa kissed his mother on the forehead. "I'll be careful, Mother. You don't need to worry."

"But we *will* worry," Orena interjected, suddenly appearing at his side. One slim, alabaster arm slipped around his own. Orena kissed his cheek. Her lips were cold. "After all, you are precious to us."

"Nermesa." The elder woman clasped her hands together. "Why won't you ease all our hearts and bind yourself to Orena? It wouldn't be the marriage ceremony we planned, but a priest could be found who could quickly and officially bind you together! At least, then, she would have something of you in case . . . in case . . ."

"Now, now, dear mother," Orena murmured, stepping from Nermesa to stroke Callista's cheek. "Be at ease, for our sake."

The younger Klandes was saved from answering by Quentus, who came up, and said, "Garaldo needs to see you."

"Garaldo?" The senior knight had not been present, his duties keeping him from the ceremony. Nermesa wondered what he wanted now.

"Please excuse me," Nermesa said to the others. "I've got to go now . . . but I promise I'll be safe in the Westermarck," he added for his mother's sake. Nermesa gave his parents each a hug, then dutifully kissed Orena on her cheek. Without thinking, Nermesa gave Telaria, who had silently watched everything, a quick smile before bidding everyone good-bye.

As the newly anointed knight followed his servant out, he grumbled, "I've got to admit it, Quentus, but, for once, if

Garaldo wants to chew me out for doing something wrong, I'll be happy to suffer through it."

The bearded man grinned. "Oh, you won't have to suffer much, Master Nermesa. Garaldo doesn't want to see you. I just did that because it looked like that she-wolf had nearly trapped you . . ."

"It was a lie?"

"Another minute, and you would've been standing before a priest, my lord. She had your mother all worked into it."

It had been clear even to Nermesa that Orena had been talking to Lady Klandes. "I still have to marry her when I return, Quentus. My parents will demand it then."

"Maybe, if you're lucky, your head'll end up on a Pict spear."

"Don't jest like that." Still, although he *would* do his duty when he returned, the time out in the Westermarck did seem more like a reprieve. Of course, Nermesa was no fool. Eventually, there would come a point when all he would be able to think about was riding back to Tarantia, riding back to his family, his friends, and . . . yes . . . even Orena.

But that point was surely far, far off . . .

THE GREEN LANDS stretched for as far as the eye could see. Rolling hills covered in forest led into thick, grassy fields. Oaks, cedars, birches, and firs mingled freely. Flowering bushes abounded, adding highlights of color to the rich, emerald scene.

Gray clouds muted the lushness only slightly. The strength of the wilderness surrounding the newcomers was clearly strengthened by moisture such as the clouds promised and, in fact, the air was far more wet than back east.

Through the bucolic panorama moved the column, a striking contrast of silver, black, and gold against the green. Knights of Aquilonia astride their horses—both riders and animal armored well—held high and proud their long, tapering lances. Behind them, mounted men-at-arms followed suit. More than a score of wagons trailed after, and, in their

wake, came those on foot—more men-at-arms, archers, pike-
men, and so on.

The banner of King Conan fluttered high above, the
golden lion overlooking his domain. The column followed
the only road in the area, one beaten smooth long ago by
those who had preceded the soldiers on it. The soft, consistent plod of the horses' hooves accented the constant rattle
of armor.

Ahead at last lay the fortified town of Scanaga, the destination so eagerly awaited by those in the column since
they had left the capital some weeks earlier. The moment
should have been one of tremendous satisfaction and
pride . . . and would have been, if not for the fact that the
knights had been under constant siege all day.

"Mitra! I wish I was back in Tarantia!" snapped Nermesa, smiting another mosquito on his cheek.

Quentus, the only one near enough to hear his outburst,
grinned . . . then slapped a mosquito on his arm. "But the
ladies love you here, my lord . . . at least these little, pointy-
nosed ones."

The wooden gates of Scanaga opened for them. Scanaga
was the largest settlement in all the west but, compared to
Nermesa's home, was a provincial village, albeit one surrounded by a tall, imposing wooden wall. Still, despite its
rustic flavor, Scanaga was an essential part of the realm,
the place in which the ruling power of the west resided.
True, the lands were supposedly controlled by barons who
lived much farther to the east, but here a territorial judge
appointed by the king himself had final say in most matters. The strength of his position was significantly augmented
by the military forces under the command of General Boronius and, even though Scanaga was part of the territory of
Conawaga, their authority covered Oriskonie to the north,
Schohira to the south, and even Thandara, which Nermesa
had yet to find on any of the maps he had been provided.

They rode in a column of two hundred men and wagons
and, to his surprise, forty of those were under his com-

mand. Even under Conan, some privileges of the nobility apparently still survived. By his blood alone, Nermesa had the authority to lead these men into battle . . . at the order of General Boronius, fortunately.

Most of civilian Scanaga consisted of long, wooden buildings with angled roofs—the former barracks and supply houses for the military when they had first built the facility. Now, though, these structures were used by settlers, craftsmen, and merchants. The actual military complex lay a short distance ahead, it, too, surrounded by a high, gated wall. A fort within a fort. The notion was not so ridiculous as some might have found it, for if the Picts ever made it over the first wall, the second would give the defenders a chance to regroup or at least hold out in the hope of reinforcements.

People lined the street as the column passed. Most wore armor of some sort. In truth, there were yet more soldiers than settlers here, and many of the latter had direct ties to the former. However, as the focal point of the western expansion, Scanaga was also the place where new settlers paused before venturing out to stake their claims and entrepreneurial merchants sought new markets or exotic items to take back to the old ones. The mix of people brought some comfort to Nermesa, for it was, at least, a ghost of the sort of scene he was accustomed to back home.

Scanaga had the only true streets in this part of the Westermarck, even if they were mostly of stone and gravel. The clatter of hooves and wheels marked the column's entry into the colonial capital. Nermesa eyed the guards on the walkways of the walls and beside the gates, noting how much less polished they looked compared to his own party. Yet, what they lacked in shininess, they made up for in experience. These were hardened men, veterans now. Most had been out trying to tame the frontier for more than a year and, in that time, Nermesa knew, those not up to the task had been brutally culled by the Picts.

The notion did not put fear into him, but still, he swore again to be careful. He would not make the mistakes that so many others had. He had been singled out by General Pallantides and Sir Garaldo; they surely expected great things of him.

Thinking of that, he straightened. It would not do to look hesitant and uncertain. Ignoring the ever-present mosquitoes, Nermesa began nodding directly to onlookers, his expression hopefully confident. The settlers and shopkeepers were friendly enough, many waving; but a few smirked, as if they knew better.

A sentry atop the inner wall waved down to those within the military section. The gates there opened up, and the column entered.

Five towers stood in Scanaga, one each on the corners of the outer wall and the last in the midst of the inner fort. General Boronius's headquarters lay just below it. General Octavio, the commander of the column, led his men to a waiting column of knights and men-at-arms just before one of the few stonework structures that Nermesa had seen so far. The golden lion flew high overhead, marking it as their destination.

Octavio, a gaunt, mustached veteran on his third expedition to the Westermarck, signaled the halt. As he did, a trumpeter near the door of the building sounded a single note.

From within stepped a barrel-chested figure in armor who looked nearly as powerful as the king. His craggy features were partially draped by a thick, impressive mustache that hung below his chin. Somewhere along in his career, his nose had been crushed, and the mender who had reset it had not done the best job. The results added menace to an already fearsome face.

Under a single, thick black brow, piercing brown eyes took the measure of the newcomers. Boronius kept his helmet in the crook of his arm, allowing his slightly graying hair to drop free over his shoulders. His armor was weathered but kept polished, and Nermesa noticed that the guards standing nearest also seemed neater than their counterparts at the outer gates.

"General Octavio . . ." Boronius's baritone fit his image perfectly. "Welcome back . . ."

The other officer dismounted, and the two clasped gauntleted hands together. There was that in their guarded expressions that nonetheless hinted that these two were comrades of old.

"General Boronius! Scanaga is a welcome sight, as are you."

The commander of the west laughed. "Ha! Only if you don't live here!"

Although Octavio joined him in laughing, no one else so much as breathed wrong. Neither man had given them permission to do so.

The column's leader removed his own helm. While Boronius still had a good head of hair, his counterpart had lost most of his long ago. Removing one glove, Octavio ran a hand over his sweating scalp. "I bring you a gift from King Conan and General Pallantides . . ." He indicated Nermesa and the rest. "The finest that they could muster."

Boronius gave a grunt, whether of approval or distaste, the young Klandes could not say. General Octavio turned to his men and shouted, "Riders dismount!"

The knights and those men-at-arms on horseback did so as one. With the exception of a small, personal coat of arms on the silver breastplate of each knight, they were clad almost identically. The mounted men-at-arms wore armor less elaborate in make and had no crests to their helmets, but there was little other difference. Nobles like Nermesa had brought their own armor and weapons, and the mark of House Klandes stood proud on his chest. All of them, however wore metal badges affixed to their right shoulders that bore King Conan's symbols.

"A timely reinforcement," General Boronius finally remarked. He glanced to his left. "Caltero! Take these men and see to settling them in as quickly as possible!"

Caltero? Nermesa risked tilting his head to the side just enough to see the knight with whom the general spoke.

"Aye, my lord!" With the exception of the newcomers, Caltero was possibly the most gleaming among the assembled fighters. His armor was immaculate. He wore a neatly trimmed beard that ended just below his cleft chin. His plumed, open-faced helmet did not obscure the golden locks or the merry, silver-blue eyes. The face itself much resembled Nermesa's, although it was more refined, more handsome . . . at least to Bolontes' son.

Briefly leaning forward, Quentus whispered, "Did you know your cousin was here?"

Nermesa shook his head. Although older by a good ten summers, Caltero was the eldest son of Bolontes' younger brother, a veteran soldier slain in the struggle against Xaltotun and the Nemedians. As a child, Caltero's few visits had been fun times for Nermesa, but once his cousin had decided for a permanent career in the military, those visits had all but ceased. Still, the two had remained in contact on and off during the years, and it was in part because of Caltero that Nermesa had first begun to flirt with the idea of serving the king he so admired.

Caltero stepped before the column, then waved his arm to the north. "This way! Those with the wagons, stay where you are! You'll be dealt with afterward!"

A number of other knights from Scanaga followed with Nermesa's cousin, obviously there to assist in arranging the newcomers' lodgings.

"Noble knights, your places are in there," Caltero declared, pointing at a long, oak structure with a stone base. Gesturing farther on, he added, "Mounted men-at-arms to the next . . ." The other soldiers were assigned accordingly.

"I will come to assist you at first chance, Master Nermesa," Quentus said with an apologetic bow. He hurried after the others of his rank.

Luxury was a commodity unnecessary in the eyes of General Boronius, and the quarters given to Nermesa and the others showed that. Each knight had a cot with a space next to it for storing the armor. Small dividing walls gave some semblance of privacy, and wooden hooks on them marked where Nermesa could keep cloth garments or even items such as his breastplate. The cot consisted of a thick blanket in a box-shaped frame, with another thick blanket atop. Both blankets had seen much use, and Nermesa tried not to think about what had happened to his predecessors.

"Those of you with servants attached as men-at-arms can have them assist you with your armor and belongings," Caltero called out. "Those without can call on aid from whatever common soldiers you find!"

The elder Klandes cousin started to turn, then sighted Nermesa. With a grin, Caltero wended his way through the others. "Aah! Cousin! The general told me that you were supposed to be among the arrivals!" He clasped Nermesa tight on the shoulders. Caltero stood an inch taller than his younger relative. "Look at you! A warrior of the realm!"

Caltero's enthusiasm was contagious. Nermesa grinned back and briefly hugged his cousin. "It's good to see you, Caltero! Your last letter came more than a year ago! We only had word from a friend that you were still out here and not—"

"Not decorating a Pict's spear, yes! Ha! Where else would I go? Klandes is yours, and the only thing I've ever been good at is fighting and drinking . . . and women, of course!"

"You must be good at command, from what I saw. General Boronius seemed to rely on you."

"The Boar's managed to stir up a bit of responsibility in me, yes." In a conspiratorial whisper, Caltero added, "The name's meant good, for he fights like the tusked beast in war. He even knows of it and approves . . . out of earshot. Just don't use it in his presence; he likes decorum."

Nermesa would not have even thought to do so. He was familiar with the general's reputation and respected Boronius almost as much as he did Pallantides. "I'll remember that."

"Fine! Now, then! 'Tis nearly time for the evening meal; then, afterward, you lot can unencumber yourselves and get some rest! You're to be individually presented to the general at first light, so make sure you're up and armored again!

Make no mistake about it, cousin; he'll put you to work immediately!"

"Of course."

Again, Caltero leaned close. "Tomorrow night, when things are a bit more calm, I'll have a little entertainment for the two of us to welcome you here . . ."

He slapped Nermesa on the back and strode off before the younger Klandes could ask what he meant. Barely a moment later, a bell clanged—the call to supper. Nermesa dropped the few belongings that he had carried from his horse onto the cot, then hurried with the others to the dining hall. General Octavio had wanted to reach Scanaga before dark, and so the only food that his men had been able to eat was whatever rations they could pull from their saddle packs while still riding.

The dining hall proved to be a building identical to the barracks save that, instead of cots with separating partitions, a series of three long, well-worn wooden tables with accompanying benches filled it. The new arrivals ate alone, Scanaga's contingent having eaten just prior. Nermesa and the rest of Octavio's men had come to replace soldiers either slain, heading home, or being sent off to other parts of the territories.

For the knights, the meal consisted of cooked oats with a piece of seasoned but stringy mutton. Such as it was, it was still likely better than what Quentus was eating and definitely better than those ranking even lower had for their meal. A goblet of frontier ale—tart and mud-brown—enabled Nermesa to down his food with only minimal effort.

Quentus met him outside the knights' quarters, the man-at-arms belching as his master approached. "Pardon, my lord! I think the rabbit in the stew was tryin' to hop back out . . ."

"No doubt to follow the old sheep who made up part of my meal."

"Well, we knew it wasn't goin' to be one of Ariana's specialties," Quentus returned, referring to the Klandes' cook. Originally from a region in the southern part of Aquilonia, the stout slave woman had learned how to use spices from the neighboring lands in astonishing ways.

"I expected all this, Quentus." Nermesa had, but still he missed the wonderful aromas of his home . . . them and his soft, plush bed. "Come in and help me with this armor."

With practiced hands, the servant aided him in removing the plates and other components. Quentus set them aside as carefully as he could. "Will you be leaving your quarters, Master Nermesa?"

"No. Leave everything packed for now, though. I spoke with my cousin." Nermesa told Quentus what Caltero had said about the coming day. "I don't want anything to go wrong."

"I'll be around to help you first thing, my lord." Quentus bowed and, with a clank of metal, marched off. Only after he was alone did Bolontes' son think about the fact that Quentus would have to remove his *own* armor without aid.

The cot creaked precariously as he sat down on it. Nermesa made a belated search of the blankets and, fortunately, found them devoid of unwanted bed partners. Several other new arrivals had begun their own preparations for sleep, but the clink of metal and muttering voices made no dent in Nermesa's immense weariness. Scant seconds after he laid his head down, the heir to Klandes was fast asleep.

TRUE TO HIS word, Quentus awoke him early. Nermesa noted that his companion was already clad. Quentus went about his work silently and efficiently, finishing up the task in quick order.

There was just enough time to eat before Caltero came for him. As one of the senior officers, Nermesa's cousin had quarters of his own. Looking as immaculate as ever, the elder Klandes nodded approval.

"Keep straight, and the Boar will find you suitable! Don't let me down; I've talked you up a bit!"

The knights on sentry duty saluted Caltero as the pair approached. One then knocked twice on the door.

"Enter!" bellowed Boronius from within.

The same guard ushered them inside but left the door open. General Boronius sat behind a weathered writing table. Hints of gilt on the scrollwork edges yet remained. Nermesa suspected that the desk had been out in the West-ermarck far longer than its current user.

Helm set aside on the left corner of the table, the Boar sat studying maps and reports. Half-rolled scrolls lay every-where. A tarnished, round-bottomed, brass oil lamp dangling from a chain above illuminated the room. The two windows, one on each opposing side, were shuttered despite its being day.

Boronius looked up at the duo. "So, Caltero. This one is of your blood?"

"My cousin, Nermesa of Klandes, General. Heir to our House."

"A good House, Klandes," the huge knight remarked with a slight nod. "A good House."

His tone hinted that he knew Klandes even better than his words indicated. Of course, Caltero had been stationed here for some years, so, why would he not? Nermesa po-litely nodded at the compliment to his family.

"Thank you, Caltero. You may leave us alone now."

Nermesa's cousin saluted. He closed the door behind him, the shutting of it a sound that made a tense Nermesa nearly jump.

Boronius glanced down at something in one of the re-ports and snorted in a manner that only emphasized the name by which his subordinates called him. Looking up at Nermesa, he growled, "Just another whining complaint by one of the barons supposedly in charge of these territories! Can't supply the fresh goods I've requested! Too taxing on his subjects, he says! Ha!"

Crumpling up the parchment, Boronius threw it on the planked floor. Nermesa noticed two other similarly crushed missives.

"Too taxing on their riches, I'd say!" The frontier commander gazed at the figure before him. "I'm no noble like you, *Captain* Nermesa, but I am the general in charge of trying to tame this wilderness! I started as a man-at-arms with only what my good master gave me to carry on my back, but I proved better than a lot of fancy aristocrats who came out here and got their coiffured heads cut off within a week!"

Nermesa had no idea why Boronius told him all this, but wisely chose to stay silent.

"Why've you come out here, Nermesa of Klandes? Why leave the safety of your bed in Tarantia?"

"To serve King Conan as best as I'm able, General!" the noble replied without hesitation. "To repay him for what he's done for Aquilonia . . ."

The Boar eyed him dubiously. "A Cimmerian? A pirate and thief? You know all they say about his past, and you still wish to serve that barbarian?"

His words stunned Nermesa. He knew that there were still many among the aristocracy and military elite who secretly looked down on the Cimmerian as nothing more than barbarous scum, but he had hardly expected to hear such words from the king's frontier commander.

"General Boronius, I know only what *King* Conan has done for Aquilonia since overthrowing Namedides, and I honor him for that. If this disagrees with your opinion, I am willing to be posted somewhere else—"

"Ha!" The general smiled grimly. "There's no worry about that! Hear me, young Nermesa . . . I wish there were more with your belief in our liege! It'd make my task that much easier."

Nermesa blinked. "I don't understand . . ."

Boronius waved off his curiosity. "Never mind. You're dismissed for now."

Startled anew by the sudden end to their meeting, Nermesa saluted. Yet, as he turned away, he heard the general mutter, "Damn shame . . ."

Looking over his shoulder, the young knight asked, "Sir?"

Glaring, the Boar rumbled, "*Go*, Klandes!"

Nermesa wasted no more time, fairly leaping out the door. He found Caltero waiting outside for him.

"How did it go?" his cousin inquired, smiling.

"I'm not quite certain. I don't understand half of what we discussed!"

"He has that effect on those serving him, yes." Caltero put a companionable arm around his cousin's shoulder. "The day's training is about to start. I'd recommend getting some wine to wash out the taste of your encounter, then ready yourself for a few bruises"—he chuckled wryly—"or *worse*."

5

CALTERO HAD NOT been exaggerating. The grueling training sessions through which Sir Garaldo had put him seemed like child's play compared to what General Boronius expected his fighters to suffer.

There was much dueling, but without padded ends on the blades, which forced the combatants to be far more careful. Even still, more than one knight and several men-at-arms were cut, a couple badly. The same held true for the lance work, which was performed by charging down on a wooden board with a heart painted where a Pict's would be. Simple enough . . . save that archers fired at the charging knight from behind the standing plank. Fortunately, their shafts *were* blunted, or else the corpses of Nermesa and several comrades likely would have littered the field.

There was no rest between sessions, for, as General Boronius put it before they started, "Those tattooed devils aren't going to take a pause so you can catch your breaths! They're going to keep coming and coming and coming until either your heads decorate their tents or their cursed corpses cover the landscape!"

Scanaga had not been attacked in more than three years, and that last had been easily quashed, but much of the rest of the Westermarck was not so fortunate. Every week— even, sometimes, day upon day—Picts sought out what they thought the weakest points in the territories. Most such incursions were repelled, but a few lives were always lost.

By the time the first day had ended, it was all Nermesa could do just to walk. He ate his evening meal, allowed Quentus to aid him with the armor, then prepared for an early sleep.

But Caltero had other ideas. No sooner had Nermesa drifted off than his cousin prodded him awake with one booted foot. Clad in surcoat and breeches, the elder Klandes held up a jug of wine. "Come, come, Nermesa! 'Tis far too early to call an end to the day!"

Nermesa would have argued that notion, but Caltero followed his declaration by immediately pulling his cousin up by the arm. Overwhelmed by Caltero's presence, Bolontes' son could only obey.

"At least let me put on some clothes . . ."

His cousin granted that concession but, once Nermesa had dressed, dragged him out of the building to his own quarters. A few sentries saluted them, no one seeming to take Caltero's cavalier attitude amiss.

"It's good to have some family blood around," he declared as he led Nermesa to the door. Pushing it open, he indicated that his cousin should enter first. "You are my guest! After you."

Nermesa entered, noticing at first only the single, lit oil lamp set on the wooden table next to Caltero's cot, a softer, wider thing than his own. As his eyes adjusted to the gloom, Nermesa saw that the room was several times larger than the space set aside for the new knight. Caltero had a separate area in which to hang his armor and on the right, near the bed—

The dark eyes of a *Pict* stared back at him.

"Mitra!" Nermesa reached for a sword he did not have. The Pict—a young female—crouched low. Her eyes grew lidded, and her lower lip thrust out in fear. Lush black hair spilled over her shoulders as she moved, falling down and draping over her uncovered bosom.

Caltero seized Nermesa's arm. "Gods, cousin! Calm yourself! She's no harm, only pleasure!"

The young, barefooted woman backed to the wall. She had only a dark leather loincloth that did little to cover her supple form. As Nermesa calmed, her full lips attempted a half-hearted smile.

"Look, man! She's frightened of you! Relax!"

"Caltero . . . what's she doing in the fort?"

The elder Klandes bent his head back and laughed. "Damn! It's a good thing for you that you're out of Tarantia! By Mitra, Nermesa, she's here for company, what else?"

"But a Pict—"

"They're like any other people . . ." Caltero walked over to the female, who quickly molded herself against his open arm. "Well, maybe a bit more open in their emotions. There're Picts in Scanaga, cousin. They come to trade, to be paid for scouting . . ."

"But they're our enemies," Nermesa insisted.

"Which makes it all the more exciting . . ." Sweeping up the woman, Caltero kissed her long and hard. The Pict met his attack with at least equal passion.

Pausing, Caltero thrust the jug to Nermesa and indicated a stool against the opposing wall. "Have a drink, cousin! Let's celebrate your arrival!"

Nermesa reluctantly took the jug and sat. After another kiss, Caltero led the woman to the bed. He sat down, the Pict settling herself in his lap.

"The west is different from home, cousin. You'll learn that quick enough . . ."

"I think I have." He suddenly noticed that the Pict's lidded eyes were on him. Despite having tried to ignore her, Nermesa could not help appreciating her dark, exotic beauty. Dressed like a lady of Aquilonia, she would have put most of the elegant women of Tarantia to shame, including Orena. Still, she had a predatory look that made Nermesa want no part of her.

"Her name's Khati," Caltero remarked, mistaking his gaze for desire. "If you'd like to have some fun, I could leave her with you for a little while."

"The wine's enough, thank you."

"Well, if she's not to your liking, there are some other tasty females who come into Scanaga. You won't lack for companionship here, not with the fine Klandes looks, eh?" He grinned, turning his head to show his own profile.

Caltero had always been the adventurous one, and Nermesa had, for most of his life, wanted to emulate him; but now the elder cousin had developed a reckless streak with which Nermesa felt uncomfortable. Trying not to show this, Nermesa took a sip of wine as Caltero again kissed his Pict woman.

The heir to Klandes choked, almost spitting out the wine.

The woman looked sympathetic, but the other knight laughed at his misfortune. "Forgot to warn you how strong this particular local vintage is! The one they officially serve in the camp is water in comparison! Almost spat on the Boar the first time I tried this! Had to swallow it, tears running down my eyes the whole time!"

"I can . . . well believe it . . ." Nermesa handed the jug back, Khati taking it instead of Caltero. Again, she gave him a sympathetic look but one that also somehow had a sultry, inviting touch to it.

Seizing the jug from her, Nermesa's cousin took a huge gulp without so much as batting an eye. He put the container next to him. "Like everything else, you'll become used to it, cousin." For just a very, very brief moment, Caltero's expression utterly changed. A hollowness invaded it, one that stunned Nermesa. "You'll get used to it . . . you have to."

Khati giggled, seizing the senior knight's face and pressing her lips against his. Caltero's brief melancholy vanished, and he lustily met her efforts.

Nermesa yawned, stretching his arms at the same time.

"You must forgive me. I think that wine was too much to begin with after just settling in. I'm going to get some sleep after all, Caltero."

"Sorry to hear that." Caltero looked at the squirming bundle in his arms. "But, yes, it might be better if you did."

Leaving his cousin to his pleasures, Nermesa departed. Only when he was outside did he relax. Both knew that his weariness had mostly been an excuse to leave. It had grown too uncomfortable for Nermesa. In truth, there was nothing with which he could fault Caltero, though. Perhaps, having been away from civilization for so long, the other had needed what comfort he could find. After all, unlike Nermesa's, the military *was* Caltero's future.

He grimaced. The military might be his cousin's future, but Orena Lenaro was *his* . . . and Nermesa was not so certain that Caltero had the worse of the two fates.

NERMESA HAD PREPARED himself for weeks of tedious albeit bone-battering training, but General Boronius was not one to leave his men idle—if it could be called that—for very long. Eight days after Nermesa's arrival, the general began redistributing his forces, assigning various units to where he thought them best suited. A large contingent under the command of General Octavio set out for Oriskonie, where Nermesa gathered from muttered comments there had been much trouble of late. He had hoped to be a part of that contingent, but, instead, the Boar had a different mission for him, one in which Nermesa would act as third officer.

A lanky, eagle-eyed knight with a perpetual frown stood with the general. "This is Commander Maxius," the general informed Nermesa. "He'll be leading your group."

"Klandes," was all Maxius, apparently a man of few words, said in greeting.

"Sir."

Boronius indicated charts on his desk. "Since you're unfamiliar with all this, I wanted to give you a brief rundown.

The fort in southernmost Conawaga needs refitting, Nermesa of Klandes. You'll have six wagons and fifty-one men, counting Maxius, yourself, and another knight. Six mounted men-at-arms will accompany the wagons. The rest will be men-at-arms on foot. I don't have to tell you, I think, what it means for a fort to be low on food and other essentials. Unlike Scanaga, the smaller forts aren't so self-sufficient. It's vital this reaches them on schedule."

Nermesa saluted Boronius. "I won't let you down, General."

"The course is a straightforward one, as you can see from this map. You'll have no trouble following it, and most of the men with you have gone there before. Make no mistake, though. Be wary all the time. That's how you survive in the Westermarck."

"Yes, General."

"Gather your gear." The Boar waved him off.

Outside, Nermesa briefly talked with Quentus, who did not at all like the notion of their separation. "Master Nermesa, I'm supposed to guard your back! That's why I'm here."

"I can take good care of myself, Quentus. You know that."

"You're one of the best damned fighters I've seen here, the senior knights included, if I may be blunt, my lord. Your father always said you had a natural gift, but you still can't see behind you—"

"I'm not a child, Quentus." Nermesa glanced over his shoulder. "They're readying for the journey. Help me with my gear."

"Aye, all right . . ." But the other man still did not look pleased.

With Quentus's able if reluctant assistance, Nermesa soon joined the small column. Commander Maxius gave him a nod, then turned his attention to other matters. The other knight, one Remus, summoned Nermesa over.

"You'll be back behind the wagons, with the last group of footmen," the round-faced fighter informed him. Remus looked not all that much older than Nermesa save in his eyes, which were a weathered brown. "I'll be in front of the wagons, in charge of them and the detail riding alongside. Understood?"

"Yes!"

Nermesa's anxiousness must have shown, for Remus softened a little, saying, "This will be a boring trip, Klandes. We're on the safest route in all the territories. The Picts there are subdued, and the Zingarans are too weakened by their own infighting to be a worry. Don't even need any scouts for this one."

He turned and rode off, leaving Nermesa with conflicting emotions. On the one hand, he was relieved that his first excursion would not be one in which men's lives might depend on him, but, on the other hand, he had not joined simply to be nursemaid to wagons that likely could have made the journey unescorted.

A figure near the end of the ranks caught his eye. Gritting his teeth, Nermesa urged his mount there.

"Quentus!" he muttered. "What do you think you're doing?"

The man-at-arms—his armor only half-secured—stepped away from the wagon he had been using to hide himself from Nermesa's view. "What I swore I'd do. What I want to do. I'm coming with you. I'm guarding your back . . ."

But the knight shook his head. "No, Quentus. First, there's no need. Second, I am my own man now. I can't have you trailing behind me like an ever-present shadow."

"Your father—"

"Is not out here. I am. Go back to your other duties. I don't want you getting in trouble just because of me."

The bearded fighter opened his mouth to protest, but something he saw in Nermesa's expression finally struck home. With a grudging nod, Quentus abandoned the column. Nermesa watched until his friend and former servant had stepped back far enough, then nodded. Quentus returned the nod, then slapped his fist over his heart in salute.

A horn sounded. Nermesa glanced over his shoulder just in time to see Maxius raise one gauntleted hand.

At the top of his voice, Remus shouted, "Forward!"

Their route first took them through Scanaga and beyond, the contingent exiting through the main gate in the east and retracing for several minutes the path Nermesa's original column had taken on its trek to the Westermarck. However, a few minutes past the outer settlements, the party veered abruptly south, heading along a less-traveled pair of ruts leading into a more thickly wooded region.

The column kept a standard marching pace so as not to weary those on foot, but Nermesa was soon glad that he was on horseback, regardless. While enough of the woods had long been cleared away for wagons, the going was still not all that even. Most of the footmen had to watch their steps at all times. Nermesa's horse moved with more ease, but the bouncing that did occur gave him a good idea what the others were going through.

The morning gave way to the afternoon which gave way to the evening . . . all without the slightest hint of danger. Nermesa saw that Remus had the right of it; the more veteran soldiers kept watch as they walked, but it was with some confidence that nothing watched back.

"Stop," was Maxius's sole command, when it grew too dark to continue. Remus gave orders for the camp to be set up. The men moved with practiced ease, and, as he dismounted, Nermesa realized that the location chosen was one that had served the same purpose often in the past.

"Tomorrow we stop at a location called Hawk's Ford," Remus informed him, as they sat by one of the fires to eat. "Nothing much but a stream. After that, there's a clearing overlooking a ridge . . ." He went on, detailing each of the places they would stay.

"How many times have you been assigned to this?"

The other knight gave a harsh laugh. "More than there're men in this column. It could bore me to drink . . . if I wasn't so grateful to be on it." When Nermesa looked askance, Remus explained, "When I first came out here, it was with three friends and a brother. Was certain we'd be the ones to tame the west."

"And?"

Nermesa's companion raised one hand for him to see. He folded over the two last fingers. "Two of my friends died a week after we arrived. One with an ax in his belly, the other his throat full of arrows. It happened during a try to take back parts of Conajohara."

Conajohara was a lost territory, reconquered by the Picts years ago. Although Aquilonia had managed to recross the old boundaries, they had never gotten much farther.

Remus folded in his thumb. "My brother died on a patrol in Oriskonie. They found his body completely skinned . . . done so while he was alive and bound to the earth." Even though the other knight retold it without much emotion in his tone, Nermesa could see from his moist eyes that it still pained Remus much.

"What . . . what happened to the last of your friends?"

Remus folded down the index finger. "Was on his way home, of all things. He and a merchant wagon were slaughtered only a day east of Scanaga . . . by the brigand, Khatak, they said."

"Khatak!" Without realizing it, Nermesa began searching the dark.

"Don't worry yourself about Khatak! The foul bandit went north after that. Been up there ever since. There was some sort of terrible trouble in one of the forts just a short while back. Don't know what it is, Klandes, but that's where Octavio's headed."

And Nermesa was trapped in what now was clearly a very routine task. He hid his disappointment and slight anger. He had wanted to serve King Conan, but guiding a supply train through peaceful lands seemed more the work of simple foot soldiers. Why had General Boronius even talked of it as if it were so much greater a risk?

Nermesa brought none of this up with Remus. With much disappointment, Bolontes' son finished his meal and settled down for the night, well aware that he had nothing to fear in his sleep other than some woodland pest crawling into his blankets.

This was how he was to serve his monarch . . .

THE NEXT DAY went exactly as Remus said, and the day after that. The most excitement the column had was when two of the wagons got stuck in a mud-soaked area. The struggle to free the pair put the column two hours behind schedule. Maxius pursed his lips, the only sign of his annoyance at the delay.

Although they pushed to make up the difference, night fell with them still at least an hour from the clearing. The drivers hung oil lanterns at the fronts of the wagons and designated soldiers carried torches to light the way. Most of the soldiers took the delay in stride, even though they understood that it would mean that they would lose that much sleep. Nermesa learned that such "disasters" were the worst he could expect on this particular route.

"We once lost a day to storms," Remus told him during a brief pause. "Maxius pushed us hard to make it up. First time I ever heard him put four words together at once . . . all of them bad."

The forest thickened before the clearing, forcing the Aquilonians to press closer together. Nermesa's stomach growled and, for once, he looked forward to the evening fare. His disenchantment with his service to the king gave way to mere anticipation of finally dismounting.

A bird's cry echoed in the darkness. Nermesa listened, trying to identify it.

Ahead, Maxius abruptly straightened in the saddle. "All men stand ready—"

His command, the longest Nermesa had heard from him, ended in a gasp.

The hilt of a dagger stuck out of his throat. Maxius dropped backward off the saddle, landing in a heap next to the road.

"Men-at-arms!" shouted Remus. "Face outward! Prepare to repel the enemy!"

With howls and wild whoops, a fearsome band exploded from both sides of the forest.

Many were Picts, the first of the males that Nermesa had seen. They grinned ferociously, their teeth sharpened and their faces painted in ghoulish designs. Several wore necklaces of teeth or bone or even dried ears. All had their hair tightly bound back, with parts of the skull shaven. Most brandished spears, axes, and long, cruel blades.

But with them came a number of other figures, these clad in grimy, torn shirts, pants, and worn breastplates mostly of Aquilonian make. Some even wore ragged boots obviously once belonging to knights. Despite their long, unkempt hair and savage beards, they could claim such heritages as Bossonian and Poitainian . . . and, yes, there were those who might have even been of the blood of Nermesa.

The brigands—for they could be nothing else but—poured into the column, slashing at the soldiers. One footman went down with a bolt through his midsection. Another's head was cleaved from his body before he could get his weapon up.

"Hold your lines!" commanded Remus. "Nermesa! Move them up closer to the—"

He screamed as a blade ran him through from the back of his neck, the point coming out in front. Remus, blood spilling over his breastplate, gasped and fell.

Nermesa stared in horror at the other knight's slayer.

One of the mounted men-at-arms.

Before he could do anything, a fiery-eyed bandit tried to pull him from his steed. Nermesa kicked at the man, then instinctively ran him through the chest. That this was the first time that he had slain another human being registered only faintly on the young Klandes. What was of far more immediate importance was survival . . . not only his own, but that of his comrades. A sudden determination came over

Nermesa. He had sworn to serve Aquilonia, to serve King Conan, and he would let neither down.

But suddenly he faced an attacker of a more threatening sort. The blade that nearly sheared off his face belonged to yet *another* mounted man-at-arms. Nermesa did not know the soldier's name, but that in no manner diminished the shock of discovering not one, but *two* traitors in the column's midst.

Nevertheless, he met the turncoat's attack with his own, the two trading strikes several times. The man-at-arms glared furiously at Nermesa and kept altering his attacks in the clear hope of getting past the knight's guard. Around them, men screamed, and, out of the corner of his eye, Nermesa glimpsed more than one soldier fall to the brigands' onslaught.

Then he managed to parry the traitor's thrust, pushing the other's blade high. Nermesa immediately lunged, catching his foe in the torso between sections of armor.

Dropping his weapon, the man-at-arms clutched his wound. He teetered in the saddle, then slumped dead.

Shoving past the other horse and its ghoulish burden, Nermesa went to the aid of a mounted soldier who clearly was not one of the betrayers. Bolontes' son rode down one of the three bandits seeking the defender, then slashed at a second, lopping off an ear. As the brigand ran off howling, the man-at-arms finished off the last.

Nermesa seized the soldier by the arm. "Get everyone around the wagons! Beware of traitors!"

"Aye, my lord! I saw Benaro slay Remus, and Zuvian looked to be conversing with him afterward!"

So there were *still* two more to watch and who knew how many others. Nermesa swore, then said, "Just watch as best you can!"

A sudden illumination made both men pull back. In the struggle to seize one of the wagons, the brigands had accidentally set it ablaze. A soldier standing too near ran screaming, his body half in flames.

Riding swiftly, Nermesa reached the wagon in question.

Already he could see that it was a total loss. The oil from the lamp had splattered it well, and each drop appeared to have started a fire of its own.

He cut down a Pict trying to leap at him from the driver's area. Seizing a foot solder, Nermesa commanded, "Get the wagon out of the column! Steer it out toward the brigands and get the horses moving! Let them pull it into our foes!"

The soldier jumped up and seized the reins. Nermesa helped him guide the burning wagon to the right, then, as the anxious horses tugged it forward in their attempts to flee, he slapped the hind flank of the leader. This further agitated the horse and, in turn, those following.

The wagon went rolling toward the bandits. The man-at-arms leapt off, but, as he landed, a bearded brigand with a crooked grin and a half-Pict face buried an ax in his head.

Forgetting all else, Nermesa charged toward the murderer. But as he neared, a huge figure outlined by the flames dropped down from the trees between the noble and his adversary, a figure so massive that he easily stopped the knight's horse in its tracks.

Nermesa's mount cried out as gigantic hands crushed its throat. The knight was tossed to the side, landing hard. He rolled over and over, somehow coming to collide with the burning wagon. Licks of flame scored Nermesa's armor and singed his face.

He looked up to see the giant approaching him. There was something not quite right about the way this monstrous brigand moved, but Nermesa could not worry about that. He desperately searched the ground for his sword, but could not find it.

A harsh, barking laugh made him look to his left, where the bearded, wild-haired brigand watched in amusement. Nermesa stared at the face and the Pictish tattoos, recalled bits of accounts he had heard . . . and knew then that it was Khatak the Butcher who so reveled in his imminent demise.

He tried scrambling back as the silent, silhouetted figure neared him, but the crumbling wagon chose that moment to tip to the side, sending a rain of burned bits of wood and ash over Nermesa. A large, flaming chunk of timber landed just to the side of his head, the heat so tremendous that the hapless noble was instantly drenched in sweat.

He heard rapid, heavy breathing and a stench like none he had ever smelled filled his nostrils. Before Nermesa realized what was happening, a huge hand roughly grabbed him by the back of his collar and dragged him up as if he weighed nothing. In the background, Khatak's laughter took on an ominous tone.

As he was lifted, Nermesa again reached desperately for some weapon. His hands closed on the burning piece of timber, the heat almost scalding his skin inside his gauntlet. Yet, somehow the Aquilonian managed not only to hold on, but bring the flaming wood upward.

A blood-chilling howl filled the air. Nermesa's giant foe tossed him back like a rag doll. The makeshift torch flew from his grip.

The howl continued as Nermesa tumbled into the forest. As he bounced to a stop, he heard a loud crash, and the howl receded in the opposite direction.

Dragging himself up, Nermesa stumbled his way back to the battle. As he neared, he saw that the first soldier that he had given orders to had managed to get most of the remaining fighters to the wagons, but several were still cut off.

Seizing the rusting sword of a dead bandit, Nermesa lunged toward his men, slashing at whatever foes stood in his way. He surprised a Pict about to spear a wounded man-at-arms, cutting the tattooed attacker across the chest as the latter turned to meet him. Nermesa stunned another with the flat of his blade, then leapt past to join the other defenders.

"Strengthen that line! Archers! Focus on your left!" Commands flowed from his mouth. Nermesa was not certain that anyone would listen; he only shouted out whatever made sense.

The sudden reappearance of command revitalized the Aquilonians. They pushed back the encroaching enemy, their lines straightening.

"Sir!" A rider brought a second horse to Nermesa, who

gratefully accepted. Mounting, he glanced to his right, where some of the other survivors remained cut off.

Nermesa did not hesitate. He rode toward the desperate band, unaware that, as he did, the mounted man-at-arms and several foot soldiers followed.

A brigand swung wildly at him with a mace, but only managed a glancing blow. Nermesa jabbed, catching the man in the shoulder. As the bandit pulled away, Bolontes' son made the horse rear. Front hooves kicking out, the horse bowled over two more attackers.

The brigands before him broke away as those behind Nermesa joined the struggle. To the members of the party he had come to rescue, the noble called out, "Pull back to us! Take the wounded with you! We all retreat to the wagons!"

They obeyed in quick fashion. Nermesa led them back, then surveyed the situation again. The Aquilonians were putting up such a powerful resistance that the brigands finally began retreating.

But a sharp voice hounded them back. Khatak stood near the smoldering wreckage, berating his followers and even cutting one who tried to run past him.

Something made Nermesa urge his mount forward. He only knew that, if Khatak escaped, the deaths of Remus, Commander Maxius, and the others would be for naught.

A roar went up as he advanced. The Aquilonians took his action as a command for them to take the attack to their foes. They came at the already-disorganized bandits. Several turned and fled despite Khatak's admonitions, but some paused to halfheartedly make a stand.

Nermesa all but rode over one . . . then Khatak stood before him. The brigand chieftain still wore the crooked smile, but there was a glimmer in his gaze that bespoke of a fury. With a roar, Khatak leapt at his mounted adversary.

Khatak's ax caught the horse near the shoulder, biting deep. The animal shied, and it was all Nermesa could do to slip off before it threw him. He slapped the startled beast on the flank, sending it away.

The horse turned aside . . . and Khatak filled Nermesa's

view. His grin wider, the black-maned villain tried to chop Nermesa in two, the ax barely missing. The Aquilonian slashed, but the chieftain battered the blade from his face. Nermesa realized that Khatak was a skilled fighter and quickly backed away to think.

But Khatak would not permit him that luxury. He threw himself toward the knight, cutting an arc of death before him.

Nermesa brought up the sword as the ax head closed. It managed to stop the attack, but shattered in the process.

Without thinking, Nermesa flung the remnants in Khatak's face. The brigand reacted instinctively, putting up one arm to deflect the object.

Nermesa lunged at his foe, sending both crashing to the ground. Khatak's ax dropped a short distance away.

Growling like a mad wolf, the half-breed sought Nermesa's throat. The Aquilonian did the only thing he could think of, swinging a mailed fist at Khatak's jaw.

He struck a solid blow. Khatak grunted, and blood from his mouth splattered Nermesa's own face.

The bandit chieftain went limp.

Gasping, the knight looked up, fully expecting another brigand to pounce on him at any moment. When he saw none, he stumbled to his feet, grabbed Khatak's ax, and used his other hand to drag, as best he could, the unconscious villain.

The mounted man-at-arms with whom he had earlier spoken rode up to him as he and his burden neared the road. The soldier held a torch in one hand. "They're on the run! The column's been saved!" He peered down at what Nermesa dragged and almost dropped the torch. "Mitra! It's Khatak! You've captured Khatak!"

The ax slipped from Nermesa's grip as the full realization of what he had done finally sank in. He had indeed captured Khatak the Butcher, Khatak the Beast.

He had beaten in battle the Terror of all the Westermarck.

6

THE FORT TO which they had been ordered to deliver the supplies lay within easy reach, but with such a startling turn of events, Nermesa could not simply finish the journey and then head back. He feared that to do so would give Khatak's men time to plan another trap, one from which the remaining Aquilonians might not escape. There remained only twenty-eight men, counting himself, and some of those were wounded. Worse, they had, in addition to the brigand leader, the two surviving traitors and five other bandits to guard.

Hoping he judged correctly, Nermesa sent eight men on with the wagons and had the rest of the party immediately reverse direction. He disliked splitting the force further, but could not think of what else to do.

He was forced to have Khatak gagged, the half-breed otherwise mouthing obscenities and threats at a breathtaking, unceasing pace. With their arms bound tight behind them and nooses linking each prisoner to the one following, Khatak and rest were led along by Atalan, the mounted man-at-arms with whom Nermesa had worked during the battle. At the prisoners' rear, the other remaining mounted fighter kept watch. The foot soldiers finished up the much-depleted column.

And so it was that, three days later, Nermesa rode at the head of a sight that froze settlers in their work and left guards riveted at the gates and atop the defensive wall of Scanaga. Most recognized that this was part of the troop that had gone out to restock one of the forts, and so its sudden return—with less than half its contingent and several prisoners in tow—created a great stir of concern.

Someone finally had the presence of mind to sound the alert. The gates opened and Nermesa, although weary from the grueling trek, rode in sitting as straight as he could. All those left from the original contingent moved with an air of pride, for they knew what a prize they had. With each step, more and more people began to understand just who it was behind Atalan's horse, and concern gave way to awe.

The rest of the prisoners staggered, but Khatak walked as tall and straight as the Aquilonians. He made no sound, but his eyes burned through anyone foolish enough to meet his gaze. No one doubted that, given half a chance, he would seek to escape and wreak his vengeance.

Yet, his defiance could not much dampen the growing mood of Scanaga's inhabitants. Cheers arose, first scattered, then becoming one loud chant. The capture of bandits and Picts was always cause for relief, but the taking of the terrifying Khatak was an event of historic proportions.

Horns blared ahead, and as Nermesa's group neared the inner fort, the gates opened to reveal a full squadron of soldiers and knights awaiting the column's arrival. Sentries above forgot their duties for the moment in order to jabber at one another in excitement and point at the brigand.

As he entered, Nermesa caught sight of his cousin. Caltero stood at the doorway of his quarters, mouth open in disbelief. Next to him was his Pict female, who stared round-eyed at the display, then looked at Nermesa himself with renewed appraisal. The younger Klandes suddenly felt his cheeks redden under such a perusal.

Turning, he spotted Quentus, who also wore a look of wonder at what his master had accomplished. He finally shook his head and grinned at Nermesa.

Nermesa called a halt before Boronius's headquarters. A guard at the general's door tapped on it once and almost immediately the Boar stepped out. He wore his full armor, even his helmet. The commander of the west kept his eyes on Nermesa at all times as he descended the steps. Boronius wore an expression that Nermesa found unfathomable, some cross between relief, fury, and many other emotions.

"Nermesa of Klandes," the Boar muttered with a shake of his head. "What've you gone and done?"

Bolontes' son was taken aback. "Sir?"

But the general had already moved on to the prize Nermesa had brought back with him. "Khatak . . ." Boronius suddenly grinned. He seized the brigand by the hair and pulled him close. "There's a lot of people who'd like to see your head decorating a pike, half-breed, just like you did to many of their kin . . ."

Khatak's only response was a burning glare to which the Boar seemed entirely oblivious.

The general suddenly released the prisoner's head. With a derisive snort, Boronius loudly continued, "But, that pleasure will be others'! Tarantia will soon hear of this, and I don't doubt that King Conan will be granting you a visit to his court before long . . . and then to the executioner's block shortly after!" He turned from the brigand, dismissing him as if the latter were inconsequential. "Take him away!"

As soldiers dragged Khatak off, the Boar eyed the two traitors. Unlike the bandit, they looked back at their former commander with far less bravado. The worst thing that one could do was betray the Aquilonian military, especially in the west, where even the slightest thing could mean the deaths of many.

"I should hang you here and now . . . and let the birds peck away at your dangling corpses for weeks to come . . . but that's also a pleasure the king might enjoy." He stared the two down. One man-at-arms shook his head; the other closed his eyes. "But you've got a chance to escape Traitor's Common," Boronius went on, referring to the area outside the capital where the bodies of those like the pair were left to rot in dishonor. "Mayhaps you can even buy your way out of the Iron Tower, if you cooperate with us."

One man quickly nodded. General Boronius summoned over Caltero. "Take these scum and see what information you can wring from them! The same goes for the brigand trash with them! Give me something, Caltero!"

"It shall be done!" snapped Nermesa's cousin, as serious as his commander concerning the heinous situation. "Guards!"

As the prisoners were herded away by Caltero's squad, Boronius returned his attention to Nermesa. "Klandes, I want you to clean that road filth off you and get some food. And while you're doing that, lad, think very carefully about all that happened! I'll be wanting to see you in my quarters right after to hear everything in detail! Understood?"

"Yes, General!"

"Dismissed!" Boronius hesitated, then, almost as an afterthought, added, "Oh . . . and good work, lad."

"Thank you . . ."

As the Boar retreated into his quarters, Quentus and others came up to congratulate the arrivals. Nermesa accepted backslaps and handshakes as he dismounted, but his thoughts were on his impending report to his superior. Boronius had looked none too pleased about the entire incident, and the knight did not understand why.

Quentus put a hand on his shoulder, guiding him and his horse from the well-wishers. "Come, Master Nermesa! You heard him! We'd better get you taken care of as quickly as possible! Wouldn't want to leave the Boar waiting!"

Back in his own meager quarters, they quickly removed Nermesa's grimed and bloodied armor. Quentus brought him a basin of water, and the young Klandes immediately washed his face. The cold water felt good against his skin and shook away some of the cobwebs. He began to recall things with tremendous detail. Sharpened images from the battle replayed. Nermesa saw everything again—

"Mitra save me!" His legs collapsed. He fell against the basin, spilling the water on the wooden floor.

Quentus seized his arm, but Nermesa shook him off. Gasping, Bolontes' son shivered. He had seen men slain . . . and *worse*, he had slain men. Only now, here in the safety of Scanaga, did it all hit him. For all his dreams of serving the king and Aquilonia as a knight, the realities had not sunk in until the attack.

"Master Nermesa?"

The noble fought down his shaking. Slowly, the horrific memories receded. They did not disappear, but at least they faded . . . a little. Nermesa exhaled and finally allowed Quentus to help him up.

"I—I'm all right, Quentus. Thank you."

"Master Nermesa, what—"

The knight's eyes narrowed. "Don't call me *that*, anymore."

His companion frowned. "I don't understand."

"Never call me 'master'! Not now, not ever again! I release you from all obligations! I free you of all that binds you to House Klandes. You'll call neither me nor any other man 'master'!"

Quentus opened his mouth, then closed it. After a few seconds of brooding, he quietly picked up the basin and put it aside. "We'd better hurry. The general will be waiting."

"Did you hear me, Quentus? You don't have to help me, either. Just pack your things and get back to Tarantia—"

"And leave my friend and brother behind." For the first time, Quentus glared at his lifelong companion. "I could've ridden off on the way here if I'd so chosen, Mas—Nermesa! I am as much Klandes as you, and we've grown up together! Now, enough of this talk! The Boar doesn't like to be kept waiting!"

Although they continued their task in silence, Nermesa felt both relief and gratitude. He had been afraid that Quentus might actually go but knew that his friend had deserved the chance to decide for himself. When they finished with their work, Nermesa impulsively clasped Quentus's hand, then marched off to give his report to the general.

As Nermesa walked, soldiers continued to come up and congratulate him. While shaking hands with one, Nermesa happened to glance at Caltero's quarters and saw that his cousin's Pict woman again watched him. When she noticed him staring back, she lowered her eyes and smiled shyly before slipping back inside.

Boronius awaited his arrival. The bearded knight sat ready behind the table, a half-finished note to Tarantia already lying before him. He set the silver stylus down as Nermesa stood at attention.

"There's the Nermesa of Klandes I expected the day you arrived," Boronius cryptically remarked. "Clean and pampered, like so many young nobles." The Boar's brow furrowed deep. "But you're not that now . . . and you never were, I think, despite what I was told."

"General?"

A flask of wine sat on the commander's left, with it two matching silver goblets that had seen better days. General Boronius poured some rich red wine that in no manner could be mistaken for a local vintage into one goblet . . . then into the second, too.

"Brought for me at some expense from Tarantia, lad. Join me in a drink."

Somewhat disconcerted, Nermesa reached over and took the second cup. Boronius leaned back and, with his goblet, saluted the knight. The veteran fighter took a deep swallow, then stared down Nermesa until the latter finally did the same.

"The least of your rewards for such a feat," explained the Boar. "I've hunted Khatak. Great nobles and veteran commanders have hunted Khatak. Some of them found him, much to their despair. You, though, you caught him and lived to tell the tale."

"It was chance, General, nothing more! Chance!"

"Chance is the true commander on the field of battle." Putting down his goblet, Boronius indicated a chair to the side. "Drag that over where you are. I want you relaxed while you tell me everything. Everything."

Once seated, Nermesa described the incident as well as he could remember. Again, the terrible images of men being slaughtered filled his thoughts, but he kept, as best he could, any of his emotions from showing through.

Boronius listened silently, eyes never straying from Nermesa's own. He wrote nothing down and gave no indication of belief or the lack thereof.

"Finish your wine," General Boronius ordered, when Nermesa had completed his retelling. As the younger knight drank, the bearded commander sat in obvious thought.

Finally, the Boar said, "I've heard different."

"General?" Nermesa went over the details in his head, recalling nothing misspoken.

"I've had five men in here already, Atalan among them. You remember him? Good. He's an honest sort, especially, but every one of them pretty much agrees on what happened . . . and that you played a far greater role than you yourself described, Klandes."

"I've told all as it happened . . ."

This brought a snort from the Boar. "Humility. Not all that common among the nobility, Klandes. In fact, damn near impossible to find. Well, Pallantides and the king will hear *everything*, I promise you that."

Nermesa was not quite certain he liked the way Boronius said the last, but there was no protest he could make. He set down the empty goblet and waited for the general to dismiss him.

But Boronius was not yet done with Nermesa. "One last thing, Klandes. Something I feel's due to you after this. I want you to know, though, that it was done with good intentions."

"I don't—"

"Hear me out first," the Boar said with a growl. "This concerns your father."

"My father?" Nermesa had no idea of what the senior knight spoke. How did the elder Klandes fit into the conversation?

"You've not much idea about Bolontes' past, do you?"

Nermesa said nothing, assuming the general had a good reason for asking such a thing.

Boronius nodded. "Smart answer. Most children don't pay much attention, but pretend that they know everything about their parents . . . usually in a bad way. Truth be told, your father was among the most honored men in our realm's military . . . and one of the most controversial."

"Him?" Nermesa imagined his staid parent, who always seemed to follow traditions.

"Bolontes of Klandes served two kings, the tyrant Namedides and Namedides' father, Argaen II. Argaen was nothing like his son, by the way, and there are those who firmly believe he was poisoned by Namedides."

Such rumors still abounded, and no one in the court of King Conan saw any reason to put an end to them. Nermesa grew anxious, picturing his father as a loyal servant of the despised Namedides. It certainly explained Bolontes' hesitancy to have his son serve the barbarian who had slain the tyrant.

"Calm yourself, Klandes. Don't assume." The Boar poured himself more wine. After a sip, he continued, "Namedides would have had your father's head twice if not for Bolontes' reputation. He dared not touch him although the temptation was always there. Bolontes, in turn, was a traditionalist. He despised Namedides, but the bastard was of the bloodline of the kings of Aquilonia, and so your father did nothing despite much secret urging. When his brother died, he took the prestige he had gained and used it, during some particularly troubled times that followed, to preserve House Klandes . . . and the infant son he'd just been blessed with."

"What . . . what happened, then?"

"When the Cimmerian started his bid for the throne, a gathering of nobles called on Bolontes to stand up for Namedides in the name of the ancient Houses and his lineage. This could've rallied hesitant troops and supporters. But Bolontes refused outright. If he hadn't, Conan might still have won, but it would've been an even more terrible struggle, and there's no telling if Aquilonia would've survived the aftermath."

Nermesa sat stunned. None of this had he ever heard from anyone, let alone his parents. Caltero, who probably knew something of it, had remained silent, too. "But . . . what does this all have to do with me?"

"When Bolontes commanded in the military, he came to know many young soldiers who admired him, some of them not even Aquilonians. I was one. Pallantides was another. You'll likely not be surprised to know at this point that Count Trocero of Poitain is a friend of his as well. I'd wager that even King Conan understands the part Bolontes played in tipping matters at the end."

"My father knows *all* these men?"

"Aye . . . and so asked Pallantides and me to protect you, his only son and heir, as best we could, when he knew that you would be sent out here. When he found out about you joining, lad, he contacted us immediately. And, knowing him, we did just as he asked."

Which explained to Nermesa why his first mission in the Westermarck had been the most routine possible despite what General Boronius had said prior to it. Nermesa could scarcely believe how his father had manipulated matters behind the scenes. While on one level he could understand why Bolontes had done it, on a more basic level Nermesa felt a fury growing. He had been played so easily!

"You'll dampen down what I see in those eyes of yours if you know what's best for you, Klandes!" The Boar rose. "Your father did what he thought right, whether it was or not, to protect you. You don't think you'd do the same for your heir?" He shrugged. "Besides, the point's moot after what you did. Pallantides and I built you up to your face so that you'd never suspect what we planned, but I can see that we pretty much underestimated you."

"General, I—"

Boronius waved him off. "I've got a report to finish.

You've done well, Klandes. Very well. This won't be the end of the matter."

Nermesa saw that he would not be allowed to say any-thing. In truth, he was not certain just what he planned to say. What the general had told him had left the younger knight utterly disconcerted.

The guards snapped to attention as he departed. Other fighters, be they knights or foot soldiers, treated him almost as if he were Boronius. Word was spreading quickly . . . too quickly.

It was not only the Aquilonians who acted differently. Some of the other Pict females who stayed at the fort had gathered by one doorway. When they saw Nermesa, they giggled like the young women admiring the palace guards back in Tarantia. Despite himself, Nermesa's chest swelled at the admiration.

"Master warrior?"

The feminine voice stopped Nermesa in his tracks. He looked to his left to discover Khati. She wore simple, cir-cular breastplates that did little to obscure her glory and the slim loincloth in which he had first seen her. The other Pict females became vague memories in her presence.

"Master warrior," she repeated, gazing up at him with half-lidded eyes. "The spirit of your totem is truly great . . ."

Nermesa had not been aware that she spoke such excel-lent Aquilonian, but it did not overly surprise him. After all, she had spent so much time in Scanaga, especially in Caltero's company.

"Thank you," he replied, not knowing what else to say.

She reached with perfect, tapering fingers to touch the emblem of Klandes on his surcoat. "The lion," Khati mur-mured, her lips pursing as she traced the animal. "Strength. Determination. Power."

Even through his thick garments, her touch unsettled Nermesa as no other woman's had, save Orena's. However, where the Lady Lenaro's had repelled him, the Pict's did the opposite.

He suddenly recalled just what she was and, more important, *whose* she was. "Where's Caltero?"

"He still talks with prisoners. Much time it will take. Very much time."

The last she said with the clear hint of invitation. Nermesa gently disengaged himself. "If he asks of me, I go to rest. I'm feeling very tired and wish not to be disturbed."

She did not hide her disappointment, and her pout made Nermesa almost regret turning down her offer. Nonetheless, he bowed to her—only afterward realizing that he had treated a savage as he would have a lady of the court—and hurried off to his quarters in the hopes that, when next he stepped out, the world would be more as it had been before he had taken his fateful journey.

7

YET, NERMESA'S HOPE was not to be, for, if anything, the days that followed only saw further glorification of his questionable achievements. Word spread throughout Scanaga, throughout all of Conawaga and beyond. The territorial judge, an elder statesman by the name of Flavian, summoned both Boronius and Nermesa to him for yet another retelling of the events. Standing before the desk of the cadaverous, black-gowned man, the general went over the betrayal of the party and the capture of Khatak as Atalan and the rest of the survivors had claimed the situations had taken place. Nermesa was called upon only to verify details, not tell his own, somewhat differing version.

Flavian awarded him the lion cross, a medal of honor issued by King Conan that resembled the roaring head of the golden beast, and gave lesser honors to Atalan and various others. Nermesa wanted nothing more than to hide the medal, but by the judge's "request," he had to wear it over his breastplate for the following week.

General Octavio returned a few days later, and, after jesting that Nermesa had deprived him of his prey, congratulated the young knight. He also reported that the Picts had suddenly grown quite silent, even withdrawing from some lands recently contested. Khatak had been a tremendous influence on them, and his capture had evidently demoralized the tribes.

"Haven't seen the wilderness this peaceful since King Conan himself was out here, before he seized the throne. He'd beaten the savages at their own game, putting the fear in them like few others . . ." Octavio smiled. "Likely more than a few chiefs know *your* name now."

That suggestion filled Nermesa with a new anxiety, one in which he imagined every creak at night to be some Pict who had slipped by all the guards and now walked upon the roof over the knight's head, seeking entrance. Nermesa had also not forgotten Khatak's brutish minion. At best, he had been burned somewhat, but surely such a strong villain would soon regain his strength and seek revenge . . . and the freedom of the brigand chieftain.

As for Khatak himself, he had said nothing since his mouth had been ungagged. Instead, according to all reports Nermesa heard, the wild-haired bandit merely stared and smiled that crooked smile, as if expecting something dire to happen at any moment.

Despite dogged interrogation by Caltero, the two traitorous knights could only tell that they had been paid by a hooded figure whose voice they could not recognize save that it was male. The general decided to leave further questioning to those more adept back in Tarantia.

"Terrible business, this," remarked Nermesa's cousin when next they were alone. He had sent away Khati so that the two knights could talk undistracted. "Aquilonians betraying their own kind for base gain! I recommended to the Boar that he just string up the two traitors, but he knows better, I suppose."

"They might still tell us something. I'm sure the king's interrogators will do better."

Caltero took a sip of wine, brooding over the matter. "Yes, I suppose they will."

"I, for one, will be very happy when they and the brigands are all on their way to the capital." Nermesa nursed his wine, wanting to keep his head clear for as long as Khatak and the other prisoners remained the charges of Scanaga.

"Can't say as I blame you. The sooner that scoundrel is away from here, the better! The Boar's posted extra guards on both walls and around his cell. Wouldn't do to let such a prize escape, eh?"

But Khatak remained the prisoner of the fort for over three weeks while General Boronius inquired what Tarantia desired him to do. Khatak's foul deeds had long been constant news in the capital, to the point where some people imagined him skulking around in their own homes. Tarantia would wish to have their say in his fate.

Nermesa tried to stay away from the prisoner, but, eventually he was drawn to the cell. The sentries outside saluted him, and when he requested to see Khatak, he was instantly granted access, which surprised him.

The knight had expected the brigand to act like a caged animal, pacing back and forth constantly. But when he confronted Khatak, it was to see the black-maned villain simply sitting and staring at him.

"So . . ." The eyes brightened as Nermesa had seen a cat's do before lunging at its dinner. "You come, Nermesa of the lion totem."

It so startled the Aquilonian that Khatak would know his name that he could not prevent himself from gaping. This brought a chuckle from the captive, who leapt to his feet with the grace of the feline to which he had just referred.

"Welcome to this one's humble home," Khatak said with a bow, again chuckling.

No longer certain why he had come but not wishing to let the prisoner see him flee in anxiety, Nermesa stepped closer to the cage. He warily watched the figure within, not wanting to risk an attack.

Khatak lunged.

He flattened himself against the bars, stretching as hard as he could to reach Nermesa, who had stopped dead in his tracks. The bandit chieftain's grimy fingers missed the knight by more than a foot, but Khatak did not seem disappointed. Rather, he was again amused by his captor's reaction.

"So you will know where it's safe to stand, my friend."

Silently cursing at how well Khatak could read him, Nermesa stayed where he was, studying the prisoner. Khatak looked no worse for wear despite the interrogations. There were scars, yes, and a few more bruises, but little else. Boronius wanted Khatak more or less intact for the journey to Tarantia. Once there, whatever happened during *those* interrogations would be out of the general's hands.

The brigand abruptly stepped back and began a short jig. He laughed loud at Nermesa's startlement, then said, "Have I amused you now, friend?"

"I didn't come for your jests."

"No?" Once more, Khatak became a predator. He leaned close to the bars. "Then, why?"

"You could save yourself a lot of pain by telling them whatever you know about your band or what the Picts might be up to," Nermesa responded somewhat lamely. He had not had any real reason for coming, that much he realized now, save to assure himself that Khatak was still secure.

The bearded half-breed chuckled, a sound that already grated on Nermesa's nerves. "The people of the forest are creeping up on the fort. They wish the heads of all! My men, they are robbing all caravans! The wilderness is filled with dangers!"

Letting out a loud whoop, Khatak spun around and returned to the bench on which he had been sitting. As he dropped, he folded his arms and positioned himself as he had when the knight had first entered.

Lips tight together, Nermesa turned to leave.

"Son of the lion . . ."

The young Klandes paused and, despite himself, looked over his shoulder at the brigand.

Khatak's expression was terrible to behold. He gazed at Nermesa from under his shaggy brow, and the crooked smile had stretched long and narrow. There was no humor in that smile, though. The bandit did not blink, his eyes boring into the one who had brought him here.

"Son of the lion, Nermesa of Klandes . . . I will devour you. I will find your throat in the dark of night and rip it out. Your heart I will sacrifice to the Four Brothers of the Night and Gullah, The Hairy One Who Lives in the Moon! Yes . . . especially, Gullah . . ."

To his credit, Nermesa steeled himself against Khatak's words, simply replying, "A hard thing to do without your head."

Khatak laughed, the sound echoing in the Aquilonian's ears long after he had left the jail.

Growing more restless with each day that Khatak remained nearby, Nermesa finally requested of General Boronius some mission that would take him from Scanaga, at least for a short while. With the Picts unusually quiet and Khatak's band nowhere to be found, the Boar returned him to the supply caravans. However, this time, Nermesa was in command, something unusual for one so recently made a knight. As such, Nermesa was able to pick his own men, and so Quentus rode with him.

They made two journeys, both uneventful save for a bit of rain, but being out in the forest did as Nermesa hoped. His nerves calmed, and he began to recall just why he had wanted to serve his home and his king.

The second trek was of the most interest, concerning bringing goods to one of the "friendly" tribes paid off by Aquilonia. For the first time, Nermesa faced Picts who smiled humbly—at least in his presence—and who offered food and drink, not bloodshed. Pictish huts came in more than one form, but were generally tall, rounded, and made from frames and skins. Most of their race were far shorter than he, and his height, above average for his own kind, made Nermesa a marvel to some of the natives. The women seemed especially fascinated, giggling whenever he looked their way and finding reasons, however feeble, to be in his path.

Few Picts spoke much more than broken Aquilonian, so an interpreter was required. Riding with Nermesa's band was a Pict named Kyonag, whose right hand had, in his youth, been mangled by a bear. Kyonag had once been of the Fox Tribe, but his injury made him unable to hunt, a terrible thing for one of his race. He had early on come willingly to Scanaga, for there he at least had a use to someone . . . even if it was invaders.

Nermesa and Kyonag met the chieftain of the tribe in the circular area in the middle of the village, the area where gatherings and ceremonies took place. The totem of this particular village—the owl—perched high overhead. The chieftain and all the males wore feathers from the bird in their hair, a common practice among other Pict tribes named after avians.

General Boronius had warned Nermesa to act with caution even while with this "friendly" tribe, but the Owl people all but fell over themselves to please him. He received little disagreement with anything he passed along from Scanaga, the chief's head bobbing up and down continuously throughout the conversation. Nermesa was constantly offered Pict delicacies—salted squirrel, river fish roasted over the fire, and such—and various gifts, including a knife with a bone handle that Kyonag, with a grin, assured him had come from an elk, not a human.

The Picts offered Nermesa one of their huts in which to sleep, and he gathered from the expression of the young female standing near it, she was included in the offer. Nermesa politely declined, and when he had looked at the woman, another's face—Khati's—had briefly overlapped it. Shaking off such thoughts, the knight returned to his men and settled down.

The Owl people came out in force to bid his troop farewell, chanting as Nermesa passed. He finally had to ask Kyonag if this was typical.

"Is you," the tame Pict declared, grinning. Although long a resident of the fort area, his teeth were as pointed as those of any of his wild cousins. "The totem of the lion defeated the totem of the Gullah, Khatak's totem! All were amazed! Khatak had god himself! All the People of the Forest know you fought both and won!"

His explanation only opened the door to more questions, but Nermesa at least understood one thing. His capture of the legendary brigand was known to the Picts, and many thought Nermesa a man touched by the lion spirit—both part of his House emblem and that of King Conan.

But what Kyonag had said about Khatak confused him. Nermesa had heard the name Gullah mentioned before, but none among the soldiers understood exactly what creature or god it was supposed to be. A monstrous, hairy man who, as the bandit chieftain described him, lived in the Moon. Nermesa recalled the huge bandit who had attacked him and wondered if he masqueraded as the supposed deity for Khatak. The knight could recall little about him save that he had worn furs that stank and been tremendously powerful, but, certainly he had been no horrific god. Mitra was the only true god in the world.

But if that were the case, Mitra was a more capricious god than Nermesa supposed. Upon his return to Scanaga, the young Klandes was met by his cousin, who immediately announced that Tarantia had finally sent word about the brigand's fate.

"He and the others, including the traitors, are to be marched off tomorrow to the capital! The Boar wants to see you immediately about it!"

"Me? Why?"

"That's for him to say, cousin!"

Quentus followed him as far as the outer door. "I'll be here in case you need me for anything."

Nermesa nodded, although he knew as well as Quentus did that there was nothing the man-at-arms could do even if something *did* happen. Besides, what danger could there be in the general's quarters?

"Klandes," Boronius greeted him. Standing, the Boar came around and clasped Nermesa's hand. Ignoring the latter's startled look, the general asked, "All went well with the Owls? They give any trouble?"

"None, General."

"Well, then, you can fill me in on the mundane details after we talk over why I wanted you to come to see me the moment you returned. Sit!"

After Nermesa had done so, Boronius returned to his side of the table. However, he himself did not sit, instead lifting up a piece of waxed parchment that, from what Nermesa could see of the cracked seal, contained some message from the capital.

"From Pallantides himself. I'll tell you right away that the first part is congratulations to us—you, especially—for the capture. The whole palace is talking about it! Word's racing through Tarantia and beyond like wildfire."

Feeling his face redden, Nermesa muttered, "My part in it was small, General. It—"

"Yes, yes! We've been through all that, Klandes! What's important is what follows the congratulations. They want that bastard marched off as soon as possible . . . and good riddance, I say! Pallantides has convinced the king that Khatak must be made an example in front of the people in Tarantia. The questioning's only part of it, though a vital one. Khatak knows how the Picts think and work. He can tell us much, with the proper . . . *encouragement*."

"As you suggested."

"Yes. Once that's done, it'll be the chopping block for him. Word of his execution will spread all the better from Tarantia! It'll reach the right ears in every surrounding kingdom! Pallantides thinks it'll demoralize a few folks with intentions of causing trouble elsewhere. Khatak's been making Aquilonia look bad for too long and fools like Stygia, Zingara, and even blasted Nemedia always take that as a sign we're ripe for deviltry."

Mention of Nemedia in particular made Nermesa tense. The story of Xaltotun resurfaced in his memories. General

Pallantides had the right of it; make the fate of Khatak known to all and Aquilonia's enemies would think twice about causing her trouble. The quiet of the Picts was a prime example.

"He should be sent with all haste, then," Nermesa stated.

"Quite right. I know you can be trusted to see he's no trouble on the way."

Nermesa almost jumped out of his seat. "*Me?* What about General Octavio or Caltero or—"

The Boar shook his head solemnly. "Octavio's out in the wilderness again. This peaceful attitude of the Picts could shift at any moment, and we need to be watching, especially when we send Khatak on. Caltero's a good man, but Tarantia wants you, specifically."

"But why?"

"That's the last part of this letter." Boronius waved the parchment. "You're to be honored by the king *himself*, Klandes. You're to be presented to the people as a hero of the Westermarck, a way of promoting success out here, not disaster."

Tarantia . . . Nermesa already missed the city, but to go back meant confronting unsettled matters, such as Orena. Worse, although he was grateful that the king wished to congratulate him for his efforts—something he had dreamed of since first desiring to join the military—Nermesa was not one for public spectacles. Even the granting of the medal by the territorial judge had been too much.

"I see that look, Klandes. You're going to go to Tarantia and represent all that's right out here and get the accolades you deserve in the process! That's an order, lad!"

There was no arguing with Boronius. Nermesa nodded.

"Good!" The Boar sat on the edge of the table, which creaked ominously under his immense mass. "Now, there's just one more thing to discuss. That's Khatak himself."

Nermesa understood immediately. "You think he might try to escape along the way?"

"Or someone'll try to help him. It's been too silent around that bastard. He sits there, either grinning or laughing, as if waiting. Waiting for *what*, though? I've got guards all around, and no one can get to him, but I still don't trust the situation. There's another traitor yet, you know that. The one who paid the men-at-arms. But, whoever he is, he can't make a move in the fort."

"Outside, though," interjected Bolontes' son. "He might."

"Aye, he might. But you'll be with a full contingent of troops, and Khatak'll be watched day and night by different men. You got that, Klandes?"

He did, whether he wanted to or not. Yet, despite his concerns, Nermesa no longer sought some excuse by which to escape his duty. He had no fear of escorting Khatak to Tarantia, only the clamor that would follow once he delivered the villain into Pallantides' hands.

"Yes, General, I do."

"Then, go take care of yourself . . . and steer clear of any wine with your cousin. You've got to be prepared to leave at first light. I won't be happy until that bandit is dangling by his wrists in the Iron Tower."

Saluting, Nermesa left. True to his word, Quentus still awaited him outside.

"What is it? Can't be tellin' a damned thing from your expression!"

"We're going back to Tarantia."

The man-at-arms grew agitated. "You've been cast out? For what? How could they do that after—"

"Calm yourself!" interrupted Nermesa. "Just the opposite. I'm to be honored before the king himself." He quickly detailed what Boronius had informed him.

Quentus's expression changed from fury to exhilaration. "Ah! Now that's the thing! Well done, Master—well done, Nermesa! Wonderful!"

"What's all this?" Caltero marched up to the pair. "A celebration without me?"

Quentus quickly filled him in. Caltero listened to all of it with an ever-widening grin. When the man-at-arms had finished, Caltero slapped his cousin hard on the back.

"Ha! I knew some of it, Nermesa, but not all! I'm proud

of you! Come! Let's go to my quarters for a proper toasting of the hero of all Aquilonia!"

Nermesa recalled General Boronius's warning and declined. "I need to rest. We'll be up well before dawn. Remember that, Quentus. You're coming, too."

"Aye, you're right! Pity not to have one drink, though," the bearded soldier urged. "This local stuff 's grown on me. Just one wouldn't be that bad, would it?"

The declaration made Caltero laugh. "Well, if my cousin won't drink to himself, let's you and I do it for him, man! Come!"

"Nermesa?" pleaded Quentus.

"I'd recommend it stay one drink. It's a long journey to the capital."

"One, it'll be!" his cousin promised.

"Aye!" swore Quentus. "One . . ."

As they walked off, Nermesa hurried to his quarters before anyone else could slow him. He had much to think about, much to prepare. He had hardly expected to make the journey home and under such complicated circumstances.

That was assuming that he made it home at all, of course.

NERMESA HAD EXPECTED sleep to elude him completely, but barely minutes after he laid his head down, the young noble had already drifted off. Dreams soon infiltrated his mind, some of them pertaining to the capture of Khatak, others to the honors he would receive in Tarantia.

One had to do with his family.

In his dream, Nermesa was waving to the crowds as they honored his feat. Somehow, the celebration ended at the steps of his home. He then found himself standing in the high hall, his parents, Caltero, Quentus, and the servants all congratulating him. They all had goblets of wine in their hands.

His father toasted him, their disagreements for some

reason not a part of the dream. "To the future of Klandes, my pride and my son, Nermesa!"

"To Nermesa!" the others shouted.

"Congratulations, Nermesa . . ." said a melodious voice.

He turned and found Khati dressed like one of the noble-women of Tarantia, her hair up and her face made in the manner of Aquilonians. She smiled, and that smile filled his gaze.

But then her face shifted, becoming another beautiful woman whom at first he mistook for Orena. Yet, this one was dark-haired like Khati, and her features, though so very close to Nermesa's betrothed, were softer.

Then the face did indeed become Orena Lenaro's. "My love," she cooed, reaching up and stroking the side of his neck with her smooth, cool fingers. "Let me hold you tight . . ."

Her fingers stretched, becoming sinewy and moving as if with a life of their own. They encircled Nermesa's throat, tightening. They continued to tighten until he could no longer breathe. He grasped at them, but they were wrapped around one another, intertwining.

"Let me hold you tight, my love," Orena repeated.

She smiled, revealing two long, dripping fangs—

At which point, Nermesa woke . . . and found the con-striction around his throat a living nightmare.

A hiss near his right ear was the only warning that saved him from an even more foul fate. Nermesa instinctively froze, lying as still as the dead.

The serpent hissed again, but did not strike. The tight-ness around Nermesa's throat lessened enough for him to breathe. He did so, but as minimally as possible.

The serpent slowly unwound from him. Nermesa con-tinued to keep motionless even after the creature had aban-doned his throat. Listening carefully, the knight tried to judge its location.

When he sensed that it had started to move away from his head, Nermesa cautiously slid his left hand to the side until he found where he had set his dagger. The occasional hiss of the serpent kept him apprised of the creature's whereabouts.

His fingers fumbled with the hilt.

He felt movement, and the next hiss sounded closer again. The serpent had veered back toward him.

With a short oath to Mitra, Nermesa twisted around, thrusting.

The serpent gave a loud hiss, then began wriggling violently. Nermesa waited for it to bite him, but, instead, the creature suddenly went limp.

Gasping, the Aquilonian felt his blood calm slightly. In the gloom, he made out the serpent's body. His dagger had pierced it through the neck just below the head. Nermesa could not take credit for such a strike, though. He thanked Mitra for luck being with him.

Voices rose around him as others became aware of something amiss. Two other knights came to his area, one carrying a lit lamp.

"By Mitra!" the man with the lamp growled. "A rock viper! You should be dead! Be you certain you're not bit?"

"Their poison is strong," added the second. "He'd not be alive right now if he had been."

Others gathered. With more than one lamp illuminating things, Nermesa, now standing, saw just how close he had come to death. The serpent had fangs more than an inch long, and drops of venom stained the blanket beneath them. The entire creature was over three feet in length, which made it all the more amazing that he had not noticed it slowly crawling over him until it had begun encircling his neck.

Someone must have sounded an alarm, for Caltero abruptly appeared. Half-clad, he looked aghast at the sight.

"Let me through! Let me through!" Nermesa's cousin bent down by the bedside, first glancing at the younger Klandes, then taking both serpent and dagger from the bed. "A very, very close call, cousin! How did it happen?"

Nermesa related the story as best he could. The gathered knights murmured to one another as he finished.

"They generally don't like to leave their burrows after dark," commented a mustached fighter.

"Could be it made a new burrow under the building . . ." suggested a second figure.

Caltero called a halt to the speculations. "Wherever it came from, you know such a beast lives alone. There won't be another. Come the morrow, someone can seek under the building and check. Likely, it was simply lost. Not the first time we've had such a thing happen, you know that."

"First time one made it all the way into our quarters," grumbled the knight who had suggested a burrow beneath them.

Ignoring him, the senior knight dropped the carcass back on the blanket, then wiped the dagger off there, too. "The blanket's ruined already. Someone find him a new one. I'll take the carcass and have it burned, cousin." He handed Nermesa the dagger. "The Picts hear of this, they'll truly think you protected by a powerful spirit . . ."

The others began drifting off. The first knight who had arrived traded lamps with Nermesa, taking his unlit one away. Grateful for the continued light, Bolontes' son finally began to calm down . . . and think.

The fear that some Pict or brigand had purposely dropped the serpent in the building came to mind, but Nermesa quickly saw that such an act would likely have been impossible. They could not have hoped that the creature would go to the correct victim. No, for this to have been some fiendish plot, the perpetrator would have almost had to stand over Nermesa and lay the serpent on him.

Too foolish, he decided. The incident had merely been an almost-unfortunate accident. No one, not even the traitor they still sought, could have arranged this.

Yet, Nermesa could not sleep, not immediately, for the encounter made him think of the coming day and the journey to Tarantia. He was not a superstitious man by nature, but the serpent felt like an omen. It was a long way to the capital, and there were men who would seek to free Khatak, no matter what the cost.

Men far more dangerous than the most poisonous viper . . .

8

THE IMPORTANCE OF Khatak's arriving in Tarantia was emphasized by the more than two hundred men escorting him and the other prisoners east. General Boronius had judiciously picked men from wherever he could at short notice so as to not weaken any of the outposts. Still, more than a few settlers clearly watched the column depart with mixed emotions. Most were glad to see Khatak off to his doom, but the sooner the soldiers returned, the better. Every good sword was needed out west.

Some twenty knights rode with the column, and while most had many more years of experience than Nermesa, they deferred to his command without the slightest rancor. Another forty mounted men-at-arms—Quentus and Atalan among them—followed, with seventy soldiers of various types making up the rest. There were also three wagons in the center. The first held the brigand chieftain and the other captives, while the second and third supplied the column's needs.

The banner of King Conan fluttered high and proud as they traveled, and the mood among the men was high. Nermesa masked his own concerns with a look of determination befitting what the rest expected of the one who had defeated and captured the terrible Khatak. Yet, despite his doubts, he could not help but glance back on occasion and be secretly awed by the might under his command. Such numbers were enough to make any villain pause, and the farther east they got, the less and less opportunity anyone seeking to free Khatak would have.

Quentus rode near enough so that the two could talk. Nermesa's former servant had full confidence in him, which helped ease the noble's mind a bit.

"Nothing's going to happen," he assured Nermesa not for the first time. Quentus kept his voice low, so as not to draw attention to his friend's concerns. "I've talked to some of the others. This direction's been pretty much cleared of all but the smallest bands of thieves, and they wouldn't risk their necks for anyone, even the great and powerful Khatak."

"Let's hope so."

"Atalan told me again how you saved them, Nermesa. Your father's going to be truly proud when he hears the full story." The bearded fighter grinned. "And make no mistake about it! I'll be sure to tell him if you don't!"

"He likely knows already." Of that, Nermesa was certain. Either Boronius or General Pallantides or both had no doubt sent word to Bolontes of his achievements. The true question was whether the senior Klandes would be so proud. He had tried to keep his son from just such situations. For that matter, what would happen between the pair when Nermesa confronted him with what he knew of his father's maneuverings behind the scenes?

Escorting a dangerous villain across half the realm began to seem the easier of young Klandes' tasks.

To reach Tarantia, they would have to cross the Shirki River by use of the bridge at Galparan. General Boronius had decided on the man-made crossing rather than the natural stone bridge to the south, near the fortified city of Tanasul, trusting to Aquilonian construction over nature. Nermesa had been commanded to give his papers only to the officer in charge at Galparan, then proceed on. The more the prisoners were kept from other people, the less chance of something happening, so the Boar thought. Nermesa could hardly disagree.

After the Shirki, they would continue east—or rather, *southeast*, in truth—along the flat wide valley of the same name to another river crossing, then on to the plains of Tarantia. The latter half of the trek was, to Nermesa's belief, the point where the column could begin to relax its vigilance ever so slightly.

Of course, before all that, they first had to get through the Westermarck and the Bossonian Marches.

They made good time the first day, Nermesa eager to make the best of the weather and road. When he finally called a halt, he placed Khatak's wagon in the center of a circular formation with more than a dozen guards in eyeshot of the brigand himself. The half-breed eyed the sentries with wry amusement, but his expression turned darker when, at one point, he and Nermesa locked gazes.

The knight met Khatak's glare squarely. "We're a day closer to Tarantia."

The bandit chieftain scowled. "A day closer to your doom, Aquilonian."

Yet, despite Khatak's threats, nothing happened that evening or the next. The western edge of the Bossonian Marches soon beckoned.

"Will we have any trouble with the Bossonians?" Quentus asked of him as the column made camp.

Nermesa shook his head. "The papers from General Boronius will give us passage, and he said we could rely on the Bossonians as much as we can our own."

"Strange, though, that they live in Aquilonia but aren't subjects of it."

"General Boronius also said not to forget that fact when we speak with them."

Representatives from the nearest town came just as the

soldiers finished their meals. Their leader stood several inches shorter than Nermesa, but was more broad-shouldered. He, like the rest, was clad in simple but well-crafted brown-and-green garb more suited for farming or hunting. However, lest anyone think that the Bossonians were not here on serious business, one only had to notice the longbows slung over the shoulders of each.

"Hail to you, Aquilonian," greeted the head Bossonian in an earthy voice matching his stolid appearance. "I am called Ranaric. We've had word of your coming."

His accent was strong despite his excellent command of Nermesa's language. The knight met Ranaric's steady, brown eyes and read in them a man he could trust. "Hail to you, Ranaric. I am Nermesa of Klandes, commander of this column and serving under General Boronius."

"How is the Boar?"

Behind him, Quentus chuckled. Ranaric smiled at Nermesa's expression. Ranaric clearly knew Boronius well.

"He sends this personal note." The knight handed the Bossonian a small letter that the general had written for this very man. Nermesa had been ordered not to give it to anyone else.

Ranaric tucked it in his leather belt. "And from you?"

Nermesa produced the orders. The Bossonian leader read them over carefully, clearly an educated man despite living in such a frontier land.

With a nod, Ranaric gave back the documents. "A dangerous business, this. Will you visit our town?"

Despite the fact that Bossonian towns were well fortified, Nermesa had been ordered to stay clear of them. Even among Ranaric's folk, there were those who might prove sympathetic to Khatak.

"I must decline, thank you."

Ranaric shrugged. "Then I must at least promise you the protection of our men."

Nermesa was about to remind Ranaric that he had over two hundred trained fighters, including archers of their own, but several of the men behind the Bossonian leader immediately began fanning out in a manner that showed they knew the area far better than any Aquilonian. Within seconds, they had vanished among the trees, leaving no trace. Yet Nermesa could sense that the archers were watching.

"Nothing will harm you in this forest," promised Ranaric with the assurance of one who knows that he speaks the utter truth. He bowed to Nermesa, then, all alone, turned in the direction of the distant town.

"But we can't allow you to journey back alone!" the knight insisted.

Without looking back, Ranaric answered, "I will be no more alone than you."

Which meant, Nermesa realized, that more Bossonian archers watched the land ahead. If they were safe anywhere on this entire journey, it was clearly here in the Marches.

Several of the men who had watched the tableau unfold now eyed the foliage above. Quentus shook his head. " 'Tis true what they say about them! Like shadows!"

"Which in no manner means that we can relax our guard. I want everyone to continue to keep a sharp lookout."

Whether because of the Bossonians' presence or the Aquilonians' continued vigilance, the night passed without even the hint of trouble. Come the morning, one of Ranaric's archers suddenly materialized out of the forest to report to Nermesa.

"All passed well," he grunted. "Ranaric bids you good journey."

They saw none of the other Bossonians, but as Nermesa had his column mount up and continue on, he remained aware that the party was constantly scrutinized.

"The Marches are fairly narrow," the man-at-arms Atalan informed him as they rode. "By late tomorrow, we should be at the eastern border—the unofficial one, of course. After that, Galparan's the next civilized stop. Once across the Shirki, we are as good as home, sir."

"When I see Tarantia ahead on the plains, we'll be as good as home," Nermesa replied.

The forest began to thin out some, which comforted

him. Too well Nermesa recalled the night of Khatak's capture. The fewer trees, the less opportunity for surprise by
the brigand's cohorts.

Yet their prime prisoner seemed not at all put out by the
growing odds against his escape. Khatak continued to ignore all save Nermesa, to whom he offered death with every
glance.

Reluctant as he was to call a halt, Nermesa finally did
so. Despite more hospitable surroundings, he did not re-
duce the number of sentries around the wagon. Even if the
unknown traitor was in their midst, it would be impossible
for him to get past all of the safeguards.

"Can you not rest yet?" asked Quentus, as Nermesa
brooded by one of the fires. "He'll be going nowhere, especially not this night. If you had any more soldiers standing
guard over him, I'd think he was the new king of Aquilonia!"

"I just can't shake the feeling that something will still
happen."

"We're almost out of the forest, and the trees are thin
enough that no band of cutthroats could sneak up on us,
even in the dark."

"I know, but I just want to be . . . careful."

Quentus shook his head and walked off to get some water. Nermesa sat staring at the flames, unable to shake his
concern. When the foliage of a nearby tree briefly rustled,
he all but leapt to his feet, one hand already reaching for
his sword. Yet, despite a serious survey of the area in question, Nermesa saw nothing. It was a scene that he had already repeated more than once this evening.

Quentus brought him some of the salted rabbit stew that
served as the column's chief source of sustenance. Nermesa ate in silence, gaze constantly shifting from the dark
surroundings to the activities of the camp. Despite his worst
fears, however, he saw nothing to worry about and, after
making a final walk around the perimeter, finally forced himself to go to sleep.

To his frustration, the dreams that came to him were all

ones in which Khatak escaped, leaving all dead but Nermesa. The knight, his arms limp, could only watch helplessly as the brigand and an army of followers ransacked the entire kingdom of Aquilonia.

After what was perhaps the thousandth repetition, Nermesa finally woke. Scowling, he left the camp just far enough to deal with matters of nature, then headed back to his bedroll.

But with the memory of his dreams still fresh, Nermesa decided to make another check of the prisoners. Perhaps when he saw that all was as it should be, his slumber would become more peaceful.

He grew encouraged when he noted that the first sentries were still in place. They saluted Nermesa as he approached.

"Everything quiet?"

"Aye, sir," answered the senior one. "That mad dog must sleep with his eyes open, though! I've not heard anyone who's seen him shut them once on this whole trek."

"Oh?" Steeling himself, Nermesa went to the wagon and peered inside.

Snores emanated from most of the prisoners, but, as the man-at-arms had said, Khatak sat up straight. Worse, he stared directly at Nermesa, and any thought that the bandit *did* sleep with his eyes open was eradicated by a short but harsh chuckle.

Nermesa pulled back. Had Khatak been waiting all this time just for this encounter? Impossible . . . and yet . . .

Approaching the guard again, Nermesa asked, "He sits like that . . . all the time?"

"Aye."

What was it Khatak expected . . . or was he merely bluffing?

The branches above rustled, causing Nermesa to jump. Fortunately, the sentries, having also reacted, failed to notice his lapse. Nermesa silently cursed. Khatak still had such an effect on his foes even while imprisoned.

"Keep wary," Nermesa commanded the sentries. He turned back toward his waiting bedroll—

A heavy thud echoed in the woods to the north.

Nermesa immediately pointed at three of the guards. "You! Come with me! The rest of you stay vigilant! This may be nothing, but then again . . ."

He summoned other soldiers as he hurried along. Several men woke as he and the others ran past. Seizing their weapons, the sleepers leapt to their feet.

Grabbing a torch from a guard on the perimeter, Nermesa led the way into the forest. A dozen men now followed him, with more on their way.

The knight paused to listen, but only the silence of the dark greeted his ears. He knew that he was near the spot from which the sound had come, but the torchlight revealed nothing out of the ordinary.

Unwilling to take a chance, Nermesa led his growing search party on. Such a noise could not have been caused by nothing. He would not leave until he had discovered the reason.

"Over here!" cried someone to his right.

Following the voice, Nermesa saw Quentus ahead. His friend stood over a large mound with a frighteningly familiar shape. As Nermesa arrived, Quentus turned the grisly form over.

" 'Tis Iolon!" gasped another soldier. "But he was left guarding the far perimeter on the southern side!"

"His back's cracked in half, and his throat's torn out!" said another. The stunned soldier gazed wide-eyed at their surroundings. "Some demon got him!"

"Silence!" Nermesa spun around, first surveying the forest, then intently studying the treetops. There was a broken place in the foliage above and, when, the knight looked down again, he saw that there were twigs and leaves caught in Iolin's armor.

But *what* could possibly have carried off an entire man, especially one clad in plate, without him being able to cry out?

Then, something moved in the trees above. All eyes skyward, the Aquilonians froze.

Behind Nermesa, a soldier cried out.

The search party turned in time to catch a glimpse of the man's boots as he vanished upward into the thick greenery.

Two archers immediately readied arrows, but had no target. The missing soldier's scream cut off harshly.

The tree next to Nermesa shook and, as he raised his sword to defend himself, a heavy object dropped on him.

"Nermesa!" Quentus leapt to aid him, but it was too late. Under the massive weight, Nermesa sprawled on the ground, stunned. His torch went flying. A face rolled against his . . . a face that, even in the dark, he could see was staring fearfully even in death.

The soldier who had just been seized.

"Get that off him!" Quentus demanded. "Atalan! Douse that fire!"

The weight was hefted away. Nermesa pushed himself up on his elbows and watched with sickened heart as the others laid the second body by the first.

Then, the foliage rustled again.

"My sword!" he demanded. As someone handed to him, Nermesa also ordered, "Stay away from the trees! Archers, to me!"

Others had joined the search, some of them fortunately with bows. Nermesa now had five archers, but was that enough?

Something else suddenly occurred to him. This bizarre attack was too coincidental for his tastes. "Atalan! Make certain that the prison wagon's still secure!"

"Aye!"

More leaves moved.

Two of the archers immediately fired at the location, but clearly to no effect. As they readied their bows again, the other three waited for a chance.

A monstrous roar echoed in the night.

A roar very close to them.

"Watch out!" a man-at-arms shouted. There was a crashing sound and what seemed like half the tree above Nermesa came tumbling down. He leapt aside, but one of the archers was not so fortunate. The heavy wood bowled him over and crushed in his skull.

And in the midst of the chaos, a gargantuan *thing* landed on the ground in front of Nermesa.

There was no torch near enough to enable him to see the figure clearly, but the same stench the knight had smelled previously was identification enough. Here was the bestial brigand who had almost slain him before Khatak's capture.

Although Nermesa tried to bring his blade up quickly, the fur-clad figure moved swifter. A hand as huge as the Aquilonian's head seized him by the collar.

"Nermesa!" cried Quentus. "No!"

The bearded fighter dove toward his friend, sword slashing at the giant. His blade caught the attacker's arm, but the blow was glancing.

Yet, it was still enough to infuriate the fearsome figure. With a snarl, he tossed Nermesa hard against a tree. The knight collided with the trunk and all but blacked out.

With terrible ease, Quentus's opponent seized the man-at-arms by the wrist. Pulled forward, the former servant lost his balance. He fell into the waiting arms.

"Save him!" Nermesa managed. He tried to join the struggle, but his head pounded, and his legs would not work yet.

Three other soldiers closed in on the pair. The mysterious bandit placed one hand on the side of Quentus's head . . . and twisted it sharply.

A horrific cracking sound accompanied the action.

"Nooo!" Nermesa staggered forward, aware that it was already too late to help.

With a mad roar, the giant effortlessly tossed Quentus's limp form at his nearest foes. Then, before anyone else could close with him, he leapt *up* to the branches, pulling himself out of sight in less than the blink of an eye.

Two of the remaining archers managed belated shots, but to no avail.

Nermesa slashed at the area under where his friend's murderer had last stood. Tears streaming down his face, he

THE GOD IN THE MOON

growled, "Come back, damn you! Come back! I'm here! Here!"

But the leaves did not shiver, and no giant leapt upon him. The area was silent save for his harsh breathing.

In frustration, Nermesa finally thrust his sword point down into the earth. He went to Quentus's side, hoping despite everything that his childhood friend might still breathe.

But life had already long fled the former servant. His head lolled to the side, the broken bone visible through the flesh. Death had been instantaneous, but that brought no relief to Nermesa.

"You came out to protect me . . ." Bolontes' son murmured. "But, when it came to it, I should've protected you . . . and didn't."

Fists tight, Nermesa looked up . . . and thought of Khatak.

"Carry the bodies back!" he snapped. "But gently!" Seizing his sword, Nermesa added, "We'll give them a decent burial come the morning!"

With that, he trod off, only one thought left to him. Quentus's death—the deaths of all the men—could be laid at the feet of the brigand chieftain. It was his horrific henchman who had so brutally slain the soldiers . . . and now Nermesa intended that Khatak *pay* for that act, regardless of orders.

His expression must have been terrible to see, for the first sentry he came across gaped and backed up a step before saluting. Nermesa ignored him, heading directly for the prison wagon.

Several soldiers moved about the area. Atalan was speaking with one of the original guards, who looked harried. The wagon looked untouched, which surprised but did not deter Nermesa.

The senior man-at-arms noticed him and saluted. "Did you find the—"

"Khatak!" Nermesa spat. "Is he still in there?"

"Yes, but—"

Bolontes' son strode past him without another word, concerned only with reaching the brigand. Seizing a lit lamp hanging on the wagon, he looked inside. The other prisoners grouped in the back of the cage, their postures indicating a fear of the lone figure seated cross-legged near the door.

In the lamp's light, Khatak gave him the crooked smile. The half-breed's eyes glittered like a cat's. The brigand chieftain looked unruffled, even relaxed, which made Nermesa all the more furious.

"The son of the lion," greeted Khatak.

Nermesa started for the captive, fully intending to run him through . . . but then hesitated. Butchering a caged prisoner was something he would have expected of the man before him. Nermesa was tempted to unlock the cage and give Khatak a weapon with which to defend himself, but that might be just what the bandit had been hoping for.

"My friend is dead because of you!" he rumbled.

"Because of this one? But I have been sleeping here so restfully all night." Khatak grinned. "Well . . . there was some noise that woke me. Thought it was singing . . ."

He meant the cries of Quentus and the others. Nermesa felt his blood boiling again but fought it down. Khatak wanted him angry and careless.

Gritting his teeth, Bolontes' son looked over the cage. At first glance, it appeared untouched despite the damage to the wagon's top. One of the bars above had been bent a little, but that was all.

"Your friend . . ." Khatak interjected. "He died horribly?"

The question was asked with amusement. Once more, it was all Nermesa could do to keep from running his prisoner through.

He chose not to answer, concentrating again on the interior. All those deaths, and Khatak had not even come close to being freed.

Retreating from the wagon, Nermesa summoned Atalan over to him. "Were the guards here at all times?"

"From what I gather, yes."

"Did you search the wagon?"

The senior man-at-arms scratched his chin. "It was not something that came to mind, sir. The trouble seemed outside." He hesitated. "Did I hear you say—"

Nermesa cut him off. "Get the prisoners out and search them and the wagon . . . very carefully!"

Atalan had the guards pull Khatak and the rest out. The brigand chieftain continued to smile as he was brought past Nermesa, but his eyes now appraised the Aquilonian differently. Nermesa did not care what Khatak thought at the moment, interested only in the results.

The soldiers looked over their captives from top to bottom, even stripping them down. None of the group had been allowed sandals or boots, the better to keep them from running off should they escape the cage.

While this went on, Atalan and others searched the wagon. As time passed, and they discovered nothing, Nermesa grew frustrated. Had he been wrong?

Then, Atalan emerged with a long, slim object . . . and a narrow dagger with it. The dagger had cryptic symbols on both the short hilt and the blade. "Found this under the cage, between the wood frame at the bottom."

A Pict weapon. Nermesa understood its purpose, but the piece discovered with it made no sense at first, until he thought of the fact that the cage was sealed with a lock. Ordering someone to bring the lock in question to him, the noble closed it, then tried to use the object on it like a key.

On his third attempt, the lock opened.

"This wasn't in the wagon when it left Scanaga," he declared. Nermesa eyed Khatak, whose expression had not altered in the least, then asked Atalan, "You made certain that there was nothing else hidden anywhere?"

"I'd swear my life upon it!"

As that was exactly what would be at stake if the prisoners ever did escape, Nermesa took him at his word. Clutching the dagger and the picklock, he ordered the traitors and bandits back into the cage.

Yet, as Khatak passed, Nermesa could not help pulling

him out of the line by the collar and bringing him almost nose to nose.

"Another day closer . . ." he whispered to Khatak. "We'll be seeing the walls of Tarantia soon . . . and then you see nothing but the inside of the Iron Tower."

Shoving the outlaw to one of the guards before Khatak could respond, Nermesa walked off to plan the burials for Quentus and the other victims.

9

IT WAS IMPOSSIBLE to discover just who had passed on the dagger and the tool during the chaos—supposing that it had even happened *then*—but Nermesa did his best to solve, at least temporarily, the problem of further assistance to Khatak by alternating the guards more often and having them in pairs at each station. The odds that two soldiers standing side by side would both be traitors were not so great, he felt.

Quentus was buried alongside the others and his belongings, including his armor, were gathered for return to his family. Only when they were being loaded aboard one of the supply wagons did Nermesa realize that *he* was the nearest thing his former servant had to family. That resurrected anew his bitterness at his friend's horrific demise, and he silently swore that, once in the capital, Khatak would not escape justice.

The crossing at Galparan days later was a blur to him. He recalled the officer at the gate of the bridge and the presenting of papers to him. What the man had said was lost, as was the actual march across the wide, lined bridge. A clattering of hooves, the curses of men trying to push one of the wagons forward . . . those were the sum total of his memories of Galparan.

The lands beyond fared little better with his attention. The hills gave way to a more level region and occasional forest—the latter nothing as worrisome as out in the Westermarck or the Marches—and one or two nameless villages, which, per Boronius's orders, they avoided.

Only when the column reached the edge of a vast plain spreading to the horizon did Nermesa stir. He knew this land well. It was *home*, even if his actual residence was still days ahead.

The Plains of Tarantia.

But although only small, wooded areas greeted them on this last part of the trek, he nonetheless kept vigilant. The nearer to Tarantia, the more he wanted to make certain that nothing else happened. He rearranged the guards again, hoping that, by doing so, it kept the traitor in their midst from calculating a new escape plan.

And, at night, Nermesa himself stayed awake whenever they were forced to camp near trees.

Then, late one overcast day, a tall structure came into sight. Nermesa stood in the saddle, squinting in the hopes of making out better detail.

It was not Tarantia, but it was almost as good. An estate, such as his family owned in addition to their residence in the capital. As the column neared it, more detail came into view. The main house was particularly imposing, with battlements atop it and a wide stone wall upon which guards walked. Arched windows marked the upper floors, and a sculpted grove lay within the protective wall. Banners fluttered atop the house, a blue field upon which the black silhouette of a tall bird wielding a weapon stood.

The banner stirred some memory, but Nermesa quickly buried it again. What mattered was this was one of the Tarantian estates. That meant that they would surely reach their goal within another day.

"Justice will be served, Quentus," he whispered to himself. "I swear it . . ."

They came in the view of peasants working the fields. Many of those toiling stopped in their tasks to watch the column pass. Nermesa slowed his horse to talk to a thin man barely older than himself.

"Who is your master?"

Round cap clutched tight in his dirt-encrusted hands, the peasant anxiously replied, "Baron Antonus Sibelio."

"Sibelio?" Nermesa glanced back at the banner. Small wonder it had struck some memory. A heron with a sword.

The worker bowed. "I shall go alert the master to your presence—"

"Not necessary," Bolontes' son quickly responded. "We must be on our way."

But he was not to escape so readily, for from the main house there suddenly emerged a band of riders in the familiar blue-and-black garb Nermesa still recalled from his first encounter with their master.

And sure enough, Baron Sibelio rode at the head of the party, his cloak flowing behind him. The Gunderman, Betavio, followed directly behind. Aware that a meeting could not be avoided, Nermesa ordered the rest of the soldiers to stand down.

"I am Baron Antonus Sibelio, and I welcome you to my lands, sir knight—" The aristocrat paused to study Nermesa's face. "By Mitra! It is you! The heir to Klandes!"

"Good evening to you, Baron," Nermesa said, nodding to an equal. Behind the other noble, Betavio bowed his head but remained silent.

"The last I heard, you were out west and . . . aah!" Antonus studied the long column, his eyes especially pausing on the wagons. "The tale is true, then? Is the famed bandit in one of those?"

Keeping himself formal, Nermesa answered, "We are returning from the west at the order of the throne. I regret to cut this short, Baron, but my orders are to proceed to Tarantia with all haste, and I intend to march us there tonight."

"With men on foot, you'll not arrive until virtually dawn! Please! You and these men must be my guests! There is an area to your right not being used this season for growth. The soldiers can camp there, you and your officers may stay at my humble house!"

"You are most gracious, but I must decline. My orders come from General Pallantides himself."

The baron's eyes briefly widened. "Aah! You have the right of it, then, young Klandes! Very well, I will not hold you any longer save to ask how your family fares? I've not spoken with them since you and my cousin, Bertran, last stood before the king."

"So far as I know, they're doing well." Nermesa made to turn his horse back to the road.

"Lady Orena said so, but I wondered."

The comment caused Nermesa to hesitate. "You've spoken with her?"

The master of Sibelio shrugged. "The business affairs of my House have, of late, included contracts with that of Lenaro. As she is its mistress, we have met on occasion."

Why that should have bothered Nermesa at all, he could not say. Forcing aside uncomfortable thoughts, he saluted the baron. "Thank you again for your offer of hospitality."

"Think nothing of it. I hope to offer it to you again in the future." Baron Sibelio signaled his men to turn. With a last nod to Nermesa, the other noble rode back toward his home.

Nermesa glanced at his hands, which had tightened around the reins since the baron's arrival. Frowning, he returned to the front of the column and waved for the march to resume. Never once did he look back at the Sibelio estate.

THE WALLS OF the capital were a welcome view even though glimpsed in the gloom of night. Nermesa had never experienced coming to Tarantia in such a manner. Most of his excursions outside of the city had been to various estates, and those trips had lasted overnight at most, making the returns home rather mundane. Now, though, after so long out in the Westermarck, Tarantia loomed larger than life, more the mythic capital that he knew pilgrims and foreigners saw upon their first visits.

The broad walls loomed like giants as the column approached. Torchlight illuminated the top, creating a divine halo over Nermesa's beloved city. Other fires marked the area leading up to the gargantuan iron gates. Scores of guards monitored the vicinity from both atop the wall and at the arched entrance.

A patrol leader rode out with a small band to meet the column. His heavily scarred face and the three-fingered hand he raised to call a halt marked him as a veteran who had seen much fighting.

"Ho, there! Present your orders!"

Nermesa dutifully did. The hawk-faced soldier peered at them, his serious expression suddenly breaking into a gap-toothed grin. He looked at the young fighter with new respect.

"All in order!" The patrol leader handed everything back, then, grinning again, added, "And welcome you are, Nermesa Klandes! *Much* welcome!"

"Thank you."

"We'll lead you in. Should've arrived in the daylight! We could've had quite a crowd for your homecoming! Everyone wants to see the bastard and the man who at last caught him!"

More grateful than ever that he had avoided just such a spectacle, Nermesa simply nodded to the officer. The veteran turned toward his own men, signaling with his maimed hand that they should take up escort positions.

"We could still ride in with horns blaring," he suggested to Nermesa. "Draw quite a crowd yet, even if from their beds."

"That won't be necessary. General Pallantides wants the prisoners secured as soon as possible."

Mention of Pallantides' name finally settled the matter. The officer gave some further commands to his soldiers, then guided the column toward the gates.

Like the mouth of a dragon opening high to swallow them, the pointed gates rose to admit the newcomers. Everywhere, soldiers lined the area in the hopes of catching a glimpse of Khatak . . . or even Nermesa, for that matter. A few early-rising workers and merchants also gathered, curious as to what the fuss was all about.

Despite the long day's march, Nermesa's men moved as if fully rested. Some little of the glory of Khatak's capture rubbed off on them. Several of the Tarantian guards gave cheers and slapped the backs of the new arrivals. Nermesa grew a little nervous over the slacking of attention. It would be a fine jest if somehow Khatak escaped at the very walls of the capital.

But no such horrific incident occurred. The column moved on from the gates. The patrol leader pulled his own troops aside and saluted Nermesa as he passed.

Beyond the gate, there were few yet awake. Bracketed torches in the sides of buildings and walls lit the stone streets, revealing the tall, arched buildings that made up much of Tarantia. The king's banner flew everywhere, and occasional patrols marked important intersections. Every soldier paused to watch the column move along.

From the second floors of several of the beige-toned structures, some sleepy residents stepped out onto barred balconies to see what was happening.

"What's all going on down there?" demanded a portly man in a blue silken robe to one of the soldiers on patrol duty.

"They've brought that devil brigand back in a cage!" the armored figure responded. "Khatak, the Beast of the West!"

"Khatak!" The man pulled his robe tight in momentary concern.

"Aye," continued the soldier, suddenly pointing at Nermesa. "And there's the one who captured him!"

How the soldier could know for certain that he pointed at the right man, Bolontes' son did not know, but the act brought more and more attention Nermesa did not desire. Word spread from balcony to balcony, street to street, some-how moving swifter than the column. Despite Nermesa's intention of sneaking into Tarantia, groups began to gather ahead, citizens so interested in seeing the monster and the hero that they stood in their nightclothes, unconcerned about appearances. Even the fact that they soon realized that they would only see a wagon instead of the actual bandit did not dissuade them. Worse, many pointed at Nermesa, gesturing to one another and talking animatedly about him.

But this was what you wanted, wasn't it? he chided himself. *To return home the conquering hero, the envy of all and the champion of the king?*

A hint of light upon the horizon began bringing Tarantia to life. Tall, spiraling towers formed in the distance, marking the main temple of Mitra. Like so many of the other towers, including those of the palace, they were blue and gold, though both colors were muted in the twilight.

But then another structure arose, one that in its own unique manner signified the near conclusion to the long trek. Narrow, a stark gray, the Iron Tower was a dread reminder of times past and present. During Namedides's reign, it had been filled to bursting. It had not mattered whether any of the prisoners were guilty or innocent, the city guard under Namedides had taken the slightest hint of disrespect as reason enough to drag someone off to the sinister tower. To speak of the clawed structure then was to do so in whispers for fear that ears within it would somehow catch notice. Only the uppermost level of the tower had windows ... two red burning gaps that, as a child, had reminded Nermesa of blazing eyes.

Thankfully, the area ahead opened up, and a vast, regal estate situated within the city center filled his gaze. Even though it had only been a few scant months since he had last seen the palace, Nermesa eyed the sight with tremendous pleasure. The spiked wall and the sculpted grove within were, at this point, as welcome to him as his own home.

Nermesa suddenly noticed that there was a welcoming committee at the gates of the palace. A dozen riders wearing the garb of the Black Dragons sat at attention, eyes on the approaching column.

General Pallantides, looking as neat and orderly as always despite the odd hour of Nermesa's arrival, sat at the forefront. He cocked his head when he saw who led the arrivals.

"Welcome back, young Klandes," the king's commander calmly said. "You've made good time in your return."

"I'm glad to be back, General."

Pallantides peered behind him and, without preamble, asked, "The first wagon?"

He meant Khatak. "Yes, General. All the prisoners are secured there."

"Any trouble on the way?"

Memories of Quentus and the others suddenly sought to overwhelm Nermesa. Fighting down his bitterness, he managed to reply politely, "There was some, but nothing successful."

Yet, the skilled Pallantides evidently read some of his grief. "We shall speak of these things later," he said, his tone more somber. "Once the villain is dealt with and you and your men have had an opportunity to rest."

Now that he was back home, and Khatak was all but in the hands of the most trusted officer in the kingdom, Nermesa's exhaustion finally caught up with him. "I—we'd be very grateful for that, General."

Pallantides summoned one of the Black Dragons to him. "Edric, take charge of the prisoner wagon and see to it that it's taken directly to the Iron Tower. You know the preparations I've demanded of them for our special guest. Make certain that everything is as it should be."

"Aye." The brawny Edric, followed by three other Dragons, headed back to where Khatak and the others were held.

"You came during the night," Pallantides commented to Nermesa. "Others would have chosen the high day, when the crowds were fullest and the opportunity for glory greatest."

"I thought—"

"You thought correctly, Nermesa. Such would have

been the inclination of ambitious nobles, not a true servant of the realm." The stern face softened some. "We underestimated you. I speak of your father, myself, and others. I already know that Boronius has had words with you on this matter. I can only say that someone I respected almost as much as the king asked of me a favor, and I granted it . . . but I freely admit now that I'm glad it went awry. You are a natural soldier, a natural commander, Nermesa . . . and Aquilonia is always in need of such."

Nermesa was glad that the gloom hid his no-doubt-reddening cheeks. "I am honored by what you say."

"We'll speak more tomorrow. You should dismiss the men and sleep this coming day in your own home." Suddenly, Pallantides' gaze went past him. "Your man . . ."

"The—the troubles I spoke of earlier."

The commander of the Black Dragons frowned. "I see. Go to your family, Nermesa. That would be best."

With that, General Pallantides veered off to the palace, the other Black Dragons following close. Nermesa watched the famed soldier vanish into the dimness, then glanced over his shoulder.

The remaining Dragons already had the wagon out and were guiding it away from the area of the palace. The Iron Tower loomed close. The trek would not be a long one. Before the hour was ended, Khatak would find himself a resident of the fabled prison.

And perhaps then, Nermesa could indeed rest.

HIS FAMILY DID not know of his arrival, and he forbade the servant who came to the door from telling them. Nermesa headed directly for his room, which he found exactly as he had left it. Despite the grime of the long journey, the young Klandes simply dropped his armor and garments on the white marble floor and tossed himself onto the opulent, silk-sheeted bed. His head had scarcely hit the down-filled pillows before Nermesa fell fast asleep.

He awoke to bright sunlight and the excited chatter of voices, one of which he recognized as his mother's. A moment later, Callista burst in, looking as if the Picts had just poured over the walls.

"Praise Mitra, you're awake at last, my son!" She flew to the bed and hugged him tightly. Nermesa returned the hug, momentarily forgetting all that had happened since he had last left the Klandes residence.

"When Simonio told me you were back, I thought it was some cruel joke, but there you were in your bed!" She pulled back, giving him a stern expression. "You should have had us roused from our beds! How could you torture your mother so?"

"The boy needed sleep," came his father's voice from the hallway. Bolontes stepped in and, as he did, his voice all but trembled. "Still . . . it would have been nice to know."

Nermesa sat up. "I'm sorry. All I could think of was wanting to go to my bed."

"Understandable, lad." The patriarch frowned. "When we discovered Quentus was not with you, I had someone ask about it." He cleared his throat. "I'm sorry for the loss of a good man, Nermesa."

The admission stirred up the terrible memories again. "I'm sorry for the loss of a brother . . ."

"Yes, he was like that to you. I take blame for his death. I sent him after you—"

"No." Nermesa would have none of that. Any animosity toward his father in that regard had quickly faded. Quentus had very much desired to follow his master and friend no matter what the danger. If Bolontes had not suggested it, Quentus no doubt would have. "He did what he wanted to, and I was glad for his company. There's no one to blame for his death but that brigand and his monstrous servant."

"Well, you've got the one," reminded his father, trying to raise Nermesa's spirits. "Word is everywhere! Nermesa Klandes is spoken of throughout the city! Nay! Likely throughout most of Aquilonia, by now!"

"I'm just happy that you're alive," Nermesa's mother added. Her fingers stroked a scar. "My poor child!"

"I'm all right. I truly am." Something suddenly occurred to him. "Has there been any word for me?"

Bolontes straightened. "As a matter of fact, there's been several. Mostly from friends and associates—"

"And Orena, of course!" interjected Callista.

"—but you mean something *official*," the elder Klandes continued. From his robes, Bolontes produced a small, waxed parchment. "This arrived but an hour ago and bears the seal of the king."

"The *king*?" Nermesa all but leapt from the bed. Fortunately, in his weariness, he had left on a simple tunic, else he would have made quite the spectacle before his parents. With a smile, Bolontes handed the sealed letter to his son.

Nermesa cracked the seal and read.

To his amazement, it was written by King Conan himself. That what some considered a barbarian could write in such fine script amazed even Nermesa, devoutly loyal to him.

Nermesa, son of Bolontes of House Klandes, will come to the palace to be honored for the capture of Khatak, the bandit. The family and friends of Nermesa will also come. The time will be three days from this letter at the second hour past midday.
Well struck, warrior.

It was simply signed *Conan, King of Aquilonia*.

Knowing what he did about his monarch, the sparse, straightforward speech in the letter did not surprise Nermesa in the least. His hand shook as he reread the contents. Boronius had prepared him for just this event, but still it struck Nermesa to his very core.

I'll be honored by the king!

"What does it say that stirs you so, my son?" Callista asked.

He told them. His mother clasped her hands together

and looked so very proud. His father was more cautious, but, after a moment, Bolontes also smiled.

"It is a great thing to see my son honored," he said. "And better by this man than Namedides."

The statement meant much to Nermesa. He had worried that his parents, especially his father, just might not wish to be there.

"We shall have to tell Orena," his mother went on, suddenly summoning a dark cloud into the situation. "She would want to be there, son."

As she was his betrothed, Nermesa could not deny the suggestion. Perhaps things would be different, though. Perhaps when he and Orena met again, the trials he had been through would make their reunion a loving one.

Perhaps . . .

IN THE CAVE deep in the Pictish wilderness, the hooded figure waited patiently by the fire. Occasionally, a slim hand would reach out and toss certain powders into the flames, causing the latter to erupt briefly. A hiss would arise from the fire and tendrils of red smoke would dance.

The effects would last but seconds, yet there were still enough to be significant to the form. The portents were not good, yet, there was still hope. *He* had not returned. So long as that was the case, the chance of success existed.

The hood shifted toward the entrance. There, a fearful bandit clad in a stained silken shirt and pants—loot stripped from the corpse of a long-dead merchant—stood waiting. Like many of those in the band, he had some trace of Pict blood in him, in this case revealed most by his blunt nose and the shape of his wary eyes. He bowed low as he entered. In his hands, he carried a bowl filled with a dark, crimson liquid.

"The others," the newcomer anxiously growled. "They get nervous! Ask questions! Want to know one thing! Has Gullah looked down on Khatak without favor?"

The one to whom he spoke did not reply, instead reaching

for the bowl. Hardly hiding his growing irritation, the robber handed it over. The hooded form ignored him after that.

With a cautious glance outside, the bandit pressed the point. "They say that Khatak is in the stronghold of the Cimmerian devil who rules these pale Aquilonians! The Picts speak of the Cimmerian as a spirit who walks among men and cannot be slain! If Khatak is his prisoner—"

At this, the shrouded figure vehemently hissed. One hand slipped to the powders and, with catlike reflexes and swiftness, tossed a pinch at the questioner.

He tried to duck away, but failed. As the white substance hit his face—and his eyes—the shaggy-haired bandit shrieked. "Aaaiee! My eyes! They burn like red embers!"

He stumbled to his knees, searching frantically somewhere for water. His wild search led him back toward the cave mouth . . . just as a hulking, shadowed form entered.

Even through tearful eyes, the brigand could see enough to grow panicked. He rolled away from the entrance, but the giant stooped down and seized him by the throat. The brigand looked into a face out of nightmare . . . and promptly *fainted.*

A muffled sound erupted from the watcher by the fire. The shadowy giant looked up, then silently took the robber and dragged him outside, where he would eventually wake up and flee to his brethren, telling them of his narrow escape from the god. It would keep the rabble under control for a while longer, or so the hooded figure thought.

The shaggy, shadowed form returned. He sat in the darkened corner, growling.

Another hiss escaped the watcher by the fire. So, that was it, then. Failure. Something else would have to be done. The Aquilonian pig would have to live up to his promise or suffer the consequences. One way or another, Khatak would be freed.

Then there was the warrior, the child-faced knight who had the luck of the spirits with him. His luck would have to be turned. He would have to be brought back to the land somehow and made to suffer horribly so that the tribes would understand his weakness, the weakness of all the invaders.

But first . . . first there was the fort with which to deal.

First . . . there was Scanaga.

10

RATHER THAN HAVE Orena visit his home—and, thus, have their uncertain reunion take place under the gazes of his parents—Nermesa chose to meet his betrothed in her own abode. It was not that he expected anything wrong to happen, but it would be difficult enough to speak with Orena without having to be concerned with other ears.

Like Klandes, Lenaro had an elegant residence in Tarantia within sight of the palace. It followed the standard design of the mighty Houses—fluted columns at the entrance, high marble steps, the symbol of the House carved above, and the vaulted roofs. A great white gate surrounded the Lenaro mansion and two mighty oaks, supposedly as old as the bloodline itself, flanked the stone serpentine entranceway. Sentries in the livery of Lenaro—white with silver lining—stood guard at the wrought-iron gates. Banners with the Lenaro emblem—two crossed blades with a four-point crown above them on a field of white—flew in the light breeze. The images were silver, and the crown represented the fact that Orena's House could also claim Aquilonian kings in its blood.

Arriving near the steps, Nermesa handed his mount over to a waiting servant. As the noble strode up, the doors swung open. It was not, however, Morannus who greeted him, as Nermesa had expected. For a moment, he thought that Orena had somehow darkened her hair, making it auburn, then realized that this woman was slightly shorter and also younger. Her features were softer, too.

Those features lit up at sight of him. "Nermesa! You've come!"

"Telaria?" The woman before him was not the boyish figure he had last seen. Nermesa recalculated the time he had been gone and marveled at the sudden change in Orena's sister. "You surprised me. You are looking grown-up!"

She flushed, then quickly urged him inside. "Morannus was to answer the door, but I wanted to greet you! I won't get much chance once you're with Orena."

He joined her. As she shut the door, Nermesa said, "Well, I appreciate the trouble. It's very good to see you, too."

Up close, he could see even more differences, most of them subtle but combining to create a transformation Nermesa saw would someday soon enable Telaria to rival her sister in beauty . . . if not surpass her. Her auburn hair, which was, for one of the few times that he could recall, unbound, flowed around her face and cascaded below her shoulders. Telaria's dress—which to Nermesa's eyes was not much more elaborate than that of the servants—clung to her in a pleasing fashion . . .

"Good morning to you, Master Nermesa," rumbled Morannus's voice. "It is a pleasure to have you back. All Tarantia speaks of you and your feat."

The noble quickly looked from Telaria to the Gunderman. A sense of guilt pervaded Nermesa, although he had not truly done anything wrong.

"Hello, Morannus. Is your mistress about? She should be expecting me."

"Aye, she is, my lord. She awaits you out on the terrace."

"I can guide you there," Telaria immediately offered.

The Gunderman shook his head. "My orders are to take charge of Master Nermesa, my lady. Your sister wished to remind you that you have tasks to complete."

The animation in Telaria's face utterly vanished. She bowed her head slightly. "She is correct, of course." Without looking up, Telaria said, "It was good to see you, Nermesa. If you will excuse me?"

"It was my treat. You'll be at the ceremony?"

Now, the auburn-haired woman looked at him. "No," she said with a frown. "I'm unable to come."

Turning, Telaria all but scurried from the hall.

Morannus stood patiently by a bust of Orena positioned on a pedestal. "If you would follow me, Master Nermesa?"

A bit disgruntled, the noble nodded. Morannus marched him through the long, main corridor bisecting the Lenaro residence. Friezes of the lords and ladies of the past lined the wall, each image bordered by silver. Unlike the images in his own home or of those of many of his friends, Lenaro's were all stark white marble. If not for the silver borders, the entire hall would been most blinding, especially with the sun now shining through the windows. It was a very sterile view, and yet somehow it fit its present mistress perfectly.

Nermesa fought back a frown. His attitude toward Orena was unbefitting one who was to be her husband. This was a time to begin anew, for the two of them to prepare for the future. The honor he was to receive raised Nermesa to a new level among his peers. Much more would be expected of him from here on, including in his personal life.

As they stepped out onto the terrace, Morannus announced, "My lady Orena, Master Nermesa is here."

She was draped across a small couch set near the stone rail running along the boundary of the terrace. At that moment, Nermesa truly thought that he had wronged his betrothed, for the vision she presented was so striking that he could see why other nobles envied his position. Orena's hair had been artfully sculpted around her face, then bound toward the back. A silver band decorated her like a crown.

Her half-lidded gaze somehow magnified the effect of her
eyes. She wore a slight smile and had touched up her lips—
not to mention her cheeks and eyelids—with skillful use of
colors accenting her alabaster flesh. The gown in which
Orena had clad herself was a silken wisp that managed to
balance itself perfectly between modesty and allure.

Sitting up, Orena gracefully stretched forth her hand,
and murmured, "My love, come to me."

He did without hesitation. Morannus vanished back into
the house.

As he started to sit, her eyes shifted to the sword sheathed
at his side. Even though he was home, Nermesa continued to
wear the weapon. He did not know why, for in Tarantia he
was not on duty, but the sword's presence comforted him.

"Can we not have that removed for the moment, my
love?"

Hiding his reluctance, Nermesa undid the sheath and
placed the sword behind his side of the couch. Lady Orena
nodded satisfaction, then again gave him her hand.

As he kissed it, she pulled it back, leading his face to hers.

Yet, if Nermesa expected more life from her lips than in
times past, he was sorely disappointed. Although the kiss
was long and lingering, it was as cold as ever. It felt calcu-
lated, not caring.

When they parted, though, Nermesa gave no indication.
A smile crossed Orena's perfect features, one that somehow touched him as triumphant . . . as if with the kiss she
believed she had conquered any reluctance on his part.

"I am so very proud of you, my love. I fear I might have
shown what some could mistake as anger when you so suddenly chose to leave on this adventure, but it was merely surprise and concern! I feared for you, I did, my love, and not
without good reason, it seems!" She touched his cheek, her
fingers as chill as her lips. "Those savages out there! Horrible to think about! But you!" Her eyes narrowed like those of
a cat about to devour a plump mouse. "You conquered them
all . . . and brought back the greatest bandit in chains! All of
Tarantia speaks only of that tremendous deed, my love!"

Despite her praises of him, Nermesa could only think of the many times that she had so far called him "my love." Did Orena imagine that by repetition of the term she would make him so? Nermesa did not at all imagine that the lack of love in their betrothal was his fault alone. Orena cared little for him personally. He had hoped that he was wrong, but that was not the case. All her acting was part of an effort to wind him around *her* finger and convince others that she was something she was not. When he had first come to consider that notion years ago, it had begun the widening of the gulf that now stood between them.

But a betrothal between Houses did not depend upon love or even liking. It was, if nothing else, a business transaction.

"I was . . . fortunate. Quentus was not."

"Quentus?" She paused for a moment and, to Nermesa's hidden dismay, he realized that Orena *truly* did not recall the man at first. This, despite Quentus's having accompanied them on countless outings as servant. "Ah! Yes . . . poor soul . . ." That was all. For Orena, there was only one topic at hand. "The ceremony to honor you is to take place in the coliseum, is it not? At least, that is what I heard."

"Yes. They want to show me off before the people."

"And rightly so!" Her eyes grew so wide, so vibrant, that they startled Nermesa, who had never seen them so. "Think of it, my love! The adoration of the population! The envy and admiration of the nobility! You are the favored of the throne and have the ear of men like Pallantides and others of the inner circle! The potential for elevating this into permanent reward is staggering! When we stand there, we stand facing our future—"

He was not certain that he heard right. " 'We'?"

Orena paid his interruption no mind. "A celebration must take place afterward, too, of course! We shall hold it here, in our house! It will be the perfect point at which to announce the day of our binding! Then—"

Feeling as if every brigand in the Westermarck had suddenly fallen upon him, Nermesa cut her off. "What are you talking about?"

Eyes veiled again, Lady Lenaro smiled. "Why, now that you've done with your adventure, we can continue on with what has been too long delayed . . . just as you promised. I know that your dear parents think the same. After the king honors us, it only stands to reason that we make the expected announcement of our marriage! In fact, it would not be out of the question, I think, if we even included him and the queen among our guests . . . and General Pallantides as well, of course!"

Nermesa blinked, certain that he had gone mad. How else to explain what he was hearing? Orena had turned a twist of fate—a twist filled with tragedy, yet—into a plan intended to further her desires for greater prestige among the nobility.

"There won't be any celebration after," he bluntly stated.

"Of course, there will be! I—"

"No celebration . . . I won't turn a matter filled with the deaths of so many brave men into a ball. I don't even want this ceremony, but it comes at the decree of my king and Pallantides. I will get through it . . . alone . . . and then the matter will be done. Hopefully, soon *forgotten*, too."

For just the briefest of moments, her eyes threw daggers at him. "You don't appreciate what chance has given you! This is more than many ever achieve! To waste such potential—"

"Is better than treading on the bodies of the men who died in the capture. I'm honored to serve my king, Orena, but it ends there." He stood. "If you'll forgive me . . ."

Most likely, she would not. Nevertheless, Nermesa strode into the house and through the corridor without glancing back. His betrothed, thankfully, did not summon him back. Had she done so, Nermesa could not have promised to hold his temper in check.

As he neared the door, though, he again saw Telaria. Orena's sister peered carefully after him, then, as Nermesa neared, muttered, "I'm sorry. I—I couldn't help overhearing about Quentus. He was . . . You always seemed like brothers . . ." A tear streaked the left side of her face. "He was always so good and cheerful and never wanted to hurt anyone . . ."

Nermesa's anger dissipated. He put a hand on her shoulder, causing her to gaze up into his eyes. The concern, the softness that he had not seen in Orena's, was there. It overwhelmed him that Telaria, who should have been far less interested, understood exactly how Nermesa felt.

"Thank you, Telaria," he murmured. Her hand rose to squeeze his. Nermesa fought back his own tears, which had suddenly threatened to burst free. "I'm sorry you won't be able to come to the ceremony. My parents would have liked to have seen you."

She started to reply, but then Orena's strident voice called, "Telaria! Come here! I want you! Now!"

The younger woman immediately broke free of him. Her eyes had a wide look to them that startled Nermesa. "I have to go!" Telaria blurted. "I have to go!"

She scurried down the hallway. Nermesa's brow furrowed as he watched her run almost frantically toward the terrace.

"Your horse awaits," a voice suddenly announced. Morannus stood by the doors, his abrupt appearance worthy of a ghost. The Gunderman gave him a sympathetic look.

"Thank you." Nermesa was more than happy to leave. He exited quickly, trotting down the steps outside. The servant who had earlier taken his mount stood ready with the stallion. As the noble mounted, Morannus closed the door.

Nermesa urged the animal on. However, he had only made it midway to the gate when the absence of weight at his side made him tug on the reins. To his misfortune, he saw that he had left his sword inside. It was tempting to abandon the weapon, but then Orena might use that as an excuse to come visit him at his own home, where she would no doubt make her case to his more amenable parents. The very thought of that made Nermesa quickly turn his mount around and return to the Lenaro house.

The servant had vanished, so Nermesa tied his horse to a nearby shrub. He leapt up the steps to the door. Nermesa almost knocked, then thought better of it. There was a chance he might be able to steer clear of further trouble. Slipping open the door, the knight peered inside, then walked quietly down the hall toward the terrace.

Orena's voice rose from ahead. Nermesa grimly pressed on. He fully expected to have to confront his betrothed again, but then noticed that her voice came not from the terrace, but rather from a chamber to his right. So much the better. If a continuation of their argument could be avoided, Nermesa would be grateful.

The sheath was exactly where he had left it. Nermesa did not waste time reattaching it, deciding that such a minor thing could wait until he was far away.

As he started back, Orena's voice rose higher, almost becoming shrill. However, not until he heard Telaria's tentative one responding did he grow interested.

The door to the room in which the sisters likely were was right next to him. Nermesa glanced around, but the servants were oddly absent, even Morannus.

Then, a harsh slap echoed in the corridor. Nermesa stiffened as he realized that the violent sound had come from where Orena and her sister spoke.

He heard Orena say something, then Telaria responded in what was almost a gasp. There was another slap, this one even louder and more severe than the first.

From Telaria, Nermesa heard a whimper.

Conflicting emotions raged through Nermesa. He struggled, but, in the end, he could not control himself any longer. Grabbing the handle, he flung the door open.

Telaria knelt on the floor, sobbing. The left side of her face was red, but not from the tears.

Orena stood over her, face contorted into a monstrous visage of anger, her right hand open and raised high.

The two women looked in his direction. The gazes of both widened.

"Nermesa . . ." uttered Orena. The horrific expression vanished abruptly, replaced by the cool mask with which he was far more familiar. She saw his own expression and noted his eyes shift from her to her sister and back again. Reaching down quickly, Orena said, "You should be more careful, Telaria, slipping like that! You could have broken something . . ."

The auburn-haired young woman turned her face from Nermesa. "I'm sorry, Orena," she managed. "I—I was so clumsy."

The playacting did nothing for Nermesa. Clutching the sheathed sword, he stepped up to Orena, staring down at her. For the first time, a moment of uncertainty—even anxiety—flashed in her eyes.

"Never again . . ." It was a command, not a request, and Nermesa was certain that she understood that.

Thrusting his free hand to Telaria, he helped her to her feet. Once up, though, the younger woman fled from the chamber.

"Nermesa—" Orena began.

His furious gaze cut her off. "Never again . . ."

He left her standing there. As Nermesa returned to the hall, the Gunderman reappeared. Morannus looked a bit distressed.

"Master Nermesa! Please! If I could but have a moment of your time, it—"

But the knight went past him, throwing open the main door and all but jumping down the steps. Tearing the reins free, Nermesa mounted. He urged the stallion on with all haste, shouting at the guards at the gates so that the entrance would be open for him by the time he reached it.

Not until he had left the Lenaro residence far behind did his pulse begin to calm.

HIS PARENTS DID not understand the alteration in his mood, for Nermesa told them nothing about the monstrous incident. His mind roiled as he considered what best to do, but nothing seemed right. Yet Nermesa knew that he could not leave matters as they were.

When the day of the ceremony arrived, he was no nearer

to a solution. Nermesa hoped that the event would be over quickly, for there was not a shadow of a doubt in his mind that Orena would come despite his wishes. He prayed that he would not create a spectacle because of her presence.

Nermesa wore his full armor, which had been meticulously polished. In honor of Quentus, he carried the former servant's dagger in his belt. Nermesa still felt it wrong that he was honored when others had perished. There were those like Atalan who had played their parts; they had as much right to stand before the king as he did.

But it proved impossible to bring this up with either Pallantides or the king, and so before the crowd gathered in the coliseum, he marched alone to where the king and queen awaited him. The vast, oval structure, with its columned upper level, was impressive. Fifty rows of seats encircling the sandy floor upon which Nermesa trod enabled a great portion of Tarantia's population to witness any spectacle. Bracketed banners lined the very top of the high wall surrounding the playing field, and heralds stood on platforms every few yards apart, their long, brass horns raised to their lips.

A fanfare announced his entrance through the grated wooden gates. As a further sign of the significance of his deed, Nermesa was escorted to the center by six Black Dragons, three flanking him on each side. While honored, Nermesa was aware that they were also there to protect their monarch . . . even from the heir to Klandes, if necessary.

His parents had been given the seats directly before the spot where he was to stand. Nermesa did not have the opportunity to see if Orena had joined them and could have done nothing if she had. Instead, he concerned himself only with the event, which he prayed would be one of the typically short ones King Conan preferred.

The horns lowered. Drums began to beat, their rhythm matching the march of Nermesa and his escort. He had expected the king and queen to make their entrance afterward to even greater acclaim, but the Cimmerian-born ruler had already led his bride to the center, where they now stood in their finery, watching him approach. It bothered Nermesa that they should await him, but the Black Dragons and the drummers evidently had their set notions as to what pace should be taken, and so he could not speed things along.

Queen Zenobia wore a gown of dark, emerald silk with a matching cape. A jeweled necklace hung from her neck, the five-pointed centerpiece resting on her chest. She smiled graciously as Nermesa neared. In her slim fingers she held a small, rounded box made of some stone, perhaps rare jade.

King Conan was King Conan. A score of Black Dragons surrounded him and his queen, but they hardly seemed necessary. An imposing, impressive figure, he looked very much like he could take on every man on the field at once and beat them handily. His garments were identical to the last time Nermesa had been presented to him. At his side was sheathed the very sword with which he had knighted the young noble.

There were several high-ranking officials with the royal couple, but Nermesa was familiar only with General Pallantides. The rest appeared to be military officers and public officials, the most trusted of King Conan's circle.

Nermesa's escort paused just beyond arm's reach of the king. The drums ceased. A stillness swept over the crowd.

A slim, robed figure with only a circle of gray rimming his otherwise bald head stepped forward. He unrolled a parchment. His voice, when he began, startled the young noble for its deepness. The acoustics enabled all to hear his words, which were about Nermesa's accomplishments.

"Citizens of the realm, people of fair Aquilonia! Let it be known that on this day is honored Nermesa of House Klandes, a hero of the land!"

The horns sounded. The crowd cheered Nermesa, who wanted nothing more at that moment than to sneak away. He had only done what he could and had survived by pure luck where others had not.

"Nermesa of House Klandes, son of Bolontes of House Klandes, himself hero of the battles of Shamar and Dartha . . ."

Nermesa blinked. He had never heard of those battles from his father.

"Nermesa of House Klandes, who, as a knight serving his majesty, Conan I, did join the western forces and thus become the bane of the Picts . . ."

The embellishments that followed sounded so outrageous that Nermesa more than once closed his eyes in embarrassment. Even the one that mattered—the capture of Khatak— had been turned into a battle in which hundreds seemed to have fought.

His gaze accidentally alighted on General Pallantides. The officer met his eyes with mild amusement and sympathy. Nermesa had sat in audiences when Pallantides and others had been previously honored, and he now suspected that the general had felt much the same as he during those spectacles.

Then, at last, long past when Nermesa thought he could stand it no more, the accolades ended. The robed elder rolled up the parchment and returned to his place with the other dignities. The horns sounded again, and King Conan and Queen Zenobia approached. Nermesa sensed his escort tense as the two came within reach of the noble. He did not understand their concern; not only would he have never thought of attempting to harm his lord, but his sword, sheathed at his side, was bound tight.

Conan drew his own weapon. Nermesa knelt. The king tapped both shoulders, much as he had done upon knighting Nermesa. Conan then resheathed the weapon and turned to his mate.

Zenobia opened the box lid . . . revealing a gleaming golden medallion shaped like a roaring lion's head, mane and all. Although it followed a similar theme in terms of animals, it was even more elaborate than the medal given to Nermesa by Flavian. Black gems made up both the eyes and the nose of the noble beast and small crystalline diamonds composed its teeth. The skill with which it had been crafted awed Nermesa.

Conan raised the medallion, which was connected to a

gold-link chain. He held up the award for all to see. Nermesa expected a speech, but the king simply turned to him and set the chain around the knight's neck.

"Rise, warrior," the former barbarian quietly commanded.

As Nermesa stood, King Conan slapped a powerful fist against his own chest where his heart was. He then nodded, his eyes meeting Nermesa's own. In them, Nermesa saw approval, the greatest reward he could have imagined.

Pallantides suddenly stepped forward. Gazing at the assembled throng, he called out, "All hail Nermesa of House Klandes, hero of Scanaga, captor of Khatak the Black Fox, and knight of Aquilonia!"

The crowd roared. Nermesa shook. When King Conan actually offered his hand, it was all Nermesa could do not to shiver as the two men shook with one another.

"Well fought," murmured Conan.

The words came blurting out of Nermesa. "Your—your majesty, I only reacted! I only did what I had to do!"

"Crom, man!" responded the king quietly. "What do you think I always did?"

He stepped away before Nermesa could recover, Queen Zenobia taking his place. She gave a smile that dazzled Nermesa. This near, he realized that she was not much older than he.

"Congratulations," she said. "Aquilonia owes you a debt! For what you've done, if there is a boon I can grant, you've but to ask it."

A sudden thought stirred within him. Nermesa had no idea how it could have formed so complete in such a minute time, but it seemed the right thing . . . if the queen meant what she said. "There is . . . there is one thing, your majesty."

Her eyes encouraged him.

"If you would have a place among your ladies-in-waiting, there is one Telaria of House Lenaro I would beseech you to summon to your service."

She smiled. "A beloved?"

"A . . . friend."

The smile only widened. "Certainly a tiny boon! And if she is cared for so much by you, I suspect her company will be more than welcome by me. In fact, I will see to it this very day."

With that, Zenobia joined her husband, leaving the way open for Pallantides.

"Congratulations, Nermesa. I saw your father's reaction. Tears, though I'd wager he'll deny it when you talk with him."

"This is all too much, General! I'm not deserving of it!"

The veteran commander smiled ruefully. "Savor it while you can. Whether by Mitra, *Crom*, or merely chance, the world has a habit of turning on its head. Tomorrow, you might be wishing desperately for this day." The smile vanished. "You may trust me on that. I speak from experience."

The general moved on. As his place was taken by one of the nameless dignitaries, Nermesa fingered the medallion and thought of what had happened since he had decided to fight for his beloved Aquilonia. Thought about it . . . and knew that Pallantides had spoken all too true.

11

THE WESTERMARCK CONTINUED to be quiet. General Octavio found that quiet both pleasant and disturbing. The wilderness was a beautiful place, true, with lush, green forest and a breeze that helped cool him in his stifling armor. Octavio even occasionally thought of retiring to the west as a settler . . . but first the land would have to be cleansed of the foul Picts.

And that was the disturbing part. The savages were never more worrisome to him as when they seemed up to nothing. Picts lived for mischief and bloodshed, so the general believed.

He and his troop of some two hundred men were on their way back to Scanaga to report to General Boronius. For all his time out here, Octavio had nothing to show for it save two minor bandits caught and hanged several days back. The pair had claimed to be trappers, but the evidence in their wagon revealed that they had slain the true owners and taken the skins for their own gain. Unfortunately, they had given no evidence indicating they had any link with Khatak.

Octavio had left them dangling where they would serve as a long-term reminder to both brigands and natives that the Aquilonian military meant business.

The general's trained ears heard a rustling of leaves from his right. There were few Picts in this region, and the largest tribe, the Fox people, were scarcely worth even the notice. Against a force such as his, they would have been easily butchered. Still, that did not mean that a few young warriors might not try some foolhardy stunt like picking off a man or two with their bows and melting back into the landscape.

But it was not a warrior whom Octavio caught a glimpse of slipping into the forest, but rather a young, barely clad Pict female. Octavio had a taste for them, especially after almost two weeks on the march, but pleasure was not on his mind just now. The woman could not be that far from her tribe. Whatever knowledge she had of their where-abouts and activities might be of some interest to him.

Then, perhaps he would take his pleasure . . .

"Sir Hedric! Four men! Into the forest after that Pict! I want her brought back now for questioning!"

"Aye, general!" The knight in question waved forward several mounted men-at-arms. With Hedric in the lead, they quickly rode after the female.

Barely a minute passed before he heard her protesting voice and the laughter of one of the men-at-arms. General Octavio frowned, determined to punish any soldier who let his duty slip due to lust. Duty always came first.

Then, the laughter turned to an outcry. There was a heavy, pounding sound.

The first cry was followed by shouts of dismay from the other pursuers. The clash of arms echoed throughout the area.

"All men! Ready weapons!" Octavio drew his own sword. "Into the forest! Double pace, but maintain order!"

The force rapidly advanced. The general quickly veered toward the exact point Hedric and the others had gone. Even as he did, though, the fighting died away. What sounded again like pounding briefly arose, then also ceased.

The Aquilonians slashed at the undergrowth, hacking it to pieces as they would those who had attacked their comrades. Precious moments slipped away.

It took longer for them to make their way through than Octavio had bargained for, but at last the gaunt commander spied a pair of figures standing tight against the trees ahead. The glint of light on them marked the pair as his own men. Both were peering around the trunks toward the wilderness farther on.

As he drew nearer, Octavio saw that one wore the armor of a knight. There was no sign of the men's horses or the other two soldiers and the Pict female.

"Hedric!" he shouted. "Hedric!"

But the knight did not answer. In fact, neither man moved.

Only then was the general near enough to see that something stuck out of the area of Hedric's neck where the helmet met the breastplate.

It looked the head of a large iron nail.

He glanced at the man-at-arms and saw the same there. Belatedly, General Octavio noted that the hands supposedly gripping the trunk had also been hammered into the wood.

"Mitra!" The veteran officer had witnessed many Pict atrocities over his career, but this was a new and particularly abhorrent one. That the pair likely had been crucified only after already being slain did nothing to assuage his fury.

General Octavio's rage grew. Despite their incredible swiftness, the Picts could not be far from their victims. He would teach them a lesson against which this travesty would pale.

Something red and furred caught his gaze. The tail of a small animal, with a bone pin at the end.

A fox tail . . . and one that had been worn by an attacker.

"The Fox people . . ." He knew who the culprits were. The fools! Octavio would slay ten of the savages for every man of his slaughtered. He would wipe out the entire tribe!

A figure far ahead of the lines stumbled in the underbrush. A head briefly popped into view. The young Pict female. There was a red stain on her cheek, and she moved as if one of her legs had been badly injured. There was no hesitation in her actions; she tried desperately to move as fast as she could.

"After her!" snapped the general. He did not rule out a trap, but his men were more than capable of anything a handful of Picts could devise.

A hissing sound gave the only warning before two men staggered and fell, arrows through their throats. A few more feathered bolts bounced harmlessly off armor and shields. Octavio made a quick estimate and counted no more than a dozen bows. One of his officers called out, and the company's own archers, some of them Bossonians, responded to the fire with their own bows. Cries rang out from the woods, and at least four Pict bodies slumped forward.

The forest thickened, but not enough to slow the advance. Even the horses were able to keep pace, and, from what he could see of the land ahead, matters only improved. Octavio grinned. The natives had outsmarted themselves.

With the soldiers drawing so close, a few Picts fled from their hiding places. As for the female who had lured his men to their doom, she was only seconds from being run down by his own animal. Any earlier desire he had for her had transformed into utter hatred. He would do to her as her kind had done to Hedric and the others.

"Scour this place!" Octavio roared. "I want it washed clean with the blood of these beasts!"

The female slipped, disappearing in the high undergrowth. The general eagerly rode over the spot, but his horse's hooves landed on nothing but earth. He cursed and glanced back at the area, but she was nowhere to be seen.

General Octavio decided that he could worry about her after the warriors were all slain. One maimed Pict female would not make it far.

They came out into a clearing. The panicked Picts, some twenty or so, were trying desperately to reach the far side, where the forest would give them renewed if naive hope of escape. Already, the company's archers were getting into position to unleash a volley that would likely bring down at least half of the savages. This part of the battle was already almost finished. After the last had been run to the ground, Octavio would lead his men into the village itself and raze it to the ground. It would be a good, grim reminder to other tribes of what happened to those who defied the military.

The Aquilonians spread through the clearing. The archers raised their bows high. The slaughter was imminent.

And then, from the other side, more Picts than General Octavio had ever seen in his entire career in the Westermarck poured out of the forest toward the stunned soldiers.

The commander tried to make a quick estimate and failed. He stared in disbelief that there could be so many. It was as if there was far more than one tribe—

The general looked from one Pict to the next. There were those of the Fox Tribe, as he had expected, but many warriors wore feathers of varying types or skins of animals other than the one he had expected.

It was not one tribe they faced, nor even two or three, as had sometimes happened in the past . . . but rather a banding together of at least half a *dozen*.

Octavio opened his mouth to call for an ordered retreat, but even before a single sound escaped his lips, other cries rose from not only the right and left flanks . . . but the rear as well.

There were *more* Picts.

"Form squares!" he shouted. "Form squares!"

The soldiers hurried to obey, but the Picts were too close. A flight of arrows fell among the Aquilonians, downing several. Men in the rear line turned just as the first savages collided with them.

A shouting warrior with a club swung at Octavio. The general stabbed the Pict through his tattooed chest. A man-at-arms only a few feet away cut off the hand of another warrior, then fell with an ax in his throat.

Farther ahead, two Picts dropped as a few of the archers got off shots. Two knights trampled an overzealous savage, then cut a swathe through the milling enemy.

General Octavio's hopes swelled. There was still a way to salvage most of the company—

A hideous roar briefly overwhelmed all other cries. Octavio reined his mount to a halt, searching for the source.

Something dropped on the two mounted knights, bowling them off their mounts. The Picts eagerly fell upon the two helpless fighters, pounding them to pulp inside their armor.

"What in the name of—" The knights had been taken down by a huge piece of wood that might have been the stump of a dead tree. The gaunt general eyed the forest nearest the stricken pair. It had almost seemed as if the missile had dropped from the foliage.

The Picts fought with more lust than ever, seemingly galvanized by this bizarre and frightening attack from the trees. Octavio watched his lines collapse as if made of paper. The Aquilonians were pressed on all sides. For every savage to die, one of his own perished . . . and there were far, far more Picts.

Distracted, he noticed the warrior near his left too late. The Pict tried to drive his spear through a space between the plates protecting the general's torso. The veteran soldier managed to deflect the point down, but it still sank deep into his leg at the joint.

Biting his lip so hard that he drew blood, General Octavio slew his foe, but the pain from the wound made him shake. The Pict's spear had gone most of the way through, tearing muscle and sinew.

"General!" A knight seized his reins. "We've got a square formed! There's still a chance for some of us to—"

But a Pict arrow ended the other's words. With a gasp, the dead knight fell into Octavio's arms.

At the same time, two tattooed figures leapt onto the general's mount. Octavio kicked one away, but his arms, tangled with the corpse, prevented him from doing anything about the second.

Giving the Aquilonian officer a grin filled with filed teeth, the Pict buried his spear just below Octavio's throat.

Choking, the general flung the dead knight away. The Pict's spear broke off just below the head. Octavio batted its wielder away, but the dark deed had been done.

The world spun madly. General Octavio caught glimpses of desperate soldiers pinned back-to-back, swarms of Picts spilling over them, and what he thought was the same young female who had led them into the trap. She was grinning.

And then the general saw nothing more.

DESPITE HIS WORRIES and the general's warning, the week that followed eased some of Nermesa's apprehensions. He had no confrontation with Orena, and his parents did not question him about her. However, news came to him that Telaria had received an invitation to join Queen Zenobia's ladies, an honor, he knew, that Orena dared not refuse her sister. Ironically, by gaining this for Telaria, Nermesa had also given his estranged betrothed some of what she desired, for it would grant Orena an excuse to visit the palace. It was a worthy price to pay, though, to remove the younger sibling from Orena's direct power.

Friends and associates continued to shower Nermesa with praises, and his father appeared to have forgotten any distaste he had expressed for the king in the past. Klandes had also gained several lucrative agreements over the past few days, all of them owing to the throne's favor.

Nermesa had expected to be sent back to the Westermarck immediately, but no orders had as yet come. He thus spent much of his time riding through Tarantia—even once visiting the family holdings in the countryside—and twice prayed for Quentus's soul at the temple of Mitra, all to take his mind off of his inactivity and avoid the inevitable concerning Orena.

But the latter situation at last caught up with Nermesa. As he readied himself in his quarters for another evening ride through the city, he heard a familiar voice in the hall below. Morannus's. The Gunderman was speaking with his father. The conversation lasted only a few seconds, but that was far more than enough.

Moments later, Bolontes caught him as he attempted to depart through the back of their home. "Nermesa! I wish to speak with you, son!"

"Father, I—"

The elder Klandes cut him off. In his hand, he held a letter with the Lenaro seal on it. "Nermesa, what is between you and Orena?"

"Nothing, Father. Between us, I can swear by Mitra that there is *absolutely* nothing." The vehemence in his tone surprised even him.

His father was taken aback by it. "What are you saying, son?"

Aware that he could no longer avoid saying something, Nermesa bitterly added, "I intend to break our betrothal. I will not marry Orena Lenaro."

"What?" Bolontes looked aghast. "Our two Houses planned this long ago! It's set! Lenaro will be a tremendous addition to our holdings, and Orena is certainly no hag! You could do far worse, my son."

"It would be difficult to do so!" Nermesa snapped. Taking a deep breath, he gave Bolontes an apologetic smile. "Just trust me, Father, that what I do is not just for me, though I'll be grateful for cutting the ties! I will *not* marry Orena Lenaro for any benefit to me or my House!"

"Nermesa—"

But Bolontes' son, trying to keep from further argument, strode past the patriarch. He rushed down the stairway and out of the house to his waiting mount. He grabbed the reins from the startled servant and, leaping into the saddle, rode off into Tarantia.

Nermesa rode aimlessly throughout various parts of the vast city. He paid little heed to either his surroundings or the people with whom he came into contact. His mind was a storm of conflicting emotions. He regretted speaking so with his father and knew that he should have broken the news in a more subtle manner, but Orena's letter had come at just the wrong moment. Confronted, Nermesa had been unable to stop the words from issuing forth.

He would make it up to his family somehow. There were other matches that could be made, good ones that would benefit House Klandes and be tolerable for Nermesa.

Nermesa did not realize how long he had been riding until he began to notice a lessening of the crowd. He tugged on the reins and peered around, unfamiliar with the area. Taverns that had seen better days populated the vicinity, and those exiting and entering them were clearly of a less fortunate stratum than the knight. A few unsavory faces peered suspiciously his way. Nermesa only then realized that, in his haste, he had left his sword back home.

With an air of casualness, he turned his mount and headed away. Fortunately, despite the darkness, the torches atop the palace towers were visible. Nermesa grimaced at how small they appeared, though; he knew now that he had ridden all the way to the opposite end of Tarantia.

Despite the lateness of the hour and the emptying of the streets by all but the hardiest of souls, the return was a slow one. The streets of Tarantia had been built as the capital had grown over the centuries. This meant many winding paths that suddenly ended, more than once forcing Nermesa to take an alternate route.

Eventually, though, he made it back to the proximity of the palace, a place much more well lit than many through which the noble had passed. Nermesa relaxed as he rode by the great edifice, the innate power of the king comforting him. He thought suddenly of Telaria, who would be within, and hoped that she understood that he had only tried to help her. Nermesa decided to visit her when the opportunity arose and see how she was faring.

The light of the palace began to fade behind him and suddenly Nermesa had the unsettling feeling that someone sinister watched him. He surreptitiously gazed around but saw no one. Yet, the sensation of being watched remained strong . . .

He looked over his shoulder.

The fiery twin lights of the Iron Tower gazed down imperiously at him.

Nermesa quietly swore, startled to find that his childhood fears of the place had come back to haunt him. The dark prison served a better purpose now that Conan ruled Aquilonia. Its present residents were *supposed* to be locked away, unlike in times past.

In contrast to much around it, the Iron Tower never slept. That was made more apparent by the three figures near the entrance to the ominous structure. Two were clad in the armor of the city guard and the third was a disgruntled, scarred male in grungy garments who looked like a thief of some sort.

The sight reminded him of Khatak within. Nermesa urged his mount to a more active pace, his desire to be home increasing. He wanted to forget completely the imprisoned brigand.

While he did pass some areas still frequented by various elements of the populace, Nermesa's path was, for the most part, quiet save for the occasional patrol. More than once, he rode through places where the torches had either not been lit or had gone out, but, fortunately, those places were near to home and thus familiar to him. By now, his tensions had all but slipped away, simple exhaustion taking over.

It was with weary relief that he saw at last the Klandes house ahead. The torchlit gates welcomed Nermesa. He urged his stallion on, eager to be in his bed. Tomorrow, he would somehow make things right with his father.

"My lord Nermesa?"

He started, not having noticed the cloaked figure coming out of a side street. Nermesa relaxed almost immediately, though, for the shadowed newcomer wore the armor of the Aquilonian military.

"Who are you?"

"Forgive me, my lord. I tried to see you earlier, but you were away. I've been waiting some time for you to return." The man pulled his hood back slightly, revealing in the torchlight a bearded face that struck a chord.

"I know you, don't I?" Nermesa leaned down. "You were in the column . . ."

"Aye, my lord. The column. 'Tis why I've come." He glanced around furtively, as if fearful of being discovered. "I need to speak with you on a dire matter dealing with the bastard brigand we brought back . . . and those who'd see him free . . ."

"What?" Nermesa tensed. The matter of the traitor who had sought Khatak's release during the trek had not been resolved. Nermesa had assumed that, once the bandit had been incarcerated in the Iron Tower, the treacherous soldier had simply given up. "What do you mean? What have you heard?"

Again, the man glanced about. "My lord, can we not move out of the light? This involves some of my own, and should anyone see our conversation, I fear word might get back and endanger things."

"Very well." Nermesa urged his horse to the darkened side of the street near where the soldier had materialized. He then dismounted and joined his companion in the shadows. From what he had so far gathered from the soldier's concerns, the betrayal must have gone deeper than one man, information that had to reach General Pallantides as soon as possible.

"Is this better?" he asked.

With a swift survey, the soldier—a man-at-arms, the noble finally recalled—nodded. He bent close to Nermesa. "They seek to free him this very evening."

"Who—you don't mean *Khatak*?"

"Aye . . ." The man gazed past him. "He may even be free by now . . ."

Nermesa took him by the shoulders. "And you stood here waiting for me? You should have gone to the palace with this news! Why wait here in the shadows for me?"

"Because it is what I wish," said another behind him.

Nermesa spun toward the new voice. He caught a glimpse of wild hair and eyes that seemed to glow like embers in the darkness.

And despite the shadows of night, he also saw the crooked smile.

Khatak struck him on the side of the head with the hilt of a dagger.

Nermesa tumbled into the waiting arms of the traitorous soldier . . . and knew no more.

12

CONSCIOUSNESS, WHEN IT returned, did so accompanied by pain. There was more than one type of pain, too.
There was the throbbing ache in his head, especially harsh
where he vaguely recalled the brigand chieftain striking
him. But there was also the tight constriction around his
arms, legs, and throat, the last most stifling when he moved
just the wrong way.

Worst of all was the shameful pain that Nermesa had
fallen victim to Khatak's ploy. Oddly enough, it was not for
himself that he feared, but rather those who would die because he had not slain the bandit when first they had fought.
Nermesa had no doubt that Khatak would mark his return to
the west by wreaking havoc on the territories as never before.

With effort, he forced his eyes open . . . and saw nothing
but darkness. Nermesa at first thought that he still lay in the
shadows of the street, but quickly realized that he was in
some sealed chamber. There was no floor, only soft, moist
earth. The reason for the constriction around his limbs and
throat was a simple one; someone had bound him quite

thoroughly, then looped one end of a rope around his neck, guaranteeing that he could do little to free himself without choking to death. It was a wonder that Nermesa had not done so already while unconscious.

But where was he? Still in Tarantia or somewhere much farther west? Why had Khatak even bothered to leave him alive? He already knew why the brigand had taken the chance of recapture to come after the Aquilonian. Khatak was vain, arrogant, to the point of megalomania. Nermesa had done what no one else could and, in the half-breed's twisted mind, to regain his fearsome reputation, Khatak had to prove that he was the master of the two to those following the bandit.

But it would have been simple enough just to cut off his head and drag it back to the Westermarck. That Khatak had left him breathing surely meant he had something more dreadful in mind. Nermesa's death was to be a spectacle to put awe and fear in the ruthless Picts.

They had stuffed his mouth with cloth and bound another piece around his head so as to prevent him from calling out. Again, it was a wonder that Nermesa had not suffocated because of their thoroughness.

Unable to do anything else, the captive knight pondered Khatak's escape from the seemingly impregnable Iron Tower. There had to have been other traitors besides the man-at-arms, and at least one of those others was someone of prestige. How else to gain entrance to the prison?

From that point, however, Nermesa reached a dead end. He could think of no one who would wish to aid the nefarious bandit leader. The notion that any Aquilonian of reputation would do so was beyond comprehension. What gain could there be worth such a vile act?

A sound caught his attention. A voice . . . *two* voices. They drifted nearer and nearer until at last Nermesa found himself able to understand portions of the conversation.

". . . foolish gesture . . . risks all . . ." said the first, a voice the heir to Klandes did not at all recognize.

The second voice responded and, although unintelligible, could not be mistaken for anyone other than Khatak.

The bandit's companion spoke again. ". . . of here as soon . . . dark! The wagon—"

"Enough!" snarled Khatak, suddenly much clearer. "Understand all very well!"

"Then understand . . . foolish to . . . alive! . . . Not out of here . . . cut his throat myself!"

Nermesa strained to identify the other voice, which remained more distant. That it was of Aquilonian blood was most likely, but the walls muffled it too much otherwise. Of course, even if he could have heard the traitor clearly, doing so might not have helped at all. Nermesa did not know every noble of Tarantia—assuming that the speaker even *was* one—and even of those he did, most were not familiar enough to him to recognize them under any conditions. Assuming it was not that of a stranger, the voice could have belonged to a hundred or more acquaintances.

Nermesa expected someone to enter, but both Khatak and his companion moved on. The stillness bothered Nermesa more than the voices, for it made it too easy for him to imagine various unsettling scenarios. He became determined to find some manner of escape.

With great caution so as to avoid strangling himself, the Aquilonian rolled across the chamber. His face slipped into the earth more than once, but at last he made it to the other side. The arduous trek proved a disappointment, however, for Nermesa discovered nothing but a blank wall. That it was impossible for him to stand proved frustrating, for it meant that any hooks or such even at what would have been shoulder level were far beyond his reach.

With effort, he turned himself to the side and began rolling again. Unfortunately, the results were no better. Nermesa appeared to be in a rectangular chamber likely used for grain and such—at least, that would have explained the seeds over which his face occasionally crossed. Whether it had been cleared out prior to his arrival, he could not say.

What mattered was that he had found nothing with which to unbind himself, and, failing that, he was surely doomed.

No . . . there had to be some way out of this predicament. Nermesa considered his garments. His captors had emptied his pouches, but had left him clothed. That, however, helped Nermesa very little. If he had been in armor, perhaps there might have been a jutting piece of metal he could have used to cut the ropes, but most of what he wore was cloth, entirely useless to his cause.

At a loss, Nermesa flattened himself against the nearest wall and started to inch along its width. Perhaps his rolling search had made him miss something. It was all that was left for him.

But the first wall gave him nothing, and the second proved no better. Desperation crept into his thoughts, yet Nermesa pushed on.

In order to move, Nermesa had to undulate in a manner that forced his head up and down. More than once, he caught his throat, forcing him to pause to regain his breath. The strain began to tell—

The back of his head rubbed against something sharp and metal.

Nermesa cautiously slid his head across it. A small hook or brace about two feet from the floor. It was only an inch across. What purpose it served, Nermesa did not know, but perhaps it might prove his salvation.

He shifted ahead, trying to match it with his wrists. In order to place the bonds there against it, the captive knight had to arch himself painfully. That was a small price to pay, though, for survival.

Nermesa began rubbing the rope over the sharpest edge he could find. The metal was rusted and slightly loose. He feared that it would break off, but after several minutes, it still remained in place.

While Nermesa could not entirely be certain, he thought he felt the first strands begin to give way. Pulling his wrists as far from each other as possible, he increased his pace, rubbing back and forth, back and forth . . .

His hands abruptly shifted. They were not free, but clearly part of the rope had been severed. The Aquilonian worked harder, knowing that at any moment he might be discovered.

The metal piece suddenly wobbled violently. Caught up in his efforts, Nermesa paid it little mind . . . until the brace *snapped* off.

Clattering once against the wall, the metal dropped onto the dirt floor. Nermesa wanted to cry out in anger. He tugged violently, trying to see if he could reach the piece and hold it well enough to continue on.

The last of the rope ripped apart.

Nermesa felt his left hand come free. The right one was still partially bound to the rope running from his throat to his ankles. Nermesa sought to undo the other hand, then realized that he would be better off untying his neck first.

He struggled to undo the knot. With only one hand, the effort was difficult, but in the end, it came loose. As the rope fell away, Nermesa reached for the cloth binding his mouth. More than anything else, he wanted to take one decent breath before continuing.

And at that moment, he heard a key rattling in the unseen door.

Slipping his free hand behind him, Nermesa pressed his back against the wall. A creaking sound echoed in the chamber and light filtered in.

Nermesa all but shut his eyes, leaving just the barest slits so that he could have some idea of what was happening. Pushing the door closed again, a lone figure bearing a square lantern stepped down a single stone step, then proceeded toward the prisoner. From what Nermesa could make out, it was the very same traitor who had caught his attention in the street. The man was unarmored now, but still wore his sword and dagger. His harsh breathing echoed loud in the otherwise silent chamber.

As the soldier brought the lantern close, Nermesa closed his eyes the rest of the way.

A hand shook him roughly. The captive made no sound, even when the jerking movements almost cut off his air.

"Still out, are you?" grumbled the traitorous man-at-arms, ceasing the shaking. "Well, you'll be sleepin' forever soon." There was some shifting, then the other said, "Nice boots. Look to be about right. Maybe I can slip them off, considerin' you won't need them, my lord."

He chuckled. Nermesa sensed the light shift toward his feet. He heard the man-at-arms set the lantern down. Trying not to tense, Nermesa cautiously opened his eyes. The traitor's attention was on the boots. From the present angle, the fact that the rope around them no longer extended to Nermesa's throat was not so obvious, but the captive noble could not hope that it would go unnoticed much longer. He clenched his free hand, ready to strike his foe as best as possible . . . then noticed that the man's sheathed dagger was well within reach.

It was his best—if also most desperate—hope. With the utmost caution, Nermesa slid his hand out and stretched it toward the dagger. His captor was focused on how easiest to free the boots, not realizing that all he had to do was pull hard.

Nermesa's fingers were only an inch from the dagger. He held his breath.

"What's this?" the man-at-arms suddenly growled, studying the area near Nermesa's ankles. "These shouldn't be loose—"

Thrusting himself to the side, the knight seized the dagger, pulling it free.

His captor felt the motion and started to turn.

Nermesa buried the dagger in the traitorous soldier's upper back, shoving it in all the way to the hilt.

With a gasp, the man-at-arms grabbed frantically for the blade, but it was out of his reach. After a moment, the effort proved too great. Body quivering, the villain fell forward. Perhaps he tried to call out, but the sound that emerged was but a grunt that could have meant anything.

Slithering, Nermesa rolled on top of the dying man. He covered up the soldier's face to avoid a second possible attempt at giving warning. His effort, however, proved unnecessary, for the man-at-arms shook once . . . then went limp.

Wasting no time, Nermesa crawled back and removed the dagger. Ignoring the dripping blood, he used it to completely free his other hand, then severed the rest of his bonds.

Rolling the body over, the noble undid the belt holding the dead man's sword sheath, then placed it around his own waist. He thrust the dagger in the belt, then tugged the larger blade free from the corpse's grip. The guard's sword was a capable one, if less honed than Nermesa would have preferred. He swung it twice to test its weight and balance, at the same time using the moment to stretch his cramped muscles.

Hurrying as best he could to the door, Nermesa listened for any immediate threat. Hearing nothing, he slowly opened it and peeked outside. The area beyond was a dimly lit hall that revealed no secrets concerning his whereabouts but at least also contained no menace. Nermesa paused to listen again but heard nothing from either direction.

Slipping out of his prison, the noble took a guess and turned left. As he silently made his way, he debated what to do. On the one hand, it made sense to escape and give warning to Tarantia. On the other, Khatak could easily use the time Nermesa needed to reach help to flee.

What choice he would have made was taken from him by the abrupt appearance of a breastplated figure emerging ahead of him. The mustached soldier gaped at the sight of the escaped prisoner, then, with a warning cry, drew his sword.

Cursing at his lost advantage, Nermesa lunged at the other. The man met his attack, parrying it and attempting one of his own.

"This time, you'll die!" growled the villain. "Like you should've on the supply run!"

Nermesa blinked, finally recognizing his adversary as one of the men who had betrayed the supply column the night he had captured Khatak. That meant that whoever had freed the brigand had managed to release the others as well. That bespoke someone with tremendous influence working with Khatak.

Their blades came together with a harsh ring. The other man-at-arms was capable, but Nermesa knew that, had he not been bound and gagged for so long, he could have already taken his foe.

Voices shouted from somewhere outside. Nermesa realized that the longer he did battle with this man, the worse his chances became. Despite the agony to his body, he had to end this fight immediately.

The mustached soldier swung hard for his chest. Nermesa deflected the blow downward, then ran his blade across the man's throat. He only grazed his adversary, but it was enough to put the other off-balance. Nermesa chopped at his sword hand, severing more than one finger and causing the man-at-arms to drop his weapon. The noble finished his foe with another jab to the throat.

Leaping back from the collapsing body, Nermesa turned and headed away from the shouting. He dashed through a windowed corridor, catching a glimpse of the walls of Tarantia in the distance. They had not taken him as far away as he had feared. If he could but find a horse, he could make good his escape and warn the city guard. Nermesa ran faster, eager to be rid of this place—

However, as he turned down another hall, he all but collided with a pair of brigands. Reacting faster than either, he smashed one in the jaw with the hand wielding the sword, then cut the other across the chest. As the wounded man fell forward, Nermesa hit the first bandit again, this time in the back of the head.

Although very brief, the struggle sapped him of more of his flagging strength. Worse, the shouts of others in search of the missing captive grew more ardent.

Leaving the duo behind, the Aquilonian came to an open balcony. The house clearly belonged to someone of moderate wealth but lacked any sign of habitation other than his captors' presence. Nermesa suspected that its sole purpose was for such nefarious deeds as smuggling and his kidnapping.

A clatter arose in the hallways. Nermesa glanced over the rail, judging the distance down. Hesitating only a moment, Nermesa sheathed his weapon, climbed over the rail, and jumped.

He landed in a crouching position, his bones shaking from the impact. Immediately, Nermesa sensed a figure behind him. He spun around, sword drawn as he moved.

The tip of his blade ended just before the heart of a stoutish man in the robes of an aristocrat. He quivered before Nermesa's weapon.

"Please! I am unarmed! I am Lucian, once master of this house before those fiends took over!"

Nermesa frowned, uncertain as to whether or not to believe the man. Certainly he did not seem the sort with whom Khatak would consort, but he also looked too healthy and clean to have been a prisoner.

"Where are the stables?" he finally demanded instead, deciding that he had nothing to fear from this round figure so long as Nermesa was the one with the sword.

"Th-there!" stuttered the other noble, pointing to his left.

His voice, somewhat high-pitched, did not sound like that of the one with whom Khatak had been speaking earlier, but Nermesa could not be absolutely certain. He would have to take a chance. If his companion spoke the truth about himself, the bandit and his cohorts would certainly slay him for having aided Nermesa in his escape. There was only one choice, however questionable it might be.

"Do you want to escape with me?"

There was no hesitation from Lucian. "Yes! Please! Yes!"

"Quiet! Come with me, then!"

With the heavyset aristocrat plodding beside him, Nermesa headed for the stables. Behind them, the clamor in the house continued to escalate. Nermesa prayed that they would continue to think he was still inside, at least long enough for the two of them to saddle horses and ride off.

The stables, a flat-roofed, wooden structure, beckoned ahead. The building was dark, and the only sounds were some unsettled snorts from the horses. As they arrived at the entrance, Nermesa had Lucian stand back in case someone hid within. The estate owner was only too glad to comply.

Sword ready, the knight stepped inside. A horse greeted his entry with another snort. Nermesa gazed past the animals, trying to see any sign of danger in the gloom.

Again, the one horse snorted. It tried to come in his direction, but could not. Stepping closer, Nermesa smiled. It was his own mount. The animal had recognized his scent.

Confidence rising, Nermesa glanced back to the entrance, quietly calling, "It's safe to come in—"

The pitchfork grazed him at the shoulder, only his chance turning saving Nermesa from being impaled from the back.

The round form of Lucian pulled back the tool for another strike.

"In here!" cried the treacherous noble, his expression vicious. "I've got the fool in the stables!"

He plunged the pitchfork at Nermesa.

Shoulder stinging, the knight backed up to his horse. Lucian's strike hit the beam next to him, the sharp prongs burying themselves in the wood. The portly estate owner attempted to pull the makeshift weapon free, but his earlier momentum had driven the pitchfork in too far for him to remove it.

As Nermesa straightened, his betrayer let go and tried to run. The knight flung himself at Lucian, taking down the latter. All of the fat noble's bravado vanished, replaced by the quivering fear that the knight had first witnessed.

"No! Please! I didn't mean to!" Lucian's lip quivered.

His pleas were lost on Nermesa. He dragged the heavyset man to his feet. "Enough! You're going to lead me out of here—"

Lucian shook uncontrollably. He started to speak, but instead slumped back. His eyes rolled up. Startled, Nermesa repositioned his grip.

Only then did he feel the dagger hilt sticking out of the estate owner's back.

Outside, someone cursed. And lights began congregating.

Nermesa tossed Lucian aside, then retreated back to his steed. He released the animal, but dared not take time to saddle it. Although Nermesa had ridden bareback in the past, he was not so skilled at it that he did not attempt the trick now without risk. Yet, the approaching lights and angry voices told him that he had no other choice.

Two figures—one wielding a torch—barged in just as he urged the stallion forward. The huge beast forced the startled men aside as it raced out. Nermesa took a slash at one, but his need to clutch the horse's mane prevented him from doing any damage.

"To the gates!" someone called.

Nermesa hung low, trying to make himself less of a target for anyone who might have a bow. He steered the horse past another man with a torch and searched for the gates in question.

There! They were open, too, which could only mean that none of Khatak's cohorts had yet reached them. If he could get beyond the walls, there would be no stopping his flight to Tarantia.

Shouts continued from behind him, but they were farther back now. Nermesa was but seconds from freedom. The arched entrance loomed before him.

And from it, a figure dropped down on the Aquilonian, sending both of them crashing to the ground. They rolled over and over several times, Nermesa's attacker ending on top.

"Your head I will have!" Khatak growled. "Wanted to drag you back, to be flayed alive slowly for all Picts to see that I am the most favored! That Gullah watches over me!"

Nermesa managed to get a knee up into the brigand's stomach. He pushed Khatak from him, then rolled away in search of his sword.

"Luck is not with you now!" mocked the half-breed. From

somewhere, he produced his own sword, which he instantly used to nearly behead his quarry.

Still rolling, Nermesa landed on top of what had to be his weapon. He kicked wildly at Khatak, forcing the brigand back a step.

It was all Nermesa needed. He seized his sword and brought it up just as Khatak attacked again. The clang of their swords resounded throughout the darkened estate.

Unfortunately, it could not be long before some of Khatak's comrades would join the struggle. In his present condition, Nermesa had no illusions as to his odds against two or more opponents. He had to get away.

A snort from beyond the gates made him realize that his horse had come to a halt outside. Unfortunately, Khatak stood between him and the stallion.

The brigand came at him. Khatak laughed as he slashed again and again and again. He knew that all he had to do was delay Nermesa until the others came . . . and judging by the calls, they were but seconds from arriving.

Nermesa's gaze darted left and right, finally fixing on a set of stone steps leading up to a walkway on the wall surrounding the house grounds. Perhaps, if he could beat Khatak to the top . . .

He pretended to lunge at his adversary, and when Khatak moved to deflect his strike, Nermesa surprised him by instead racing off toward the stairway. The wild-haired half-breed cursed and gave pursuit.

Racing up two steps at a time, Nermesa reached the top. He spun around and kicked out, knowing that Khatak would be right behind him.

The bandit chieftain grunted as Nermesa's boot caught him squarely in the chest. He tumbled back, barely keeping from plunging headfirst off the side.

Turning back to the wall, Nermesa bent over the edge, seeking some way down the outer side. The height was such that to jump would not kill him, but he likely risked a broken leg, maybe more.

Tromping feet warned him that his time was running out.

From his right, two armed men—the lead one also bearing a lit torch—charged him. Another villain had raced up past a stunned Khatak and was only steps from the top.

Nermesa ran to meet the one on the steps, taking advantage of his higher position to come over the other's guard. His blade sank through near the breastbone, and the brigand tumbled off the steps to the ground.

Beyond the dead man, Khatak began to rise. Nermesa had no time to worry about him, for the other pair were nearly upon the desperate noble's position. He met the sword of the first, forcing his opponent back against the second cutthroat. Their collision only gave Nermesa a momentary respite, though, for the second man then slipped by his companion, coming at the Aquilonian in earnest.

Nermesa used the man's aggressiveness against him, letting the bandit stumble forward on the narrow path. With his free hand, the knight caught part of his adversary's garment and pulled as hard as he could, flinging him off the walkway.

Flames filled Nermesa's view, the heat alone almost scorching him. He backed away as his remaining foe swung wildly at him with the torch. Nermesa deflected the fiery staff, then barely dodged a thrust by the other's sword. As he struggled against his foe, he heard more footsteps coming up behind him.

Dropping down, the Aquilonian kicked out, tangling the torch wielder's feet. As the man fell toward him, Nermesa twisted, throwing him to the side. Dropping both his weapons, the brigand frantically sought to grab hold, but his fingers only grazed Nermesa.

The torch dropped on Nermesa. He quickly batted it away, then smothered a small fire starting on his sleeve.

A sharp pain in his arm made him cry out. He threw himself away from the direction of the pain. A moistness spread down his arm.

Glancing over his shoulder, Nermesa saw Khatak bearing down on him.

"The lion is strong in you," complimented the half-breed.

He beat his chest. "But He Who Lives in the Moon is within me!"

He slashed twice more at the wounded Aquilonian. Nermesa slid backward, seeking his sword. Khatak laughed, and in the gloom of night he looked more like a fearsome demon than a man.

Nermesa continued to search blindly as he sought to avoid Khatak's relentless assault. He suddenly pulled back his fingers, their tips nearly burned by an unexpected encounter with the torch he had flung from him moments before.

Khatak used the distraction to try to cut a ravine in Nermesa's chest. The edge of the blade ripped through the Aquilonian's clothes and lined his torso with a stream of crimson, but the wound, however stinging, was very shallow.

Nermesa seized the hot torch and threw it at his opponent.

Although his aim was good, Khatak saw the fiery missile coming. He backed up and swung at the torch, batting it far over the estate grounds.

Nermesa leapt at him.

He collided hard with the brigand chieftain, almost sending both of them off the walkway. Khatak snarled. The half-breed thrust his head forward, trying to bite off Nermesa's nose. Despite a slight height advantage on the Aquilonian's part, Khatak's animalistic nature made it difficult for Nermesa to match the bandit. The black-maned fighter began pushing him back.

"Your blood I will drink, its strength to add to my own . . ." Khatak uttered in all earnestness. "Your dried head will I carry wherever I go!"

He flung Nermesa hard against the wall, jarring the noble's already-battered body. Nermesa fought to maintain his grip and avoid Khatak's sword at the same time. Trapped between them, the edge was mere inches from the knight's face.

Khatak again swung him against the wall. Nermesa momentarily bent over the edge.

Chuckling, the brigand pulled him back for a third toss. Nermesa tensed.

Khatak flung him at the wall . . . and the Aquilonian threw his own momentum into the swing. Now, it was not only Nermesa who flew against the wall, but his adversary as well.

Caught off guard, Khatak not only collided with the wall, he toppled over it.

Nermesa released his grip . . . but Khatak did not. To his horror, Nermesa followed the villain over. The black ground outside the estate raced up to meet him . . .

The landing was jarring, nearly bone-breaking, but it did not kill the Aquilonian or even knock him unconscious. Stunned from the landing, Nermesa at first did not know why he had survived . . . until he looked down to discover the angry eyes of Khatak staring up at him.

Or rather . . . staring up at *nothing*.

Khatak's head was bent at an impossible angle, and his arms were splayed to the sides. The crooked smile was forever branded on his face. He was the miracle that had preserved Nermesa, for the half-breed had cushioned his foe's fall.

Unfortunately for Khatak, doing so had cost him his own life.

Gaping at the corpse, Nermesa almost expected Khatak suddenly to rise and take him with him into death. When that did not happen, Nermesa struggled to his feet, aware that there were others inside who would eagerly fulfill the dead brigand's desires.

Through tearing eyes, he finally located his mount, which was chewing on some grass. Nermesa stumbled toward it even as voices rose near the gates.

Reaching the stallion, he climbed atop and, clutching its mane, urged it on. The horse instinctively headed toward home. Nermesa planted his head against its neck. His wounds and injuries began to tell, and he feared that he might lose his grip and slip off. The voices behind him grew faint, but Nermesa did not know whether that meant that he was farther from them or that the pounding in his head had just drowned out the sounds.

"Keep going . . ." he gasped to the steed. "Keep going. Home. Home . . ."

The horse snorted. Nermesa buried his face in the mane. He passed out.

13

VIOLENT IMAGES ASSAILED Nermesa. He was hunted by silhouettes of men on horseback as he desperately tried to crawl toward his house. Thunder roared overhead, ever ending in a malevolent chuckle.

Despite every inch he managed, Nermesa never got closer to home. He peered frantically over his shoulder, to see that the sinister silhouettes had grown to monstrous proportion. A fat, full moon shone down on them, yet still Nermesa could make out no detail save huge yellow fangs.

Tearing his eyes from his horrific pursuers, he stared directly at the moon.

Khatak's distorted visage stared back. Like the black creatures hunting the Aquilonian, the brigand chieftain had sharp fangs, which he gnashed at Nermesa.

Both the fangs and the monstrous hunters drew closer and closer. Nermesa tried to push himself to his feet, but his legs would not work.

His parents suddenly appeared on a balcony thrusting out of the front of the house. Nermesa tried to call to them, but he had no voice. He waved wildly, but although his father and mother seemed to be looking in his direction, they did not react.

Someone joined them on the balcony. Orena Lenaro put a comforting arm around each of Nermesa's parents, then smiled at him. The house suddenly receded from the struggling knight, falling farther and farther out of reach.

Khatak's thundering chuckle again assailed his ears. Shadows overlapped him, and when Nermesa looked up, it was to discover himself surrounded by his nightmarish pursuers.

The moon descended toward him, Khatak's gigantic maw opening. The brigand chieftain roared, "I will drink your blood! I will drink your blood!"

The shadow men seized the Aquilonian by the limbs. They raised him high and threw him up to the moon.

Khatak's mouth stretched wide.

Nermesa cried out—

And woke shaking in his own bed.

A startled house servant stood by the entrance, a small, silver tray with a goblet of water held precariously by her shaking hand.

"Stand aside!" called his mother's voice. Callista all but bodily lifted the young woman out of the way as she rushed in to see what was happening to her son. Her eyes lit up, and relief spread quickly across her expression as she gazed down at him. "Praise Mitra! You're awake!"

Nermesa started to move, but every nerve in his body chose that moment to scream. He fell back, gasping for air.

"Lie easy, my son," his mother urged, coming to his side. Glancing back at the servant, she snapped, "Go summon your master! Now!"

As the other woman ran off to obey, Callista stroked Nermesa's forehead. She murmured soothing sounds.

"How—" he at last managed.

"A guard from the watch had you brought here! He said that your horse rode up to the city gates with you clinging to its back. You kept mumbling, but they couldn't understand you. Someone recognized your face, though."

"A damned good thing that they did," added Bolontes, entering the chamber. The severe look in his face shifted to one matching his wife's when he saw Nermesa. "Thank the heavens that you've finally woken. How do you feel, son?"

"The fire's receding." Nermesa dared to try to sit up again. There was pain, but not so much as during the first moments. However, with the return of lucidity came memories of what had taken place. "Father! Khatak's—"

"Dead, son. When news of you at the gates reached General Pallantides, he added it to the bandit's escape and concluded that the pair of you had run into each other. With the king's permission, Pallantides sent out a band of Black Dragons, who retraced your path."

"Black Dragons . . . for me?" The elite unit was rarely used for any incident that did not directly involve King Conan's safety.

"You and Khatak, of course." Bolontes went on to tell Nermesa how the soldiers had ridden all the way back to the estate of one Lucian of Karaban, a disreputable figure of a noble whose House had fallen years before because of its support of Karaban's treacherous count, Volmana. After Volmana's death at the hands of the king, most of Lucian's holdings had been taken save for a lowly estate near Tarantia that he had inherited afterward from a relative. Lucian was not the most competent of owners, but with the estate so secluded, no one had much bothered checking up on it.

"A mistake, clearly. The place was a smuggling front," Nermesa's father went on. "According to Pallantides, it was a shell of a building, nothing more." The elder Klandes frowned. "When the Black Dragons got there, they found six bodies, but nothing else. One was Lucian's, dead in the stables with a dagger in his back. Another was Khatak's, his body broken in a fall." He eyed his son. "Was that you? Was all that you?"

Nermesa nodded, his mind awhirl. The events had happened so fast that they were still a jumble to him, but to hear from his father that he had slain *six* men—no, Lucian had been killed by another, perhaps even Khatak—startled him. "All but the Karabanian. His friends slew him . . . by accident, I think."

"And Khatak? What caused your paths to cross again?"

The young noble described the trap laid by the brigand and the treacherous soldiers. Bolontes shook his head at hearing of so much betrayal from Aquilonians for the cause of one bandit.

"Gold has replaced the soul of many a man," he muttered, when Nermesa had finished.

"Mitra be praised for miracles," Callista added, refusing to let such talk bring everyone down. "You are alive and safe, Nermesa! I won't let you leave us again, do you hear?"

Bolontes stepped up beside her. "That's not up to us. I would like to speak with him alone for a moment, my dear. Then, we'd best let him rest again for a while. Three days is hardly enough."

"Three days?" blurted Nermesa.

"Fever from the wounds had you until this morning. When the healer announced that it had broken, we were all very relieved." To his wife, Bolontes said, "Callista? If you please?"

Nermesa's mother was reluctant to leave. She finally would do so only when Nermesa promised that he would try to eat the broth that she would have sent up to his room.

Alone with his son, Bolontes suddenly looked more stricken. He dropped down on one knee by the bedside and gripped Nermesa's hand. "By god, I thought you were dead, my son! When you did not return after your ride, I feared the worst, and when I heard that Khatak had escaped, I could not but help wonder if there was a connection."

"He wouldn't leave without me, Father. He wanted to show his followers and the Picts that his totem had power over mine. He intended to have me flayed alive before the headmen of the tribes."

The elder Klandes grimaced. "Never tell your mother that part, please."

"I won't. I'm sorry to have frightened all of you."

"This was not your doing . . . but I cannot help but feel some guilt of my own. If not for our argument, you might have escaped the trap."

Nermesa shook his head. "He wouldn't leave Tarantia without me. His pride wouldn't let him. Somehow, he and his cohorts would have found some method by which to catch me alone."

"Well, the beast is dead, and good riddance! They should have strung him up the first day he was turned over to the Iron Tower." Bolontes grunted. "A great mess that! They've arrested two others there on suspicion of aiding the brigand."

"Did Lucian really have the influence to get him out of the Tower?" Nermesa suddenly asked.

"You'd think not, but there's no trail leading elsewhere, and Lucian of Karaban will be telling us nothing more."

Which perhaps is why they made certain to kill him, Nermesa could not help thinking. The men with whom the aristocrat had dealt had been far more desperate than he. Greed had caused Lucian to make a terrible error in judgment.

Nermesa suddenly felt very tired and hungry. He must have shown some of this change, for Bolontes looked more concerned. "I should let you rest. I daresay the food will be up here at any moment, and your mother will want you to have the strength to eat it." He hesitated. "But, if you can, there is just one more matter I would quickly discuss with you."

"What?"

"Orena."

Nermesa desired nothing more than to ignore that particular subject, but allowed his father to go on.

"What you said," Bolontes began cautiously. "You mean it still? You would end the betrothal?"

"I would," Nermesa replied, trying to sound as strong as possible. "Don't ask me why, just understand that I have good reason."

"It would have to be, for you to do this. She has asked about you, Nermesa. More than once."

"If she truly wishes to know I'm well, tell her, but that doesn't change the situation."

"You are as a great boulder in this. Unmovable."

Nermesa nodded again. Thought of Orena, however, made him wonder about another. "How is Telaria? Do you know if the palace treats her well?"

His father's expression became unreadable. "As a matter of fact, she also asked about your health. I understand that the queen is quite pleased with her." Bolontes cocked his head. "And you had something to do with the invitation from the palace in the first place, as I recall. Interesting . . ."

If he hoped for an explanation from Nermesa, it was not forthcoming. Nermesa would respect Orena's position that far. He also desired no embarrassment to fall upon Telaria, an innocent in all this.

He was saved from further discussion by the appearance of the young servant, this time with a bowl of steaming broth on the tray. Smelling beef, Nermesa suddenly felt an immense chasm in his stomach open up.

His father stepped away. "Enjoy the food, if you can. Rest afterward. I understand Pallantides may be visiting before long."

Hunger and pain were momentarily forgotten. "The general? Here?"

This drew a brief smile from Bolontes. "Of course. You're the conqueror of Khatak the Terrible . . . twice."

With that said, he left Nermesa to his food. The knight toyed with the broth as he tried to digest what had happened to him. It was truly a miracle that he had survived. Only Khatak's desire to bring him back alive to torture before the Picts had enabled Nermesa to lie in his bed now.

He had not intended any of this when he had joined. Nermesa had assumed that he would see battle, naturally, but never had he dreamed that he would personally be thrust into such dire situations.

But this is the end of it. Things will calm after this, the heir to Klandes thought as he took his first sip of broth. *They have to.*

Surely, they had to.

GENERAL PALLANTIDES DID not come for three more days, perhaps having kept track of Nermesa's condition without the noble knowing. When he did arrive, it was without fanfare. He wore a simple but elegant tunic and pants, with high leather boots, all draped by a travel cloak.

"I see you are faring well, young Klandes."

His wounds still stung, but otherwise Nermesa felt much better. He said so to the commander, adding, "I'm honored by your visit."

"You honor me with your presence," Pallantides returned. "I bring the congratulations of King Conan to you." The leader of the Black Dragons drew from under his cloak an elegant blade, its sheen evidence of its recent forging. The silver handle had a rearing lion etched into it. "He thinks you've had enough of medals and would prefer a worthy weapon instead."

Nermesa straightened, unable at first to express his gratitude. The sword had clearly been crafted from the finest steel. In the hilt were three exceptional emeralds. When Pallantides handed it over to him, Nermesa could immediately sense that the balance and weight were perfect.

It was a fabulous weapon, a gift of great significance. "I don't deserve this . . ."

"You are possibly the only one in Tarantia who believes that. You are an exceptional fighter, Klandes. When the king gives out such a gift as opposed to the medals so many sycophants prefer, it's because he admires your abilities . . . and thus, you." The general grinned. "I've been honored so myself, so you can take my word for it."

"Please . . . thank him for me."

"Of course." Pallantides undid the belt and sheath. "This

goes with it, of course. I brought it in like this because your father thought your mother might be a little upset with such an offering just now. Reveal it to her in a couple of days." He cocked an eyebrow. "She believes that you'll be calling an end to your military career now. That isn't so, is it?"

"No! Of course not!" Nermesa almost blurted out, *I still hope to become one of the Black Dragons* . . .

"Glad I am to hear that. Good swords and level heads are needed now."

Nermesa did not miss his change in tone. The young knight's grip on the sword tightened, as if something might very well happen in his room at this very moment. "What do you mean?"

"News came to us just yesterday. The Picts are massing in numbers unbelievable. They've attacked three different areas, in two cases massacring large contingents of soldiers." Pallantides scowled. "I believe you rode briefly with General Octavio."

At first, Nermesa could say nothing. He recalled Octavio and even the faces of some of the men he knew would have been riding with the veteran commander.

"General Boronius is organizing a sweep that will hopefully push them back into the wilderness, but he is short on dependable subordinates and has requested you in particular to return . . . if you should choose to."

"Me? But why me in particular?"

"The Picts are a superstitious lot. Khatak was a man of power to them, one with the favor of their chief god . . ."

"Gullah . . ." Nermesa muttered, recalling the brigand's mention of the creature more than once.

"Gullah," the commander agreed. "There is no greater and more feared deity among the Picts . . . and you overcame his chosen warrior. More important, word should soon be reaching the frontier concerning your having slain Khatak in combat."

"What? But how—"

General Pallantides did not look apologetic. "Winning a war is as much about the mind as it is the sword, Klandes.

So the king would tell you, too. Whether or not you were able to return west, we thought it best to spread the tale of Khatak's demise so that it reaches the tribes and perhaps demoralizes them. It might save many Aquilonian lives . . . and your actual presence there might save even more."

That it might cost Nermesa his own in the process, the recovering fighter also understood very well. Yet, despite that, he felt no inclination to refuse. His parents, especially his mother, might wish otherwise, but to turn his back on those in the west would have seemed to Nermesa a betrayal worse than that perpetrated by Lucian and the men-at-arms working with Khatak.

"I'll go."

The commander of the Black Dragons raised a hand in warning. "I'm grateful for the enthusiasm, but think it over while you recover. I want to send no man there whose head was not clear when he made his decision. There are deaths enough on my conscience, though I could have done nothing to prevent most of them."

Shaking Nermesa's hand, Pallantides bid him farewell. Long after the general had departed, the recovering noble continued to stare off into the air. His hand stroked the hilt of the new sword as he considered all that the man had told him. It was not a simple thing that Pallantides requested; Nermesa understood that, for all their possible respect for the slayer of Khatak, the Picts would seek his death. Yet, if he could turn the tide of battle . . .

He raised the sword, twice swinging it as best as he could while sitting in bed. Its pristine blade gleamed.

But not for long. I go to the west, and it'll soon be stained red.

General Pallantides had insisted that he think it over while he continued to recuperate, but Nermesa knew his decision would not change. He would return to the Westermarck and do what he could to stave off the Pict assault.

And if Mitra chose that he would perish there, he hoped that it would be fulfilling his duty.

• • •

A WEEK PASSED before Nermesa was well enough to prepare for the journey. His mother insisted that he rest longer,
but news continued to filter out of the Westermarck. Settlements were being burned, patrols attacked. Khatak's band
of brigands seemed at the heart of the matter; but whenever General Boronius sent out soldiers to run them down,
either the bandits were nowhere to be found or the hunters
discovered themselves in a trap.

"I *must* go," he told his mother and father. "I might be
able to help in some way." Nermesa had attempted to explain Pallantides' reasoning as to why the Picts might hesitate with him in the Westermarck, but Callista was having
none of it. "I might save some lives."

"And what of your own life?"

"Mitra will watch over me," was the only reply he had,
one that did not at all satisfy her. Still, in the end, she had no
choice but to acquiesce. Nermesa intended to go whether
his parents approved or not.

To his surprise, this time his father was more supportive.
Clearly, Bolontes did not wish him to leave, but he seemed
to understand. "If Pallantides and you believe this necessary, I can only wish you a safe journey . . . and ask you to
come back to us again."

Nermesa hooked on his belt. The grand gift from his king
hung at his side. Callista eyed it with venom, even though it
would be her son's first and last line of defense.

Bidding his parents farewell, he rode to the palace,
where General Pallantides surprised him with a column of
soldiers some two hundred strong . . . all under Nermesa's
command.

"Boronius recommended it, and I agree," stated the commander. The king led his first such fighting force when he
was still several summers younger than you. I led mine when
I was perhaps a year less your age."

He handed Nermesa his orders, which essentially read
that the column was to head to Scanaga. There, he would

report to Boronius for further instructions. Riders had already gone on ahead to spread word that the warrior who had taken down the favored of Gullah was returning.

"Ride wary, Klandes, and forgive me for putting the bull's-eye center on you."

"I understand."

"The Poitainian knights under Sir Prospero are massing in the southwest. Should matters grow dire, they'll be riding up from there to aid."

Nermesa remounted his stallion and prepared to order the column out. Pallantides caught his attention first, though, and pointed up toward the palace. "I believe someone else wishes your attention."

Glancing back, Nermesa noted a feminine figure standing on one of the balconies. Elegantly clad in a flowing gown, she was at first a stranger to him. Only when he saw that the cascading hair was auburn did he realize that it was Telaria. Her expression taut, she waved farewell to him.

Grateful, he nodded back to her, then took charge of his troops. Drawing his sword, Nermesa pointed toward the gates. A mounted man-at-arms sounded the horn, and the column began marching. The gold-and-black lion banner of King Conan was raised high.

The journey back to the Westermarck began.

14

THE COLUMN LEFT Tarantia in sunlight, but as the days brought them nearer to Scanaga, the sky grew overcast. Thick, black clouds threatened, and the winds turned violent. Their progress quickly slowed.

If there was one bit of fortune, it was that they encountered no other obstacles along their way. With a force of two hundred men, Nermesa might have been expected not to worry about surprise attacks, but, though still distant from the wilderness, the lessons of General Octavio—and, more importantly, *Quentus*—bitterly remained with him. It did not pay to be overconfident even in "safe" regions.

At last, the Bossonian Marches, which to Nermesa signaled the true beginning of the west, rose ahead. Nermesa ordered the column to be extra vigilant despite the security Ranaric's people themselves provided. In this area, it was still possible for Picts to sneak through, although they did so at tremendous risk.

The forests began to thicken. Nermesa eyed each tree

warily, still recalling the horror of the night when his friend had perished.

And it seemed his concern had merit, for, midway through the Marches, the new commander suddenly noticed the foliage in one tree shake as if something large perched among the branches.

Drawing his weapon, Nermesa called up the archers.

"Hold your fire!" a voice from the tree called. A second later, a green-and-brown clad figure with a bow slung over his shoulder alighted easily on the path.

The Bossonian waited until Nermesa gave him permission to approach. "I seek the knight, Nermesa. Would that be you?"

"It is."

The local bowed. "Commander Nermesa, I bring the greetings of Ranaric. He was told that you'd be passing this way. There's a line of foul weather coming this way. He advises a route taking you just north of your usual one until you're a day or two from Scanaga to avoid the worst storms."

Even as the man explained, Nermesa felt a drop of moisture strike his cheek. The path directly ahead did look the darkest. "Thank him and say that I hope his arrows ever fly true."

The Bossonian looked pleased that Nermesa would know one of his people's most favored oaths of luck. He bowed again to the Aquilonian, then silently slipped back into the forest.

The rain started in earnest only minutes later. The moment that it was possible, Nermesa began guiding his men northward. Ranaric's suggestion proved an excellent one, enabling the column to avoid some areas that their commander recalled would have been reduced to mud by now. So near the Pict regions, being bogged down in such a manner could have resulted in catastrophe.

The rains continued through much of the rest of the journey, growing more intense as the Aquilonians passed into the Westermarck. Nermesa doubled the guards and kept the camps well lit, but no trouble occurred. In that sense, he thought, the terrible weather had actually aided his cause.

It was with tremendous relief that he sighted the settlements just east of Scanaga some days later. Even more of a relief was the fact that they appeared untouched. Nermesa had secretly feared that he would arrive to find the territorial capital in ruins, its inhabitants slaughtered.

The torrential rain kept most of the settlers in their simple homes, but a few braved the weather to view the newcomers. Nermesa could read nothing from their expressions; they showed neither relief at his coming nor disappointment that he did not bring more men than he had.

The wooden walls of Scanaga finally loomed. A horn blared, and the gates opened to receive them . . .

And, at that moment, a sense of foreboding coursed through Nermesa.

There was no reason for such a dire feeling, yet the knight could not shake it. His uneasiness grew as he rode through the town. Everything appeared normal enough, but there seemed a tension pervading the area. It was not featured in the faces of the locals, but Nermesa was certain of it nevertheless.

Only when he reached the inner fort did some physical hint of his concerns reveal itself. The sentries on the wall eyed his column's arrival with mixed expressions. They looked as if they wanted to cheer the reinforcements' arrival, yet were not certain if doing so was somehow premature.

As Nermesa called a halt, he was surprised to see that it was Caltero, not Boronius, who came to greet him officially.

"Welcome back, cousin!" The elder Klandes' grin was not as it had once been, even Caltero's mood dampened by events of late. "You *are* a sight for sore eyes!"

"It's good to see you again," returned Nermesa, dismounting. "I'd expected the general to—"

"The Boar's busy planning," Caltero interjected just a bit louder than his cousin appreciated. "Now that you're here, the grand assault can get under way!" He indicated

Nermesa's men. "If you'll put one of your officers in charge, the general wants you to come right in!"

Following Caltero's suggestion, Nermesa turned over the column to a knight far more experienced than he and followed his cousin to Boronius's headquarters. The sense of unease swelled even though all looked as it should.

The sentries saluted Nermesa sharply. He noted that they seemed more interested in their duties than he had ever noticed during his previous tour. It was almost as if they guarded something very precious within.

Only when the door was shut behind and Caltero had led him into the back room did Nermesa see that what they protected was the truth concerning General Boronius.

The Boar lay in his bed, looking as if he had been unfortunate enough to have crossed paths with a pack of his namesakes. His body was bruised and broken. One eye was puffed up so much that the general could not possibly have seen with it—had he been at all conscious, that is. From his rasping breath and his stillness, Nermesa doubted that Boronius had been awake for some time. More important, he wondered if the frontier commander would *ever* wake again.

"What—what—"

"Keep your voice down," Caltero urged. "There are few who know . . . at least, so we hope."

In a whisper, Nermesa blurted, "No word of this has reached the palace! I'm sure of it!"

"There wouldn't have been time . . . even if someone had sent word yet. This happened but two days ago. The Boar wasn't even out in the forest! He was riding—with guards accompanying him yet—through one of the settlements just beyond the east of Scanaga. You rode through it yourself on the way here."

Nermesa recalled the villages again. They had seemed safe enough.

"The Boar always likes to ride out among the locals, show them that he's confident and in command. He even likes to share an ale or some local wine with them, sometimes."

"Then . . . what happened?"

The last of Caltero's once-carefree attitude faded into a deep frown. "Night fell, and there was no sign of his party. Seven men not far from Scanaga. I sent out a search party. They found what was left."

Nermesa steeled himself. "Tell me."

"It wasn't pretty. The search party discovered them in the small stretch of forest between Scanaga's gates and the nearest of the lesser settlements. The Boar and his guards were scattered over the area as if a great gust of wind had picked them up bodily, then tossed them about like so many leaves! Their horses were gone, too. Three of the bodies had Pict arrows in them, but the others, including the old man himself, looked as if some monstrous *beast* had torn them apart! Only Boronius and one other man still lived— if you can call this living. The other poor soul perished from his wounds before the rescuers could bring the pair back, though."

"Horrible . . ." gasped the younger cousin.

"The search party was wise enough to keep the entire situation quiet, even bringing back the bodies in secrecy," concluded the other knight. "If news got out about the Boar's condition, the locals would panic, and the damned savages would only increase their attacks."

"Who's in command?"

Caltero sighed. "That would be me. Not my first choice." He prodded Nermesa in the breastplate. "And you, dear cousin, would be second now."

"Me?" Nermesa blinked. "But there are others—"

"The territorial judge has decided otherwise and, yes, Flavian has that authority thanks to provisions by the throne."

"What do we do, then?"

The senior knight shrugged. "I was rather hoping that you'd tell me."

Nermesa had been all too willing to return as General Pallantides had requested and had even been honored by the command he had been given, but this was far more authority than someone of his experience should be wielding.

Worse, he was beginning to see that Caltero, someone he had counted on for guidance, truly was not cut out for his own role.

And if the Picts discovered the truth concerning the Aquilonian military's current leadership, they would indeed likely soon assault Scanaga itself. Small wonder that Caltero had tried to keep Boronius's condition a secret from the settlements. That would have only further incited the natives to attack.

Nermesa tried to think. "I was told Khatak's band is part of this uprising."

"Part of it? They're leading it. Someone's taken over for him, but the friendlies haven't been able to tell us just who. When I tried to ask, they just mutter that Gullah may be watching them and scamper away."

"But Khatak's brigands and their new leader are the key to this. We need to track them down. Where were they last seen?"

Caltero seemed to regain some of his focus. He took Nermesa by the arm. "The Boar's got some good maps still on his table. Let's leave him be, and I'll show you."

Shutting the door to Boronius's personal quarters, they went to study the maps. Fortunately, the general was the sort of man who insisted on constantly updated charts. There were notations everywhere, including all previous reports of appearances by the brigands. Caltero pointed at one two days northwest, near a settlement whose name was marked out.

"Don't bother," his cousin murmured. "They left nothing of the place . . . not even the settlers."

Nermesa grimaced. So many lives lost for no good reason. Slowly, his anxiety gave way to anger.

"What about—"

They were interrupted by banging on the door. The cousins glanced at one another. Caltero finally called out, "Who is it?"

"It's Konstantin, sir! With an urgent scouting report for the general!"

Nermesa's cousin exhaled in relief. "Konstantin knows," he whispered. "We can let him come inside." To the man beyond the door, Caltero called out, "Enter!"

A knight with red hair and beard slipped past the door, shutting it quickly behind him. He eyed Nermesa with some concern.

"My cousin," Caltero pointedly said. "Nermesa."

Konstantin's gaze widened noticeably. "Ah! Mitra be praised! I was gone when you were here last. It's good to have you back, Nermesa. A capable head and arm are sorely needed now!"

"You've news?" Caltero pressed.

"Aye! The Picts are on the move! They're heading in the direction of Anascaw!"

Nermesa stared at Caltero. "Anascaw's not that far from us! We must move to meet the Picts there!"

"Impossible," returned the elder Klandes. "It's too late! By the time enough men are ready and armed, the settlement will be burned to the ground, and the Picts will be gone again. All we'll do is run around through the woods chasing ghosts and maybe getting trapped like dear departed General Octavio." He shook his head. "Would that we could help Anascaw, but we can't . . ."

Unwilling simply to accept that, Nermesa looked to Konstantin. "If a force could leave now, would it make it in time?"

"Aye . . . I think it could."

"It can't be done," Caltero insisted. "We're better off waiting for another chance—"

Despite his cousin's reluctance, Nermesa pressed. "My column just arrived! They'll still be all but packed! It's the only chance!"

Konstantin eagerly nodded. Caltero glanced from one to the other, unable, it seemed, to make a command decision.

Nermesa grew frustrated with his cousin. To Konstantin, he ordered, "Gather up whatever other men can be available in five minutes! I'll reorganize the column! Hurry!"

The third knight ran out to obey. Nermesa seized a chart

of the area in question and ran out without regard to Caltero. They could argue about this later. There were lives in danger.

He only prayed that his column would indeed arrive in time . . .

KONSTANTIN GUIDED THE way. In addition to Nermesa's men, the other knight had managed to gather another fifty. The column presented an imposing sight, but Nermesa rode well aware that the Picts had a good number of warriors of their own and had likely not marched a long way prior, as those who had followed him to Scanaga had. Fortunately, word of the attack seemed to have spurred Nermesa's original complement on. They seemed as eager as he to push back the savages.

If that could be done.

Caltero remained in Scanaga. Nermesa had come to the unhappy conclusion that his cousin, however capable as a subordinate officer, was not yet prepared for the role of commander of the west. Nermesa prayed that General Boronius would somehow recover and recover soon.

A pair of scouts rode up to meet him. "Swarm o' Picts ahead, my lord!" spouted the seniormost. "Back beyond that wooded ridge, about a mile!"

"We did it! We caught up! We're almost between them and Anascaw!" Konstantin declared.

Nermesa glanced at the chart. "If we follow this course here, will it get us to the top of this ridge before they do?"

"Aye, and grant us the advantage . . . but we'll have to move fast to do that."

"Then, we'll move fast." Nermesa would have been more than willing to let Konstantin, more familiar with the territory, take command, but the redheaded knight, a strict follower of rules, was also aware of Flavian's edict granting Nermesa seniority despite his lack of years. Concerned with saving the settlers, Nermesa did not push on the subject, only silently praying to Mitra to guide his decisions.

Each passing moment, Bolontes' son expected to see a wave of Picts rushing down upon them, but the column continued to climb upward without incident. The scouts came back twice to report on the enemy's position and with the good news also came the bad.

"The ridge and its advantage'll be ours," the chief scout reported. Rubbing his chin, he reluctantly added, "You wanted a number on the savages . . ."

"And?"

"We've pretty much agreed they have twice as many as us, maybe a bit more even . . ."

"So many?" growled Konstantin. "That's not possible, save for some of the biggest tribes! Are you certain?"

"Aye! Lots o' different feathers and furs and such! Small tribes like Fox, but all addin' up to a mean horde."

The other knight eyed Nermesa. "What should we do?"

"What we intended to do."

The Aquilonians moved up into position and, as they did, Nermesa got his first good look at the Picts. They flowed through the forest like a dark, sinister flood, heading relentlessly in the direction of Anascaw and other nearby settlements. Nermesa had no doubt that they knew of the soldiers' presence and eagerly anticipated the bloodshed.

Konstantin peered at the oncoming force. "At this rate, they'll be upon us in minutes."

"We must be ready for them."

Archers hurried into position. Men-at-arms readied swords. The banner of King Conan flew proudly before the assembled soldiers.

As they neared, the Picts coalesced into individual warriors with tattooed bodies and wide, screaming mouths filled with sharp, filed teeth. They brandished axes, spears, and swords, and many wore dented and stained breastplates, helmets . . . and necklaces made of human ears of a much lighter hue than those of any of the warriors.

Nermesa raised his sword. He would not allow them to add more such grisly souvenirs to their collection.

"Sound the horns!" General Boronius should have been

leading this attack. Caltero should have been leading this attack. Even Konstantin. Almost anyone other than Nermesa . . . and yet, circumstance demanded it of him now.

Father, Mother . . . Mitra . . . pray that I have not just foolishly led us all to our deaths . . .

The Picts came into range.

He slashed the blade downward.

A score of archers unleashed a volley. Hissing filled the air and, but a few scant seconds later, the first line of Picts virtually dropped as one.

As the archers readied their bows, a second line behind them sent a volley at the enemy. It hit the Pict lines with only half the force of the initial one, the natives now better aware what they faced.

"They're closing the gap," Konstantin muttered.

Worse, from seemingly nowhere a flight of arrows dropped upon the Aquilonians. Several soldiers cried out. At least half a dozen men in Nermesa's range of view collapsed dead. Several more sprawled injured.

"One more volley!" he commanded. "Ready everyone for the charge!"

The archers unleashed their third assault. Perhaps three or four Picts perished.

It was time. Nermesa raised his sword again. As he slashed, one of the men-at-arms blew loud and long on the horn.

Roaring, the Aquilonians charged down on their foe. Their shields formed a long wall upon which spears and arrows bounced. Behind the first row of men came a second and a third. Behind those and riding at a slow pace so as not to trample their comrades on foot came Nermesa and the mounted contingent.

The Picts eagerly ran to meet the line. The two forces were only seconds from collision.

"Now!" shouted Nermesa.

As the horn sounded once more, the foot soldiers spread to each side. Those in the second rank joined the first, expanding both flanks so that the new line stretched farther than that of the Picts. The third rank replaced the second, leaving a great hole in the center of the Aquilonian advance.

And through it charged the knights and mounted men-at-arms.

The unorthodox charge caught the Picts flat-footed. Nermesa, Konstantin, and the rest barreled into the warriors, trampling several in the first moment. Lances pinioned Picts through the chest, and swords cleaved skulls in two.

A man-at-arms fell, his face ravaged by an expertly tossed ax. The clash of weapons resounded, and screams constantly cut through the air. Nermesa's mounted fighters continued to push forward, bisecting the enemy horde. In their wake came what had been the third line. They now swarmed in to fill the space.

Shields kept tight together, the Aquilonians pressed. Men were lost, but far more Picts perished.

Nermesa cut open the chest of a foe, then slashed another in the arm. He glanced left and right and saw that those who followed him were managing to do as he had commanded. He measured the still-growing length of each flank, then the positioning. The now-longer Aquilonian lines had taken on a shape like an upturned horseshoe . . . with the Picts caught within.

Nermesa hoped to separate the natives into two trapped groups using his mounted force to do that dividing. The war leaders of the Picts must surely have recognized that by now, though, for the riders were being pressured more and more. The main Pict attack now centered on Nermesa and those nearest. Even as he watched, two knights were seized from their saddles and taken down out of sight. The savage, gleeful cries of the Picts were evidence enough of the men's horrific fates. Elsewhere, the steed of a mounted man-at-arms suddenly tumbled, a spear through its chest. The Aquilonian soldier was tossed, whether to perish because of the fall or an ax in his chest, Nermesa had no chance to discover.

A Pict with the skin of a fox draping his shaved skull leapt on Nermesa. As the two fought, the horse—its reins constantly tugged on—began turning in a mad circle.

The painted face of his foe filled Nermesa's view. The Pict grinned, his panting breath full of the stench of one who was a ritual cannibal. The monstrous figure swung at the knight with an ax, Nermesa barely deflecting the blow with his armored wrist.

"Nermesa!" shouted Konstantin, trying to come to his aid. Unfortunately, a pair of Picts grabbed at the other fighter's legs, as if they hoped to tear him in half. Konstantin slashed at one, cutting him across the face, but the other avoided his swings.

As for Nermesa's foe, a sudden transformation overtook his expression. Uncertainty spread like the plague over his face. The Pict faltered.

Nermesa took immediate advantage. He struck his foe hard in the chin with his sword hand, using the hilt for added strength.

Arms flailing, the tattooed warrior slipped from Nermesa's horse. One hand knocked the Aquilonian's helmet off.

The Pict fell under the horse's hooves and was trampled before he could even cry out.

At first unaware of this, Nermesa slashed furiously at where he had last seen the native. When he finally caught a glimpse of the corpse, the knight immediately looked up again, certain that another Pict was ready to pounce. Instead, Nermesa discovered himself oddly devoid of adversaries.

In fact, the Picts seemed to be suddenly going out of their way to avoid him. He caught a few furtive glances and saw one warrior make a sign that reminded him of the ones he had seen the friendlies in the fort use to ward off evil.

Nermesa gritted his teeth and charged the nearest. To his astonishment, the fearsome figure at first simply stared at him, only belatedly attempting any defense. Nermesa easily avoided the halfhearted swing, his momentum such that when he thrust, the force of the blow sent blood splattering over his face and armor and his sword strike lifted the Pict's dying body several inches above the ground.

Nermesa twisted the blade, letting the dead warrior drop. Blood streamed down the weapon, dribbling onto his hand.

Gazing around, he was shocked to discover that the gap between him and the Picts had grown greater. More astounding, now he realized that they were clearly retreating from his presence. When Nermesa tried to ride after them, the gap only flowed farther ahead. The Picts would have nothing of him.

Konstantin rode up next to Nermesa, the red-maned fighter sharing in his disbelief. However, where Nermesa's expression was grim, Konstantin's held wonder and hope.

"They *fear* you, Nermesa! They actually *fear* you!"

Impossible as it was for Bolontes' son to believe, the other knight spoke the truth.

He then remembered Konstantin shouting his name within earshot of the foremost warriors. Word of Khatak's capture, perhaps even of the brigand's death at his hands— however accidental in Nermesa's mind—had indeed filtered through to the Picts. Nermesa had proven himself stronger than the supposed favored of Gullah, a powerful thing in the minds of the superstitious natives.

General Pallantides' plan had worked after all, it seemed.

Still, there were men dying and a risk of the Aquilonians failing to defeat their foe. Nermesa could hardly revel in his own seeming invulnerability while his comrades died around him.

"Gather the rest behind me! We can't rest until they're driven back!"

Konstantin waved to the other riders, who quickly reformed the wedge. However, as Nermesa led them forward, he heard his second suddenly cry out his name.

As if encouraged by Konstantin, the rest of the mounted fighters took it up like a war cry. "Nermesa! Nermesa!"

He would have twisted back and ordered them to stop such foolishness . . . but then he saw that the cry was having an *effect*.

The Picts were beginning to run, and it was all because of him.

The trained soldiers immediately made use of the natives' chaotic behavior, pushing forward in orderly but swift movements. The pincers began to close, cutting off many Picts from freedom. They fought and fought well, but their hearts were no longer in the battle.

And they continued to do their best to steer clear of Nermesa, although that was not always possible. Most astounding, when forced to face him, they did so as if already resigned to their deaths. That made it easier for Nermesa to grant them such, but, at the same time, he felt oddly guilty for being so readily able to slay them.

It became more slaughter than battle. Picts by the scores fled into the deeper forest. A far greater number than those fell to the victorious Aquilonians. Memories of those comrades who had been massacred in previous attacks, of those settlers whose homes had been ravaged and who themselves had been tortured before death, drove the soldiers on.

Nermesa himself did not call an end to the butchery until there was no one left within sight to kill. Even though they were Picts, it still sickened him; but to let them live might someday soon cost the life of one of his own people.

He signaled a halt before his eager troops could follow after the survivors. To hunt Picts in the densest areas of the wilderness was to invite disaster such as had struck down General Octavio. Nermesa would not turn victory into disaster if he could at all help it.

Konstantin was all for following. His face as bloody and sweaty as Nermesa's felt, the grinning knight rode up, and shouted, "We can make it a perfect victory! I can take a party and pick off the survivors! Give me thirty men—"

"No." When Konstantin looked to argue, Nermesa stared down the other Aquilonian. "This ends here. We've broken the back of this band, but most of our men have been on the move for days! We ride to secure Anascaw, stay there a day to recover while the scouts tell us if the Picts re-form, then, if it's safe to do so, head back to Scanaga."

He expected the veteran knight to pull experience on

him, but Konstantin instead saluted Nermesa.

"As you say," he answered without rancor.

Nermesa considered what he should do next. He decided to follow what he believed to be common sense. "Make certain that all our wounded are taken care of. The dead should be gathered, too. I want none of the bodies to act as a source of Pict mementos."

"Aye, I'll be happy to make certain of that." Konstantin rubbed his chin. "And the savages' dead?"

While he hated to act coldly, Nermesa saw no choice. He had to demoralize the Picts in whatever way possible, if only to salvage the fates of those he hoped to protect. "Strip them quickly of anything of ours they wear, then leave the bodies. We'll let the wilderness take care of them."

"Aye."

As Konstantin rode off, Nermesa suddenly shuddered. The full impact of what had just happened finally hit him. Tears tumbled down his cheeks, but fortunately, no one was near enough to realize that it was anything other than sweat.

He had served his king and his country . . . but at that moment, Nermesa wished that he had never left home.

15

OVER THE DAYS that followed, scouts reported a renewed hesitancy among the Picts. The tribes withdrew beyond the acknowledged border between the Westermarck and the wilderness. However, there they sat, simply seeming to wait. That they did not disperse meant that they remained a significant concern for the Aquilonians and Nermesa, especially, for it seemed that his name was the only reason for the halt to the natives' incursions.

"You've become the scourge of their people," Caltero commented almost blithely, as they sat in his quarters sharing wine. "Especially after riding out and crushing that attack so neatly."

"It wasn't neat at all." Visions of the dead still continued to haunt Nermesa.

"Well, as battles go, it was better than many. From what Konstantin and others described, you must've looked like a demon as you rode down the savages! Small wonder that they fled!"

Nermesa stared into his mug. "It was all part of General

Pallantides' plan, that's all. He spread word weeks ahead that Khatak's slayer was returning to crush those who'd followed the brigand and his god. Pallantides deserves the credit, really."

At that moment, the door opened, and Caltero's Pict woman reappeared. Khati gave Nermesa a shy smile.

Caltero held out a hand toward her, saying, "But the truth is, you *are* the man who captured, then slew the brigand! The Picts set a lot by such deeds! Trust me, I know them well." He pulled the female into his lap, kissing her hard before she could even settle down. Looking up at his cousin, Caltero added, "I know them very, very well."

Nermesa suddenly felt very uncomfortable. Putting down the mug, he rose. "I've some things I need to check on. Forgive me."

Khati looked as if she wanted him to stay, but Caltero waved him on. "By all means, cousin! Always on duty, you! Scanaga's in safe hands . . ."

But it was not Nermesa's hands that were supposed to be protecting the territorial capital. Since Nermesa's return from the battle, his cousin had completely abdicated any true responsibility. He left everything to Nermesa, who felt utterly overwhelmed yet could not leave things to fall apart. Nermesa continued to pray that either Caltero would stir himself to resume his designated role or that Flavian would deem it necessary to appoint someone of greater experience to the position. Neither hope, however, was a likely one. Nermesa's victory had only cemented his "reputation." Flavian, like Pallantides, clearly sought to use it to Aquilonia's advantage, whatever the young knight's protests.

The cadaverous magistrate had come to the fort the day after Nermesa's return, ostensibly to make a routine visit, but, in truth, to see to General Boronius's condition. Despite efforts, rumors were spreading as to the commander's health. The sources of these rumors could not be uncovered, but Flavian had not appeared overly concerned anymore.

"A terrible, terrible thing," the judge had said in his nasal voice. Looking much like a vulture in human form, he peered at Nermesa. "But not so terrible as it once would have been. After all, we have the hero of the Westermarck with us."

"Aye, that'll make them think twice," Caltero—no help at all as far as Nermesa had been concerned—had chimed in.

"Tarantia is aware of Boronius's situation. I await their word on what should be done."

This had done nothing to soothe Nermesa. "Surely, they'll make some decision soon!"

"We can but continue to be patient," was Flavian's reply.

But in the ensuing days, Tarantia remained silent. Nermesa found it astonishing that General Pallantides, whatever his opinion of Bolontes' son, would risk the west on a much-untried fighter such as he. Surely, at least King Conan understood the risks, having fought the Picts himself as a young mercenary. What could they be thinking?

With no other choice, Nermesa continued as de facto commander of the fort. He made the rounds, went over details with Caltero and Konstantin, and constantly prayed silently for his deliverance from this situation. If Mitra heard him, however, the god chose to stay as quiet as Aquilonia's ruler.

Yet another day passed without word. On this one, Nermesa had spent hours seeing to the organization of supplies to the frontier forts. His cousin and Konstantin had finally retired, but Nermesa had not ceased his work until certain he had missed no detail, however minor. That done, he found himself reluctant to go directly to bed. Nermesa had new quarters—both Flavian and Caltero having insisted that, as one of those now in charge, he move to a private building appropriate to his rank—but, the heir to Klandes was not yet comfortable with them. Thus, although he had already done so earlier, Nermesa chose to make the rounds of the fort again.

Despite his own questionable opinion of himself, he found that his presence did indeed seem to boost the morale of the other soldiers, even the senior knights to whom he should have been subordinate. The late inspection also turned out to be a good decision for him; the evening air cooled his head, so often burning with concerns, and the walk itself proved therapeutic. His tensions began at last to ease.

As he finally headed back to his quarters, though, he suddenly had the notion that he was being followed. In the military fort of Scanaga, that should not have been possible, but Nermesa could not shake the feeling. On a hunch, he spun around.

A dark, female figure gasped.

Nermesa leaned close. "Khati?"

The friendly Pict lowered her eyes. "Forgive this one, lion warrior! I meant nothing . . . I only wanted . . ."

As she trailed off, Nermesa demanded, "What are you doing out here? Where's Caltero?"

"He sleeps." Khati said it with what sounded like a hint of relief. "He sleeps much."

Caltero did have that habit, especially after emptying another wine jug; but where it concerned his dealings with the Pict woman, Nermesa felt uncomfortable hearing of it. "And you didn't want to sleep with him?"

"Yes . . . and no." Her long, straight hair bordered her exotic face perfectly. She stared into his eyes, and Nermesa knew exactly why the female had been following him. "Less now."

He could very well take her offer now and his cousin would probably not think a thing about it. Nermesa was tempted, too. Khati was beautiful, and her body was full of lush curves barely obscured by her simple garments.

"You should go back to him . . ." the knight managed. Nermesa did not wish to be distracted by anything, however wonderful that distraction might be.

Khati placed a soft, slim hand on his. "No . . ."

She suddenly leaned up and kissed him.

Fire coursed through Nermesa, and he returned the kiss. All thought of Caltero faded.

There was a crash from the direction of General Boronius's quarters.

Pulling free, Nermesa left a startled Khati and ran toward

the building. As he neared, to his horror he noticed that both of the general's guards were missing and the door was ajar.

Sword drawn, Nermesa burst into the front room . . . and beheld, sprawled on the floor, the bodies of both soldiers. In the dark, he could not tell how they had perished, but he thought he saw blood near the throats.

From his right, a figure leapt out at him.

The Aquilonian brought up his blade, catching the other's sword squarely. The figure did not move like a Pict or wear the armor of a soldier. What Nermesa could see of the assassin's garments—some sort of pants and jerkin—reminded him of the night Khatak's bandits had attacked the column.

The brigand, if that was what he was, fought with the ferocity of one well aware that every second made capture all the more likely. He desperately thrust at Nermesa, nearly slicing off the side of the noble's neck. Nermesa slashed at the villain's sword arm, cutting into the unprotected wrist.

The assassin cried out. His wounded limb could not hold the weapon, which dropped to the floor with a clatter.

"Surrender—" Nermesa began, but, with a snarl, the shadowy figure lunged at him.

Startled, the Aquilonian, his sword still held ready, backed up a step.

There was a clatter, and Nermesa's foe slipped awkwardly. The knight reacted, thrusting with his blade.

The brigand grunted, his body quivering. He slumped against Nermesa, impaled. Belatedly, Nermesa realized that the rattle had been the man's foot slipping on the fallen sword. The assassin had, in part, caused his own death.

There were shouts from far outside, but Nermesa had no time for them. Tossing aside the body, he raced into the general's personal quarters.

Boronius lay quiet in his bed, in the dark looking much as he had when last Nermesa had visited. However, as he neared, Nermesa heard no sound of breathing.

Nerves taut, he reached out and touched Boronius's chest, hoping to feel it rise and fall.

"Mitra . . ." Nermesa murmured. A horrific moistness

covered the general's upper torso, sticky to the touch. There was no movement. No breathing.

He stepped back as the enormity of the black scene overcame him.

The floorboards just behind him creaked.

Nermesa whirled, already aware that he turned too late. He sensed another figure in the dark, one that could only be up to deviltry.

But the second assassin, little more than a silhouette, abruptly twitched, then groaned. As Nermesa brought his sword into play, he watched in astonishment as the figure *dropped* at his feet.

Dropping to one knee, the noble checked to see what had happened. As his free hand ran across the assassin's back, he discovered the hilt of a knife sticking out just below the neck.

Someone else approached. Nermesa glanced up just as torchlight from outside gave the general's quarters some illumination.

Khati's anxious gaze met his.

Nermesa looked from the Pict to the body. The knife had a bone handle, like all Pictish weapons.

"Did you do this?" he asked.

She nodded mutely. The next instant, soldiers clambered into the room. One immediately seized Khati, but Nermesa called him off, then commanded, "Seal the door! No one enters without direct permission!"

The Pict female continued to gaze from the body to Nermesa and back again. He realized that she was not certain that the assassin was dead. Nermesa nodded grimly.

"One side!" Disregarding the soldier trying to stop him, Caltero strode to Nermesa. He took in the image of his cousin, the two dead bodies, and then Khati.

"She shouldn't be here," the elder Klandes snapped to a guard. "Take her out and let her go back to my quarters. The rest of you leave, too, except for you pair. Not a word out of anyone as to what's happened here . . . not that it all won't come out soon enough."

Khati allowed herself to be guided away, but not without one last glance at Nermesa. He gave thanks that the struggle had already colored his face red.

"Bring a lantern here," commanded Caltero. Taking the light, he swung it over one body, then the other. Both were revealed to be as Nermesa had assumed them. Brigands in worn, likely stolen, clothing. One was a half-breed. The other looked as if his parentage could be traced back to the plains of Tarantia.

"Khatak's men," Nermesa's cousin announced. "No others would be so outrageously bold or seek vengeance so adamantly."

"And they succeeded."

"Oh?" Frowning, Caltero stepped beyond Nermesa to the general's bed. With a sharp intake of breath, the other knight muttered, "Damn . . ."

Finally rising, Nermesa gazed at the murdered officer. "How did this happen? How could they have gotten this far?"

"Whoever's now master of Khatak's band is as wily as he was. This was done to prove that the Picts need not fear us . . . or rather, you."

"Me?" Nermesa had not even given that notion a consideration. This was all about him?

"Think of it," Caltero went on. "If you can't preserve the Boar's life—much less keep the ruffians out of Scanaga itself—then the spirit the savages think watches over you must not favor you anymore. The brigands'll be able to urge them to new attacks!"

"But why? Why would they want the Picts to do that?"

"Who knows? Easier looting of the dead? Possibly. Maybe much more. It was said that Khatak had ambitions above and beyond being just a dread bandit chief; I heard that he wanted to rule the Westermarck, maybe even stretch such a kingdom to the Bossonian Marches. Wouldn't be the first thief with such desires. Just look at our beloved monarch."

Nermesa purposely ignored Caltero's gibe at King Conan's colored past. "We need to find out how they entered."

"Assuredly! I'll see to it myself." Caltero shook his head.

"Damn! I was always fond of the Boar! This shouldn't have happened!"

They sent a trusted man to Flavian, who came himself in the middle of the night. The territorial judge looked upon the matter with grave concern. "I'd hoped that General Boronius might recover yet. This is dire. I shall have to put together a new message to Tarantia immediately."

"Still no reply from your previous missive?" Nermesa asked.

"None. There may be other matters of greater concern. Nemedia has been reluctant of late to fulfill the agreement made after the king retook Aquilonia from them. That would require much focus by the throne."

"Not a good time for trouble out here, eh?" growled Caltero.

"By all means, not. Still, we must make certain that they do not overlook the significance of this terrible event."

Nermesa's cousin looked resolute. "I'll make certain that some good, trusted men carry it as swiftly as possible, your honor."

Flavian nodded satisfaction. "The two of you must continue to keep the situation out here in check." He looked pointedly at Nermesa. "Your reputation among the Picts is more important to us than ever."

"I understand."

"A pity both men perished. Perhaps if one had lived to be questioned, we might know more about this would-be successor to the bandit chieftain. In the meantime, however, I must suggest you take action, young Klandes. If you would ride out at the head of a strong column, make a few passes near the savages' lands, that might cut off any thought the villains have of using Boronius's murder to stir up things."

"Would they even know of it? We caught both."

"But were they *all*? I'm afraid we must consider that."

Nermesa saw his reasoning. The assassins had gained entrance somehow. It was very possible that another traitor had helped them or that they had simply slipped past an unwary sentry. Unfortunately, it was likely that the full truth would never be known. Yes, Flavian was indeed correct; the Aquilonians had to consider the worst.

"You can rely on him," Caltero remarked, slapping his cousin on the back. "He'll have them running with their tails between their legs."

"I would be satisfied if they simply stayed put in their villages." The territorial judge bowed his head to both men, who responded in turn. "Leave the matter of Boronius to me. I have agents with me who will secure the body. Tomorrow, it will be announced that the general succumbed to an illness. He struggled to overcome it, but died in his sleep."

"Not exactly the way the Boar would've wanted to go out."

"But the way he will to preserve the safety of all. I would say 'good night' to the pair of you, but we can hardly call this eve *good*."

As the elder departed to summon his agents, Nermesa shook his head. "Would that I had come a few minutes earlier."

"Then, you, too, might have perished." Caltero frowned. "Your death would trouble me, cousin."

The somberness with which Caltero uttered this touched Nermesa. He glanced again at General Boronius's form, now respectfully draped with the commander's dress cloak. The lion symbol of King Conan filled much of the center.

"Why don't you go try to get some sleep?" his cousin suggested. "I'll stay with the Boar for a while." Caltero's face softened. "Say my last farewells to him."

Nodding, Nermesa stepped outside. The four sentries came to attention as he did. After the easy death of the two previous ones, the Aquilonians were taking no chances. While it was true that Flavian wanted no curious soldiers taking a peek, that was not his main concern. It was not outside the realm of reason to think that the brigands might return and try to take some grisly evidence of their success back to the Picts.

In contrast to his earlier reluctance, Nermesa could now

think of nothing more important than reaching his bed and going to sleep. He wanted to forget, at least as much as possible, the tragedy of this evening. But as he stepped into the darkened room, he immediately sensed that he was not alone. Nermesa drew his weapon at a shadowy figure standing near his bed, the tip of the blade coming within inches of the intruder's throat.

And for the second time tonight, a female gasp met his ears.

Withdrawing the blade, Nermesa leaned close. "Khati?"

As his eyes adjusted, he saw that she stood unclad in front of his bed. The darkness only enhanced her exotic beauty.

Soft, warm fingers caressed his cheek. "You are safe?"

"I am . . . thanks to you."

"Good . . ." This time she did not simply invite. Khati leaned up and kissed him, stirring again the fire in Nermesa.

After all he had been through this evening, his resistance easily crumbled. He wrapped his arms around her, returning the kiss. Somehow, they removed his armor and garments without him actually realizing it.

And, for a time, his wish to forget what had happened came to pass . . .

SHE WAS GONE when he rose the next morning. Nermesa wondered if Caltero had been searching for her; but when he ran into his cousin at the morning meal, the latter acted as if he had not even noticed her absence from his own bed.

"I sent out riders first thing at dawn to the lesser forts to find out about any sudden resurgence of activity among the Picts," Caltero informed him. "Let's pray that there's none."

The first reports to trickle in gave no evidence that the truth concerning General Boronius's death had reached the tribes. The official cause announced to the Aquilonians—that he had succumbed to illness—appeared to have been accepted by most. Death by disease or accident was not uncommon in the territories.

Caltero made the suggestion that perhaps it would be

good for them to follow the general's example by taking turns riding out on routine patrols. "Let them see that all continues as it should. People like familiarity in their lives."

Nermesa recalled that it was on such a patrol that Boronius had been attacked, but still saw the merit of his cousin's suggestion. For the next several days, the pair did as Caltero had recommended, riding among the inhabitants of Scanaga and the nearby settlements. The action proved to do just as they hoped; the people, somewhat anxious after the "accidental" death of the territorial commander, began to return to their own routines. By the time two weeks had passed, Scanaga seemed almost to have returned to normal.

What had not returned to the way it had once been was Khati's relationship with Caltero. The Pict woman remained with Nermesa, who no longer fought against his emotions. His cousin seemed untouched by this betrayal, even taking another female within a day of her departure from him. Nermesa's guilt faded whenever he looked into the deep forest eyes of the woman in his bed. He knew that his parents would have been aghast, but Khati's presence helped Nermesa to continue on.

Yet, if the loss of his woman did not appear to bother Caltero, the duties of the fort finally seemed to take their toll. Caltero's drinking increased to the point where, when it came time for his turn on patrol, he could scarcely walk, much less ride.

"I'm in an awful state, cousin," he admitted from his bed. His new woman, Mahana, lay next to him. Unlike Nermesa, Caltero did not try to keep his trysts from the eyes of the men, which disappointed the younger Klandes. Mahana, a thin thing with a pinched face for a Pict, was unclad.

"You should stop the local wine," Nermesa bluntly suggested. "This isn't good for you or Scanaga, Caltero."

"Yes, well if the damned fools back in Tarantia would get back to us with news of some new commander coming to take over, I'd maybe do that, but where are they? They think you and I can run this forever? I was perfectly happy as the Boar's subordinate, and he was supposed to be in command forever!" Caltero swung his hand as he talked, causing a bit of the wine in the jug he held to splatter his blanket.

"I'll ride for you tonight," Nermesa finally said, sighing.

"May the blessing of Mitra be upon you!" The other knight suddenly groaned, as if his own voice had been too loud for him. He gave Nermesa an apologetic look. "It won't happen again. I'll clean myself up, cousin."

Although not at all certain that Caltero would keep that promise, Nermesa nodded. As he left, he thought once more about how the image that he had built up over the years concerning his cousin had proven so different from the reality. For a brief time after Boronius's murder, it had looked as if Caltero had pulled himself together, but this new incident had established that Nermesa had simply been deluding himself.

Khati was not in his quarters when he arrived. Nermesa prepared himself for the patrol as quickly as possible, already becoming skilled at slipping on the unwieldy armor without the aid of another. Briefly, he thought of Quentus and how his friend and former servant had so readily and willingly adapted to becoming a soldier of Aquilonia . . . and in great part because of Nermesa. After seeing Caltero in such a ruinous state, Nermesa missed Quentus more than ever. He had not gotten over his guilt for his friend's death, not even after Khatak had paid the ultimate price.

Konstantin had the patrol waiting for him. The red-haired knight saluted, his expression indicating that he knew exactly why it was Nermesa and not Caltero who rode this evening.

"I will endeavor to do what I can to assist your cousin, Nermesa."

"Thank you." Mounting up, Nermesa surveyed the dozen men with him. He knew most by name and respected all. They, in turn, treated him almost as if he were General Boronius. He did not feel that he deserved such an honor and hoped that he could live up to it.

Raising his hand, he shouted, "Forward!"

They rode out of the fort and through Scanaga with their heads held high, the picture of strength and determination. There could be no sign of hesitation or uncertainty. The people had to know that all was well.

Even if the man leading the patrol did not believe that himself.

Four men held torches to keep the way lit. As Scanaga gave way to the forested lands beyond, the members of the party shifted positions, two men riding up before Nermesa and two others flanking him. Despite his own desire to ride foremost, security demanded that he, as one of those in command at Scanaga, be protected. It grated Nermesa, but it was one order he could not countermand.

Local sentries in the settlements gratefully acknowledged their presence. As had become his practice, Nermesa paused to speak with a few. Not only did he feel that it reassured them, but it gave him the opportunity to discover any rumors of significance.

But this night, there was nothing more dire than that a calf had been slain by a wolf or panther. It was a valuable loss to the owner, but not, unfortunately, uncommon. Since the locals had already set out traps and planned a hunt for the next day, the matter was no concern for the military.

They met a long-range patrol on its own circuit, discovered no news, and headed back toward Scanaga. Nermesa realized that Caltero, even in his dire state, could have made this evening's ride. The night air likely would have done his cousin much good.

The distant, torchlit walls of the territorial capital called to them as they rode along the forest road. Nermesa felt a sudden yearning for Khati and hoped that he would find her when he returned to his quarters.

A harsh hissing sound—like that from a nest of angered serpents—suddenly cut the silence.

Four men, including two of those bearing torches, cried out. One slumped in the saddle while the others dropped limply to the earth.

From out of the trees leapt dark figures. Three more of

the Aquilonians were torn from their mounts before the
rest could react. Nermesa drew his sword and did battle
with a bare-chested bandit. He ran the man through, but not
before two more came to take up the battle.

"Keep together!" Nermesa urged. "And drive forward!"
If they could push ahead of the ambush, they would leave
their adversaries in their wake.

There was no use calling out to Scanaga for aid. The
daring brigands had chosen a location just far enough away
to make certain that neither the fortified town nor the next
nearest settlement could hear the struggle. Visions of the
terrible scene discovered by those searching for General
Boronius flashed before Nermesa's eyes, but he fought
them back just as he did the squalid villains before him.

Then, a voice speaking Pict shouted what sounded to
be a command. Nermesa's brow furrowed; there was
something about the voice that did not sit right. It was almost as if—

A great mass akin to a blanket fell upon him. He heard
curses from the soldiers and knew that they were likewise
encumbered.

The brigands had thrown a net over the party.

Nermesa brought up his sword in hopes of cutting
through the thick rope, but as he did, the bandits pulled the
net. The knight was torn from his saddle.

The collision with the ground shook his bones. Fighting
against the jarring pain, Nermesa managed to slip partially
free of the net. A snarling bandit tried to tackle him, but the
Aquilonian slashed him across the stomach, sending the
latter sprawling back.

The sounds of battle continued around him, but they
were far fewer than in the beginning. Anxiety growing,
Nermesa cut free his remaining limbs from the net and
turned to aid the others.

Then, a horribly familiar stench invaded his nostrils. He
turned to find a huge, fur-covered shadow towering above
him.

The voice Nermesa had heard before shouted again in

Pict . . . and this time the Aquilonian realized why it had seemed so odd the first time.

The voice was female.

But as this registered, the giant suddenly roared. Nermesa stared in shock as the face came close enough for him to at last make out some shadowed details.

A gargantuan fist barreled into his face.

16

DRUMBEATS WERE THE first sounds to penetrate the fog surrounding Nermesa, drumbeats with an evil rhythm to them.

Pict drums.

Realizing that, the knight struggled to wake, but a clinging, seductive scent kept luring him back into the enshrouding fog. He fought it unsuccessfully time and time again, but, at last his desperate perseverance defeated the scent, and gradually reality began to coalesce around the Aquilonian.

What he awoke to was a nightmare.

The heads of the men who had ridden with him stared back in what seemed to Nermesa accusation. Of the bodies, there was no sign. In some cases blood still dripped from where the necks had been brutally severed from the torsos. The heads perched on the ends of long, wicked spears whose sharp points had been buried in the earth.

Tearing his stricken eyes away from the gruesome display, Nermesa finally noticed that he lay in a cave. Torches beyond lit the entrance of a passage likely leading out. Others brilliantly illuminated the ghastly vision to which he had awakened . . . and which his captor had intended him to view first, he realized.

That he was in the hands of Picts, Nermesa had no doubt, but there was also no question that Khatak's brigands had executed the ambush itself. Once again, they could have not done so without the aid of some traitor in the fort. Someone knew exactly what path the patrol would be taking. That they had captured Nermesa was an added gift . . . if they even knew it was him. Had Caltero ridden as planned, it would have been the elder cousin who lay here now.

But why *had* they preserved his life when the others had all been slaughtered? Whether or not they knew just who it was that they had seized, Nermesa guessed that he was to be used for some sacrifice that would strengthen the Picts' will. Among the tribes, the ritual slaying of a senior warrior of the enemy was believed to give his might to his captors.

But what would happen if they discovered that they had the man who had captured and killed Khatak? How much worse would his fate be then?

With that nightmare to urge him on, Nermesa struggled to free himself. His first attempt was short-lived, and only then did it register to his still-awakening mind that he lay with limbs splayed on the cave floor. His wrists and ankles were bound to stakes hammered in the ground, and his mouth was bound with a leather strap. To taunt him further, his sheathed sword hung to his right on a small outcropping in the wall.

A swift tug on his bonds revealed very quickly that he was held very, very tight. Nonetheless, Nermesa tested each limb over and over, hoping that the ropes holding one of them would loosen.

A scraping sound in the passage beyond made the noble immediately stop. Shutting his eyes to mere slits, he waited for his captor.

What emerged was a figure so cloaked that, at first, Nermesa had no idea as to whether it was even human. The

hooded form leaned close to him, the face buried deep
within. Nermesa continued to pretend that he was still unconscious. Perhaps his captor would undo one of his wrists.
If so, then, perhaps as he had done with the man-at-arms in
Lucian's estate, a swift motion might enable the knight to
overcome the hooded figure and free himself.

But instead, the silent intruder reached with his long
sleeves into a small, clay pot sitting nearby. As he turned
back to Nermesa, the latter quickly shut his eyes. No sooner
had he done so when something powdery landed on the
closed lids.

Nermesa's eyes suddenly burned as if with fire.

He could not help gasping and shaking. A raw scream
finally escaped him. Desperately, the Aquilonian tried to
blink away the agony. Had his hands been free, it was very
likely that Nermesa would have torn out his eyes, if only to
be rid of the horror.

"The pain will fade shortly," a feminine voice declared
maliciously. "At least . . . *that* pain."

Sure enough, after a few more seconds of torture, Nermesa was able to tolerate the burning. His eyes still stung,
causing them to water, but he no longer felt as if he wanted
to rip the orbs from their sockets.

As he came back to his senses, the knight swore at his
captor. The torture through which he had just suffered had
all been to see whether or not he was pretending to sleep.
Nermesa glared at his tormentor, who at first remained a
murky blob. Determined to face his foe, the Aquilonian
blinked until his vision at last cleared. As it did, the figure
obliged his curiosity further by pulling back the hood.

Khati . . .

The smile that played over her soft lips had a crooked,
cruel bent to it that Nermesa had never seen on the Pict before. Despite her beauty, the evil in her expression repulsed
him utterly.

"The lion warrior . . ." Khati spat in his face. "Gullah
will feast on your bones . . ."

"Why do this? What do you want?" he managed, his own voice coming out as more of a croak.

"Your skin to be worn like this cloak," she replied, removing the garment. "Your head to be on a pole! Your soul to be devoured by He Who Lives in the Moon . . ." The Pict spat again. "And only then will my brother be avenged! My brother, *Khatak* . . ."

"Khatak?" Nermesa could not contain his consternation. He could have never tied the Pict with the half-breed, not even, he belatedly thought, through the similarity of their names. There were many Picts with similar names. Besides, Khati had been a friend of the Aquilonians, even sharing the beds of Caltero and Nermesa.

Where she could learn all she needed for her brother, Nermesa realized. He and his cousin had been played for fools, their lusts betraying them. Small wonder that Khatak had been so brazen in his feats. Still, Nermesa had been careful never to say anything of significance to her . . . but Caltero had probably babbled his head off.

"I'm sorry about your brother . . ." More likely, *half brother*, from the looks of things. If there was any Aquilonian or other eastern blood in her, he could not see it. "But I had no choice."

"You will have no choice, too, when you die horribly." She ran a finger over his chest, causing him to shudder involuntarily. His armor had been removed, and the garment beneath cut open to reveal his upper torso. Nermesa expected each moment for Khati to drive a knife through his heart.

Then he recalled how she had actually *saved* him from General Boronius's murderers. "The man you killed for me—"

She leaned close enough to kiss him. "He might have spoken if tortured, so had to die. I was not ready for you yet. Besides, there were others coming."

So it had been to save her own skin, not his. Nermesa wanted to spit back in her face, but his mouth felt as dry as Stygia's fabled deserts.

She laughed lightly at his anger, then kissed his cheek as if tasting him. He twisted his head away, which only made her laugh more.

"But you will also serve another purpose, besides vengeance! The headmen of the tribes will see how Gullah's favor is now with me," she murmured. "I have the feared lion warrior roped like a goat for milking, and soon He Who Lives in the Moon will break your living body into pieces before their eyes . . ."

Her excellent grasp of the Aquilonian tongue did not surprise him anymore. To act as a spy for Khatak and herself, she had to understand the enemy well.

More to buy time for himself than out of any hope that he could convince her of the error of her intentions, Nermesa said, "You don't have to do this, Khati. Your brother fomented trouble between your people and mine. He caused deaths on both sides just for his own gain."

With an unsettling laugh, she shook her head. "No . . . *our* gain." Her eyes lit up at his confusion. "*Our* gain, lion warrior! His *and* mine! Think you that my brother could have planned all this alone? Khatak, he was like Gullah, ferocious and strong, but I . . . I am quicker here." Khati touched her forehead. "Quicker than him, quicker than you, quicker than all!"

Nermesa could certainly not deny her cunning. She had made fools of the Aquilonians and had certainly looked to have the cunning to guide her brother in his deeds.

"The headmen will see," the Pict continued, caught up in her triumph. "They will know that I am the blessed of Gullah and that to follow me is to drive your kind from the lands of the People!"

Picts did not normally follow the females of their race. It said much for Khati's power already that she could even make them consider such a thing.

"And then you'll become queen? Is that it?"

"Yes . . ." Once more she laughed, then suddenly leaned down and kissed him again. He tried to turn his head, but she held it tight until she was done. Pulling back, Khati mocked,

"A final gift to you for your sacrifice! You will bring me much power with your doom!"

Rising lithely, the Pict retrieved a jug of water from one corner of the cave. She brought the jug over to her captive, setting the opening to his mouth.

When Nermesa refused to drink, she gave him a crooked smile, then put her own lips to the jug. Some of the water dribbled out of her mouth as she drank, coursing down her neck and over the slopes of her breasts. After several swallows, Khati again presented it to the Aquilonian. "Drink."

Seeing that it could not be poisoned or drugged, Nermesa gladly did. To his surprise, she let him drink his fill, even taking care that he did not choke.

"Thank you," he managed after he was done.

She chuckled. "You must live long enough to be sacrificed!"

Setting down the jug, Khati swept out of the cave.

Nermesa again struggled with his bonds, but they proved no more receptive to his efforts than previously. He laid his head back, shutting his eyes so as not to have to look upon what had been done to his men. Their faces were ingrained into his memory well enough already, and he would not be able to avenge them contemplating his guilt.

Yet how could Nermesa even free himself? He had no knife and, even if he had, it would have been impossible to manipulate the weapon well enough to sever the ropes around his wrists.

Eyes still shut, Nermesa tried to think of any other avenue of escape. However, perhaps because of either lingering traces of whatever Khati had first used to keep him unconscious or the simple knowledge that there *was* no other way to free himself, Nermesa drifted off again . . .

But he stirred immediately when some inner sense warned him that he was once more no longer alone. How long he had been out, the Aquilonian could not say. Nermesa only knew that footsteps echoed in the passage beyond, footsteps that were made by someone much clumsier than a Pict.

All but one of the torches had died out, leaving Nermesa

in almost complete shadow. The knight wondered if he had slept all the way to the time of his sacrifice.

As he had the first time, he kept his eyes only slits. Judging by the noisy steps, the intruder was likely one of the brigands. Should that be the case, Nermesa had some slight hope that he might be able to trick the newcomer into freeing him.

The clink of metal preceded the arrival of the figure and enabled Nermesa to determine that it was indeed no Pict. His hopes rose. Greed fueled bandits. Nermesa could use that fault to his advantage.

Yet, it was not one of Khatak's cutthroats who entered, but rather someone who was such a sight to the captive that Nermesa could not help but open his eyes wide and gape.

"Praise be, you're conscious. I was afraid that I'd have to try to rouse you . . ."

Nermesa stared. "Caltero! But how—?"

His cousin knelt by his side. "We can talk later. Best if we're away from here before that brigand's body is found. I didn't have time to drag it far."

From his belt, Caltero produced a dagger and began cutting at the ropes around Nermesa's wrist. The other knight wore his breastplate over cloth garments. The clinking had come from his sword, sheathed at his side. A voluminous travel cloak the color of the forest draped over his hunched form.

"That's one free!" Caltero grunted quietly. He slipped back to Nermesa's ankle. "See if you can undo your other hand while I deal with your feet."

Twisting, Nermesa fumbled with the ropes while his cousin first cut one ankle free, then the other. Caltero helped him remove the last around the wrist, then pulled Nermesa to his feet.

"No time to lose! Follow me!"

"My armor—"

"Will be no use if you spend the time trying to put it on and get captured again!" The elder Klandes stood at the entrance. Sweat covered his face. "Now, hurry!"

Seeing the sense in Caltero's words, Nermesa reluctantly abandoned his armor. But just as he was about to leave, he thought of something else. The younger knight twisted out of his cousin's tight grip and returned to his equipment. Before Caltero could retrieve him, Nermesa pulled free his sword and sheath.

"Leave that thing," Caltero all but growled. "I've another weapon waiting by the horses!"

But this was the sword given to him by King Conan, and Nermesa somehow felt that it would give him the extra edge should they be forced to fight. He slipped it on, then stared expectantly at Caltero. Shaking his head, the other Aquilonian turned. They wended their way through the tunnel and out into what proved to be the night.

"A full day?" Nermesa muttered.

"Two."

That should not have surprised him. That his skull had not been cracked by the powerful blow to it had been a miracle, but between that injury and whatever substance Khati had used to drug him, two days could have been *four* or more.

Caltero grabbed his arm, pulling him to the right. "This way."

The pair dove into the thickest part of the forest, heading up a gradual incline. Far back, Nermesa heard the beat of drums. He prayed to Mitra that no one would come for him until long after the Aquilonians had made good their escape.

How he had underestimated his cousin. Caltero had risked his own life to come to Nermesa's aid.

"How did you ever find me?" he murmured, once they were far from the cave. The moon was only a sickle this night, an omen, perhaps, but one whose lack of light at the moment aided them quite well.

The other knight fought past a low branch. In an equally low voice, he replied, "When we discovered the remains of your patrol and saw that your breastplate was not among the torsos, I knew that the Picts or the brigands had you.

Then I saw Khati looking eager to leave Scanaga, and so I followed her . . ." Caltero's voice trailed off. "Khati . . ."

"She's Khatak's sister. She's the one leading his band of brigands . . . and trying to draw the Picts to her cause, too."

"She could do it. Khati is very persuasive."

Nermesa did not have to be reminded. "She must be stopped! I've listened to her. She's more dangerous than he was!"

"Of that, I can wholeheartedly agree." The elder cousin paused. "The horses should await us just ahead—" Caltero suddenly froze.

Nermesa leaned close. "What?"

"Thought I heard something behind us." He readied his weapon. "I'll slip in back of this tree while you move on as if nothing's amiss. In the dark, they won't notice me."

"I'm not going to leave you alone to face—"

"No arguments!" muttered Nermesa's cousin, pushing him forward. "I'll be fine . . ."

Rather than risk their plan coming undone because of his hesitation, Nermesa nodded and continued his way through the brush. He tried to act as if nothing was amiss, even mumbling just loud enough for anyone following to think that Caltero was still with him.

Ahead, Nermesa heard a slight snort. He sensed movement from there and cautiously drew his weapon.

A sigh of relief escaped him. It was a horse . . . Caltero's horse, from what Nermesa could see of it. The animal was tied to a tree. It looked the knight's way, perhaps thinking that its master had returned.

Nermesa started toward it . . . then stopped. Frowning, the knight looked around but saw nothing.

There was only the one horse.

Instinctively, he spun, sword raised.

"Ungh!" A sharp point dragged across his back and side, even flickering over his arm. Blood trickled from the long but thankfully shallow wounds.

His would-be slayer cursed.

"Why couldn't you just have stood still!" growled Caltero. "Why couldn't you have let me make it swift and at least relatively painless? Damn you! You can never leave well enough alone, can you?"

"Caltero . . ." Nermesa finally managed. "Are you mad? Are you under some sort of Pictish spell?"

"A Pictish spell? You might say that, cousin. She *is* a witch, although not in the mystical sense! Oh, she knows about some interesting powders, but her magic goes deeper . . . straight to the head and heart! You'd agree with that, wouldn't you?"

Caltero suddenly lunged, almost catching Nermesa off guard. Their blades clashed several times, with Nermesa, unwilling to do anything but defend, forced back.

Pausing, his cousin continued, "I can't think without her, or breathe without her! She fills my dreams and my waking moments! I tried drink, but that only made me more pliable to her desires, not defiant to her will!"

"This is insanity, Caltero!"

"It is, isn't it? But I've no choice, you see. This is as much as I've been able to defy her, bringing you here. She'll be very mad with me, but I'll make it up to her with the others!"

His words made absolutely no sense. Here he was trying to slay Nermesa for her, and he called it *defiance*?

"You're my *cousin*, after all, cousin!" Caltero went on, still seeking an opening by which to kill the figure before him. "We've been as close as brothers, we two. When you first arrived, I was thrilled! When your man, Quentus, died, I mourned him in my way. When Khati said that she intended to take to your bed in order to lull you into false security, I made the sacrifice, no matter how it pained me to see her with you!"

"And now you'll gut me to win her favor back?"

The other knight laughed. "Is that what you think? Cousin, I'm trying to spare you much grief! If you knew what sort of torture and grotesque fate Khati intended for you, you'd thank me!"

The swords clashed. Grimacing, Nermesa asked, "Why didn't you just slay me while I was bound?"

"You're the dearest of my blood and my closest friend," Caltero returned blithely—and quite madly. "I couldn't just cut your throat while you lay there like a calf tied up for the butcher! I was trying to give you a good, clean, and noble death! You would have died thinking you were free, thinking that you could still save the day." He shrugged. "It was the least I could do for family."

Caltero talked as if he truly meant it, which made the situation even more grotesque. Trying to think of a way out of this insanity, Nermesa continued to ply his cousin with questions. "Then why didn't you kill me as soon as we were outside? I had my back to you more than once."

"You took that damned sword with you even though I told you we didn't have time! I've seen your handiwork, cousin! Not as good as mine, but worthy of respect! I had to revise my plan, and that took most of our trek. Thought I'd finally figured it all out perfectly—and then Mitra must've whispered in your ear that I was behind you, damn him!"

Without warning, Caltero once more lunged. This time, his blade caught Nermesa's wrist, almost making Bolontes' son drop his sword. Grunting in pain, Nermesa stepped back again . . . and collided with a tree trunk.

Caltero thrust.

His blade would have skewered Nermesa just below the throat . . . if his target had still been there. Nermesa barely managed to roll around the trunk. He heard the tip of Caltero's sword bury itself hard in the wood. Bits of bark pelted Nermesa's face.

"Caltero! This makes no sense! We are cousins and Aquilonians! Why can't we just return to Scanaga? I'll tell no one what happened!"

The elder Klandes shook his head. "I can't betray her *that* far, Nermesa! She *needs* your body! She needs you, the slayer of her brother, dead! I have to give her that, don't you see? She'll forgive me for keeping you from the horrors she intended, but she'll expect that you'll still perish! It's the only way!"

Nermesa did not have to see his cousin's expression to know it would be filled with madness. Caltero's desire for Khati had led him to allow countless soldiers and settlers to die. His twisted attempt to ease his guilt over his betrayal of Nermesa only further emphasized how deep was the Pict's hold on him.

Breathing heavily, Caltero slashed at the trunk, following Nermesa as the latter tried to avoid the attacks. Nermesa tumbled back through the forest, trying desperately to think of what to do against his own blood. He had never imagined having to face one he had held dear to him, but there was no convincing Caltero to cease.

"Let it end swiftly, cousin!" Caltero snapped. "You keep this up, and the Picts or her brigands will yet find you . . . and then they'll drag you back to face Gullah's hunger!"

"Would it be any worse than being murdered by *you*?"

The other Aquilonian laughed harshly. "Oh, yes! You'd be praying to Mitra that he somehow let time flow back to this moment so that I could run you through! You'd scream to her to end it, but she wouldn't! Trust me on that, cousin! I'm doing what's best for all concerned!"

He renewed his attack, but Nermesa met each of his blows. Yet, continued defense would not serve Nermesa much longer. The combination of his captivity and this terrible revelation had drained him significantly. He had to do something, and quickly. It was not just for his own life, either; if he perished, it would, as Caltero had said, help stir up the Picts, send them out once more in search of Aquilonian blood.

Though he himself would be dead, the slaughter of many would be on Nermesa's hands.

Caltero lunged yet again . . . and to his surprise, found Nermesa not only parrying his attack, but countering with one of his own.

"What do you think you're doing?" growled the veteran knight.

"What I have to."

His treacherous cousin cursed as Nermesa drove him back toward the horse. It was immediately clear that Caltero had underestimated both Nermesa's resolve and ability.

"You'll ruin everything! She'll never forgive me! I should've left you in the cave!"

"You should have never betrayed me or any of our people in the first place," the younger Klandes declared grimly.

He lunged, his blade clanging off of Caltero's breastplate right where the heart was located.

The other knight began to attack with some desperation. His swings grew wilder, which in some ways made them deadlier. Nonetheless, Nermesa deflected each and continued to push his cousin back.

Then, in the distance, the sounds of drums echoed again. They had a frenetic beat to them, as if building up to some dire climax.

"You hear that?" Caltero muttered. "That's the call of Gullah! That's how they summon He Who Lives in the Moon to come to claim his prey! Khati promised them you this night, and they know that she speaks as the favored of the god! I barely got you out of the cave in time!" He cut at Nermesa, almost severing an ear. "And for this you show me such gratitude?"

"Caltero, you must stop this! I swear I won't say anything!" Nermesa would not, either. Somehow, he would help his cousin recover from this obsession.

The other fighter hesitated, then, suddenly lowered his weapon. He looked down, shaking his head at the same time. His other hand fell to the side. "What am I thinking? What's she done to me?" Caltero glanced up again. "Nermesa . . . you have to *help* me!"

Nermesa lowered his own blade. He stepped toward his cousin. "Caltero . . . this will remain between the two of us. Come! Before the Picts arrive, we've got to be away—"

He cried out as Caltero's other hand came up and plunged a dagger into his forearm. Nermesa's sword dropped.

Despite the wound, he attempted to retrieve the weapon. However, as Nermesa bent, he sensed Caltero draw back his sword.

"This is for the best for all of us," the traitorous knight muttered.

The foliage above them rustled. Both Nermesa and Caltero looked up into the dark trees.

With a blood-chilling roar, *something* dropped down on Caltero.

He tried to fend it off, but before he could get his sword up, it was upon him. In the blackness of night, it resembled most an inky blob, but the familiar stench told Nermesa exactly what had come upon the pair.

Khatak's fur-clad servant, a being Nermesa no longer believed could be human.

And then a name came unbidden to him . . . *Gullah* . . .

The massive shape turned from the startled Caltero toward Nermesa. The latter fumbled for his sword, aware that he would not be ready in time.

But, in his shock, Caltero made a dreadful mistake. He slashed at the thick body of the attacker. The angle ensured that his strike did not even cut the skin, but it was enough to draw the ire of the fearsome being.

With a roar, the man, beast, or *god*, seized Nermesa's cousin in one huge hand and lifted him up into the air.

Nermesa went to the aid of Caltero, but a random swing by the unnoticing giant struck the would-be rescuer in the head with such force that it flung him back. Nermesa collided hard against the horse, which was frantically tugging on the tied reins.

The giant threw Caltero to the ground. Caltero screamed, and in his agony, continued to make desperate, foolish swings that only served to further enrage his horrific adversary. The furred form fell upon him again.

Stunned and still not fully recovered from his captivity,

Nermesa stumbled in the dark, trying to focus. As he glanced back at the struggle, he saw Caltero raised toward the face of the giant. A memory from the attack on the patrol flashed through Nermesa's muddled mind, a vision of deadly fangs. He started forward, still hoping to save his cousin despite the latter's treachery.

But Nermesa's head suddenly throbbed where Gullah had struck him. His legs grew unsteady, and the only thing that saved him from falling was clutching to the horse.

The giant shook Caltero like a rag doll and raked the man's chest with his nails. Caltero screamed.

Even through the throbbing, Nermesa realized that he could no longer do anything to save his cousin. In fact, in his present condition, he only presented Gullah with an easy second victim.

More important, the fort had to be warned of Caltero's betrayal and Khati's ambitions. Despite a part of him screaming that he rush to Caltero's aid, Nermesa knew that he had but one choice. He twisted around, seeking in the dark the horse's reins.

But at that moment, the panicked horse reared, ripping the reins free from the tree where Caltero had tied them. It turned from the struggle and prepared to race off.

Nermesa saw his chance—Scanaga's chance—slipping away. With his free hand, he lunged for the saddle. He managed to grab the straps just as the animal moved.

The horse ran, and as it did, it dragged Nermesa along with it. In his other hand, he clutched his sword tight, aware that it was his only weapon should the creature come after him.

The frenzied steed pulled him farther and farther from Caltero. Exhausted, his wounds throbbing, Nermesa simply did what he could to hold on. The uncaring mount dragged him against trees, branches, and brambles. He shut his eyes for fear that they would be poked out.

Far back, he heard his cousin cry out. The scream shook him to the core . . . then cut off with a terrible finality.

Nermesa mourned Caltero, even knowing him for what

he was and what he had tried to do. He choked, the tears catching in his throat.

The horse had no apparent sense of where it wanted to go. It merely dragged Nermesa on and on. The sounds of the drums receded, but he felt certain that, at any moment, the thing that had slaughtered Caltero would drop on them from the thick foliage above.

Then, the horse suddenly stumbled, falling toward the side on which the Aquilonian hung. The movement battered Nermesa against a thick oak.

He tore free of the saddle. Stunned, the knight spun around. His sword flew from his grip.

Crashing to the ground, Nermesa rolled through the brush. He collided with a rock.

And with a groan, stilled.

17

CHANTING PIERCED THE darkness.

Chanting in the Pictish tongue.

Nermesa woke with a start, certain that he was once more Khati's prisoner and that his sacrifice to the natives' god was imminent. He pulled at his wrists, hoping to free them . . . and discovered only then that they were not even bound.

In fact, only one ankle was tied, and that loosely. It slowed the Aquilonian down just long enough for him to register his surroundings as other than the cave of Khatak's villainous sister.

Instead, he lay in a frame-and-animal-skin hut. The skulls of various animals hung from leather straps affixed to the wooden frame above. To his side stood a variety of clay jars that reminded Nermesa of those that Khati had kept in her sanctum.

The sensation that he was being watched made the knight look left. There, seated before a low fire—the only source of light in the hut—was what at first looked like the mummified remains of a Pict elder clad only in an old loincloth. The tattoos covering his body had a faded look and on many parts of his torso had collapsed in on themselves. The mouth barely had lips of which to speak, the flesh even curled back. Yet, no mummy had such black, penetrating eyes that even now stared back at Nermesa.

A shaman.

Nermesa reached for his sword . . . and found the sheath empty. The scrape of metal made him look again at the Pict, where he discovered the wizened, bald figure now presenting him with the gleaming weapon.

"The lion's bite." The shaman's voice sounded like wood crackling in the fire, yet there was something about the horribly gaunt figure that warned Nermesa not to take him lightly.

The elderly Pict continued to hold out Nermesa's weapon until the Aquilonian finally rose to retrieve it. Even though the knight loomed over the almost-naked figure, Nermesa had no desire to attack. Thus far, his host had only given him aid.

Although why any Pict, especially one of their revered shamans, would do so, concerned Nermesa more than he revealed.

"Thank you," he said as he sheathed the blade.

The Pict nodded, then, with a bony hand, indicated for Nermesa to sit across from him. Not certain just why he should, the Aquilonian nevertheless obeyed.

The elder cackled. "The lion outplays Gullah again . . ."

Mention of Gullah sent shivers down Nermesa's spine. He recalled Caltero's hopeless struggle and that last, soul-wrenching scream. The Aquilonian's grip instinctively tightened around the sword's hilt.

"Be calm. The lion's bite is not needed here . . ."

Nermesa in no manner relaxed. He eyed the shaman with open suspicion. "You know my tongue well."

"To know how the enemy thinks is to have power over them. I learn long, learn well. Use well, too."

"If your people and mine are enemies, why did you bring me here? Why not slay me while I was unconscious?"

The skeletal figure did not answer at first, instead taking from a pouch a pinch of powder and tossing it into the low flames. At the same time, he muttered some unintelligible words.

Nermesa fell back as the fire exploded upward, the flames turning a startling green in the process. The display lasted but a few scant seconds, though, the fire then returning to its previous state.

Behind the flames, the wizened Pict's gaze took on an unsettling aspect. He appeared to be staring beyond Nermesa into another world, and when he spoke, his voice carried the timbre of someone much stronger than his gaunt frame indicated.

"The invaders will be swept from the lands of the People, and many heads will decorate the ceremonial fires. Fallen warriors will be honored. Blood will rule the day and night. The tall villages of the invaders will burn, and their totem will be trampled. The People will fall over their lands, and the memory of their arrogance will be all that remains of the invaders . . ."

The knight shivered despite himself, aware that his host spoke of Aquilonia in such dreadful terms. The shaman said all with a tone of certainty, of finality, as if this was the only future for the realm.

Nermesa clenched his sword tighter. He would not sit idly by while Khati's followers spread death through the territories and beyond.

But as Nermesa started to stand, the Pict elder suddenly shifted his gaze and, sounding like himself again, added, "But that day is far, and enemies must sometime become shield brothers against others." He cocked his head at the wary Aquilonian. "The bear must join with the lion . . . even if it is against Gullah."

Only then did Nermesa notice the ursine skull positioned so dominantly above where the other sat. The ferocious jaws were open wide in defiance, and even though no flesh remained, he almost felt as if the black pits stared back at him.

"Gullah is strong, lion warrior. To defeat him, you must be stronger."

Nermesa met the gaze of the shaman. "I don't understand a word of what you say! If I am no prisoner, then let me depart. I have to get back to the fort. If you try to stop me—"

"I am old," the Pict remarked with a grin. Of his sharpened teeth, only a handful remained. He dismissed Nermesa's threat with a wave of his gnarled hand. "An old Tokanu is no danger to you."

Nermesa was not so certain of that. Besides, it was not only the shaman with whom he was concerned. How many warriors waited outside, ready to charge in at a single call from their holy man?

As if reading his thoughts, Tokanu gestured toward the flap leading out. "Please. Look for yourself. No harm will there be."

Drawing the blade, Nermesa went to the entrance. He heard no sounds from without, but Picts could be very silent when the situation demanded it. Prodding aside the leather skin flap with the tip of his blade, the Aquilonian peered outside.

It was still dark. Nermesa hoped that this meant that he had only been unconscious for a little while, not an entire day or more.

Then he noticed something else. Tokanu had spoken the truth when he had said that no harm awaited Nermesa outside. That was because there were no warriors, no village whatsoever. The shaman's hut sat in the middle of the forest, hidden so well by the surrounding trees and brush that Nermesa doubted that he would have seen it had he stood only ten yards away.

Slipping back inside, the noble faced the placid Pict. "What goes on here?"

"The Bear people follow the favored of Gullah. They believe the false words that this is the day of the People. Tokanu knows better. Tokanu knows that day is not. That day still comes, but many seasons must pass, and Tokanu and all here now will be long dust."

"Tokanu was not believed," Nermesa hazarded, ignoring the rest. "Tokanu was cast out, wasn't he?"

His rescuer spat. "They believe the she-devil over Tokanu! A female! First the mongrel, then the she-devil . . ."

She-devil. Khati. Nermesa suspected that Tokanu had been a powerful and respected shaman before his objection to her and Khatak's plan. He had probably been fortunate to escape with his life, considering how merciless the pair were. "Tokanu doesn't fear Gullah?"

"All should fear Gullah," the skeletal Pict warned. "All." His fingers closed on a tiny pouch around his neck, one bound with a long leather loop. He held it for Nermesa to see. "But Gullah and his children can be discouraged," Tokanu added cryptically.

"What do you mean?"

With astonishing ease, the shaman rose to his feet without any use of either his arms or aid from the Aquilonian. Standing, Tokanu turned out to be taller than average for his people, but still several inches shorter than Nermesa. He removed the pouch from his person, reached up, and hung it around the startled Aquilonian's own neck. A slight, unsettling odor that Nermesa could not identify emanated from the tiny cloth pouch. He wanted to remove it, but thought better of it for the moment.

Tokanu muttered something in Pictish, then touched the pouch reverently. In Aquilonian, he then added, "Let it touch the heart, for there it will gain strength."

Nermesa assumed that the elder meant that he should slip it under his shirt. Although not certain why he did, the knight obeyed. At the very least, Tokanu had so far done him only good, taking him from where he lay and tending to his wounds. The dagger thrust by Caltero did not even hurt, only throbbed, thanks to some poultice bound to it. For now, Nermesa would humor the Pict. He could always remove the pouch once he was far away.

The question was . . . which way should he go from here? He had no idea where the horse had dragged him.

"I thank you for the gift, Tokanu."

"It is not a gift. It is a weapon." The hairless shaman indicated what appeared to be a water sack and a thick pouch next to it. "That is a gift. Water. Food. Take. The lion must be strong against Gullah. It is the only hope."

Nodding, Nermesa took the offerings and stepped outside. Tokanu followed. The Aquilonian gazed around, trying to get his bearings but not succeeding.

"There," said Tokanu, pointing ahead. "There must you go."

"That will lead me back to Scanaga?"

"It is the path you must take," his benefactor answered curtly. He eyed the sky. "The spirits of the wind and clouds feud again."

By that, Nermesa could only assume that Tokanu meant that there was bad weather brewing. The nighttime heavens had already grown overcast, the clouds thick and turbulent. The battered noble steeled himself; whatever the elements chose to do, he had to reach Scanaga. They had to be told what Khati intended. Nermesa had no doubt that through Caltero and her own wiles she knew far too much about the territorial capital's defenses.

And if Scanaga fell . . . the rest of the Westermarck would soon follow.

He turned to bid farewell to Tokanu, but the shaman had already disappeared inside his rounded hut. Within, the ancient Pict began muttering, but his words were in Nermesa's language, not his own.

"The fires cleanse the land of the Lion . . . the People come from the forest . . . the heads will be many. . . ."

Gritting his teeth, Nermesa trotted off. Even though Tokanu's voice quickly faded away, what he had said remained with the Aquilonian. Nermesa had no notion as to whether in the end the shaman had been referring again to his prediction of the distant future—one with which the knight would have argued—or the current threat. He only knew one thing: He had to do whatever he could to keep catastrophe from sweeping over the Westermarck.

Even if he had to face the god Gullah himself.

• • •

DAWN, SUCH AS it was, arrived perhaps two hours later. With it came thunder and lightning and a harsh wind. The threat of rain was imminent.

With the dawn also came a terrible realization . . . that Tokanu had sent him in the opposite direction from that which the Aquilonian had desired.

The first glimmer of daytime was a vague lightening of the darkness at the horizon from pitch-black to a heavy gray. Unfortunately, this occurred *behind* Nermesa, which meant that he was not going east, as he had supposed, but rather west, *deeper* into Pict country. That the shaman had tricked him should not have surprised Nermesa. Recalling Tokanu's words, the Aquilonian saw that the wizened figure had simply said that the direction he had pointed was the path that Nermesa *had* to take . . . at least, where the shaman was concerned. Tokanu's interest did not involve saving Scanaga but rather creating trouble for Khati.

Nermesa swore. He immediately turned around and headed the way *he* wanted to go. He would not trust to some secret plot by the ousted shaman. The only hope of avoiding terrible bloodshed on both sides was for him to reach the capital as soon as possible.

But that might take days on foot, assuming he even lived that long. Nermesa had to hope that he would come across a horse at some point. The Picts made use of them. If he came upon a lone scout or hunter, perhaps there was hope.

In the meantime, he had to keep walking.

The wind howled at his back and more than once Nermesa thought that he heard the cry of the thing that had killed Caltero. Again, Nermesa thought of how the murderous figure could not merely be some monstrously gigantic brigand; whatever had slain so many, including Quentus, was not human, not quite.

Was it indeed Gullah?

Rain started coming down, and although the storm did push him forward, it also made his footing unstable. He slipped on wet tree roots and rocks and caught his feet in mud. It was only a matter of time before he would fall on his face.

Grasping onto a tree trunk for support, Nermesa paused to chew on some dried meat—and at the same time found himself staring into the face of a Pict warrior.

The tattooed warrior was as startled as he, gaping wide at Nermesa with his filed teeth displayed. Only when lightning flashed the next second did he react . . . but by then the Aquilonian had already thrust.

The Pict let out a short cry as the sword sank deep into his stomach. As Nermesa pushed the body away, he heard excited voices. The scout had not been alone after all. Cursing, the knight shifted to the south, hoping that he could avoid the warrior's companions. The storm made the going slow, but Nermesa hoped that his pursuers would suffer as much as he.

He was not so lucky. Another Pict leapt out of the trees on his left, taking Nermesa down. The Aquilonian struggled as the savage warrior gained the advantage. Grinning, the Pict tried to bash in Nermesa's skull with his ax, but the noble managed to bring it to a halt just above his forehead.

The other voices drew near. Calling upon manic strength, Nermesa twisted the Pict under him, then jammed his fist into the latter's throat. As the Pict gasped for breath, Nermesa struck him hard on the jaw.

Leaving the stunned warrior where he lay, the Aquilonian continued to stumble south. His feet seemed to snag on every weed or root, but still Nermesa made progress. The voices started to drift farther west.

He had been fortunate. If not for the foul weather, the practiced hunters would have tracked him easily. As it was, there was still the possibility that some followed. With that to urge him on, Nermesa quickened his pace. He was no coward, but warning Scanaga came first.

On and on he ran, at times not even aware of the trail. Eventually, though, his path led him up a high ridge, which, despite the storm, Nermesa hoped would give him a chance to gain his bearings.

Pausing at the top, Bolontes' son surveyed the land before him. A river lay ahead and, farther on, areas where the forest actually gave way to open lands. And, farther yet to the east—

Farther yet to the east moved a mass that Nermesa, wiping his eyes momentarily dry, was certain was a column of soldiers.

What they were doing out here, he did not know. Very likely they had come in search of Nermesa, whose body had not been among the dead. Whether or not they found him alive, the Aquilonians had to strike back after yet another harsh slaughter in their very midst. The security of the territories demanded reprisal.

Nermesa opened his mouth to call out, then clamped it shut. Not only would they not hear him from such a distance, but his cry might instead draw the Picts to him. He had to get nearer to the slowly moving column.

Hopes renewed, Nermesa wended his way down the other side of the ridge, half-running, half-sliding. Reaching the bottom in one piece, he leapt through the forest in the direction he estimated would best enable him to meet his comrades. Nermesa had to try to run ahead of the column or else risk having it pass him by. If that happened, he doubted that he would have the strength to catch up to them.

The rain lessened. Nermesa saw it as a sign from Mitra. Luck was at last with him—

A thundering roar ahead made him slow.

He had never heard such violent rumbling. With no idea what could be its cause, Nermesa continued on, but more warily.

And at last, the river he had seen from high above greeted his dismayed gaze . . . a river monstrously swollen by the storm.

The water poured over the banks, spilling almost up to where Nermesa stood. During normal times, it probably would not have been very difficult to cross the river by swimming, but such an attempt at this juncture would have been suicidal.

Yet it stood between him and the others. Nermesa gazed up and down the river, trying to decide which one might better lead him to a possible crossing point. He finally chose downriver, that putting him nearer to the front of the column.

Praying that he had not made the wrong choice, Nermesa raced along the side. He could not see the column from his current vantage point, but prayed that the weather conditions kept it from moving along too swiftly. Besides, surely at some point they, too, would have to cross the rampaging waters. Even a bridge would be risky under these conditions. That might slow them enough to make up for his own trials.

Then he came upon a place where the river narrowed. It was still too dangerous for Nermesa to swim in, but near one turn he spotted three trees lying tangled across it. The swollen river had ripped away the earth holding them. It meant some cautious climbing, but it was the best for which the Aquilonian could hope.

One tree was turned at a precarious angle, but it seemed to support the other two well enough despite that. All the foliage was on the opposing side, which meant that Nermesa would have little obstruction for most of the way.

Climbing over the roots, he tested the firmness of the makeshift bridge. The main trunk constantly shook, but seemed to stay in place. Water washed over it, but Nermesa felt that if he kept his legs wrapped around the trunk, he would be safe.

Sword sheathed, the knight put himself in position, then began sliding his way across. Progress was slow, but at least consistent. It was hard to maintain a grip with his hands, the tree was so soaked. Yet, inch by inch, Nermesa neared his goal.

Utterly drenched as even the rain had not been able to do to him, he finally made it to the first branches. Unfortunately, this also proved his first obstruction. Nermesa was forced to draw his sword and hack away until he created a gap. Only then did he dare sheathe the blade again.

He was forced to rise. The trees continued to rock, but

Nermesa had become accustomed to their motion. He started to climb his way through the tops of the fallen giants, the other bank now enticingly close.

A rumble momentarily shook his resolve. If the storm began again in earnest before he reached the other side, it would cause him much trouble. He pushed faster, taking a bit more risk in exchange for the extra distance covered.

The rumbling continued without pause, even building up in intensity . . . and Nermesa realized only then that it could not be thunder. He looked upriver, the direction from which the deafening sound came.

A great wall of water came rushing toward him.

Nermesa tore through the foliage, trying to reach the bank. Only a few more yards, and he would be safe.

His foot tangled in the branches. He tugged it free, but then had to continue to battle through the maze of greenery.

The knight looked up as the thundering reached a crescendo.

Water engulfed Nermesa and the trees. He used the branches to maintain his hold, hoping that the worst of the surge would soon play out.

A low, lingering groan arose from beneath him. The trees shivered violently . . . then began to shift.

The one to which Nermesa clung began to turn over, sending him toward the raging water. The surge pounded at him, half-drowning the Aquilonian even before he plunged into the river.

Nermesa feared that the tree would keep turning until he was completely under it, but it became further entangled with one of the others. He was left with his head just above the surface. The tangled trees turned in the swollen river, following the harsh flow. Nermesa had no choice but to hang on as he was swept along.

The savage waves battered at him. The wriggling branches scraped his flesh. The Aquilonian gritted his teeth and prayed to Mitra that he would somehow survive. He had to reach the others and warn them of Khati's evil and Caltero's treachery.

The trees bounced madly as they continued their wild trek down the stormy river. Nermesa's grip slipped, only the mangled mass of branches—most now stripped of their leaves—keeping him from being lost. He grabbed for one particularly thick one, then succeeded in pulling himself back to the trunk.

His lungs felt filled. Nermesa coughed and choked, but the river would not let him completely regain his breath.

Then, with a collision that almost jarred the knight free again, the trees came to an abrupt halt. For several seconds afterward, Nermesa, certain that the reprieve was only temporary, continued to clutch the trunk tight. When at last he concluded that the trees would not be moving immediately, the weary Aquilonian dragged himself up out of the water.

Straddling the trunk, Nermesa glanced ahead. A bend in the river had soundly caught the trees and other debris. The continued force of the water would likely break them loose again eventually, but Nermesa hoped that he would be on dry land long before that happened.

Still deluged by water, Nermesa crawled toward the bank. He had no idea where he was. The landscape rose high in this region, and the forest was thick. Despite his desire to reach his comrades, Nermesa had no choice but to return to the side upon which he had originally found himself. He could only hope that at least his tumultuous ride had sent him closer to where his fellow soldiers would cross.

The tree rocked as he wended his way, but did not come free. When Nermesa finally set foot on solid—if soaked—earth again, he immediately dropped on his face. For some minutes, the battered noble lay there, forced to waste what he considered precious moments for his own recovery.

The instant that he thought that he could, the Aquilonian pushed himself up and started moving. One hand clutched tight his sheathed sword, whose continued presence he saw as a gift of Mitra. That Nermesa might not have the strength to draw it—much less use it—was a concern he would worry about if the necessity arose.

The rain came down, but after what Nermesa had suffered

in the river, it hardly bothered him. His garments clung to him, and beneath his shirt he could feel the shaman's pouch. Nermesa thought about tossing it away, but decided not to waste even that much strength. Reaching his goal was all that mattered.

That proved more difficult than ever. Both banks continued to rise, the river cutting a channel through what had once been a single high hill. Nermesa had no choice but to ascend, which made each muddy step feel like five.

Lightning flared. Nermesa constantly glanced across the river but did not see the column. For all he knew, the rain had forced them to halt for the day. If so, while it would mean a longer trek, it would also ensure that he would reach the crossing before them.

Again came the lightning . . . and this time Nermesa froze; the outline of a Pictish warrior had been revealed in that flash.

He ducked behind a tree, then fumbled for his weapon. Dark though the day might be, it was still possible for the Pict to see Nermesa if he looked hard.

Sword free, the Aquilonian came around the other side of the tree. The Pict remained where he was, his attention focused away from Nermesa. The knight moved as quietly as he could to a nearer tree, then another.

Closer and closer, Nermesa came to his quarry. Once, the tattooed warrior glanced over his shoulder toward where the Aquilonian stood, but clearly did not see his enemy approach.

At last, there were no more trunks between Nermesa and the Pict. A few scant yards separated them. Nermesa could cross the remaining distance in seconds, but those seconds could also be enough for the Pict to notice him and prepare to defend. Weary as he was, the knight feared that he would not be able to take on the native without the element of surprise.

Nermesa took a deep breath, raised his sword, and stalked quietly toward the Pict. Each step was measured to prevent some noise from alerting his foe.

The Pict shook off some of the rain that had settled on his shoulders . . . and as he did, he happened to look Nermesa's way.

The desperate noble lunged.

He drove his sword through the turning Pict's side, the steel halting at the rib cage. Nermesa's foe grabbed at the blade, cutting his fingers as he sought to pull free. The native called out, but thunder drowned out his warning. Nermesa continued to shove the sword, at the same time clamping a hand over the warrior's mouth.

The wound proved too much for the Pict. His eyes grew glassy, and his body shivered. The hands fell to the side . . . the Pict himself dropping moments later.

His breathing rapid, Nermesa eyed the body. Only now did he wonder what this Pict had been doing here. It had almost seemed as if he had been a sentry . . . but for what?

Nermesa belatedly realized that the land ahead sloped downward again. Forgetting the Pict, he trudged forward a few steps, trying to make out any hint of the column. It was possible that they *had* moved on and might even now be across the river.

But as lightning flashed, it revealed instead a sight that left Nermesa colder than the foul elements did.

The land below swarmed with tattooed warriors armed to the teeth.

A vast force of Picts was moving east . . . toward the unsuspecting column.

18

THE HORDE BELOW made the warriors he had fought
against in the battle near Anascaw seem a paltry handful.
Even from a distance, Nermesa could see that their numbers
included many more tribes. The Aquilonian swore, knowing
that these must be the ones summoned by Khati in the name
of Gullah.

She had moved swiftly after his escape. How she had
convinced the headmen of her continued favor by the savage god was a mystery. She had intended his sacrifice as
the sign of her supreme power.

A horrific thought came to Nermesa. Had she used Caltero's ripped and bloody form instead? Possibly she had
been able to convince them that it was Nermesa's. That
made the only sense.

And now Khati intended to further prove the favor of
her god by trapping and slaughtering the column.

She had no doubt known through his cousin that a
search and reprisal assault were being organized. It made
for the perfect show of might. With so many Aquilonians

slaughtered, there would never again be any questioning of her leadership.

More than ever, Nermesa had to get past the Picts and warn the others.

Then, the sound of drums drew his attention farther westward. He peered through the rain and mist . . . and saw Khatak's sister astride her mount, the supposed camp follower now riding like a warrior queen. She wore a high, feathered headdress such as he had seen on great chieftains, and her face was painted with jagged, black lines that gave her a predatory, feline look. Her breasts were cupped by brass, and at her side she carried a sword of Aquilonian make. Behind her flowed a fur cloak from what Nermesa guessed had been a bear. Both beautiful and fearsome, she radiated utter confidence.

Adding to her daunting image was a horrific display attached by rope to the saddle of her horse. The heads of Nermesa's men hung in a bundle, their vacant eyes staring out. They were not the only ones, either, for the stunned knight also saw at least half a dozen Pict heads, likely from foolish rivals. The grotesque ornaments bounced against the leather and mount as if cheap goods carried by a merchant, not the grisly remains of unfortunate souls.

Around Khati, scarred, foreboding warriors moved as if in the presence of a goddess. When she barked an order, they hastened to obey like frightened children. Impressively, for all the size of her force, the Picts barely made a sound as they moved, and what little they did was certainly drowned out from the ears of the column by the storm.

Nermesa glanced to the east, then back at Khati. A grim determination overcame him. His odds of reaching the soldiers had grown to nil with the coming of the Pict horde, but there was one way yet by which he might avert disaster.

If he could capture Khati, the knight might be able to tear apart her coalition. The tribes were held together by fear and power. If Nermesa proved that Khati was not Gullah's favored, then the horde might break apart.

It was perhaps a mad notion formulated by an exhausted

mind, but it was the best course of action Nermesa could devise. He planted himself against the nearest tree and studied the Picts. Somehow, he would make his way to Khati and seize her.

Surveying the throng, an idea came to him. In addition to her own kind, Khati's force also consisted of the brigands who had served her half brother. They were a disreputable-looking, filthy bunch that included not just half-breeds like Khatak, but exiled Aquilonians, Bossonians, and more.

And as he presently looked, Nermesa could have easily passed for one of them.

He tore off any traces of his military aspect from his garments. The boots were no trouble, being caked with mud and scratched badly by his journey. Nermesa looked as if he had looted a merchant or dead soldier. Only his sword risked giving him away, for the rain had washed it clean, and its newness still shone through. He sheathed it, instead grabbing the ax the dead Pict had carried.

Hoping that he passed for one of the bandits, Nermesa worked his way toward the back of the horde. He watched those nearest, waiting to make certain that no one would notice when he joined in the march.

The moment it seemed safe, Nermesa slipped from his hiding place, matching the pace and stance of those who had just passed. With each step, he shifted toward the center, where Khati rode.

As Nermesa looked again at the mounted figure, one of the brigands next to her glanced his way. Nermesa immediately grinned as savagely as he could and raised the ax as if in anticipation. The brigand grinned back and brandished his rusty sword.

Emboldened, the Aquilonian picked up his pace. At the same time, he studied those mounted bandits near Khati. They would be his greatest threat when he grabbed her.

Time was rapidly running out. Nermesa had a fairly good notion as to how far the Picts and brigands still had to journey before they reached the place they intended to ambush the column. If the knight was to make his move, it would have to be soon.

He was almost within range of her. Intent on the tableau before her, Khati paid no mind to one more minion. Her thirst for power and revenge had her so focused that Nermesa believed that he could walk up next to the woman, look her in the eye, and still not be recognized.

He casually looped the ax on his belt. Both hands would need to be free for what he planned.

Nermesa could almost touch the horse's flank now. The bobbing heads often twisted his way, almost as if to remind him that if he failed, he would soon be one of their number. Some of the Pict heads were even fresher than those of the Aquilonians—

And one of those, wearing an almost toothless grin of defiance, was *Tokanu's*.

The appearance of the shaman's head among Khati's horrific trophies must have so startled Nermesa that he had made some sound, for Khati immediately turned in the saddle and glared down at the knight.

He had been wrong; the intense blaze filling her eyes gave clear indication that, despite his wild appearance, Khati immediately recognized Nermesa.

"You . . ." she growled like a wolf. "The lion warrior!"

Nermesa attempted to seize her arm, but she twisted out of reach. Several of those around them looked to see what the commotion was about.

"Take him!" Khati demanded to the brigand who had earlier locked gazes with Nermesa. "Quickly!"

Somewhat befuddled, the shaggy, scarred bandit nonetheless obeyed quickly, swinging hard at the Aquilonian with his sword. Nermesa pulled free the ax and parried the attack, then retreated. Caught by surprise, his adversary stumbled, allowing Nermesa time to drop the ax for his favored sword.

Khati reached for the blade by her side, one that Nermesa suspected she could wield as well as—if not even better than—Khatak. Aware that he now faced certain death, Nermesa quickly lunged at the brigand, running him through. He moved to meet Khati, but two more of her followers ran toward him.

Nermesa made a quick estimate and realized that his chance to capture her had utterly disappeared. He was forced farther and farther back from Khati.

The first of the pair to reach the Aquilonian proved no match whatsoever, perishing from a stroke across the throat. The second was more competent, if wild. He survived mainly due to his rapid, wide swings.

Others began converging on the hapless noble. Nermesa cut his foe deep in the sword arm, forcing the other away, then was nearly ridden down by a mounted bandit. As the rider neared again, Nermesa desperately slashed at the other's leg.

His blade cut true. Clutching the long gash across his thigh, the brigand cried out. At the same time, he accidentally pulled on the reins, bringing him back around to Nermesa,

Aware that he could do nothing more here, Nermesa seized the opportunity afforded him by the rider's instinctive action. He pulled the wounded brigand from the saddle, tossing him headfirst into the ground. Even before his adversary hit, the Aquilonian had jumped atop the beast.

A Pict attempted to do to him what he had done to the bandit. Nermesa rewarded him with a solid kick to the face. With an audible crunch, his boot struck the warrior full in the nose. As the bleeding Pict stumbled around, Nermesa veered his stolen steed around and rode for the forest.

Cries warned him that he was vigorously pursued. Daring to look back, he counted at least five men on horseback, with that many more on foot following.

He also saw Khati. Curiously, her expression had relaxed. She watched the pursuit calmly, almost confidently. The "lion warrior" was proving himself no danger to the favored of Gullah.

Nermesa entered the deeper forest. All sight of Khati

and the horde vanished behind him. The sounds of pursuit, however, grew nearer. Nermesa urged his mount to greater speed, but the uneven ground and tightly bunched trees made it difficult going. Those giving chase seemed less bothered, perhaps having ridden through this region before.

His horse stumbled. Nermesa managed to escape being thrown, but the near accident stole valuable time from him. He heard movement from his right.

A sword slashed at him. Had the Aquilonian not instinctively ducked, his head would have been in the next instant bouncing against the trees. The bearded cutthroat who had almost decapitated him swore loudly, then jabbed at Nermesa's side. Nermesa twisted, but this time was only partly successful in evading injury. The edge of the blade scraped along his thigh, leaving a thin, red trail.

Ignoring the sting, Nermesa thrust at his foe, but trees came between the two mounted fighters. The knight watched for the bandit, but neither could reach the other.

But if he had lost one adversary, Nermesa quickly gained two more. From his left rode in a heavyset giant wielding a twin-edged hand ax, which he promptly attempted to bury in the neck of Nermesa's horse. Behind him came a more lanky bandit upon whose body several belts holding daggers hung. The smirking figure had two in his free hand and looked more than capable of tossing both simultaneously. He tried to maneuver around the ax wielder, but the latter, laughing with gusto, continued to make wide swings at Nermesa. The Aquilonian knew that, unless he did something quickly, sooner or later, by sheer luck alone, the huge brigand would land a fatal blow.

Nermesa ducked under the giant's guard. He jabbed twice, drawing blood both times, but his attacks only seemed to infuriate, not incapacitate, the bandit.

A dagger flew by Nermesa's ear, burying itself but a moment later in the tree next to him. The second cutthroat readied another toss, then had to pull out of the way as the path narrowed.

Seizing the opportunity afforded by one less foe, Nermesa

slowed his own mount. The ax wielder growled as his target fell behind. He twisted back, weapon raised.

Bending low, Nermesa sliced through the strap holding the bandit's saddle on.

The saddle slipped to the side. With it went the giant.

The brigand struck hard against a tree, bending around it as if suddenly spineless. The harsh sound of his collision shook even Nermesa. The tree shook violently, then stilled.

His own mount suddenly shrieked. The animal staggered. A red streak, quickly diluted by the rain, coursed down the horse's leg.

A dagger stuck out of its shoulder. The Aquilonian did what he could, but the blade lay deep. The horse twisted in pain, turning Nermesa this way and that.

The first of his pursuers suddenly reappeared, slashing at him from the other side. His seating precarious, Nermesa nonetheless met each attack with a counterattack, finally cutting through his adversary's guard and catching him in the stomach.

As the brigand toppled, Nermesa's mount stumbled. Weakened by its wound, it lurched to the side, tossing the Aquilonian off.

Nermesa collided with a tree as he fell, but fortunately the blow was glancing. He slid to the ground, momentarily stunned. His wounded horse continued on, oblivious to his predicament.

Two other horses raced past, the dagger thrower and another brigand pursuing what they thought was Nermesa. The knight kept still, aware that he was too shaky at the moment to fight them. As they disappeared beyond him, he considered what to do. His foolish attempt to capture Khati had gone completely awry. All that remained for him was to find some way he still might warn the column that they were riding into disaster.

Keeping an eye out for other pursuit, Nermesa headed back. If he could sneak around the Picts and bandits, he still had a chance, however remote. Yet, there was nothing else the knight could think of to do.

The clatter of hooves warned him of the approach of a rider from behind him. Nermesa whirled . . . just as another dagger buried itself deep into the trunk nearest him.

Swearing profusely, the brigand pulled another blade free.

Nermesa charged him.

The mounted bandit tossed the new dagger, but the Aquilonian deflected it with his sword. As the lanky figure reached for another, Nermesa came up and sliced him across the stomach.

Life fluids pouring from the savage wound, the dagger thrower slumped. Nermesa grabbed for the horse's reins, but the animal, spooked by the fighting, pulled out of his reach. The noble made another desperate try, managing to snag the reins with two fingers. He wrapped them tight and tugged.

The horse slowed, acknowledging his mastery. Nermesa moved to sheathe his weapon—

A monstrous shape dropped from the foliage above, unleashing a terrible roar as it landed before the Aquilonian.

The bandit's mount shrieked. Seeking to escape the hulking monstrosity, the animal whirled away. In doing so, it tore the reins from Nermesa's tenuous grip, almost ripping his fingers off in the process.

The all-too-familiar stench assailed the knight. A gigantic fist hammered him. Nermesa flew back several yards, landing between a pair of oaks. His other hand jerked, sending his sword flying to the side.

Somewhere beyond, he heard the horse flee. Then, a shadow loomed over him. Blinking frantically to clear his vision, Nermesa stared up at his unearthly nemesis, the thing that had hunted him for both Khatak and Khati.

"Mitra . . ."

It was covered in coarse, thick fur, brown overall but with streaks of silver around the head. Seen clearly for the first time, Nermesa gauged the giant to be almost twice as wide as he, with huge muscles. The hands were clawed and reasonably human, but the feet . . . the feet almost resembled hands themselves, and the toes bent much as fingers would.

A simple loincloth was all the monstrous figure wore. There were numerous scars across the heaving torso, possibly the result of manic scratching by the victims of its bestial wrath.

And the face . . .

There was a man there . . . and yet, there was not. The brow was low and the eyes black and animalistic in their ferocity. The nose was broad and flat with huge, flaring nostrils. The mouth . . . the mouth was round, thick-jawed, and filled with yellowed teeth, including savage, scarred fangs and a huge, blood-colored tongue.

It was the god of the Picts, He Who Lives in the Moon . . .

Gullah.

Gullah roared, his cry both human and not. He lunged down, seizing the Aquilonian before Nermesa could recover from his astonishment.

The god's strength was incredible. Nermesa was lifted as if he weighed nothing. Huge arms pulled the knight into a crushing embrace. Gullah breathed into his face, the sickly-sweet smell of the giant's carnivore breath by itself almost enough to kill Nermesa.

The Aquilonian struggled to free himself, but Gullah had arms of iron. Nermesa's bones were crushed together. The air was shoved out of his lungs.

Gullah snorted. His face contorted into something even more hideous.

With a sudden rage, he released Nermesa, who tumbled backward. The man-beast took a step away, again snorting as if somehow the human was more offensive in odor than he. Gullah swatted his own nose, seeking to rid himself of some smell.

Coming to rest on the ground, Nermesa wondered at his amazing reprieve. Khatak's god moved as if having been sprayed by a skunk or worse. Somehow, something about the noble drove the giant mad to the point of distraction.

The sight served to wake Nermesa to the fact that this

was no invulnerable deity. Gullah this might be, but it was a very mortal Gullah . . . which meant that it could bleed.

Or so he hoped.

Nermesa sought his weapon. The sword lay a few yards to his right. He would have to get to his feet, then hurry to it before his horrific foe recovered.

With no other choice, Nermesa leapt for the sword. The instant he moved, Gullah roared angrily. Breathing heavily, the god bore down on the Aquilonian as Nermesa's hand closed on the hilt.

The furred demon spun him around. Nermesa managed to hold on to his sword, but the awkward angle prevented him from making any use of it.

Once more, Gullah lifted the human, pulling Nermesa until the latter's chest was nearly against the god's nostrils. The yellowed fangs came menacingly close.

But with a howl, the man-beast flung him back again. For a second time, Gullah reacted as if Nermesa radiated the most noxious odor possible.

It was clear, though, that the thing would not abandon the hunt. Gullah kept back only enough to cleanse his nostrils of whatever offended them, his fearsome orbs remaining fixed on the knight.

Nermesa touched his chest . . . and felt the soaked pouch the shaman, Tokanu, had given to him. Some herb, concoction, or other item within was anathema to the murderous creature. Thinking of the shaman's head hanging among the other grotesque trophies, Nermesa realized that the elder Pict had so desired the downfall of his rival that he had sacrificed to the Aquilonian his own protection from Gullah. It had likely been the one reason that the defiant shaman had lived so long.

But without the pouch, Tokanu had been easy prey for the man-beast, who had likely not been far behind the knight's trail.

And now, the tiny bag was all that had saved Nermesa, but for how long?

Not daring to wait long enough to find out the answer to that, the bedraggled fighter steadied himself. Gullah growled, the hairy giant sizing up his would-be victim. In that moment, as their gazes met, Nermesa knew that here stood an intelligent being, not an unthinking animal. It momentarily unnerved the Aquilonian, for he again wondered if this was indeed the Pictish god. However, then he recalled the effect of the pouch. This might be some being who wore the form of Gullah, but he *had* to be flesh and blood.

Nermesa lunged.

Gullah—Nermesa knew not what else to call his ferocious foe—snarled, then leapt up. One hand seized hold of a thick branch and the man-beast swung up into the trees. Nermesa took a last stab, but the brutish figure vanished among the soaked foliage.

But he had left his mark on Gullah. The blade's tip was newly daubed with crimson. A small wound, but a telling one. Gullah was still a nightmarish thing, but was very much mortal, indeed.

A harsh, cracking sound echoed from above.

What seemed half the tree came crashing down on Nermesa. A branch as huge as himself nearly crushed him, the knight barely dodging at the last moment. Unfortunately, no sooner had he avoided that when he heard another crack above and a second collection of great branches rained down on him.

This time, he could not avoid them all. One of the larger branches caught him a sharp blow in the side. With a pained grunt, the Aquilonian fell against another tree, his sword hanging limply.

Only barely did he hear Gullah leaping down behind him.

"No!" Gripping his weapon as best he could, Nermesa swung wildly. He encountered resistance.

A thundering howl filled the region.

But barely a moment later, a savage fist pummeled his back. Thrown forward by the blow, Nermesa stumbled through the forest. In his wake, he heard grunting and the shaking of foliage above. Aware that at any moment the trees might again come falling, the Aquilonian kept moving.

In spite of his own precarious situation, Nermesa still worried about his comrades. The Picts and brigands had to already be where they could ambush the searching column. Time was running out.

Ignoring his injuries and wounds, Nermesa turned in the direction of the upcoming battle. Perhaps he could lose Gullah somehow.

There was no sound from above, but that did not mean that he was safe. Nermesa kept watch on the canopy, hoping that if his horrific adversary did follow, he would at least be able to glimpse the creature before it was too late.

He came across the body of the huge, ax-wielding bandit. Nermesa thought of adding the heavy ax to his defenses, but found its weight imposing. Searching quickly through the corpse's pouches, the Aquilonian found a small bit of dried meat. It was salty and tough, but it was sustenance. He took it with him, eating on the run.

Where was Gullah? Had he returned to his mistress? Where they had found this man-beast was a question that burned in Nermesa's mind. The wilderness was a place of remarkable and exotic creatures. Was Gullah one, or had he come from elsewhere?

He doubted that he would ever discover the answers and, in truth, the secret of Khatak's god was one that could wait, supposing that Gullah himself would permit that. All that mattered was the column.

Nermesa heard the rustling of leaves. He flung himself to the right, hoping that his random decision would not lead him directly into Gullah's clutches.

Something round and very massive buried itself in the earth exactly where he had but the moment before stood.

The rock was far greater than any Nermesa could have lifted even at his most fit. In truth, Nermesa doubted that two men could have hefted it. Certainly, they would have been unable to toss it with such incredible accuracy.

He anxiously looked above, seeking the monstrous entity.

Gullah's arms wrapped around the startled knight from behind, squeezing the life from him.

Nermesa groaned as his ribs threatened to cave in. He felt the hot breath on his neck.

Some inner sense warned him of further catastrophe. Nermesa twisted his head forward. Gullah's fangs, intent on his neck, instead scraped his shoulder. Nermesa gasped as they tore his skin.

He frantically reached for the pouch. Gullah's grip had caught him on an angle, which just enabled Nermesa to free the shaman's token. Unable to do anything else, he tossed the pouch over his shoulder, the leather loop wrapping around his throat like a hangman's noose.

The pouch must have bounced against the giant's face, for Gullah shrieked, releasing a gasping Nermesa a moment later.

Summoning his strength, the Aquilonian whirled, bringing his sword around for a hard slash.

He caught the furred behemoth across the chest, the sharp blade leaving a rich, deep valley over the center. The bestial maw opened in what in a human face might have been shock.

Gullah stumbled back. He touched the bloody ravine, then sniffed his crimson fingers.

Nermesa lunged.

The blade bit deep just below the wide cut. The new pain stirred Gullah again. He angrily grabbed at the Aquilonian, only to cut his fingers on the sword. Deep red tinged the widening black orbs.

Howling, the man-beast reached to his left and tore a branch from the nearest tree. Swinging the makeshift club, he attempted to swat Nermesa. Gullah's breath came in heavy pants as he lumbered forward. Despite both that and his wounds, however, his strength was still phenomenal. With his heavy weapon, the gargantuan figure batted away whatever lay in his path. One strike of the branch would shatter Nermesa's skull.

Nermesa felt his own strength waning. If he did not act

fast, Gullah would surely catch him. The knight studied the swings, trying to estimate how long each took. He would have one opportunity and one only.

But midway into another swing, the creature released the branch. Instead of a club or pike, it became a missile. Caught unaware, Nermesa left himself open.

The branch struck him in the stomach. Nermesa doubled over.

Gullah roared lustily and leapt.

The Aquilonian attempted to retreat, instead slipping on the drenched ground. The demonic giant filled his wide-eyed view.

Gripping the sword with both hands, Nermesa swung at the oncoming behemoth.

The god of the Picts fell upon him.

19

KHATI'S EAGER EYES watched as the Picts and bandits took up their positions along the hilly forest path. The easterners would soon be passing over the river and from there would have no choice but to enter here, the place of their destruction. This victory would ensure her supremacy. There would be no doubt among the People that He Who Lives in the Moon favored her. She would be queen of the Picts, her kingdom expanding all the way through the so-called Territories and beyond.

Even reaching, eventually, the home of the invaders, Tarantia.

A hirsute brigand who acted as one of her officers rode up to report. Although he was of Aquilonian origins himself, when he spoke of those in the column, it was with as much venom as any Pict. "The soldiers're comin' along at just the same pace as before! They'll arrive like we hoped!"

"Do they suspect?"

"Not a bit." He laughed. "Like sheep to the slaughter!"

She nodded, then gave him an imperious wave of

dismissal. All fell into place as Khati intended, a sign that she was truly favored by the spirits. Gullah truly watched over her.

Thinking of the god brought her focus back to the bane of her existence, the cursed lion warrior, Nermesa. The spirits had been strong in him, and his countless escapes from death had perturbed her more than Khati had let on to her followers. His sacrifice before the headmen of the tribes would have not only solidified her influence over them but eased her own qualms.

The outlander had to be dead by now, though. He was clever like the fox and as ferocious as the badger, but this time he would not escape his doom. Her Gullah would tear him apart, rip open his throat, then bring the mangled pieces back for her pleasure.

It had been she and her brother who had first found the giant in the northern hill lands. Khatak's band had retreated there after the invaders had attempted a strong thrust to rid the wilderness of his troublemaking. Her brother had been all for standing and fighting them to the death—his death most likely—but, as she had always done, Khati had counseled him into a more sensible decision. As she had suspected, the Aquilonians had not followed into the unexplored northern hills—a land plagued by unpredictable earth tremors— giving the brigands a chance to regroup and recover.

And while they had been doing so, she had come across the cave. Khatak and she had intended it for use as a place to store their ill-gotten gains, for who would search in such a desolate region? Even the rogues they commanded would not be able to find it.

But the cave proved an unstable place, with treacherous ceilings that crumbled loose when a new tremor struck. It proved not to be the first such catastrophe to occur in the cave of late, either. The two found evidence of another, very recent collapse . . . and in the process discovered that they were not alone.

He lay pinned under the shattered ceiling, injured and stunned. Clearly he had lain so for several days. Khatak uttered the name that had forever changed their lives. *Gullah*. The being before them had looked as the god was described by the shamans, but clearly no god could have been held prisoner by mere stone.

Khatak had been for leaving the unnerving man-beast to his fate. Yet Khati saw immediately the potential for such a being. Convincing her brother to help, they alone freed the imprisoned giant and she had, over the next few weeks, treated his wounds by herself. During that time, her quick wit had enabled the Pict to learn much about their new companion.

Most important, there had been a mind behind those black eyes, and it seized upon the brother and sister as saviors. Gullah—what more appropriate name for him?—was clever, to a point, quickly learning and obeying the signals and gestures they taught him.

When Khatak's band learned of the giant, they reacted just as Khati expected . . . with fear and awe. It was then that her plan grew. Khatak's father had been a brigand like himself, an eastern exile who had chosen life among the People. He had been a man of power, and when he had died, Khatak's mother had married one of her own, Khati's father. Through Khatak, Khati had learned to see beyond merely the tribal ways. Her ambition to be more than the mate of a warrior grew, and she had no difficulty convincing Khatak, wise enough to see her intelligence, of her value as a spy and planner.

But the discovery of Gullah had given her an even greater ambition. Together, she and Khatak could use him to draw the People to their efforts. As the easterners had their single rulers, so, too, would the Picts.

That Khatak had perished before that day could come had angered her. She had also feared that her people would slip away now that there was only her—a female—to lead them. Fortunately, Gullah had removed the first with such intentions, and the rest, seeing how the "god" had punished those turning against Khati, had fallen back into line.

She glanced over her shoulder, but there was no sign of

him. By now, he should have caught his prey. Perhaps the riders had gotten in his way. Khati shrugged; if they were foolish enough to do so, then they deserved whatever he did to them.

She shook off all concern about the lone Aquilonian's surviving. His blood would be hers. Gullah wanted him as much as she did. She had learned how to read the giant's emotions. Gullah would let nothing keep him from destroying Nermesa this time.

Just as she would destroy the unsuspecting soldiers ahead.

Khati rode tall, thinking of the victory, the many heads that would decorate the People's spears. Her puppet, Caltero, had made that possible. She had wrapped the lovesick fool around her finger and made him willing to sell his own kind for the pleasures of her body. Only with his cousin had he felt some guilt, and for that failure to her he had paid. His own battered, torn corpse had made an adequate imitation of Nermesa, at least as far as the tribal leaders had been concerned. The resemblance between the two had been sufficient, especially since the battering his face had taken had removed any noticeable difference. Besides, the headmen of the tribes barely knew one Aquilonian from another.

Her reverie was interrupted by another brigand far ahead. This one waved, then pointed eastward. The moment was nearly at hand. Her followers were in position, and the unsuspecting column crossed the river.

Khati smiled, and though her teeth were not filed in the manner of a warrior of her kind, they was no less predatory. She could smell the invaders even from so far away. The Aquilonians carried a stench upon them that revolted any of the People. Soon, that stench would be erased. Khati could already taste the many deaths to come.

Licking her lips, the Pict urged her mount on.

COME, NERMESA . . . RISE . . . you can't lie there and die . . .

The Aquilonian shook as something within him stirred. He wanted to inhale deeply, but some terrible force all but crushed in his chest. Vague memories of the monstrosity against which he had been fighting rose up. Had Gullah beaten him to a pulp and left his broken body to the elements? Could the reason that Nermesa could barely breathe be that his ribs had been crushed into his lungs?

You can't die out here . . . not you, too . . .

The voice in his head was not his own, yet, there was a comfortable familiarity about it. It gave him encouragement. Nermesa fought open his eyes . . .

And stared straight into the horrific countenance of Gullah.

The knight gasped, certain that the man-beast would next bite off his face. Yet Gullah did nothing but stare down, fanged mouth open.

Open . . . but emitting no breath.

Nermesa looked into the eyes. As fearsome as they were, he gradually saw in them a lack of focus. Gullah did not stare back at him . . . Gullah simply stared, unseeing.

The god of the Picts was dead.

Struggling, Nermesa managed to get a hand up by the giant's chest. A moistness covering the furred body almost made the hand slip, but the Aquilonian persevered. Summoning his strength, he pushed.

Gullah's limp body tipped to the side, sprawling on the ground next to Nermesa.

The effort cost him. Pain ripped through his body. Nermesa started to black out.

Don't let the darkness claim you . . . fight it . . .

He knew that voice. His lips struggled to form the name. "Q-Quentus?"

There was no response, of course. Vaguely, Nermesa knew that all he heard were his own thoughts. Quentus was merely the form his addled mind had used to drive him on.

It served well enough. Forcing himself to stay conscious, Nermesa pushed himself slowly to his feet. His eyes remained fixed on the blood-splattered giant lying next to him, as if at any moment Gullah would prove to be the god the Picts believed him and come back to life to punish the Aquilonian.

The man-beast stayed very dead, however, the blood congealing on his chest. Nermesa's desperate swing had cut a fatal swathe from the lower side of one breast up through the throat. Despite his monstrous size, Gullah must have died almost instantly. Momentum had kept the body going, however, and in death the giant had nearly claimed the knight.

Thinking of his sword, Nermesa glanced around anxiously. Fortunately, the blade lay not far away. Nermesa vaguely recalled its being knocked from his grip as his huge foe barreled into him.

He stumbled over to the weapon. In his weakened state, it felt as heavy as Gullah. Nonetheless, he gratefully gripped the sword, aware, though, that his one victory did not mean he was safe from harm. There were likely still searchers in the forest, and even if that were not the case, hundreds of Picts lay between him and safety.

The rain had ceased, and a mist covered much of the soaked region. Nermesa stood motionless for a moment, uncertain as to his next move. He did not even know in which direction lay the ambush.

A trickling sound caught his attention. Water. Either runoff from the storm or maybe even a stream. Despite the inherent dampness all around him, he turned toward the sound, suddenly very thirsty.

The source of the trickling proved farther than he had thought it would be. Nermesa slashed at the undergrowth as he searched for it. The water became of overwhelming importance to him.

At last, he came to a narrow stream coursing through a small clearing. The pristine water enticed Nermesa. He went to the edge, set the sword aside, and drank.

It seemed as if he had never tasted anything sweeter. The knight swallowed handful after handful. His thoughts cleared a little.

When he had finished drinking, Nermesa continued to

splash water in his face. That he would need to do so after nearly drowning in the river and being drenched by the storm seemed incongruous, but the splashing did help.

Finally satiated, Nermesa sat. Even though he knew that he needed to find his way back, he was also aware that his body had been through an ordeal. A few moments' rest was necessary.

But barely had he relaxed when a low growl set the hair on the back of his neck standing.

This deep in the wilderness, the presence of wolves should not have surprised him. Moving slowly and cautiously, Nermesa shifted his head so as to locate the animal.

It was not a wolf . . . not exactly. There were lupine features, but they were mixed with canine ones. This was no natural denizen of the forest but rather a mix of wolf and hound. The hound must have been a huge beast itself, for the product of its mating stood far taller than any wolf. It had a blunter nose, too, but long, sharp ears like its other parent.

A crude, spiked collar decorated its throat, the sharp, rusting nails almost as long as Nermesa's hand. The gray-brown beast eyed Nermesa with hungry orbs.

The Aquilonian began to slide his hand toward his blade.

Another low growl from the opposite direction made him freeze again immediately.

He managed to shift his head just enough to see the second creature, one clearly of a similarly mixed heritage. The second was slightly smaller than the first, but no less imposing because of that. It, too, wore a spiked collar.

A third then shuffled through the brush, its evil face bearing the worst aspects of both parents. Nermesa knew that these could only belong to Khati's bandits. Someone, perhaps even she, had had the intelligence to unleash the animals on him. The Aquilonian had certainly left enough of himself—especially his blood—for the villains to use to give their hounds the scent. The cessation of the rain had proven just what the animals needed.

Nermesa glanced around but saw no sign of their handlers. They could not be far behind, however. More to the point, the brigands likely did not even worry about catching up. These beasts appeared trained to kill . . . which, in the case of Nermesa, was exactly what their masters desired.

Again, he attempted to slide his hand closer to the sword. The moment his fingers moved, though, all three animals growled, and two took steps toward him. When Nermesa stilled, they did likewise, at least temporarily.

But sooner or later, they would have his measure; and then they would attack. Nermesa had to decide whether he wanted to instigate things or react to their move.

He grabbed for the sword.

The dogs charged.

His legs unsteady, the knight met the first beast, slashing at its muzzle. The animal howled and dropped back, a wicked red scar along the right side of the jaw. If anything, though, the wound only seemed to infuriate the dog. It snapped at Nermesa, seeking his hand.

At the same time, the other pair closed. One leapt for his throat, while the other dove low. The desperate Aquilonian kicked at the second, managing to shove it back, but the weight of the first sent Nermesa back. The knight fought to keep his balance, knowing that if he fell, the dogs would have him.

Slavering jaws snapped at his face, his throat. Doing his best to avoid the spiked collar, Nermesa used his free hand to keep the monster at bay, at the same time slashing with the sword at the other two beasts.

Claws tore at what remained of Nermesa's shirt. He grunted in pain as the nails scored his chest. With a growl of his own, the Aquilonian finally threw the beast from him. The wolf-dog whined as it hit the ground, then quickly scrambled to a standing position.

The dog to his left chose then to try to take Nermesa down. This time, the fighter was ready, though, and as the beast leapt, he skewered it through the stomach.

But as the one perished, the third also lunged. It snapped at Nermesa's leg. He struck it soundly on the head, forcing the jaws away, but not before they had broken the skin.

The two animals pulled back. Taking a chance, Nermesa leaned forward, and shouted, "No!"

The two dogs instinctively cowered at the harsh command. At this point, Nermesa looked enough like one of their masters. The reaction lasted only a moment, though, the animals rising and growling once more.

Yet the hesitation was all that Nermesa had sought. He thrust at the nearest, the sword's tip going deep in the side of the neck.

The dog let out a howl and turned away. Blood streamed from the wound. The animal was dead but did not yet realize it.

The loss of its other companion in no manner shook the last and largest of the hounds. It charged Nermesa even as he drew back his blade from the attack on the second dog.

This time, the knight could not keep on his feet. He and his canine foe collapsed in a heap of snarling fangs and grasping fingers. Nermesa's sword proved more hindrance than help, and he finally let go of it.

When at last they ceased rolling, it was Nermesa atop the beast. A primal fury surged through the Aquilonian. He had survived betrayal, blades, and the horror of Gullah. He would not let himself perish at the jaws of a hound!

Nermesa's fingers slipped below the deadly collar and tightened on the beast's throat. The dog's actions grew more agitated. Claws raked the knight, but he paid them no mind. Nermesa squeezed.

He heard the crack of bone and felt flesh and sinew give way. The massive animal shook violently in his grip, but Nermesa refused to let go.

Finally, with a last, strained grunt, the dog went limp.

It took Nermesa several seconds more to recognize the dog's death. Hands shaking, he let go of the body.

Looking up, the Aquilonian saw no sign of the third beast. He had no fear of it, though, certain of its imminent demise. Exhausted, Nermesa located the sword, then returned to the stream. He washed the blood and drool off as best he could, taking special care on his new cuts.

As Nermesa leaned forward to wipe his face, he caught sight of himself in the water. Even considering the distortions caused by the running water, the man he saw staring back at him startled the noble. Under the cuts and bruises was a face he did not recognize save that it bore some distant resemblance to his father. It was not the young, untried visage of Nermesa Klandes, not even the one of a few short days ago.

Shuddering, Bolontes' son pulled back. He remained by the stream just long enough to clean off the blade. The weapon still looked new despite the battles and deaths of which it had been a part.

And there was yet one more it needed to join.

Nermesa looked around, trying to estimate exactly where he had to go. Keeping the sword ready, he stumbled on.

The Aquilonian constantly glanced at the overcast sky. "Mitra," he muttered once. "Give me the strength and speed to make it there in time . . ."

But even if he did, Nermesa had no idea what he could do to salvage survival—much less victory—for his comrades.

He trudged through the forest, listening constantly. As of yet, no sound of battle echoed in the wilderness. Nermesa prayed that it was no trick of the land that kept the cries and clashes of steel from his ears.

Thunder roiled, and lightning occasionally flashed. No new deluge fell, but if it had, Nermesa would not have been daunted. He would reach the others somehow.

Then, in the underbrush, the knight saw a large, furred shape. It did not move, but Nermesa recalled the third dog. If still alive and very wounded, it might be crazed enough to attack.

However, the furred form did nothing as he neared, and finally Nermesa got close enough to recognize it.

He had found his way back to Gullah without realizing it. Nermesa pondered his path. He had not been moving in as straight a line as he had imagined. He had wasted more precious minutes.

The monstrous visage seemed to smile mockingly. Nermesa wondered if the Pict god had actually had something to do with his meandering trek. Was this Gullah's revenge for slaying his mortal shadow?

As he paused to rethink his path, Nermesa heard the snort of a horse. Muscles taut, the Aquilonian hid among the underbrush near the massive corpse.

Mere seconds later, an unsavory figure astride a black charger rode into sight. Long brown hair plastered to his head and shoulders, the scarred and bearded brigand looked none too pleased to be out in the forest. In his right hand he held a stained but quite usable hand ax, and at his side was sheathed a sword. The brigand wore a breastplate that had once adorned the chest of an Aquilonian knight.

The newcomer peered warily from under thick brows, his slanted eyes taking in everything. Standing, he would have been taller than Nermesa. His animal was a powerful beast, one with markings also indicating its past as part of Aquilonia's military.

Nermesa tried to keep his breathing quiet, but each inhalation and exhalation sounded in his ears like the thunder. He was certain that the bandit could hear him, yet the latter made no sign.

Then the rider abruptly straightened. He pulled sharply on the reins. The bandit glared in Nermesa's direction, almost causing the Aquilonian to leap out.

The rider urged his mount closer. He held the ax ready, but not as if he believed a battle imminent.

Just yards from where Nermesa hid, the bandit tugged on the reins again. Eyes ever staring ahead, he dismounted. Guiding his horse along, the hunter took a few tentative steps . . . and stopped at the body of the man-beast.

A string of epithets escaped the villain's lips. He halted the charger, then bent down to investigate better the startling discovery. The bearded bandit ran his fingers along the massive wound, expression one of utter disbelief.

A noise from far away made the rider leap to his feet in nervousness. Nermesa, too, all but jumped. It was impossible to mistake the sound for anything but what it was.

The distant clash of arms.

Khati's followers had ambushed the soldiers.

An intake of breath escaped Nermesa. He tried too late to smother it.

The brigand whirled.

Nermesa leapt from the underbrush, roaring as he closed on his pursuer. The startled rider deflected his first attack but made no attempt to follow through. His expression was filled with shock and dismay. Nermesa must have looked like a demon to him.

The knight gave the other no quarter. Bringing his blade back around, Nermesa sliced through his foe's weapon arm. The brigand screamed as his limb hung loosely. He scrambled to pull his sword free with his remaining hand, but the awkward angle left him wide open for Nermesa, who ran him through.

As the brigand dropped, the Aquilonian grabbed for the horse's reins. He need not have feared that the charger would attempt to flee, however. The horse was seemingly unperturbed by the bloody struggle before it. Nermesa again marked its likely training as a steed of war and thanked Mitra for delivering unto him such a fine choice.

With the charger, he could still reach the battle and at least lend his hand. That it was too late to do anything else greatly distressed the knight, but he would at least not stand idly by while his comrades perished.

As he mounted, Nermesa's gaze fell upon Gullah, the source of much of the Aquilonians' troubles. It had been fear of the god that had enabled Khatak and Khati to stir up the Picts. As his favored, they had set the entire Westermarck and wilderness on the path of destruction . . .

His eyes narrowed. Nermesa studied the horrific face closer.

Fear of Gullah drove the Picts . . .

20

IT HAD FALLEN to Konstantin to lead the column out following the disappearance of both Nermesa and Caltero. While more than willing to take on the role, Konstantin would have much preferred either of the other two to be here . . . but then, if that had been the case, the column would have never gone out at all.

It was Caltero's vanishing that most disturbed the commanding knight. He understood Nermesa's disappearance, however dreadful it had been. That had been the impetus for gathering together the finest of the Westermarck's protectors. Caltero, on the other hand, was a story with far too many questions. The elder Klandes had seemingly ridden out on his own without giving any word to his comrades. While it was most likely that he had gone in search of his cousin, Konstantin could not understand why he had first ordered this march, then had not even waited for the troops to collect.

Konstantin was wary about leading the soldiers into this area, but he was a man who followed his training. Logic said to proceed on this path and mete out retribution to the tribes. That was what his superiors had taught him. If he found either cousin alive, that was an added bonus, but not necessarily his concern. The Picts had to be taught their place; that was it.

And yet . . .

Per his training, he sent out scouts to survey the region. They all returned with reports of no Picts or bandits ahead. That did not entirely assure Konstantin, but as a loyal soldier of the realm he had no choice but to push forward.

The column reached the river without trouble. Konstantin wasted no time in sending the first elements over. Within a short period, the efficient work of the Aquilonians had more than half the soldiers over and standing ready. Even the storm-swollen waters made for little trouble, the stone-and-wood bridge designed to withstand the worst of the wilderness's turbulent weather.

But as the last of the column wended its way across, disaster finally struck.

During all this time, the scouts had not seen any sign of activity, any sign of even one Pict. Yet, from seemingly the earth itself, the land filled with howling, tattooed warriors and savage brigands. They so easily caught the column in a vise that Konstantin had to assume that somehow they knew the Aquilonians' methods as well as he did.

"Form ranks! Quickly!" he shouted. "Archers! At the ready!"

But even as his own, well-trained men moved into position, a flight of arrows dropped among them. Soldiers fell by the dozens, and lines splintered. Officers shouted more men up to the front, but the attackers were already nearly upon them.

The Aquilonians brought their shields together, forming a sturdy line of defense, and Konstantin began to relax. Then he noted that the hordes of Picts continued to come without end. Even without being able to count the enemy, the lead knight realized that the savages and their allies outnumbered the soldiers by several times.

We cannot possibly hold against so many! Konstantin knew . . . and yet, they would have to. They had no choice.

And then the Picts swarmed the lines.

Konstantin did not shirk from the battle, riding in and cutting down an overzealous warrior. Two more perished by his blade, but his effort seemed like nothing. All he could see were savages. They wore the symbols of at least a dozen different tribes, yet they fought as if one. It was far worse than even the battle near Anascaw.

It was all too well orchestrated. Konstantin could only assume that either Caltero or Nermesa or both had been tortured into relaying what information they knew about Aquilonian tactics. Someone among the Picts had learned quickly and well from that stolen knowledge. The enemy had been waiting in just the right place at just the right time and knew just what to do. It was as if their leader was as familiar with the Aquilonian military as any soldier in Scanaga.

And understanding that, Konstantin also realized that, barring a miracle from Mitra, the chief defenders of the realm's western border were going to be slaughtered to a man.

Then there would be no one to protect Scanaga and the other settlements . . .

WITH EACH CRY, with each ring of steel, Nermesa's pulse raced. Even with the charger making the best of the terrain, he feared that it would be much too late to turn the tide. Worse, Nermesa was not even certain that what he planned would have any viable effect. The Picts might be too caught up in their bloodlust even to notice him other than as an enemy needing to be slain.

Nevertheless, he urged the charger on. Hoping to make the run easier, Nermesa had stripped the animal of everything but the saddle. Now, only a single cloth sack fully filled bounced against the horse's flank. As for the Aquilonian himself, he had been forced to forgo the brigand's breastplate, which was too cumbersome for his form. Nermesa fully expected to die, but if it meant life for others, he was prepared. He had already asked Mitra to watch over his parents and had even said a prayer for the king. If the Picts won here, they would continue east as far as they could push.

Lightning flashed, briefly turning the landscape bright and surreal. Thunder roared, but it could no longer obscure the sounds of battle.

And as Nermesa pulled up at the top of a ridge, he came upon the struggle.

As he had feared, the soldiers were trapped. They could not retreat properly back across the river without opening themselves up to an even easier slaughter. Picts guided by Khati's bandits fell upon them from the remaining directions. The Aquilonians were putting up a good defense, but there were so many Picts.

Nermesa momentarily sat there, daunted. He saw now how foolhardy his desperate plan was. He would only get himself quickly slain by the first warrior to turn his way. There was still hope for him if he simply turned and fled for his life.

But the son of Bolontes could not do that. He remembered again those men who had perished under his command, especially Quentus. A grim cast to his expression, Nermesa studied the Picts, seeking the place where he might best be seen by many. All hinged on the tattooed warriors noticing him quickly.

He was certainly a sight. His shirt hung in ribbons, his hair flew wildly, and his body was etched with long red cuts. His skin was otherwise so pale from his trials that he looked as if he had perished, not Gullah.

Thinking of the savage god, Nermesa no longer hesitated. Drawing his sword, he turned to the pouch. With one swift cut, he opened up a gap large enough to remove the contents. Gripping them tight in his other hand, he seized the reins with the one holding the sword and took a deep breath.

"Yaaaa!" With that scream, Nermesa drove the black charger down among the combatants.

• • •

THE PICT WARRIORS eagerly poured forward, each hoping to gain a kill before there was no one left to fight. They pushed at the defenders, axes, blades, and spears seeking Aquilonian blood. Victory was a certainty; after all, Gullah watched over them.

Then those on the farthest flank heard a wild cry above their own and, in the next moment, a deathly white, demonic figure astride a horse of shadow barreled into them.

His eyes flared with the lightning, and his hair seemed to have life of its own. The latter spread wide, giving the astounding figure a very leonine appearance. He roared like the animal, daring any to meet him. To the Picts, his body—far more pale than that of any of the invaders—further marked him as a ghost, a spirit.

The sword he wielded cut through startled warriors as if they were but water. A neck flowed, a stomach spilled open. Such was the fury of this unnatural warrior that only token resistance was given by those caught in his path.

Eager for blood, the demon carried the reins of his shadowy steed between his clenched teeth. This not only enabled him to put his blade to good use, but allowed his other hand to hold high a large object.

And when the first Picts saw what he held forth, their hearts shriveled, and their courage waned. It was not possible. Such a thing could not be.

The leonine demon triumphantly held aloft the goresoaked head of Gullah.

There could be no greater sign of disaster. They had all either heard of or witnessed their god's power. Sacrificial victims had been torn apart, and they who had Gullah's favor had spoken of the glory that the tribes would garner. Yet now this lion spirit revealed that even Gullah was no match for him. Worse, his striking down of the People's warriors meant that he favored the invaders, not them.

Against such a vision, no Pict would fight. First one, then another turned from the battle. Those farther on who noticed this action looked for the cause and saw the same terrifying image. Outlined in lightning, the lion warrior swung Gullah's head left and right, defying any to argue with his supremacy.

The few fleeing became many. The horde faltered as even those too distant to see the ghostly rider came to understand that some catastrophe had befallen the tribes. They joined their retreating companions, adding to the masses escaping the struggle.

Those who had been facing certain death took immediate advantage. The Aquilonians finally organized their lines, pushing back those Picts still remaining. Such a shift further disheartened the remaining warriors, and the last elements holding against the soldiers began to crumble.

But the battle was not yet over . . .

AND FOR NERMESA, it had barely begun. He cut a swathe through the Picts, unmindful of his own fate. All that mattered was to keep them unsettled so that the other soldiers could make good their escape. That they might stand and fight now that the tribes were on the run did not even occur to the knight. Nermesa fully expected to die and die soon, and all he cared about was to send as many Picts to hell before him.

With manic strength, he drove through their warriors. The few spears raised against him snapped under the weight of his swing. The charger, guided by his desires, trampled more than one screaming foe. The leering head of Gullah served as well as any weapon, the staring eyes and fanged mouth turning strong fighters into quivering children.

Several bandits sought to stem the tide. With curses and the flats of blades, they forced Picts back to the fray.

Scowling, Nermesa confronted the group. The Picts eyed him anxiously but at first held their ground. The four brigands in charge of them shouted angrily, trying to get them to attack the lone rider en masse.

Hardly caring anymore if they did, Nermesa raised the god's head high. Then, with a cry, he *threw* it at the Picts.

It was enough. They turned and ran from the macabre missile as if Gullah himself were about to slay them. Khati's brigands tried to order them back again, but only succeeded in turning the warriors' frenzy against them. Axes and spears quickly slew the four, but, for once, the Picts did not take the heads. They continued on, fleeing from the spot where Gullah's head had landed.

To the east, the clash of arms grew louder. The Aquilonians were on the move, swarming over those Picts still hesitating. A few warriors paused to fire bows, but their hearts were not in the effort, and most of the shafts landed without causing harm. Knights with lances rode down an entire row of Picts, tossing some of the impaled fighters up into the air like rag dolls.

The banner of King Conan flew triumphantly over the drama. Nermesa saw Konstantin among the foremost riders. The bearded, red-haired noble swept past a pair of bandits, his arcing sword taking both in one masterful stroke. Khatak's former followers were the only real resistance left, and their numbers were quickly falling.

Pausing, Konstantin happened to glance Nermesa's way. The other knight gaped in recognition.

Nermesa raised his sword to the other Aquilonian. Konstantin returned the greeting, then quickly urged his mount toward his comrade.

"Nermesa! You live! Praise Mitra—" The armored figure looked aghast as he surveyed Bolontes' son. "At least, I *think* you live! What has become of you?"

"Never mind! Just keep pressing the Picts! They can't be allowed to regroup!"

"Aye, we'll do that all right, now that the battle's turned for us . . ." Konstantin smiled grimly. "And the reason for it must concern you, friend! I'd almost say that your appearance alone could be enough! How did you do it?"

Memory of the struggle flashed through Nermesa's mind. "I showed them that their god had feet of clay." Konstantin looked puzzled, but Nermesa could delay no longer. Turning his mount, he once more ordered, "Keep pressing them!"

"But, Nermesa! You should stay with us—"

"I can't!" And with that, the heir to Klandes abandoned the other knight.

The Picts had been routed, and the bandits would soon be wiped out, but to Nermesa, the threat continued for as long as Khati was free. He did not underestimate her, even now. She would slip once more into hiding, then somehow seek revenge. For all those who had died because of her and Khatak's ambitions—settlers, soldiers, General Boronius, and even misguided Caltero—Khati could not be allowed to escape into the wilderness.

But where was she? He scanned the area and saw no sign of her. Certainly, Khatak's sister was hard to miss. Had Khati already fled? If so, she could be anywhere.

A manic-eyed Pict attempted to spear his horse. Nermesa shattered the spear, then ran his blade through his tattooed adversary's throat. Such victories now meant nothing, not if he had failed to seize the mind behind the evil.

Then a frantic rider crossed his gaze. A brigand seeking to flee the debacle. Nermesa stiffened. If anyone knew where Khati would go, it would be one of her own.

Urging the charger to its fastest pace, he pursued the lone bandit. The latter paid him no mind, concerned only with getting as far from the Aquilonians as possible. Still, Nermesa felt certain that eventually the cutthroat would return to his mistress.

Picts continued to get in his path, but most had no lingering interest in fighting. The few who did quickly learned that it was fatal even to slow Nermesa for a moment. He brooked no interference with his pursuit. By the time the Aquilonian neared the deeper forest again, he had left in his wake a trail of wounded and dying warriors.

Twice Nermesa lost sight of the brigand, but both times he managed to catch up. Thunder and lightning continued to war above, but the sounds of the battle he had left dwindled until finally nothing could be heard.

Khati was close; Nermesa was certain of that. He clenched the hilt of his sword tight in anticipation. She would not be alone, that much he understood. Even after the calamity behind them, there would still be those who would fight to the death for her. She was a seductress, a witch of men's hearts.

Again, the bandit he pursued vanished, this time around a bend. The land here was hillier, but no less forested. Nermesa leaned into the charger's mane, seeking to cut the wind resistance as much as possible. Anything to keep on the hunt.

As he came around the turn, a brutish figure leapt from the trees above.

The Aquilonian's first reaction was to think that Gullah had come back from the dead. However, the savage face that pressed against his own proved to be, despite its ugliness, only human. The brigand tried to force him from the saddle, but only succeeded in slowing Nermesa's mount.

Thick fingers sought the knight's throat while others brought up a stained knife. Nermesa struck his adversary hard with the fist holding the sword's hilt. The added mass of the hilt was enough to crack the villain's nose. Blood splattered the eyes of Nermesa's foe.

As the brigand attempted to blink his gaze clear, the Aquilonian again smashed his face with the one fist. The snarling fighter bent back, and Nermesa used the opportunity to throw him from the charger.

But no sooner had he done so than a second cutthroat rode up to duel with him. Their swords clashed twice before Nermesa cut the man on the shoulder. However, before he could finish the bandit, another attacked from the opposite side.

Nermesa's strength and skill were tested. He had to bring the sword back and forth to meet each attack. The two ambushers struck as quickly as they could, calculating that one of them would soon get past his guard.

As he fought them, Nermesa heard mocking laughter from somewhere higher up in the terrain. Mocking *feminine* laughter.

That his struggles had now become amusement for Khati infuriated Nermesa. Adrenaline flowed through him.

Nermesa was well aware that, should he survive this, he would pay a terrible price for his abuse of his body, but he had no choice.

Taken aback by his sudden resurgence, his two opponents grew careless. Their attacks became wild, untimed chops at the Aquilonian.

Against such unskilled assaults, Nermesa easily prevailed. He caught the rider to his left under the arm, opening up a stream of red. As the brigand grasped at his wound, the knight continued his swing to the second fighter. Deflecting the other's sword, Nermesa drove his own blade into the attacker's stomach.

He immediately whirled back to the remaining bandit, easily finishing off the wounded rider. Even as the second man fell, Nermesa glanced up and around . . . but of Khati, there was no sign.

Cursing, he moved on. From the sound of her laughter, she had been standing atop one of the two nearest hills. Praying to Mitra that he had chosen correctly, Nermesa headed up the one on his right.

The forest grew thicker still as he ascended. Somewhere, he knew, Khati would have some nefarious trap in mind. Nermesa was now aware that he had not entirely made his choice to trail after her on his own. Khati had read him well and, as she had retreated, had planned for just this chase. The Pict could have simply vanished into the wilderness, but, like her brother, she had a need for vengeance that overrode all else. She had probably seen Nermesa pursuing the lone brigand and arranged accordingly.

And if she succeeded in slaying him, Khati would still likely escape. Nermesa doubted that any of Konstantin's soldiers had followed this far. There was still too much havoc going on back at the site of the battle for them to be concerned with a few escaping warriors and thieves.

Which left Nermesa all on his own.

The terrain grew more uneven. Forced to pick its path, the charger slowed almost to a crawl. Nermesa's gaze darted back and forth, seeking his quarry.

Khati's laugh came from his left. Nermesa quickly turned his head—

The Pict stepped out from behind a pair of trees and threw a handful of powder in his face. The Aquilonian had no choice but to inhale much of it.

He swung at the retreating figure. Khati laughed again, and, as she stepped back, she literally *melted* into the landscape.

Nermesa shook his head, unwilling to believe what he had just witnessed. He steered the horse toward where she had stood, trying to make sense.

His eyes burned. Nermesa tried to wipe them clean, but that only made the sensation worse. More worrisome, the forest around him had begun to take on a murky, unnatural appearance. The trees seemed to be stretching their branches toward him as if seeking to grab the knight. The ground began to dip back and forth as if a great hand tipped it, and a curious yellow mist suddenly pervaded everywhere.

"You slew Khatak . . ." came Khati's voice. "Can you slay him again? And again? And again?"

And suddenly the nearest trees began to change form. They grew human limbs and their roots combined into strong legs. Their knotted skins transformed into faces— no *one* face. One sinister and familiar face.

That of Khatak.

A full half dozen Khataks converged on Nermesa. He swung at one after another, but his blade always seemed to just miss the mark. The Khataks gave him that awful, crooked smile that still haunted the Aquilonian's nightmares, then attacked. Swords came from everywhere. Nermesa met one blade after another, but although he managed to deflect some, others cut him. Each strike, though mostly shallow, stung as if it had gone straight to his heart.

"My brother will have your blood . . ." Khati continued to mock from somewhere in the woods. "and through him, I will, too."

Another Khatak lunged. Nermesa parried, then thrust.

This time, his blade sank deep. The Khatak cried out, then collapsed.

As he did, he transformed into another bandit.

The transformation both startled and pleased Nermesa. Emboldened, the Aquilonian jabbed at another, but the tip of his sword instead slid off the face without leaving so much as a scratch.

Nermesa fought to focus. He realized that the powder was having this effect on him. It was one of Khati's sinister concoctions. This was not magic, but mesmerism. The powder made him susceptible to her words. Some of these attackers were real . . . but they were only her minions, not the dread Khatak come back to life.

Despite that certainty, Nermesa could ignore none of the blades that bit at him. Any one of them might be real.

He had no choice. Kicking hard, Nermesa urged the charger on. If he could not tell which Khatak was a true threat, then he would soon die. He had to push beyond them in the hopes that a few moments' respite would enable him to clear his head.

The animal started forward—and two of the Khataks drove their blades through its neck. The wounded steed shrieked and turned toward the Khatak on the right. Unfortunately, the stricken animal made it only a few steps before tumbling. Nermesa leapt at the last moment, ending a few precious yards from his ghostly foes.

Through the fog both within and without, he saw the blood drenching the dying animal. There was a vicious wound on the left side . . . but none on the right.

Nermesa looked up, focusing on the Khatak who had caused the wound. With an angry growl, he ran at the figure, shoving his sword through as hard as he could.

This Khatak did not avoid injury as the previous had. Instead, he gasped, then, with a shiver, dropped his own weapon. As the figure slumped, his features contorted, becoming, like the first to perish, those of a slack-faced half-breed not at all resembling the dread villain.

Shoving his foe away, Nermesa whirled. Four more Khataks remained, but one he immediately marked as illusion, it being the attacker whose weapon had made no wound in the horse's neck. He started toward the rest, trying to estimate which was the product of Khati's poisonous powder and which was not.

One of the Khataks moved more hesitantly than the others. Acting on a hunch, Nermesa assailed that one, but kept his eyes on the others. His target met his blows with increasing trepidation, then, suddenly, bolted.

Nermesa had no time to follow through, for the remaining Khataks were then upon him. They moved with utmost precision. Too much, in fact. As the Aquilonian struggled to keep the blades from his hide, he saw that, like the known illusion, one to his left moved only when the others did and even mirrored their swings.

Hoping that he guessed true, Nermesa ignored all but the last two. He thrust again and again at them, ignoring all else.

One of the latter left himself open. The knight plunged his weapon through the Khatak's stomach. As his victim doubled over, one of those he had ignored imitated the agony.

Eyes narrowed, Nermesa growled to the Khatak in front of him, "And you're the last . . ."

In response, the final ghost dropped his sword and fled. Nermesa turned to face the next Khatak . . . and found that the figure had disappeared without a trace. Illusion caused by the powder and Khati's suggestion, just as the knight had suspected.

His body screamed for rest, but Nermesa dared not falter. Instead, he raised his sword high, and shouted, "Your brother's dead again! Your tricks have failed!"

"You will still die, easterner!" Khati's voice all but spat. It sounded so very near, yet Nermesa could still not find her in the murky forest. "Your bones will I crush and my poison will burn your blood . . . my bite will tear your flesh . . ."

Nermesa's head pounded. He knew that the effect of Khati's powder had been amplified by his own weakness.

The weary Aquilonian inhaled deeply as he stumbled around in a circle. If he could clear the powder from his body with fresh air, Khati's mesmerism would surely lose its hold over him.

But still the landscape weaved—nearly sending him to his knees—and the shadows now seemed to gather together in one great mass. That mass began to move, too, undulating in a monstrous fashion.

Nermesa stepped back as a black form abruptly rose before him, a form in no manner human.

"Crush your bonesss, poissson your blood, and tear your flesh . . ." Khati repeated, her words now coming from the huge shadow. A sibilance touched her voice, one that made him think of another creature despite his best attempts not to do so.

And as he thought of that fiendish creature, the shadow *became* it.

The serpent rose high, looming several feet over Nermesa. Black as the shadows it was, and when the mouth opened, the fangs and the long, forked tongue that darted out were equally dark. Only the eyes held any other sense of color, but they were perhaps the most unsettling feature of this demonic horror.

They were the eyes he recalled from Scanaga, from the fort. And from his bed.

They were the eyes of Khati.

"Come, lion warrior . . ." cooed the giant shadow serpent. "You once desssired nothing more than my sssweet embrace . . ."

"No more!" snarled Nermesa, lunging at the thick form. Much to his dismay, though, his blade passed through the coiled body. "Rather would I bed the viper I once found in it!"

"A viper your cousssin brought for me . . ." The snake laughed. "I will show your crushed body to the tribes! They will sssee that I am stronger than he who has ssslain Gullah!"

"After this day, they won't ever believe in you, Khati . . ."

Again, Nermesa lunged, but once more his blade had no effect.

It's all illusion! he insisted to himself. *The powder is at fault! This is no more real than the Khataks or that Gullah was a god!*

"They will listen when they see your head . . ."

The long, sinewy tail shot up like a whip, snapping around Nermesa's throat with astounding swiftness. The Aquilonian seized it with his free hand, but could not remove the snake's coiled form.

The coil tightened. Nermesa's breathing was cut off. He began to choke.

"Let me caress you, hold you tight . . ." Khati murmured. The eyes bored into his own. "Let me send you to my brother . . ."

The pressure on the knight's throat doubled. Nermesa was seconds away from suffocating.

He slashed with his sword, but found nothing in terms of resistance. Yet the pressure on his throat was all too real. Khati was indeed strangling him just as readily as any serpent. But how could she?

Nermesa began to black out. He dropped to one knee. Somehow, Khati had him, but if she did not stand before him—

Fumbling with his sword, Nermesa turned it toward his own body. It grew difficult to think. He had but seconds . . .

With what remained of his might, the Aquilonian thrust the blade behind him, aiming upward.

A shriek deafened his ears. The tightness around his throat grew harsher . . . then abruptly ceased. Nermesa, starving for air, released his sword and tore at his own neck, removing the last vestiges of constriction.

The flailing tail of the shadow serpent wriggled in his palms. Refusing to accept such a vision, Nermesa bit down on his tongue until he drew blood. The pain did what nothing before had. The tail stilled, then shriveled, changing shape at the same time.

In its place, a tanned leather cord just perfect for such a treacherous task materialized.

A coughing fit overcame him. He rolled forward, fearful that Khati would still manage to plunge a dagger in his back while he was defenseless. Yet nothing happened, and gradually Nermesa found himself able to breathe normally again. As the Aquilonian looked up, he saw, too, that the mist and shadows had faded and that the ground no longer swayed.

Then, Nermesa remembered Khati.

He spun around, still certain of disaster . . . and met again the eyes of Khatak's sister.

But, like those of Gullah, they were eyes that no longer saw.

Khati stood staring, her back against an oak. Her fingers were still curled tight, as if she yet hoped to strangle Nermesa. The Pict wore the garments he had last seen her in, the garb of the warrior queen Khati had dreamed herself to be.

She would have seemed such to Nermesa even now, if not for one other adornment but recently added . . . his *sword*, buried at an upward angle just below her rib cage. The force of the Aquilonian's last hope had also driven the blade well into the tree trunk, which was why in death Khati could not fall.

Nermesa seized hold of the sword and unceremoniously tugged it free of both obstructions. Khati did not tumble forward, but rather simply slumped down to a kneeling position, her back still against the trunk. Her expression seemed one of hatred and defiance, as if she would give neither Nermesa nor death the pleasure of seeing her lying on the ground like a slaughtered rabbit.

Nermesa did not care. At the moment, nothing mattered. He had stopped the killing, had avenged those who had perished because of her and Khatak. All he wanted to do now was to find some peace.

Sword dragging, the son of Bolontes staggered from the area. He looked in vain for one of the brigands' mounts, but could not find any. With no other choice, Nermesa simply started walking. He hoped that he still had presence enough of mind to remember which direction would lead him back to the battleground and prayed to Mitra that the way would be clear of wandering Pict warriors. Nermesa doubted that he could have fought so much as a squirrel now. It was hard enough to walk, much less fight.

Yet, walk he did, trudging through the forest. With the last sounds of battle having long faded away, all that was left was an eerie silence. Nermesa stared straight ahead, focused only on finding the other Aquilonians.

As he walked, Quentus's voice again urged him on. *Not much farther . . . not much farther . . .*

Even knowing that it was his own mind using his friend's shade, Nermesa drew comfort from the memory. He straightened, not wanting to disappoint his friend.

Almost there, Nermesa . . . the voice constantly repeated. *Almost there, Nermesa . . .*

Nermesa . . . Nermesa . . .

"Nermesa!"

The knight shook his head, aware that something was different. It was no longer Quentus's voice.

"Nermesa!"

He stopped. Blinking, Nermesa looked up, discovering suddenly that he was surrounded by several riders. Immediately, Bolontes' son raised his sword to defend himself.

One of the figures leaned toward him. There was a flash of red hair. "Nermesa! 'Tis Konstantin!"

Konstantin . . . The exhausted knight's brow furrowed. Konstantin . . .

"Konstantin . . ." Nermesa muttered. "You?"

The bearded features of the other Aquilonian finally coalesced into an expression of grave concern. "Aye! We've ridden for an hour in search of you and now find you almost back at the river!"

"The river?" Vaguely, a rumbling sound pierced the fog of Nermesa's mind. The river. The river was east, near the battle.

"Praise Mitra, you're alive!"

"Alive." Somewhere deep in his thoughts, Nermesa heard Quentus's voice repeat the word. *Alive . . . Nermesa . . . alive . . .*

The other knight started to dismount. "Come! You'd better ride my horse until we can find you another."

Nermesa attempted to put away his sword, but for some reason could not find the sheath. "Is it—is it over? Did—did many die?"

"Some, but your startling arrival saved most and gave us the day! You're a hero, Nermesa! A hero!"

But Nermesa cared nothing about being a hero. He was only glad to hear that most of the soldiers had survived. The danger was over. The Picts had been routed and, without Khati, Khatak, or Gullah, they would not soon band together again.

"Over . . ." he whispered. Nermesa finally managed to locate the sheath. He slid the sword in, then smiled at the approaching Konstantin. "Praise Mitra . . ."

And, with that, he collapsed into the other knight's arms.

21

THERE WERE MORE dreams that followed, dreams and nightmares. He embraced Khati, only to have her become a giant snake that suddenly constricted around his body. Caltero was there, insisting that the snake was his but giving no aid to his suffering cousin.

Nermesa somehow struggled free of the serpent's crushing hold, only to find himself flying up toward the moon. The moon became Gullah's face, then swelled into a gigantic version of the Pict god. He pursued Nermesa through the heavens and as he did, his face transformed into Khatak's.

But the nightmares were more than overwhelmed by the other dreams. Khatak/Gullah faded away, and Nermesa discovered himself swimming in a public pool such as was found in Tarantia. The cool, clean water soothed his body, especially his worn muscles. There were other swimmers, their faces reminiscent of people he had known over the years. Most were slightly out of focus, but one feminine countenance caught his attention. For some reason, despite her features being more distinct, he could not identify her save that her hair was auburn.

Nermesa started to swim toward her, but then the scene shifted, and he was riding toward his parents. They held out their arms to him, but although he headed first for his mother, it was Bolontes who suddenly stood before him.

The elder Klandes opened his mouth. His words boomed like thunder, forcing Nermesa to clamp his hands over his ears. Bolontes appeared not to notice this, continuing to roar despite the fact that his son could not understand him.

But gradually, the words began to make some sense. "Son. Can you hear me? Nermesa . . . please . . ."

At that point, the dreams faded, yet Bolontes' voice did not. Darkness enshrouded Nermesa, but it almost immediately gave way to a dim, welcoming light.

And in that light, his father's distraught visage re-formed. "Nermesa!" The fear gave way to relief.

"F-Father?"

"Mitra be praised!" The graying patrician looked beyond his son. "Bring some water! Quickly!"

There was the sound of hasty footsteps, then Konstantin—of all people—appeared, a mug in one hand. The unhelmed knight grinned down at Nermesa as he handed the mug to Bolontes. "Looks as if I chose the perfect moment to check on you!"

Details of Nermesa's surroundings became noticeable. Armor and other gear hung on a wall opposite him. A brass oil lamp dangled from the ceiling, illuminating the scene. Nermesa's father wore brown travel garments, not the rich robes in which the son always pictured him.

To the elder Klandes, he asked, "Are we—are we still in the Westermarck?"

"Yes, son. In Scanaga."

Scanaga . . . a journey of at least a couple of days from where Nermesa last recalled being. More to the point, Scanaga was much, much farther from Tarantia, where last he had seen his father.

His father had journeyed all the way from the capital?
"How long have I—?"

"Some weeks," was all Bolontes would say in response. He tipped the mug by Nermesa's lips, helping his son to drink.

Konstantin filled in some of what was missing. "You were very ill. Wasted. Fever, chills, and more. Small wonder in the condition that you were found in. You had wounds all over your body, you'd clearly not slept or even rested for more than a day, and your clothes were shreds, giving you little protection against the elements."

"I was warned of all that when the messenger arrived from the palace," Bolontes interjected, his usually steady tone cracking. "But I insisted on the excursion out here nevertheless." He sighed, momentarily closing his eyes. "Even if it might be merely to bring back my son's body."

Nermesa managed to reach a hand to his father. The elder Klandes gratefully seized it.

Taking the mug, Konstantin added, "But by the grace of Mitra, he'll ride proudly alongside you, my lord Bolontes."

This caused Nermesa to stir. "What do you mean?"

"You're summoned back from the west! General Pallantides has demanded your return to Tarantia."

"But why?"

The other knight's brow arched. "Why? Because the king wants to see you again."

The king . . . Conan wished to see him again. For what he had done? Nermesa could not imagine why! It had been by sheer luck that he had survived and only by chance that he had managed to help the column."

Bolontes squeezed Nermesa's hand. "He will see the king soon enough, but first he must recover more . . . and his mother must be told that he has survived. Word must be sent to her immediately."

Bowing his head, Konstanin replied, "Of course, my lord. Nothing is of more importance."

Nermesa might have argued, but exhaustion overcame

him again. This time, however, it was a more comfortable, more familiar exhaustion.

"Sleep, my son," Bolontes said, seeing Nermesa struggling to stay awake. "I will watch over you. Sleep, then we shall see about feeding you. You've survived on little more than broth all this time. You're barely even bones . . ."

Nermesa did not argue with him . . . for he had already drifted off.

IT WAS TWO more days before Nermesa recalled being awake again. He woke with a horrific hole in his stomach, one that demanded to be filled before giving him any relief. Yet, despite his desire to consume whatever they could leave within his reach, Nermesa's father monitored his meals, allowing only so much at any one time.

"You will kill yourself if you eat until you want no more. I've seen it happen to soldiers held prisoner for days, then rescued. You must suffer a little more, my son, but not much."

And after another two days, Bolontes' words proved true. The hunger subsided. Nermesa could now think clearly. From there, he truly began his recovery, sitting up the next day and taking weak steps after three more.

Konstantin, interim commander of the Westermarck's military forces, visited him each morning and evening. Nermesa related to the redheaded knight all that he could recall—Khati, Khatak, Gullah, and Caltero included—and from Konstantin, Nermesa learned much about what had happened since. All reports were that the Picts had returned to their individual tribes and were now once more wary rivals of one another. More important, they had themselves begun to hunt down Khati's band to the point that more than one bandit had turned himself in, preferring Aquilonian justice to the tortures of the natives.

"The tribes blame them for the disgrace," Konstantin explained. "The Picts would take it out on Khatak and his sister if they weren't already dead. In fact, there's been more than one totem found bearing curse marks against their souls."

Nermesa found he could raise no sympathy for Khati. He had never met anyone so cruel and uncaring.

"So, there's no threat at all of the tribes gathering again?"

The other knight chuckled. "Still concerned. No, Nermesa. The Picts are very subdued, for the time being. There're tales spreading, too, of the fierce lion spirit who devoured He Who Lives in the Moon, then, still hungry, came among the warriors of the People and ate the souls of any who stood before him."

"That would be you, my son," Bolontes added.

"But—" Gazing into their faces, Nermesa saw that they made no jest. The Picts truly thought him some powerful spirit! How quickly they would have abandoned such notions could they see him now.

As if reading that thought, Konstantin continued, "The Picts know nothing of what is happening with you. I've had Scanaga cleared of them . . . especially the females who've frequented our section. While I'm here, that mistake won't happen again. I promise."

They let him rest after that, even the conversation sapping Nermesa of much of his remaining strength. The next day, the territorial judge came to see him and, not at all to Nermesa's surprise, knew Bolontes from years back. The pair had evidently served together when little older than the son was now.

"I saw his eyes that first time and knew he was you again," Flavian declared to the elder Klandes. "The blood of Bolontes of House Klandes. Just like his father!"

But Bolontes surprised Nermesa by shaking his head, and replying, "No . . . I could never have done what he did. Never."

A week more passed, then Bolontes declared his son and heir fit to travel by wagon. Despite Nermesa's protest, Konstantin provided an honor guard. As the wagon left the military section of Scanaga, people of the town lined up all the way to the outer gates to cheer him on. Nermesa wanted nothing of the fanfare, but such a decision appeared entirely out of his hands.

The wagon and its honor guard exited the eastern gates of Scanaga and, some scant hours later, the last of the territorial settlements. From there on, Nermesa slept through most of the journey and, before he knew it, the plains of Tarantia beckoned ahead.

And, as best, he could, the son of Bolontes prepared himself for once more entering the presence of King Conan.

IF ANY OTHER monarch, Conan would have insisted that Nermesa be brought directly to his court for a grand ceremony no matter what the "hero's" condition. But the Cimmerian was not like any other ruler. He had fought in many a war, suffered many a harsh wound, and so understood the realities. There was no grand assembly of the citizens at the gates of the capital, no trumpets announcing Nermesa's arrival. The wagon entered without notice, receiving only a respectful acknowledgment from those in command at Tarantia's entryway.

Conan demanded of Nermesa a week more recovery before coming to the palace, and Callista seconded his decree. She fussed over her son as if he were a newborn infant, doing tasks that one of her status would have normally left for servants. Even Bolontes could not countermand his wife in this instance.

There were no visitors, but one missive was sent to the House of Klandes that was of direct interest to Nermesa. It was an official document whose seal he did not recognize but knew that he should have.

The contents within were written plainly and to the point.

House Sibelio announces the binding of its Lord and Baron, Antonus, to Lady Orena of House Lenaro on the day of the Ram in the month of—

Nermesa crumpled the message, throwing it as far as he could across the chamber. He had chosen to end the arranged betrothal with Orena and had no regrets. If she thought that this abrupt marriage to the Baron Sibelio would somehow shame him, she was wrong. Nermesa intended to have nothing more to do with either her or her husband-to-be.

He only hoped that things would turn out that way.

AND WHEN AT last came the day when he was to stand before the king again, Nermesa found his legs shaking from something other than weakness. Pallantides it was who arrived at the Klandes residence, Pallantides in resplendent armor and with an honor guard of fifty Black Dragons awaiting them outside. Nermesa's neighbors already crowded the streets to see the spectacle, and as he and his parents—Callista in a stunning ivory gown and Bolontes in polished armor that fit him as well as it likely had as a youth—mounted, other inhabitants of Tarantia added to the growing throng, until the streets all the way to the palace were filled with cheering people.

Pallantides rode beside Nermesa, saying wryly, "The king may be one for subdued events, but the citizens of Aquilonia *should* acknowledge their saviors now and then . . . even if I must have word spread myself."

Nermesa would have preferred King Conan's way, but nodded his gratitude to the general nonetheless. He spent the rest of the trek waving to those on each side and hoping that at least in the palace there would not be such crowds.

That wish was not to be granted, however, for here the king diverged from what Nermesa knew of him and what General Pallantides had verified. As Nermesa entered the court of Conan—ahead of him, horns blaring loudly to announce the entrance of the reluctant savior of the west—he discovered that each and every one of the highest-ranking members of the king's council and the most influential citizens of Aquilonia stood waiting. At the calling of Nermesa's name by a herald, they broke into clapping that echoed much too loudly in the young Klandes' head. Face flushed, he marched along the thick golden carpet, Pallantides next to him. Nermesa's parents took up a place of honor at the front, Bolontes not at all looking reluctant to be in the presence of the ruler he had once only called "outlander."

Nermesa had even expected to see Orena and her new betrothed among those in the audience, but perhaps this particular honoring of him had been too much for her to suffer through. He gave thanks to Mitra for the blessing, then looked to the throne.

King Conan met his gaze, the Cimmerian's steely eyes taking the measure of the man before him. The muscular figure raised a hand for silence.

The clapping ceased.

"Nermesa of House Klandes," rumbled Conan, leaning forward in his throne. "I hear you've blooded your weapon well."

"Yes, your majesty," the knight returned, going down on one knee.

Conan, however, would not let him remain there. He gestured for Nermesa to stand again, then, he himself rose. Beside him, the queen smiled proudly at Nermesa. She turned to one of her ladies-in-waiting, a young and beautiful woman of the court. A woman with lush auburn hair.

A woman, Nermesa realized, who was Telaria.

He managed to hide his surprise at how much she had again changed. In truth, she now had the beauty of her elder sister but without the chill behind it. Telaria saw him glance her way and blushed.

"Nermesa of House Klandes," the king repeated louder, possibly to pull the noble's attention back from Orena's sister. "Aquilonia owes you much! First, the capture and slaying of Khatak the Brigand and now, the crushing of the Picts!" Conan grinned. "Ah! To have wielded a blade with you that day . . ."

"I did only what I had to, your majesty," Nermesa dared protest.

"But you lived . . . and you won." Conan faced the audience. "I hereby declare seven days of celebration for this man! Let all of Tarantia, all of Aquilonia, honor his name!"

The assembled nobility clapped and cheered. The king nodded in satisfaction as he looked over the throng.

Then, after the hall had echoed for several moments with accolades for the reluctant Nermesa, Conan again signaled for silence.

To the knight he asked, "Nermesa of Klandes, of all boons I may grant you, what reward now would you have? Medals, I think, are not you. A good blade have I given you already, and you seem so well matched that another would seem wrong. What will this warrior before me ask of his king? Tell it to me, and if it is in my power to grant it, then I will, by Crom!"

Nermesa had indeed expected some medal, nothing more, and so Conan's broad offer overwhelmed him. Yet, one thing immediately leapt to mind.

On his own initiative, the son of Bolontes went back down on one knee. He gazed up at King Conan—whose head was cocked in slight bemusement—and said, "Your majesty, if there's one wish you can grant me, it is this: I would serve you, serve Aquilonia as I have done so far! I would pledge my sword and my life to this task . . . and if at all possible, I would hope to do it as one of the *Black Dragons*."

Murmuring coursed through the audience. Nermesa took a quick glance in the direction of his parents. Callista frowned, but Bolontes nodded approval of his son's choice.

As for King Conan, he suddenly laughed heartily, then looked to where the commander of the Black Dragons stood. "What say you, Pallantides? Can you use a man with a fair sword arm?"

The general nodded once. "For him, my lord, I think that there can be found a place."

"Then so it shall be!" Conan stepped down to where Nermesa knelt. He placed a strong, sturdy hand on the noble's shoulder. "Nermesa of House Klandes! I grant you your boon! From this day on, you are one my elite! From this day on, you are a Black Dragon!"

Nermesa's honor guard, all members of that august group, shouted as one, "Hail, Nermesa! Hail!"

Their cry was taken up by the assembly. "Hail, Nermesa! Hail, Nermesa!"

At a signal from Pallantides, the horns sounded. King Conan bid Nermesa to rise and, once the latter had, seized his hand in a powerful shake. Nermesa gasped slightly at the strength in his monarch's grip.

Behind Conan, the queen rose to honor him, Telaria at her side. Nermesa acknowledged Zenobia with tremendous respect, but his eyes quickly shifted to Telaria. The pleasure he read in her expression made him flush.

" 'Tis an honor indeed!" bellowed the king, mistaking the reason for the reddening. "And an honor for me to accept the oath of a warrior such as you!" He turned Nermesa to face the rest. "Let us begin the celebration! All here will dine with my queen and I, Sir Nermesa to be seated in a place next to me! Pallantides! When our feasting is done, see to proper garb for my new champion! He is now a part of our court!"

"It shall be done, my lord!" the general said with a smile to both the king and Nermesa.

The cheering rose. King Conan stepped back to allow others to wish Nermesa congratulations. Men whom the young Klandes had seen only from afar and with awe treated him as if he was not only one of their own, but in some ways something more. He suspected it was a temporary situation, but it still nonetheless startled him.

Yet even through all the revelry, Nermesa did not lose sight of what he had asked of the king. He knew full well what the service of the Black Dragons entailed. Death was the most common fate of the king's elite, for there were ever those who sought either the downfall of the foreign-born king or even of Aquilonia itself. The evil of Khatak and Khati would one day prove slight compared to that of some other insidious plotter. When that happened, it might be that Nermesa would again be called upon to risk himself . . . and come that next time, Mitra *might* choose to take him up to the halls of the dead.

"Congratulations, Nermesa," murmured a familiar voice.

He looked to his side to see Telaria. Nermesa started to thank her, but suddenly could not find his voice. Was this the same young girl he had once considered only Orena's shadow? Certainly, up close, she was no longer a girl, but a true lady . . .

His continuing silence made her blush. Telaria suddenly leaned up and, before Nermesa knew what she was doing, kissed him on the cheek. "I'm proud of you . . ."

She vanished into the crowd before he could recover. The man who had battled Picts and cutthroats stared after Telaria like a lost schoolboy.

Someone slapped him hard on the back, jarring him back to the moment. A baron, whom he recognized only as a longtime competitor of his father, grinned at him as if Nermesa was his own son. "Congratulates, Klandes! We must talk soon! Perhaps you can put in a good word with the king about this proposal I have . . ."

But before the man could add more, another noble took Nermesa's attention, shaking his hand as he would an old friend's and also mouthing something about future business with House Klandes. One after another, the wealth and power of Tarantia swarmed Nermesa with suggestions of favors needed and potential profits. Everyone acted as if Conan had named Nermesa his heir.

They knew that he had the strong favor of the king, the young Klandes belatedly realized. Each hoped to benefit somehow from that, no matter what their past relationship— or lack thereof—with Nermesa and his family.

It occurred to him then that he had not considered this aspect when making his request to the king. War, he now at least understood something of. Despite its brutality, there was still a basic honesty to it. That was not the case with the politics of the kingdom, though. Nermesa even recalled how King Conan had acted when they had previously met. The Cimmerian had wished that he could come with the young noble and fight the battles out west. Better that than the intrigues of the royal court, surely a battle every day for the king.

And now, Nermesa, too, could expect to find himself immersed in the maneuverings of the nobility and wealthy, the ambitious and the treacherous. He had just stepped into the proverbial lion's den . . . with only a sword and his wits.

Yes, war could be brutal, but the politics of Tarantia . . . Nermesa realized that they might prove more deadly than any well-honed blade.

He could only pray that he would be ready when the first such battles began.

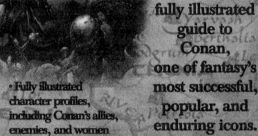

THE ULTIMATE IN
SCIENCE FICTION AND FANTASY!

From magical tales of distant worlds to stories of
technological advances beyond the grasp of man, Penguin has
everything you need to stretch your imagination to its limits.

penguin.com

ACE
Get the latest information on favorites like
William Gibson, T.A. Barron, Brian Jacques,
Ursula Le Guin, Sharon Shinn, and Charlaine Harris,
as well as updates on the best new authors.

ROC
Escape with Harry Turtledove, Anne Bishop,
S.M. Stirling, Simon Green, Chris Bunch, Jim Butcher,
E.E. Knight, and many others—plus news on the
latest and hottest in science fiction and fantasy.

DAW
Mercedes Lackey, Kristen Britain, Tanya Huff,
Tad Williams, C.J. Cherryh, and many more—
DAW has something to satisfy the cravings of any
science fiction and fantasy lover.
Also visit dawbooks.com.

*Get the best of science fiction and fantasy
at your fingertips!*